VICTIMS

A Tale of Betrayal and Revenge

Edmund Romilly

APEX PUBLISHING LTD

First published as an eBook in 2014.
First published in paperback in 2016 by
Apex Publishing Ltd
12A St. John's Road, Clacton on Sea, Essex, CO15 4BP, United Kingdom

www.apexpublishing.co.uk

British Library Cataloguing-in-Publication Data
A catalogue record for this book
is available from the British Library

ISBN: 978-1-911476-34-4

Typeset in 11pt Palatino Linotype

Editor: Kim Kimber
Production Manager: Chris Cowlin
Cover Designer: Hannah Blamires

1.
Narrative, 1979

It is a normal night at the Huffington Club. There is a buzz in the air as the chips are placed and the dice roll. The Punto Banco table is especially crowded. The bright light from the chandeliers sparks off the spangled dresses of the croupiers, who show their cleavages as they lean over the tables to deal. The pit bosses in their brown suits sit above them like lifeguards, watching for any irregularity. But the gamblers are only intent on the wheel. Men in suits and women in evening dresses sit hunched, stand or lean in a crooked fashion over the tables; there is a look of studied avarice on their faces. Some gasp in dismay when the ball settles into a particular slot of the still spinning wheel. Others squirm with relief or curse under their breath.

There is nothing quite like the sound of the roulette wheel when the ball, with a mind of its own, is deciding which number to choose. It is that of a hard, bright bead rattling within a coffin of well-tempered wood, finished in steel. Sometimes it beats like a drumstick on a porcelain plate, as quickly as the wings of a hummingbird; it goes on and on, until you think it will never stop, the sound interposing itself within the rhythm of your own heart; but with a pop-pop-pop it does eventually slow and startle by its unpredictability, the players craning their necks to see whether they have been favoured by the gods of chance.

It is quieter at the further end of the room, past the so-called cage where the cash is changed for chips and the chips for cash. Here there are the first floor windows which look onto a Mayfair street. The gaming floor was once the ballroom of a grand private residence and a century ago young couples in their finery would retire to the balconies for fresh air and maybe a chance to talk privately. Now, there are only blackjack tables, which is why it is quieter because they are emptier than the others, the punters preferring to play solo against a pretty house dealer. The player thinks that he and she can unwittingly establish a rhythm in the way the cards fall that is advantageous to him;

1

and he is right. The management, therefore, change the dealer from time to time, whenever things are getting a little too hot for the bank.

Downstairs at reception, people are still arriving, though it is past eleven; in fact the casino is at its busiest between now and three o'clock in the morning, after which comes the downturn to four, when it closes.

A man of about thirty in an off-the-peg black tie of a synthetic material is busy helping the fur coat off a coarse blonde of about forty. She is with a regular punter who always sports half an unlit cigar between his lips. You can see he's had a good dinner. He always wears a brown suit and runs a successful fruit and vegetable business. Rumour has it that he murdered his mother over an inheritance; but it is just a rumour.

As for the man in the black tie, he has a cringing manner, and his smile is too wide: it is as if the skin on his face has been pulled back from not-too-good teeth, and the stubble on his chin needs seeing to.

His name is Giles Jones, though his associates call him Gentry, and he works at the Huffington Club as a receptionist. The job entails much more than its name suggests, however, as he and the others have to be very much on the alert so far as security is concerned. At any time a pit boss might ring down and want to know who, say, the guy in the white suit and red tie is, because he is winning too much money or has been seen before in a dubious context. The receptionists have to be able to give the pit boss the information he requires within moments – how long the man has been a member, his credit history, and so on.

You get a nose for this sort of thing, a clairvoyance that even goes so far as to accurately predict which member of the club will be coming through the front door next, but you also get a nose for which of them will tip well and which won't. This is important because the receptionists couldn't begin to live off the meagre salaries the management pay them, and rely on tips to make up the difference. That is why Giles Jones is being so deferential at this moment: the man with the unlit cigar tips well if you put him in a good mood.

Sandy, the reception manager, is flattering him outrageously, as Giles Jones can hear. He himself is making a fuss over the coarse blonde, not because she might leave a tip – most women didn't – but because if he puts her nose even slightly out of joint she will almost certainly convey that feeling to her partner by subtle means, and he might therefore not be so generous. But as that gentleman flings his car keys at the waiting car jockey who is standing ready to find a parking space for him, he also presses a twenty pound note into Sandy's discreetly waiting palm.

Gamblers are superstitious people, and a lot of them tip in advance because they think it will bring them luck. Sandy waits till the couple disappear up the staircase to the gaming room before murmuring, 'Gotcha!'

The other three receptionists are looking on in approval. He puts the twenty pound note in a cardboard box they keep hidden behind the counter, where all the tips go. He presses the notes in the box and says, 'It's getting a bit spongy, eh, Gentry?'

By which he means that the tips have been building up nicely during the course of the week, prior to being split four ways on Saturday, the next day being one of their days off, as the casino is closed on Sunday.

Sandy is a good sort: ex-army, he'd made the rank of major, he is short and dapper, and keeps himself well. He has a toothbrush moustache and when it comes to leaving work he always puts on his salt and pepper overcoat with meticulous care, as if it were a prized possession worthy of such elaboration.

The other two receptionists are strictly temporary – Pete, an out-of-work actor in his twenties, thin and pale-complexioned, and Marlene, who is even thinner and by far the tallest of the four. She always wears the same black chiffon evening gown, which emphasises the slightness of her figure, and to Giles' annoyance always addresses any female customer she is attending to as "m'damn", putting the stress on the second syllable of the word "madame".

It is about an hour's walk from the casino to Giles Jones' bedsitter in Brunswick Gardens, off Westbourne Grove. After work he enjoys it: the fresh air is good compared with the fug of reception and it gives him a chance to stretch his legs, something he is not able to do in the constricted space of counter and coats. Yet along the Bayswater Road by the park he always feels fearful for his safety, particularly as now in winter time it is still dark and cold. He feels that he might get attacked and mugged, and is always hyped up just in case anybody tries it on.

Without realising it, his fists are clenched as he walks, and he looks this way and that in case someone is approaching. He feels that if anybody did try anything on with him he would kill them, acknowledging that there may be more than one. But nothing has ever happened. Once a high-powered saloon screeched past him, braked to a halt suddenly with squealing tyres and reversed till its driver was level with himself, but the man only wanted directions, which Giles Jones had been happy and able to give.

Giles Jones' bedsitter is on the fifth floor of a substantial terraced house in the middle of a square that is not really a square but a rectangle. Its housing contains nothing but more bedsitters, small flats and cheap hotels. He is lucky enough to have a window facing the straggly gardens, the dead leaves of whose trees are scattered over the grass.

It has been raining, and you can see a dewy radiance on the black metal fencing, courtesy of the powerful street lamps. Normally at this time of morning things are quiet but as Giles stands staring out of the open window, for no reason in particular, he gradually becomes aware of a noise which he cannot identify. It is regular, it is human, he thinks, but what is it? At last he realises that it is the sound of a woman having sex. He begins to listen with care. It goes on and on. It is so impersonal somehow, a deep, measured "um", that is more an expression of meditational deep breathing than carnal enjoyment. But the latter is what it is.

He turns away from the window, closes it and surveys the narrow strip of room that is his home. It is pretty basic, just a single bed, a table and a couple of chairs, some shelves and a wardrobe. An overly bright light bulb hangs shadeless from the ceiling. This bothers him but he has done nothing about it, in fact he has done nothing to decorate this bedsitter in the three months that he has been living here. The accommodation was always going to be strictly temporary and he likes to feel that he is just one more of a countless number of anonymous souls that pass through its and other walls. He walks the few paces it takes to get to the wardrobe, opens it and removes a half-full bottle of premium vodka and a glass. He pours himself a generous measure and returns to the area by the window and sits himself down at the table, where he drinks and starts to drum his fingers on its black Formica top. He is still wearing his black tie – the most comfortable piece of clothing he possesses – but has loosened the collar and taken off his patent leather lace-ups.

Giles Jones is an angular sort of man, quite wiry, with slicked back, black frizzy hair, going a little grey at the sides. His general angularity is accentuated when seated: he has the air, if not the look, of an athlete on the starting block ready to pounce at the sound of the starting gun. This is because he lives off his nerves; always has done. As for his face, it is thin and pointed. He has very bright, almost feverish eyes, which sometimes frighten people.

He is asking himself whether his hunger can wait or should he eat now before he gets down to business? He decides the latter, so he goes back to the cupboard, brings out the side of beef which he always hopes will last him the week but never does, gets the reasonably fresh loaf of bread and starts methodically to make himself a doorstep sandwich. As he does so he swigs continuously from the glass of vodka, which he keeps replenished.

The sandwich made, he munches it ruminatively while standing by the open cupboard, inside which is a tiny kitchen. When finished he closes the door to the cupboard and goes back to the table. He takes a writing pad from one of the shelves and removes his ball point pen from the inner breast pocket of his jacket. For a moment he looks up at his curtainless window and notes that dawn is approaching. A thin blue light hangs in the air and he can hear the occasional bird chirping. He strokes his chin contemplatively and starts to write.

2.
Giles Jones' Diary

I was born on 6th July, 1951, at Jones Place on the Welsh border. Or rather, my birth took place in one of the cottages on the estate, as the manor house itself had been in ruins since the war. My parents lived in London, but I think they thought it best if I came into the world in a rural setting. My father, Damien, had inherited the estate from his own father, who had inherited it from his, and so on backwards for many generations, but it was requisitioned by the government during the war and was never quite the same afterwards. In any case, my parents' lives were solidly based in London, so Jones Place became little more than a neglected holiday home. I remember going down there a few times in the summer.

My early childhood was uneventful, or at least so it appears now, as I do not remember much of it, but at the age of five I started as a day boy at the Orange School, South Kensington, which was nearby, and I remember this because it was at that time that my parents began to behave badly and irresponsibly. At first it was nothing but bickering, albeit constant, but in the next five years the situation reached intolerable levels. The cause of this I am led to believe was my father Damien's increasingly hopeless drug addiction, initially caused by his experiences as a prisoner-of-war. I tried to ignore all this and, being introverted, usually succeeded; but sometimes their space invaded mine, causing me much stress and anxiety. Of course, they tried to make sure the doors were well shut when they rowed, or they thought that I was well away from their marital battlefield when it was in full swing, but they underestimated a little boy's acuity, or were in denial as to the fall-out for others from their actions, I don't know which. Maybe they were so consumed with their own hatred for each other that they just didn't care about anyone else. Except that my father would come and tell me about it, something which my mother never did.

'Giles, you know your mother and I have not been getting on very well…'

My father said this ruefully, looking sorry for himself, late one evening when he came into my bedroom in the basement of the house. I had been in bed, reading, and tried to continue to read, in effect trying to ignore him, but it was an impossible task. He was sitting in the green armchair opposite, a picture of brooding self-pity, his long grey hair awry. He would not go away and leave me alone.

One of the reasons why I was trying to ignore him was because, even to a little boy like me, it was clear that what he had said had been an appalling understatement. In another context it would have been laughable, and now that I think about it, the best thing to have done would have been for me to have burst out laughing at him, although I know that had I done so he would have been utterly surprised, then shocked at being taken so lightly; this reaction would have led to further troubled self-examination on his part, followed by more self-pity, I have no doubt.

This state of affairs threatened to infect my life entirely, even though at school one forgot about it for the time being; even there it was not so far away, both literally and in the mind, and there were occasions when it was as stark as ever, as when, for example, one afternoon in the playground I noticed a number of children collected together round a boy of about a year older than me, whom for that reason I didn't know. I had seen him before, of course, he was a fat little boy, and his name was Colin.

He always wore the same black pair of jeans held up by a snake belt. At least I thought he did until I challenged him about it – the only time I ever spoke to him – and he explained that he had many pairs of jeans which he wore interchangeably but they all looked the same. I'm not sure I believed him but it was none of my business anyway, and it now seems an extraordinarily prim and officious challenge for me to have made; whatever, he was now crying his eyes out, his chubby cheeks red, which was why other children were staring at him with such undisguised curiosity.

My own curiosity aroused, I approached and asked a little girl what was the matter with him.

'He's got trouble at home,' she said. 'His parents quarrel all the time.'
'Oh,' I said.

I knew all about that, and walked away. His problems were not things with which I was unfamiliar, so they lacked interest for me.

The culmination of my unhappiness came very early one morning while I was still in bed. This would have been about my tenth year. I awoke to a grey light and a shadowy figure sitting at my side. It was my father. He was crying quietly, sobbing gently, if you prefer; I did not know what to do.

'Your mother's leaving,' he said finally.

Still I did not know what to do or say.

After another long pause and more tears, during which I began to feel increasingly uncomfortable, he added, 'Do you want to go with her or stay with me?'

'Where's she going?' I asked with curiosity.

'York.'

That would be to her own mother's house, who lived there with her other daughter, my aunt. They were both doctors. I often stayed there in the holidays and had jolly times. My mother would drive me up, but my father never came.

I thought a bit, then for better or worse made the most important decision of my whole young life so far. 'I'll stay with you,' I said.

I don't know why I said this; maybe it was because whatever his faults my sympathies always lay entirely with my father. Also, because by her actions my mother would be breaking up the family, such as it was – but it was better than nothing. And to my young mind she was therefore to be blamed. Perhaps weakness was at the bottom of it – my father could be very frightening and intimidating, although if I had said, 'I'm going with Mummy,' he would have accepted it.

Supposing it had been my mother who had woken me and asked the same question, what then would my response have been?

'Very well, Giles,' said my father, and slyly walked out of the room, closing the door behind him.

But in class later that morning I was summoned to the headmaster's office, a curiously small room for such a senior man in such a large building. The headmaster, who was himself on the small side, but correctly dressed, with a gold pince-nez which he kept toying with, was obviously suffering some embarrassment.

My mother was there, as well as a third person, a great, round ball of a woman whom I immediately recognised as Mrs Furze, a so-called friend of both my parents, who ran a coffee bar in Bourne Street, which all the upper class bohemians of the district frequented. She had a mass of greasy black hair. She was an emigree of some sort, and rumoured to be extraordinarily exotic. To me she was just a pain in the neck.

There was an awkward silence. Even for a small boy it was irritating to have been plucked out of one's class and summoned to this room which contained three grown human beings none of whom, however, appeared capable of speaking to me. So I said, 'I'm not going with you, Mummy.'

'Now, Giles...' began Mrs Furze.

By now I was choking back my tears and wanted to run away, out of the room, into the street, anywhere.

'Please ...' began Mr Edwards, the headmaster.

Perhaps he felt – as he certainly ought to have done – that his first duty was toward the child in his care, and he could see that the child was getting upset. Mrs Furze had turned to Mr Edwards and it was quite obvious that she was about to give him a piece of her mind in a fishwifely way until she thought better of it; because to my amazement all he had to do to stop her was raise a well-manicured finger and repeat, 'Please...'

I suppose even she was not going to risk a scene in a school.

'You have heard what the boy has said,' continued the headmaster. 'In the circumstances I cannot let you take him away.' Another silence. I was screwing my eyes up and looking hard at the floor.

'You may go back to your class, Giles,' he said to me.

I turned to the door – funny how compliant little boys can be in the face of authority – and was about to leave the room when Mrs Furze screeched, 'Aren't you even going to kiss your mother goodbye?'

From whatever quarter, this request could not be avoided, so with a great deal of reluctance I approached my mother and kissed her on the cheek. Then I left.

That afternoon, I remember, I lingered in the streets, not wanting to go home. I kicked bits of litter around and did silly walks, for example making sure I avoided the cracks in the pavement. I stared into the windows of shops whose contents could not possibly have had any interest for me, and stood with my hands on my hips as I thought an adult might, who really was interested.

At the corner of Lower Sloane Street and Pimlico Road I looked around, swinging my satchel, as if unsure which direction to take, although I knew perfectly well where my home was; and something inside said, 'Don't go. Don't go back. Go elsewhere before it is too late.'

It was puzzling: I could almost hear the words, their meaning was absolutely clear, yet how on earth was I supposed to act on them? I had nowhere else to go, I supposed I could go and see a friend – Oliver Rhodes lived just around the corner, for instance; I had often been to his house and he to mine – but to do so would have been odd. They would not know why I was there. I'd have to tell them what had happened at home this morning and I couldn't face that. Anyway, perhaps after a cup of tea and some sweets they would just take me back to my father, or try to find my mother without telling him and return me to the woman I had earlier rejected. There was nothing for it; I had to go home.

When I got to number 15, I was exhausted and terrified. But at the front door an old annoyance replaced these feelings, strong though they were: that still I had not been allowed a key and always had to ring the bell upon returning home, although it would have been much easier for all concerned if I could have let myself in. I also thought that there was this absurd notion among adults that only they were allowed front door keys, just because they thought they were grown-up.

Anyway, I rang the doorbell as usual and waited. Normally, it would be either of my parents who answered, or old Mrs Hyam, our housekeeper, if she had not already left. After a minute or two the door opened only slightly, to my surprise, and I could see my father looking at me through the gap. I thought he had an anxious expression on his face but I didn't know why. He had put the door on the chain, an unheard of thing, and so had to shut it again and take the ball out of its groove before he could let me in, which he did.

Once inside, he explained that he had bumped into Mrs Furze earlier that day in Sloane Square and had had a bust-up with her and was frightened that she would send some of her bovver boys round to his house to sort him out in retaliation. My father told me that he always suspected Mrs Furze of meddling in his marital affairs and now causing his wife to leave him and so had grabbed her by her filthy black hair and pulled her head back with force until, alarmed, she had said, 'Damien! What are you doing?' Whereupon he had desisted.

Even as a little boy, I thought it improbable that Mrs Furze would go so far as – or be able to – "send bovver boys round", as Damien had put it; but what did I know?

Nor at that stage did I appreciate quite what a melodramatic streak my father had; so far as I was concerned he simply lay about the house all day drinking tea and taking pills when he was not arguing with, or shouting at, Mummy; or pushing her up against a wall; so I let it go, and with that nonchalance that little boys have for the truly serious I went down to my basement bedroom to play a game.

3.
Narrative, 1967

On a very cold evening a group of people were sitting in the not very warm drawing room of a country house. The atmosphere was subdued. Damien Jones' ashes had been flown from America and an interment service would take place at Jones village church the next morning. Giles and his mother were staying with their cousins the Aylmer Jones of Badfield Court, whose grand but ill-kept house lay on the other side of the county. Aylmer Jones at this moment was warming his backside by the log fire, his cavalry twill trousers seeming, from where Giles was sitting, to be the largest part of him. He also wore a black corduroy jacket and a cravat, an article of clothing which Giles had scarcely ever seen before. Aylmer's young wife, Venetia, was leaning back on one of the large, comfortable but shabby sofas, toying with a glass of wine. There was a distracted look upon her pale, pretty face as it dwelt fondly upon a pair of black Labradors, each of which lay sprawled across the floor, just in front of Aylmer's feet.

On another sofa sat Mary, Giles' mother, and Giles himself, who was in a state of some distress. He was then a young man just turned sixteen, dressed very much in the fashion for his age and time. He sported a Jimi Hendrix hairstyle. They had all had a cold supper, but conversation had been awkward; nobody had very much to say and, in any case, the respective couples did not know each other very well.

Finally, Aylmer Jones cleared his throat and addressed his sixteen-year-old cousin with some formality; it was as if the speech had been prepared but its execution gone adrift.

'You know, Giles,' he said, 'there are many people round here...' He stopped and began again, 'What I mean is, a lot of people will be at your father's funeral who have had some connection with his estate or other, and well...'

He trailed off. Giles waited, bemused. He had no idea what was coming. The two women sat silently, now studying their wine glasses.

'Well, the fact is...' Aylmer Jones resumed. 'It's your hair, you see.

Many people wouldn't understand... they would be, well, embarrassed to see you like that...'

Giles was dumbfounded. So this was what it was all about! He rather thought that the embarrassment would be that of his own relatives and not these "many people" but this did not stop him from bursting into tears at what he had just heard.

Then, having said what he'd had to say, Aylmer Jones simply walked out of the room. As if on cue, Mary got to her feet and produced a hairbrush from her handbag. It was one of those spongy things, popular among women at the time, whose bristles grow from a cushion of an unpleasant pink colour. Its shape was that of a small hand mirror, and she held it up as if to reflect Giles' Jimi Hendrix hairstyle, and gently began to brush it, backwards and forwards, saying to him, 'There, there... that's right...' as if such words would soothe the now slowly weeping boy. Unlike her husband, Venetia Jones hadn't moved; she simply watched what was happening with interest.

Ten o'clock the next morning it was cold and somehow lifeless in Jones village; faint colours lay on the horizon; the pea green of the hills, the slate blue of the sky. Massive, dark trees and their branches were a dull brown, against slow-moving, silvery cloud. The sound of car tyres on gravel was cold and uninviting; people spoke or coughed or simply breathed, but whichever they did a billow of smoke would surround their heads, temporarily obscuring them. As they waited at the door to the small medieval church they seemed like crows, rooks or ravens, gathered in black for a mysterious ritual.

After a sleepless night Giles felt as frail as he ever had, not sure what to do, what to say, how even to stand. His mother was at his side, but as if at a great distance, like everyone else. These were people he had never seen before; some of them he would never see again.

They all went into the church, whose gloomy interior seemed like a mausoleum, a place of death; the bars of a few inadequate electric fires glowed orange from the floor but did nothing to dispel the cold. The dark brown wood of the pews glowed too but with a sheen that resembled ice and the pulpit, of lighter wood, seemed frozen in time as well as in fact, as did the pewter eagle above it.

He had never been here before, yet plaques to his ancestors, some distinguished, some not, adorned the stone walls next to the stained glass windows. He was placed in the front pew, beside his mother; from where he could easily see an elderly man in flowing robes in front of the altar, somehow druidical, with a kindly face. He was saying something, but Giles was not listening; if he was thinking of anything at all it was of how Venetia had looked, as he had seen her outside the church, with her short black coat concealing an even shorter black dress, and black fur pillar box hat. She was holding her arms in front, her hands hidden by a black fur muff, but her slim and shapely stockinged legs were revealed to the world. Hers had been the only legs which had been visible in the sizeable crowd; and he had wondered whether any of the others disapproved. Certainly he had seen several of the older ladies looking. The men appeared to have been ignoring the spectacle. Her pale, pretty face was crimson with lipstick and pink with rouge, her yellow hair falling in wisps from her hat and from a distance she had been giving Giles an appraising look; not unfriendly, just curious, perhaps a bit arch.

When the service was over, the congregation filed into the graveyard with the priest in front. It was a mournful parade and, later, his attention was distracted by four men who were peering into a hole in the ground. What were they doing? The priest was incanting something. Suddenly Giles saw the four men lower a small casket into the hole by means of ropes; which was unnecessary, as one of them could simply have put it in. And then he remembered; relatives in America had had Damien's body cremated in Berkeley, California, without anyone in England's knowledge, let alone permission, and these must be his ashes.

Shortly, the casket would be covered with earth and that would be that, so far as his father was concerned. Giles shuddered and the loneliness and sadness which had been welling inside him throughout the morning burst like a dam; he shook with tears. He felt an arm around his shoulder: the priest appeared to be talking to him in kindly, reassuring tones; everyone else had disappeared.

4.
Giles Jones' Diary

The next day Daddy told me that I would be going to York for the weekend; that was fine by me, as I have said I enjoyed going there. He made it clear to me that it would be for the weekend only, a concession he had made on the telephone earlier that day; and that I must be back in London in time for school on Monday.

I have no recollection of getting there, but it must have been dark when I arrived, because I still remember the gloom of the dining room, with the heavy brocaded curtains still undrawn, and a dim chandelier hanging over the Sheraton table. My grandmother was at one end of it; I was at the other. She was talking to me, and holding a book of some kind.

My grandmother always met me at the railway station when I travelled to York on my own. This time had been no different, but the pattern had changed with the absence of her usual talkativeness as she drove me to the outskirts, where her large, gloomy house stood in its own grounds. Also, no one else seemed to be there when we entered; there was a strange eeriness to the place. For some reason I felt afraid, not in the exciting way that I sometimes did when my aunt told me ghost stories, or told me that it was late and I had to get to bed because the house was haunted – which I very nearly believed – but in a cold, impersonal way that left me, as it were, battling for survival.

As I have said, she was talking to me, but I had no idea what about, her words were going through my mind but not registering; instead, it was my body that was doing so, I felt weak at the knees and tried hard to fight a feeling that I was about to collapse: I did so by clinging with both hands onto the edge of the Sheraton table, but they had become so moist that they simply slid around.

Gradually, some sort of sense came into what she was saying. Contrary to what had been arranged, I was to stay up here, at least during the holidays, for during term times I would go to the Red House School nearby, a very good boarding school for young boys. 'Oh, such a good school, you should see it, Giles,' and she showed me the book she had been holding which was, in reality, a brochure of the establishment she had been peddling like a saleswoman. She waved the glossy pages in my face, having approached me from the other side of the table.

I wish I could say that a lusty defiance at this outrageous double-cross erupted from my small being, but it didn't; instead, there came the usual dissolution into tears – odd that I always took this route as, so far as I recall, it never had the slightest effect on anybody, adult or child. But at least on this occasion I had the courage to shake my head and whimper, 'No!' Not that this keen rebellion made any headway with my grandmother, who was now babbling on about this and that, as if, having shot her bolt, she was now destined to pursue her strategy to the end. So I tried a different tack. I'd had a sudden idea. I ran out into the hallway but went in the opposite direction, towards the kitchen and scullery which were beyond the ever open green baize door. Just in front of it on a small table lay the only telephone in the house; I quickly dialled our London number, fearful that at any moment I was going to be physically stopped from doing so; but this did not happen.

The phone answered: 'Yes?' A weary voice – my father's. 'Daddy! Daddy! They want to keep me here! Come and get me!'

I went to bed that night determined not to sleep. I did not even take my clothes off, just got under the eiderdown and waited. I did not really think that Daddy would indeed "come and get me" as I had implored, but I could not be sure. In any case I was determined one way or another that my stay in York would be a short one – shorter even than the weekend arranged. But despite myself I did fall into a sort of dreamy half-sleep, as if under a mild anaesthetic; I remember this because it was disturbed by an unmistakable sound from the gravel drive outside, that of a London taxi. A faint blue light was coming through the windows, whose curtains were not fully drawn; which meant, I supposed, that it was getting towards dawn. The taxi sounded as if it were three-point turning in order to face the gate at the bottom of the drive that led to the road, because the scrunching on the gravel would stop, then start again, followed by nothing but the bronchitic throb of the engine as it idled.

I leapt out of bed and out of the bedroom, and ran across the first floor landing and down the sweeping staircase that turned back on itself toward the ground floor hall, its 180 degree bend passing the large stained glass window with a religious theme and, beneath and overlooking the hall, a little ledge with a human skull resting upon it; then through the hall whose floor clattered to the sound of my feet and into the small room which housed the front door.

In those days my grandmother and aunt, trusting doctors that they were, never bothered to lock up at night, so it was easy to get out onto the drive; and there it was – the London taxi with my father in it. I got in; he was sitting on the further side, barely visible, with his grey overcoat wrapped around him, his white hair visible in the near darkness. I think he must have been surprised that his enterprise had not been more difficult; after all, he could not have had any way of telling that I would run from the house so easily. And thinking about it years later I suppose he would simply have waited in the taxi till morning came, when no doubt there would have been a stand-off between him and the women inside. For my part, I too, could not believe that it had all been so easy; why hadn't I been stopped? Presumably because everyone else was still asleep. Yet my mother must have heard, or at least been told of, my screaming entreaties of the previous evening, so why hadn't she been on her guard to stop me going? Then it occurred to me that no one could have expected Daddy to jump into a taxi and make the two hundred mile journey to York in the middle of the night to affect a rescue. It was not what people did.

Later, my father leant toward the communicating window of the taxi and said to the cabbie, 'Can't you go any faster? My wife has a powerful Daimler...'

So far as I recall, he did not answer, nor so far as I recall, did he drive any faster; it did cross my mind that he might have been asking himself just how mad this passenger was, but again, if he did, he did not say so. I asked myself whether there really was going to be a car chase and I could not quite believe it. But the thought frightened me. In the event, it did not happen and years later I thought it had been my father just being melodramatic again. In those days he must have felt beleaguered, threatened from all sides; certainly, that was how he behaved.

We got as far as Doncaster, paid the taxi driver and took a train for the rest of the journey. Once in London Daddy started to make arrangements for us to travel to America.

5.
Narrative, 1967

Giles Jones found the others in a coaching inn in the middle of High Street of Kington, the nearest town of any size to Jones Place village. It was the sort of market town that had not changed much in many hundreds of years. Later, he was seated at a large table in its dining room, whose floor creaked and whose ceiling sloped. There were about forty others, also seated. He was in a daze, but they appeared to be making great efforts to break the ice among themselves, after the social constraint of the burial service. Alcohol was helping this; already sherry had been served copiously during the stand-up occasion just before; now a number of comely waitresses of the buxom, rural sort, were pouring wine, beer or cider from jugs into glasses.

As he watched in a sort of helpless way, Giles came to realise, as he had not during the burial, that most of the people present were unknown to him and it seemed to him that they had strange faces, almost as if they belonged to another planet. They did not share his grief. Only a sense of duty had brought them to the church and to here; that, and the opportunity to socialise, perhaps. At any rate they were now not being solemn at all: the first peal of laughter came from a man who threw his head back at something Venetia Jones had said to him; it was startling, his guffaw belied his mourning dress as did Venetia's warm smile hers.

Suddenly, she looked across at Giles and blinked. She was signalling a form of gentle encouragement to him and it must have worked a bit because, confused, Giles lowered his head and reached instinctively for the wine glass in front of him. He had not meant for his eye to be caught by anyone, perhaps especially Venetia; because without realising it he had been spying on the assembled company, as if he were nothing more than a fly on the wall, something which on objective terms he was entitled to feel, because until the moment of Venetia's glance he had been ignored.

That was because his grief was palpable and not shared by anybody else – accordingly, he was being shunned, the others afraid to engage because such grief might be contagious, or at the very least produce awkwardness. Even his mother, who had been divorced from his father for a few years now, was like that. She was listening attentively to what Derek Bradshaw was saying to her. But he, unlike her, was managing to eat at the same time, with the result that Mary's first course was growing cold. She was alone in this respect, being perhaps too submissively polite to succumb to the voracious appetite that was a collective feature of those eating at a wake.

Derek Bradshaw, Giles had been told, was his father's solicitor but this was the first time he had ever seen him and what a shock he got, not just because he had no instinctive idea why such a professional adviser should be at the funeral at all, but also because of his appearance – a thin, small man, with a mean, white face and rasping voice.

The mad Coral, who had only been married to Damien for three months before he died and who had herself taken an overdose of barbiturates shortly before his death and survived, was seated away from his mother and late father's solicitor, and next to her own father, Graham Greene. She was wolfing down her food without any regard to how she might appear or to anything else. She was displaying the unpleasant habit of splaying her elbows out as far as they would go as she manipulated knife and fork. It was as if she were imitating the very bird she was eating, as it had been in life; with her lean body stuffed into what appeared to be a makeshift black dress. Her father had had to move slightly in order to avoid being dug in the ribs by her, as had another man to her left.

This woman was later to tell Giles, without being remotely troubled by the utterance, that it was she who had sent a wreath to the church with hers and Damien's names spelt backwards upon the accompanying card, an object which he had seen at the ceremony and which he had been troubled by. He had read "From Laroc and Neimad". She explained that she and Damien had decided that if ever one of them were to die without the other that is what the survivor would do. Giles was repelled by this. But would Damien, Giles' own father, ever have done that, if by any chance it had been Coral who had predeceased him? He doubted it. Anyhow, he had thought that the accompanying card was the sickest thing he had ever seen.

Now he simply stared at her, with her flapping elbows, and couldn't believe that by mere operation of law he was, and would always be, her stepson. She too now burst into a peal of laughter at something her father had said to her, the effect of which was to disgorge some masticated food from her mouth. Her mouth anyway seemed to be merely a red oval, having nothing to do with anything human. It was horrible, but she managed to chew it down before exclaiming, 'And I expect we'll have trumpets and flying angels round it!'

They evidently were talking about a headstone for his father's ashes or, more properly, joking about it and with such a lack of taste that he was appalled. Giles looked more closely at Graham Greene. Funny that he should share exactly the name of a distinguished novelist who at that time was something of a hero of his, because he couldn't have been more adversely different from how he imagined that novelist to be. This man was coarse, though he tried to disguise the fact with a city business suit and the manners of the stockbroker belt. His little eyes were cruel and he had the reptilian habit of successively protruding and retracting his lower lip, his head always moving at an unnatural angle, darting this way and that, as if foraging for something valuable that might yet be invisible to others. It occurred to Giles that this man had not even bothered to introduce himself to him, though they had not met before. Giles only knew who he was because he had been pointed out to him, funnily enough by Derek Bradshaw, who was still monopolising his mother, if anything more forcefully than ever, having, with the flow of drink, raised his voice by several decibels, so that it could distinctly be heard even above the general cacophony.

A clear, rasping voice, it was as if he had always been, and always would be, mightily cross with the world, perhaps because, justifiably or not, he did not think it had ever given him his due. At this moment he was staring while talking at a perfectly innocuous gravy boat that sat on the clean white tablecloth, as if daring even this inanimate object to contradict anything he might have to say. '...gets everything, by which I mean all goods and chattels and so on and so forth. Of course, she...' Giles had already been told that because Damien did not make another will upon re-marriage, he had died intestate, with the result that Coral collected half his estate once her substantial statutory legacy had been paid in full. '...everything will have to be sold, of course... money will be very tight, I am afraid. I'm sorry, my dear, but there it is. The death duties will be enormous, of course, always are in this sort of case. Such a pity that dear old Damien...'

Occasionally, Derek Bradshaw's utterances would be accompanied by a fine spray of saliva, which ejection from his mouth he did not appear to notice, although whenever this happened Mary Jones tried hard to suppress a wince. '...young Giles will stay at his public school, of course... which is it? I forget now...'

'Giles was at Selwyn Mauberley College near Bath but he is now at Bishop Grosseteste's Grammar School, York,' Mary uttered in a clear tone. To Giles' knowledge, it was the first time she had spoken.

'Ah yes, of course, forgive me, I forgot... my own son will be starting at Mauberley very soon. Such a good school.'

Mary gave him an astounded look. Derek Bradshaw munched his food complacently. "Young Giles", as he was being referred to, also winced at the solicitor's utter insensitivity in talking about matters in this way, within his earshot and at his father's own wake. At this moment his mother looked guiltily across the table, for just the fraction of a second, to see if her son had been listening.

Derek Bradshaw continued, 'I did tell him, of course...' Tell him what? Giles wondered. '...of course I did. The position was fully explained, fully explained...' What was he talking about? Giles noticed that Graham Greene had stopped listening to his mad daughter and his attention was now fully upon the solicitor. '...old Damien and young Coral were quite lawfully married, quite lawful. Absolutely no doubt about that! No doubt at all. I have the certificate here...' He produced, as if it were a white rabbit from a top hat, a piece of green paper from an inner breast pocket and waved it about; next he peered at it and muttered, 'Westminster Registry Office, 3rd May, 1967... and so on and so forth... witnessed by... yes, let me see... Ronald Palmer, plumber and Mavis Pringle, seamstress.'

He then put the thing back from where it came. He looked up. 'So you see I had to explain to him, of course I did, that he needed to make another will, but did he listen? I've no idea,' said Derek Bradshaw, answering his own question. 'Alas, these things happen. Human nature, I suppose. But I did my duty.' Derek Bradshaw renewed his efforts at staring down the gravy boat and then swigged from his glass of wine.

Giles, too, took his glass, and for some reason raised it, as if to propose a toast. But it just hung there in his hand to no purpose. He felt dizzy; the wine had already got to him in any case. What little he had eaten seemed a very long time ago, still he had to wait for the others to finish before his plate would be taken away. 'Such a pity that dear old

Damien... only fifty! An appalling tragedy! Well, death comes to us all in the end, of course...' Derek Bradshaw resumed his complacent munching. Mary Jones took a sip of wine.

In contrast to Giles, his cousin, Aylmer Jones, had been the first to finish the main course and had promptly demanded a second helping. This he had achieved by grabbing one of the waitresses as she passed. Alarmed at having been accosted in this way, she turned, whereupon he held up his plate for her inspection, as if in this way he could make the meaning of his request self-evident.

She had taken his plate reproachfully and departed, not perhaps realising that she had been the only person who had communicated with him during this meal in any way at all, for such was his gluttony that his concentration on his food had been total, even to the exclusion of politely passing discourse.

Giles Jones was fascinated by this man but only because he was a blood relative. He tried very hard to see similarities between himself and his father Damien on the one hand, and Aylmer Jones on the other; but he could not, or at the least he dared not to, because if he discreetly craned his neck to the left, all he could see at the far end of the table was an absolutely gross individual some of the buttons of whose plain white shirt were popping through over-eating. Moreover, Aylmer's normally oiled hair had changed shape during the course of the meal, so that it now seemed that a weird brown bat had descended upon his cranium, become stuck and was trying to extricate itself. Or so it seemed to Giles, whose mental faculties at the moment were not the most normal. However, there was a similarity between them of sorts, he supposed, in that neither of them had once been spoken to; but this changed when Aylmer Jones finished his second helping of the main course. A lady on his left had been waiting patiently for him to do so before engaging him – good God! Do you mean to say that the man was attractive to women? It was beyond imagination, but this lady, who was something of a looker although not in the first flush of youth, and who, like almost all the others, was unknown to Giles, actually appeared to be casting admiring glances at him while she waited for him to finish. What were they talking about? he wondered. Aylmer Jones had smoothed his hair back to reveal the full totality of his slab of a face, with its pasty complexion; yet he was now smiling broadly at the lady and in that smile you could see he had charm. Strange, that! Another lady interjected – on his right this time, and she was somehow similar to the one on his left – and clearly she, too, was trying to gain his attention, speaking more assertively, perhaps more intelligently; and she had succeeded in causing him to turn his head in her direction, whereupon the first lady tapped him on the arm for his attention, perhaps because she hadn't finished the point she was making to him. In spite of himself, Giles giggled, and looked down just as a chocolate mousse was laid before him, because he really thought the two ladies were going to start a fight over this preposterous glutton.

'That's better,' he heard someone say to his left.

'You talking to me?'

The dining room had become very hot and somehow small and tight, as if about to implode and take its contents into a black hole from which they would never reappear, when Giles just about managed to realise that his manner had been rude and in need of correction. The middle-aged, grey-haired man who had spoken to him appeared kindly, however, and this made him nervous, and aware that his fingers were being watched as they tapped a beat on the table.

'Yes, I was. I thought you'd never cheer up.'

'Sorry.'

'Not at all. Must be a difficult time for you, very difficult.' A pause. 'My name's Huntley, Huntley Rupert-Smith, I'm a neighbour of the Aylmer Jones. I knew your father a bit, though not well, went to his and Mary's wedding, what, ten, fifteen years ago now? I see she's here. Hadn't seen him since. A remarkable man, quite remarkable.' Another pause. 'I'm very sorry for you, old chap. Must be awful, quite awful, to lose one's father so young.'

Giles listened politely, but felt uneasy. He didn't know how to respond. The kindly, grey-haired man whose name he had not taken in – and who had the look of a lawyer about him but was in fact a well-to-do farmer – now looked gloomily at his own pudding and dried up.

At that moment there was a movement in the room. Derek Bradshaw abruptly broke off his monologue to Mary and got to his feet, startling her; and, as if that had been a pre-arranged signal, Aylmer Jones and Graham Greene got to their feet too. 'Coffee, brandy and cigars in the smoking room upstairs,' rasped Derek Bradshaw at one of the waitresses, who nodded. The three men then marched almost in military fashion toward the oak door, although admittedly Aylmer Jones lagged fatly behind. They disappeared down the corridor. Giles had no idea why they were doing this, but he was not that curious anyway, because it didn't seem to be any concern of his. As for the others, they were perhaps too flushed with drink, food and conversation even to notice the quick departure.

Huntley Rupert-Smith was tasting his chocolate mousse. 'Not bad, not bad,' he remarked.

6.
Giles Jones' Diary

I remember our first few days in New York very well because it was so strange and novel for a little British boy – Idlewild Airport, for instance; we landed at night, in the middle of an electric storm. I had never seen forked lightning before; still less had I ever seen lightning in hot, humid weather.

The airport itself was in chaos, as it seemed to me, but it was just very busy. I have no recollection of the cab we took to the city centre, and to the plush hotel on East 60th Street that must have been recommended by the friends of my father's with whom we had stayed in Paris for a few days; but the next morning I awoke in a strange room on my own – Damien's bedroom was across the passage – beside a window through which the brightest of sunlight was flooding, a far cry from my basement bedroom in London. The morning must have been advanced because I heard many street noises outside, in particular that of construction workers who were shouting at one another. They could be heard above the din of the traffic, which itself was so loud that it was a surprise to me when I saw how far below they were; we were many floors up in a skyscraper. As I looked, I heard one of them shout "Big Deal!" and was thrilled because, although I had often read this expression in American comic books, I never thought I would actually hear it.

Later, Daddy and I met in the sitting room of the suite, prior to going out, but our exit was delayed because he was worrying about what to do with the eleven hundred dollars he had obtained in Paris for the trip. It did not occur to either of us that the hotel might have a safe in which to deposit it. I suggested dividing the bills up and putting them in different pockets of his clothes, so that if he was pickpocketed not all of the money would be taken; and he seemed to think that this was a good idea.

In the lobby a receptionist approached and told Daddy that the manager wished to see him. This was alarming because there seemed no reason for it unless the authorities in England had already been alerted to the kidnap of a child and discovered where we were. With apprehension, therefore, I waited for what seemed like a very long time before Daddy reappeared from the office at the back of the reception, looking exasperated. He became sullen and threw his hands up as if in despair. I asked him what the matter was. He told me that the manager had told him that it was not customary for men to go out without wearing their jackets in this part of town.

It was indeed hot, as I was to discover, but even so, etiquette demanded that a grown man should dress properly. So, Daddy took the elevator all the way up to our suite and a few minutes later returned with his jacket on. Not that it made much difference to the general dignity of his appearance: despite his bespoke suits my father always succeeded in looking shambolic. At the moment this was not helped by the fact that he was not wearing a tie, and his white shirt was crumpled, its collar hanging messily over the lapel of the hastily donned jacket. My father hardly ever managed to get round to having a haircut, so that his grey mane with streaks of black at the back was always too long. The appearance was certainly very striking and in fact I think it was vanity rather than carelessness that stopped him from going to the barber's too often. He once told me his hair had gone quite grey overnight, following a nightmare, but I didn't believe him, partly because of the way in which he had conveyed the information, with a curious sense of pride in his own suffering. Anyway, hair just didn't do that so quickly.

The heat of the mid-morning hit me as we left the hotel; I had not experienced air conditioning before, and assumed if I had thought about it at all that the temperature outside would not be much more than that within, but I was wrong. Also, the searing heat seemed to make the cars larger, the sides of the buildings larger, even the people larger, the noises coming at me were ever louder; it was unnerving. I looked to the large figure of my father at my side and he seemed to be wading through some shimmering substance, the loose folds of his shirt and trousers flapping oddly, but there was no wind. He had already taken his jacket off and was carrying it over his arm. I noticed that there were many men about who were not wearing jackets either, and I wondered what the manager had been thinking. It did not occur to me that maybe he was a snob who insisted on his guests turning

26

themselves out smartly. On the other hand, maybe he had simply seen Damien Jones as particularly scruffy and wanted, as far as possible, to rectify this. Perhaps any other jacketless guest of the hotel would have passed muster in his eyes.

We took a walk in Central Park, which was nearby, but the sweltering heat became dreadful. I could not tolerate it. I took shade under an awning beside a large stretch of asphalt where some black boys were playing ducks and drakes with ice cubes from a large bag they had obtained from somewhere. The cubes sped and hissed and bounced their way along the surface as if with a life of their own, wriggling like snakes as they stopped sometimes quite near me, steam rising alarmingly.

After a while Damien returned from wherever he had gone to and suggested we have lunch, which seemed to be a good idea, so we returned to the streets and looked for somewhere convenient. We went into an Automat, a branch of a very big self-service chain at the time, and were immediately caught up in the lunchtime crowd. A man standing facing me happened to place his hands on his hips and draw the lapels of his jacket back, thus revealing that he was also wearing a shoulder holster with a gun in it. Another man bent his gingery face towards mine just as I was wondering how to deal with the coin operated displays behind which lay the food. He showed me, and I begged thirty-five cents off Daddy so that I could obtain a dish of baked beans. They turned out to be deliciously hot and dry. Daddy was also trying to get something for himself. This gingery man asked if he could join us at our table and we could not refuse because the place was so busy and he had been most helpful but Daddy seemed terribly reserved about it and gave me a kick under the table when I mentioned to the gingery man that we were staying in a hotel on East 60th Street. I only did so because I was proud to be able to say the name of a street that was new and foreign to me, and the gingery man had sensed that we were from "out of town" as he put it, and had politely asked where we were from.

He was terribly polite and there was something faded about him, I thought, something old world, though I had no idea what I meant by this; maybe it was just because I found him reassuring and non-threatening; a nice contrast to my father, in fact.

'It's a vast country, a vast country...' he explained about America while Damien simply glowered at him. He was a youngish man, thirty or so, sandy complexioned, with good, clean, clear skin. However, he wore a hat which he never took off. It was a part of him, just as the other man's gun and holster had been.

Suddenly, Daddy got up and asked gruffly, 'Are you coming, Giles?'

We left the Automat in a hurry, without even saying goodbye and once outside he shook me violently by the shoulder and asked, 'What did you do that for?' in a threatening tone of voice.

'What?' This was in a whiny child's voice. I was at a loss to understand what he meant.

'Tell him where we are staying. You might have known...'

'What?'

I was bewildered and cowering with my back to the wall, against which Daddy had pushed me; he had his face within inches of mine, a habit bullies have which I have disliked ever since. '...that he was a private detective sent to find out where we are.'

This had not occurred to me, but I silently dismissed the idea as bonkers. The man had been too genuine. Nevertheless, I muttered, 'Sorry.'

'Very well, then.'

Daddy walked on. I followed.

Though the heat was still immense and the environment utterly new and not always reassuring, we continued to walk for hours, my father engrossed in his own thoughts and I trailing a little behind.

I could not have told you what I was thinking about, if anything, but on that day and for the rest of our time in America I became aware of an anxiety within my being that I had not noticed before. It was triggered, I think, by the fact that my father would nearly always be talking to himself, apparently engrossed in conversation with someone who was not there. This imaginary person always seemed to be walking ahead, but facing him, and my father appeared desperate to get his point of view across, because he would gesticulate wildly and lunge forward, as if trying to catch that person but he never succeeded, because the latter would skip away, out of reach.

When we returned to the hotel Daddy's mind was reanimated by the danger the alleged private detective had posed and once again he blamed me for giving away vital information. 'You wait till we get upstairs,' he had said menacingly while we were in the elevator. I was, of course, frightened by this but when we entered our suite he appeared to have forgotten all about it and we settled down, I to watch television in the sitting room – another thrill, this, for it was in colour – and Daddy to do whatever it was he did in the privacy of his bedroom.

Later, I went into my own bedroom and amused myself by watching the comings and goings of the visitors to the Copacabana Club, which was at street level opposite my window. A very imposing-looking doorman in green livery and top hat saluted the newcomers and hailed yellow cabs for those who were leaving. You could just about hear the tinkle of jazz music coming from inside. There were pretty tubs of flowers on either side of the portico and a plush carpet ran under the awning from its steps across the sidewalk to the road.

7.
Narrative, 1967

The three men installed themselves in the comfortable smoking room on the first floor of the hostelry. It was otherwise empty. It was low-ceilinged and, like the dining room downstairs, every bit of it creaked, just as if they were in a ship on gently lapping water. Everything was still and, for the moment, silent, for they said nothing to each other and had tacitly agreed not to until the waitress had brought their coffee, brandy and cigars and departed. Derek Bradshaw stared at the low ceiling, which bulged in places and had been painted white many years ago, and had a curving cornice all the way round it. He seemed in a kind of trance, his elbows on the rests of the deep armchair he had chosen, the tips of his fingers touching those of his other hand.

Graham Greene had filled his pipe and was now puffing at it and staring moodily into the middle distance, while Aylmer Jones had grown a little impatient and was moving about restlessly on a leather sofa of the gentleman's club sort. Presently, the waitress bustled in with a laden tray and with brusque excuses for the delay deposited it on the table in front of them. After they had helped themselves and made themselves comfortable again, Derek Bradshaw looked keenly at the other two and began. 'As you both know, old Damien Jones was an extremely rich man. But there are complexities to his estate which will entail a great deal of time to unravel. A very great deal of time.' A pause. 'In the meantime,' he continued, 'I understand you both have agreed to become administrators of his said estate?'

'Yes.'

'Rather.'

'Good. May I also take it that in your capacity as administrators you have the full approval of the other interested parties?' Nods all round. 'I am thinking, in particular, of young Giles and his mother. Naturally, in the normal course of events it would be Mary who should look after her son's interests, but, but...' The solicitor started to choose his words carefully, '...she feels her proper place is at the university, where I believe she is studying for a degree in International Relations as a mature student.' Silence. If Derek Bradshaw had hoped that his listeners would be impressed by this news, they showed no sign of it. So, he quickly went on. 'In any event, as I understand the matter, you, Graham, I can call you Graham, may I Graham?' Graham Greene continued to puff at his pipe but gave an almost imperceptible nod of the head.

'Good, good, and while we're about it, may I call you Aylmer, Aylmer?'

'Awfully sorry, old man, but I prefer Mr Jones.'

'Very well, Mr Jones,' said Derek Bradshaw drily. 'You are, of course, at liberty to call me Derek.'

'Right-o.'

For some reason Aylmer Jones had started to fondle his knees quite furiously.

'At any rate,' continued Derek Bradshaw, 'I assume we are all friends here, are we not, and as I was saying, Graham, you might have had objections to Mary Jones' involvement?'

'All academic now,' Graham Greene replied, 'as she's not on board. But for the record, I daresay there'll be bad blood between the Greenes and the Jones given the circumstances of his death, so...'

'So, indeed,' leapt in Derek Bradshaw. 'At any rate, she is a woman and this is man's work.'

Derek Bradshaw said this while casting his eyes carefully, first at those of Graham Greene, next at those of Aylmer Jones. The others took the point.

'My poor dear Coral has suffered so much,' said her father quite insincerely. 'She's never had a chance in her life. And to have met that monster – you'll forgive me I hope, Mr Jones?'

Aylmer Jones nodded. 'Never liked the fellow myself,' he said, 'even though we were kith and kin. Hardly knew him, as a matter of fact. Of course, he was far too stuck up ever to have anything to do with me. A mere country bumpkin I was, to his suave metropolitan ways.'

'As I was saying,' resumed Graham Greene, 'to have met that monster, Damien Jones, he tried to kill her! Of course, I was wholly against the marriage at the time, but she would do what she wanted to do. And now it has come to this...' His next words came out as a splutter. 'What I say is, let's screw the bastard's estate for everything it's got!' He took a large gulp of brandy.

There followed an atmosphere of relief in the room. Somebody had said what needed to be said, what they were all thinking; although Aylmer Jones ended up with a look of faint puzzlement on his face.

Derek Bradshaw looked at Graham Greene and started to smile ingratiatingly. 'Graham, I fully understand what you are saying,' he said. 'And I am of a like mind. What your daughter was forced to endure at the hands of this man must have been quite dreadful. The least we can do – I mean, is your daughter feeling quite well?'

'As well as can be expected in the circumstances,' replied Graham Greene stiffly, 'but her mental health is fragile. You have seen her on one of her good days.'

He meant his daughter's behaviour downstairs. It did occur to Derek Bradshaw that it was a strange thing for a widow to be having a "good day" on the occasion of the burial of her recently deceased husband's ashes. But of course he did not mention this. The thought had distracted him, however, so he missed the first bit of what Graham Greene was saying next. 'She has her lapses and then she has to get carted off to a private loony bin in Kent somewhere. It's not cheap, I can tell you. The doctor tells me it's only a matter of time before she has to be sectioned for good. I don't know what I'm going to do because I've taken a few duff positions on the stock market, and what with her mother not being around…' Graham Greene had started to bleat. It was embarrassing. It was as if he were rehearsing for the part of that stock type in literature, the broken man.

'There, there,' said Derek Bradshaw, with his rasping voice. 'It must be awful for you. It never rains but it pours, of course.' Derek Bradshaw knew that Anne Greene, Coral's mother and Graham Greene's wife, had died of cancer some years ago. 'I can let you have a cheque,' continued Derek Bradshaw. 'We administrators are entitled to our expenses and, in any event, your dear daughter is the major beneficiary of Damien's estate, having been his lawful wife, the precise duration of the marriage being neither here nor there.'

Derek Bradshaw continued to look at Graham Greene appraisingly, almost as if he were prey.

'If you will let me know how much, I can arrange funds for this loony bin of yours. Backdated and payable into your account, of course, as Coral is not capable of dealing with her own affairs.'

Graham Greene's discomfiture settled in an instant: now he seemed beatified, which was an odd appearance for him to have, given the essential prosaicness of his square, middle-aged, middle class features.

'I say,' piped up Aylmer Jones who, until this moment, had remained quiet because he had been struggling hard to follow the drift of what the other two had been saying to each other.

These other two now looked in his direction with some alarm, just in case what they had been slyly proposing would be shattered by a shell from a loose cannon.

'I say,' he faltered, aware of their close attention. 'If Mary is out of the picture, does that mean her ghastly son is too?' Silence. 'I mean,' he continued, 'he is his father's son, ghastly as he is, and surely he ought…'

'Giles Jones is still very young,' cut in Derek Bradshaw smoothly. 'He has his 'A' levels to think about. I understand that, regrettably, this business and, ah, other matters have affected his studies adversely. Furthermore, as administrators of this estate you are my clients and I take my instructions from you and not from Giles Jones, who is not my client and who is, in any case, a minor. My expert professional advice will be invaluable to you both, of course, but in the end the decisions regarding the estate are yours. No, no, it will be many years before young Giles sees any capital, if ever. There are enormous death duties to pay and in the meantime, he will receive a modest allowance, of course.'

'Enough to buy him a haircut, what!'

Aylmer Jones thought he had made an utterly trenchant remark and heaved himself from the depths of his sofa while grinning fatuously at the other two, in an effort to force them to concede its effectiveness. But all they did was smile slightly.

'Enough to buy him a haircut, as you so rightly say,' said Derek Bradshaw evenly.

'I was only wondering, you see,' continued Aylmer Jones, confident now of having secured the others' attention. 'Well, it's jolly difficult to explain but the farm has been making such a loss these past years, Venni and I don't know what to do. Farming's not easy at the best of times but, well, I mean it would be so awful to have to sell up, Badfield's been in the family for two hundred years, heaven knows what the county would think if we were to… well, I mean, it would be unthinkable, it, well, it just bally well wouldn't do, I mean.' Aylmer Jones' face had contorted into a look of horrible supplication. His eyes constricted with fear, his cheeks wobbled, woe was writ large upon him. He was sweating profusely. It was disgusting.

After a studied pause, Derek Bradshaw said with a rasping quietness, 'Mr Jones, as I have said, you are entitled to your expenses. If these must include the settling of the Badfield estate accounts so that you have the necessary peace of mind to concentrate fully on your duties as an administrator, which undoubtedly will be considerable, well then, so be it. If you will let me have the details, I will make certain arrangements.'

Once the solicitor's words had sunk in, Aylmer Jones slowly began to look mightily relieved and surprisingly for the first time, he gulped down half a glass of brandy and said, 'Oh, good-oh. I'll get the old accounts to you right away.'

'You must make sure you have my correct professional address,' continued Derek Bradshaw quickly, 'which I will give both you gentlemen later.' A pause. 'Bradshaw's is removing, you know, from Hatton Garden to better, I mean larger, premises in Lincoln's Inn Fields.'

Another pause and that ingratiating look came again into Derek Bradshaw's face, an expression in which, most unpleasantly, his teeth were bared.

'I must say,' he continued, 'the expense of such a removal is proving to be enormous, of course, but I thought it fitting, in view of an increasing workload and indeed the management of the estate of so illustrious a deceased as Damien Jones Esquire, that, well, my firm now has offices commensurate with his undoubted standing when he was alive; and so…'

The stockbroker, Graham Greene, knew exactly what this man was driving at but because the demand this solicitor was about to make was so outrageous, even for him, he was having uncharacteristic trouble with his words. He thought he'd nip in with a helping hand.

'My dear Derek', he said smoothly, 'I'm sure Mr Jones will agree with me when I say that any financial difficulties you might be having with regard to your removal to Lincoln's Inn should be alleviated by what funds you need from the estate of the late Mr Damien Jones. After all, you as solicitor to the administration will also need complete peace of mind. What is sauce for the goose is also sauce for the gander, eh, Mr Jones?'

Actually, Aylmer Jones hadn't expected at this point to be spoken to at all, so it was just as if he had abruptly risen from his slumbers when he said, 'What? Oh yes! Rather!' Derek Bradshaw's ingratiating smile slowly broke into a broad-beamed, wolfish grin.

'You so instruct me?' he rasped.

'We do.'

'Rather!'

The three happy gentlemen sat back with their brandies in a beneficent haze of cigar and pipe smoke, confident in the knowledge that, thanks to the untimely death of one Damien Jones Esq, a man who, when alive, was not at all well-known to any of them, their several financial problems would be relieved, if not entirely eradicated.

8.
Giles Jones' Diary

We did not visit the Automat again, which was a pity as I had quite liked it and found its coin-operated windows novel, and the question of the gingery man must have been tormenting Daddy's mind, because in a few days' time, he woke me roughly one morning and announced that we were to travel to Chicago straightaway. He had bought the tickets. He told me to pack, which I did in feverish haste because his own sense of urgency communicated itself to me, and I made myself available to do whatever his bidding directed, I suppose because I was his son. That did not, however, mean that I was not riddled with anxiety.

To my surprise we went by Greyhound bus, the cheapest form of long-distance travel in America, but when Daddy explained that he had heard from a friend in London that the courts had sequestrated all his assets in an effort to get us back to England and having also explained, in answer to my incessant questions, that we couldn't get any money, I did understand why we had to use this mode of travel. However, this was an adult preoccupation and it certainly did not distract me from more immediate experiences such as the notice above the driver at the front which read that the company aimed to serve its customers at all times without regard to "race, color or creed". This too was novel, and not just because of the spelling of the word "colour".

I was glad that the comfortable, air-conditioned interior of the coach, though crowded, was a million miles away from the cramped stuffy conditions and the groaning engines of the Green Line coaches our family had used for excursions around the countryside near London before we got a car. It meant that there was no danger of my being sick and needing the bus to stop so that everyone could watch me vomit by the side of the road. Despite, or because of these advantages, I was asleep as we approached Chicago. I know this because Daddy woke me so that I would not miss sight of its skyline, which was magical in the grey distance, its skyscrapers much more set apart than those of New York, and standing like sentinels.

At the terminal we made our way, though we did not know it, to the city's red light district where we checked into a large, but downmarket hotel, whose lobby consisted of nothing but banks of telephone booths and a drugstore at the side. A notice proudly told us that there were more telephones in Chicago than in the whole of Russia. We took the elevator to our apartment on the eleventh floor; in layout it was much like the one in New York only dowdy, and the television, I sadly noted, was only black and white. Daddy wasn't bothered about this, however, he hardly ever watched television anyway and referred to it as the "idiot's lantern". He wasn't in the least interested in how American television might compare with that in England, but I was. The adverts, for instance; how strange it seemed to be viewing houses for sale on the small screen. They looked pretty tacky, too. As did a sauce called "Adolph's" but pronounced "Ay-dolf's".

I'm telling you this because for the next few weeks I did nothing but stay in my bedroom and watch television and read comics. I would also listen to a little transistor radio I had bought for six dollars, which I played late at night under the bedclothes when I couldn't sleep. It just had pop stations which didn't interest me very much, but that was all there was. A number of them had disc jockeys who competed to see who could play the most records – or platters, as they called them – in one hour. It was funny because the only way they could hope to win was by speaking so quickly that it became impossible to understand what they were saying.

When I grew bored of this I would get out of bed and look through the window, down onto the street below. I must have been a hundred or so feet up but I could see the comings and goings, of which there were many in this part of town. There was a shop opposite whose front entrance was set back with a sort of corridor leading up to it, affording shelter for those who had nowhere else to go. I did not realise this at first, but the scruffy young men who congregated there, indeed, did not have anywhere else to go, I thought they were just socialising, until come the first faint blue streaks of dawn some of them squatted on their heels and tried to get some shut-eye. Others lolled against the windows of the interior of the corridor and tried to sleep that way. It did not look as if any of them succeeded, or if they did it was not for very long. These young men were often to be seen in the daytime parading up and down the lobby of our hotel. I don't know how they did it but they always managed to smarten themselves up after their sleepless night in the cold, some of them wore their hair so that it looked like pink or mauve candy floss, and some had the enviable knack of holding transistor radios to their ears by the shoulder, leaving their hands free, perhaps to comb their hair or fiddle with the phones in the phone booths, which reminded me of the hairdryers you saw in ladies' hairdressing salons, only covering the whole body. They were transparent so that you could see what the caller was doing but not hear what he or she was saying. You'd often see them in the soda fountain too, by the side of the lobby, leafing through magazines on sale in the stands or taking a glass of Coca-Cola at the counter. They hardly talked to each other, in contrast to the night-time when I supposed their chatter was in part an effort to keep warm. It was strange; I wondered who they were and what they were doing, but didn't dare ask. They certainly didn't appear to notice me at all. In any case I was more preoccupied with the banana milk shake I loved to watch the soda fountain man making for me; it was my favourite. Daddy always gave me the thirty cents or so with which to buy one, but he also told me that I would have to amuse myself from now on as he had important things to do without me – he did not tell me what they were and I didn't ask.

So, I roamed the streets of Chicago on my own, which was also strange but not at all frightening. Once again I was fascinated by the adverts, this time on billboards high up on the buildings, one of which read, "You don't cop out, so why should your cigarette?" I didn't know what "cop out" meant, I guessed it meant "fall to bits" or something like that. "Kent, with the micronite filter" – I didn't know what "micronite" was either.

One slogan I did understand – "Winston tastes good like a cigarette should". But I queried the grammar. I couldn't figure out why it read wrong but to me it did.

I determined to visit the Palmolive building and see if I could get to the top of it, this was because it was the tallest skyscraper at that time and had a powerful navigational beacon on its roof which circled the city at night, successively lighting it all up in a magical way. You could see it happening from my bedroom window. To my delight when I got there I discovered that anyone, including myself, could travel the elevator to the top, which I duly did.

But on the way down a strange thing happened and for the first time I was frightened. I thought I had been alone in the elevator and,

38

therefore, thought I must have been day-dreaming when I heard someone say, 'Hello, haven't seen you in a while.' I looked up. It was a friendly man's voice and he was looking down at me. I smiled back but did not say anything. Then when I got out onto the street a car drove by and a woman stuck her head out of the passenger's window and shouted, 'What's a matter with you?'

It was more of a passing scream than a shout and it was directed at me. I was puzzled, I did not know what to make of it. But the car did not stop and I carried on my way.

When I got back to the hotel Daddy came out of his room and said, 'Giles, there's someone I want you to meet.'

Her name was Valerie, she had just come from London, she was slim, dark and I would have thought attractive from an adult man's point of view. Over the next few days she was very nice to me but I never asked myself what she might be doing with us. She was obviously sleeping in Daddy's room with him, but that was no concern of mine, nor even was it of any interest. Her presence did not change Daddy's behaviour in the least, but at first they seemed to get along well together and we went looking for an apartment to live in, though it never occurred to me that the plan was to settle down in Chicago.

Valerie was not at all impressed by some of the apartments we saw; one was in a basement with a bad smell in it, or at least she thought so because while we were there she made a point of screwing up her face in disgust and putting her handkerchief to her nose. I remember this because a few days before, she had allowed me a puff of her cigarette but then told me that my lungs would be quite pink and in far better condition than hers as she had been a heavy smoker for a long time. In order to illustrate her point she had produced the handkerchief and inhaled the tobacco through it. She then showed me the brown stain that had collected there and explained that this was what happened to her lungs whenever she smoked. I was intrigued.

Valerie and I were often left alone together because Daddy claimed to be working in his bedroom and didn't want to be disturbed. She even helped clear up my own bedroom which had become so messy that the chambermaids had finally refused to have anything to do with it. We used to play games like Snakes and Ladders and jigsaw puzzles and other such stuff, but after a while she grew bored with these and one day she asked me if I would like to learn a new game. Eagerly I asked what it was and she produced a coin and dropped it down the front of her dress and told me that the object of the game was for me to hunt around in her clothes until I found it.

She then stood up and wiggled so that the coin fell further down inside and maybe lodged in a part of her body that was difficult to get at. She lay on the floor and invited me to crawl all over her and put my hands down her front and up the hem of her dress and search around. I did so with alacrity, giggling all the while – first her breasts, next her private parts. She started to giggle too; eventually we were rolling around on the floor in a paroxysm of delight. She was making it as hard as possible for me to find the coin by squirming around and contracting her muscles, which only redoubled my efforts to make sure I found it. I didn't understand why at the time but my little willy got very hard and rigid, and Valerie's giggles turned to deep breathing, and she started to make a funny, low, moaning noise. She then let out a gasp and didn't want to play anymore. I had before that for some reason looked up and saw my father stealthily watching us through a gap in the door which had been left ajar. It gave me a shock but the game carried on anyway and he didn't intervene. I don't think Valerie noticed him at all, and I never told her. I don't think I ever found the coin.

Anyway, we continued to look for an apartment and there was one in particular which I really liked because its telephones were fixed to the walls, something I had never seen before. Also the wire which connected the receiver to the base was coiled like a spring, again, something I had never seen before. They were green in colour and I could just about get my hands on the receiver if I stood on tip-toe. The rooms were pretty good too; they were unfurnished, clean, light and airy, but there must have been something wrong because on the long way back – it was quite far out of the centre of town and we had to use the Loop – an atmosphere developed between Valerie and Daddy which worried me. They were not speaking to each other and that evening I heard them rowing in the bedroom. I heard the toilet flush and an exclamation come from Valerie, so I went to see what was going on. She came out and told me he had torn up her return ticket to London and flushed the pieces down the loo. Then she turned, looked towards their bedroom door which was open and shouted, 'Damien! Don't!' I followed her in. Daddy was threatening to take an overdose of pills. In one hand he had a number of the brightly coloured capsules he was always taking while with the other he was slowly pouring water from a jug into a glass. He had a solemn, retributive look on his face. 'Damien! Don't!' she repeated; and rushed toward him. She grabbed his arm even as he was slowly moving his hand with the capsules in it to his mouth. There was a struggle. I cannot remember any more.

9.
Narrative, 1967

Giles Jones quietly excused himself from the table just as Huntley Rupert-Smith was tucking into his chocolate mousse. He also had a quiet word with his mother, who quite understood when he told her he wanted to see Jones Place for, what he thought would be, one last time. It was getting late, and he wanted to catch it before it was dark. He also told her that they weren't to wait and that he would get a cab back to Badfield afterwards. Again she quite understood, and asked him whether he had enough money. He said he had. He got a cab in the High Street, which took him the couple of miles to the place of his birth. He asked the cab driver to wait at the gate, and he walked the quarter mile or so along the straight, narrow drive to where the derelict manor house stood on a sort of platform – a raised area which ran down to the meadow on one side, a line of now scraggy golden cypresses acting as a barrier between them.

On the other side, the drive continued toward a ride, the entrance to which was overgrown and half-hidden by the branches of trees. From memory Giles knew it went along the edge of the meadow and turned back on itself, enclosing a system of pools where, apparently, a swan had made its home and only left when the old squire, Giles' great-grandfather, died. This ancestor liked to sit by the pools for hours and feel the peace of the place and, from time to time, he would feed the swan a particularly rich sort of cake of which he himself was very fond. Turning away, Giles looked across to the cottage in which he had been born; it too was on a platform on the other side of the drive, which sloped upward towards the fields and, behind it, a dense forest of beeches. Giles remembered these from early childhood as being so fantastically tall that he would marvel at them as their tops swayed gently in the wind, gently, but with great strength, producing an imperious, rolling, backward and forward susurration, like the sea. They were doing so now, and as he looked up they were no less tall than they had ever been and their presence in the darkening afternoon, and the noise they made, seemed to Giles to be the determinant of what life their surroundings had. There was a chill in the air. Giles kicked a few stones on the drive and wondered what to do next. He was fearful of entering the cottage, he didn't know why. It would be dark and empty, of course, and the lights wouldn't work; in fact now that he remembered it they had had to content themselves with paraffin lamps whenever they came down; and maybe there were ghosts there.

It had never occurred to him before, but this spot was utterly isolated, yet seemed so alive; a few shades more and it would be frightening. Maybe even then he had had an inkling of this, although he had been allowed to run naked in the grounds and had done so with all the carefree abandon of a small child. Even accidentally falling into a bed of nettles while in that state, at the side of the steps that led up to the cottage, hadn't deterred him, although he remembered the pain of it and in memory the pain had grown even worse.

At this moment the cottage was turning into a shadow. Unusually, one of its end walls also formed part of the brick wall which supported the embankment, therefore stopping it from falling into the drive; it made the building look taller than it actually was. There was no visible moon but you could see the extended wall as a pale slab which reflected what remaining light there was.

This, too, was eerie and as Giles looked toward the gate at the end of the long, straight drive he was disconcerted to find that he could not see it; only the railing that separated the drive from the meadow and that impression of flatness on the left, between the drive and the beeches, where a tennis court had once been. It was somewhere along there in the scrub that Damien had once thrown the ignition key to the family Daimler after a row between himself and Mary, who had threatened to return to London on her own.

He did not want to stay here any longer; it was past – the past, albeit his past; and he made a silent vow – which he did not keep – that he would never return. He trudged quickly back along the drive to the gate, where the cab driver sat in his car in a pool of light. He had been reading a newspaper while he waited.

The next day Giles Jones cried off the various lifts he had been offered back to London and elected to go by train instead. He wanted to be alone so that he could compose himself for what he had in mind, namely a final visit to 15 Pimlico Road, his home; where he had been brought up. But he was in for a shock, because the locks had been

43

changed and he would, therefore, have to see Mr Derek Bradshaw about getting a new set. He knew that the solicitor had travelled to the capital immediately after the wake, so he did not think there would be a problem seeing him.

Mr Bradshaw received him in his office in Hatton Garden with a singular lack of enthusiasm. Indeed, it was quite obvious that he regarded this young man with the now restored Jimi Hendrix hairstyle as a nuisance, even a potential danger. Added to which, there was the inconvenience for him that he and his firm were already in the process of moving to swankier premises.

'No, Giles, I'm afraid I cannot give you a set of keys. I forbid you from going there.'

'Why? It's my...'

'I do not have to give you a reason. I have instructions from my clients, of whom you are not one. That is all that needs to be said.'

Derek Bradshaw was twitching a little. He was a small man, even less tall than Giles, and he had the habit when standing of looking up at whoever he was speaking to, if the latter were also standing. Further, his teeth were bared and his customary rasp had now turned into a snarl, as if he were a member of the animal kingdom about to be confronted by a predator.

Jacketless, his sleeves were rolled up and his waistcoat undone. He was holding a large ornament of some kind which he had been in the process of putting into a box; now he just clutched it to his chest defensively. Behind him Giles could see what looked like large pieces of office furniture under wraps, ready to be removed, and a shapely woman going to and fro.

Giles was shocked by Mr Bradshaw's attitude, which he found incomprehensible, but most unwisely he decided not to argue the point. That was because he knew how to get in anyway; ever since he could remember, the sash to one of the windows of his basement bedroom did not work properly, with the result that a simple twist of the handle, if done correctly, would open it. Burglars were not encouraged because all appeared to be in order from the outside; on the other hand it was a method of entry Giles had often used if discretion dictated that it would be better than to use the front door. Without saying another word he backed out of the office, leaving Mr Bradshaw still clutching his ornament, a look of bafflement upon his face, and took the tube from

Holborn to Sloane Square, from where he walked down Holbein Place into Pimlico Road.

As he approached the familiar terrace of three houses, of which number fifteen was the middle, he felt a pang of remembrance, because in recent years he had not been there very often at all. His father had become just too difficult and awkward to live with. Painful memories of an unhappy, earlier childhood started to beset him, but he knew he had to suppress these otherwise he would not be able to continue with his visit. In fact, he had simply to stop thinking at all if he were to enter the house, quite apart from not wishing to be seen.

So, he quickened his pace and looked neither ahead nor back as he opened the gate and walked down the stone steps to the basement, above which were the railings that separated it from the pavement. In truth he was now anxious that the fault in the window frame might have been spotted and rectified by an officious solicitor's clerk, or that he would have forgotten the knack he had of turning the handle in just the right manner, but to his relief neither proved to be the case. With a deft twist of the wrist, the casement opened and he climbed onto the window sill, squatted there and jumped onto the floor. His basement bedroom seemed to be exactly as he had left it but was, as always, quite dark without a light on even in daytime. Nevertheless, he sat in the gloom beside the bookcase which was only half full of books as it always had been, and lit a cigarette.

It crossed his mind that he should set fire to the house since, if he could not have it, he did not see why anybody else should; but he was at that time too law-abiding to do anything more than merely contemplate this extreme course of action. Instead, after a few minutes he put his cigarette out and went into the kitchen next door.

The first thing he noticed was that the silver with the family crest upon each item was missing from the magazine in which it was kept on the dresser; as too was the tea service whose usual place was on one of the shelves above it; but he didn't think so much of this. For some reason it didn't occur to him that the articles might have been stolen. His attention was more taken by the table by the wall, around and above which so many dreary arguments had taken place; and the occasion he well remembered when Damien had threatened Mary with a knife in front of his small son. Not so long before that, he himself had been threatened with murder by his own father, because he had been whining in the corridor about something or other.

45

Those were the searing perceptions, be they past or present, against which an absence of utensils was small fry. In order to protect himself from them he left the kitchen hurriedly and ascended the uncarpeted staircase to the ground floor, but stopped when he saw the door that opened onto some stone steps which led down again to the small neglected garden outside.

He found it impossible not to be assailed by painful memories. Try as he might, he could not suppress them. As a small child, he used to play in that garden all the time, mainly doing naughty things like repeatedly cutting down next door's washing line with his pocket knife; until an angry neighbour whom he barely recognised had confronted him in the street about it and he had never done it again.

One day he had stolen about nineteen shillings in silver which his father had left upon the mantelpiece in the drawing room – Damien had a habit of emptying his pockets of loose change whenever he returned home. Giles had done this before without anybody noticing, but it had never been nearly so large a sum, so it was a reckless thing to do. He had put the money in a small, heart-shaped purse their current au pair had given him. She was German, and on the purse was a picture of a picturesque town dominated by a cathedral, with "Stuttgart" written underneath. He had dug quite a deep hole in the garden and buried the heavy, bulging purse, carefully replacing the earth so that it was completely hidden. He thought that if he did this, in time a money tree would grow, bearing silver fruit. It would be a useful addition to the weekly pocket money he was given, which he had always bitterly complained to his parents to be on the meagre side, having compared notes with other children at the Orange School.

Regrettably, however, Damien had noticed that his nineteen shillings were missing, and his thunderous face had greeted Giles one afternoon when he returned from school. He was summoned into the drawing room, where his mother squatted on the floor in her usual fashion – index and middle finger stuck together between her teeth and a copy of The Times spread out before her, which she was pretending to read. Damien had demanded to know what happened to his money but Giles, feigning ignorance, refused to say. There was a stalemate; until a temper whose eventual explosion had always been inevitable got the better of Damien and he shouted, 'I refuse to let a son of mine grow up to be a thief!'

Whereupon Damien had grabbed Giles by the hair and smashed his

46

head against a low-standing but heavy coffee table, whose pointed corner embedded itself into his temple. Giles screamed with pain. Blood started to pour onto the carpet. Damien let go and recoiled, realising that he had gone too far. He was utterly shocked by his own actions. So was Mary, who took one look at the wound and called an ambulance. By then Giles was lapsing in and out of consciousness through loss of blood. He only fully came to his senses when he became aware of a curious tickling sensation to his forehead and realised he was on a hospital bed of some kind. A man in a white coat was standing over him and putting in stitches; this man was talking to someone else about a mutual colleague who had a "dicky heart", apparently, and was living "on borrowed time". Giles felt somehow drawn into this conversation, and was pleased to realise that the terrible pain he had felt was now gone, to be replaced only by this curious tickling, which in itself was not wholly unpleasant.

Now, all these years later, he was entering the drawing room where it happened and the first thing he saw was the fluffy white rug that Mary had put on the carpet by the coffee table in order to hide the stain his blood had made, which repeated application of cleaning materials had failed fully to remove. He smiled drily at the sight of it. Then he saw by the window the studio couch on which his father used to lie for most of the day and next to that the table upon which he kept his pills. The cushions at one end were still unevenly stacked, with the appearance, even at a distance, of neglect. He knew that if he put one of them to his nose the smell of his father would come back to him, but he didn't care or dare to do this. Instead, he realised how still everything was; already this drawing room in which he had spent so many hours as a child was ceasing to have any relevance for him, its walls, fixtures and fittings seemed to be losing their substance, as if passing even now from reality to a distant past. It was heartbreaking but for once Giles did not cry.

He wanted to see whether his grandfather's service revolver was still where Damien used to keep it, wrapped in an oilcloth in the top part of one of the fitted cupboards in his study on the first floor; so he went up there and looked. He had to stand on a chair to see into the dark interior. But it was gone, as was the ammunition stored by its side in a cardboard box. It was only now that Giles appreciated that the silver downstairs had been stolen, because the gun, too, clearly had been. It was a pity because he, himself, had planned to take the latter as a souvenir and now he would not be able to. His grandfather's military bearskin, too, was missing from the attic where Giles used to play with it, together with his tops and other toys which he'd put there for secrecy's sake. One could only get inside the attic by climbing through a small trapdoor in the ceiling of the bathroom below, so someone must have been through the whole house with a fine toothcomb. Not for the first time, he wondered who.

10.
Giles Jones' Diary

Valerie did manage to get back to London, leaving Daddy and me on our own. She had also managed to defuse his play-acting, but the serious side of it remained and maybe sooner or later I would have to cope with it, although that was not something I thought about at all. I did appreciate he had a serious drug habit but that was just my father; he had always been like that. He took three sorts; Drynamil to pep him up, Sodium Amytal to calm him down and Nembutal to get him to sleep. But where did he get these drugs from? This question was particularly apposite in America, where funds were low; and once when he was in very short supply he asked me to break open the capsules and separate the tiny beads into their different colours, because he thought that each colour might have a different effect upon him. It didn't work. He swallowed a quantity of one of the colours but almost immediately as I recall he felt the wrong effect coming on, though there was a smile on his face and quite obviously he didn't mind what was happening to him.

Daddy had a friend in London who sent us money from time to time; it was always five hundred pounds in cash, in a brown envelope, and we would have to go to a bank or post office to change it. This friend, who was very close to Daddy because they had spent many years together in a German prisoner-of-war camp, did what he could, but his despatches were intermittent and Daddy always got worried when the next lot was supposed to have arrived but hadn't. After the initial eleven hundred dollars dried up, it was the only source of money we had and I suppose it all went on living things and Daddy's pills, because as I discovered the hotel bill went unpaid and one day after we had been in Chicago for several weeks he told me with a worried look on his face that the manager wanted to see him. He felt sure that it must be about the unpaid bill and maybe we would get kicked out of the hotel and have to sleep on the streets, just like the young men I could see from my bedroom window. His acute anxiety about this communicated itself to me and I felt the same. But when he returned from his meeting with the manager he looked relieved and told me that he had been given two tickets for us to see the annual fourth of July celebrations in Soldier Field, an open-air sports ground outside the city. The manager had kindly, or maybe ironically, thought we might be interested, as we were British.

These celebrations went on long into the evening so that it was night time when they finished with a fireworks display which included an enormous and very good likeness of the face of John F Kennedy, the then president. I had not known before then that fireworks could do that, and have never seen anything similar since; but the next day our money worries returned, and Daddy thought he'd better look for a job.

'I don't mind what I do,' he declared. 'I could be a dishwasher, I don't mind.'

As it turned out, this British landowner got a job selling encyclopaedias in the suburbs of Chicago. I remember him telling me that he had been told that either he could get fifty dollars a week salary but no commission on any of the sets of encyclopaedias he sold, or he could get eighty dollars commission on each set sold but no salary. He asked me what I thought. I didn't have the faintest idea, but tried to be helpful. In the end, I think he plumped for the commission without the salary but he only ever made one sale anyway.

One evening he returned smoking a cigarette, which was unusual for him, his grey overcoat buttoned up to give him that short, stout look he had; he was smiling with an inward sense of triumph. He told me that he had managed to sell a set of the encyclopaedias to a respectable young black couple who were starting a family and, therefore, wanted to "improve their education". Yet mixed with his pleasure at having sold the books (and he had been genuinely impressed by the quiet earnestness of the couple), was his sense of the callousness of the other salesmen who worked with him, of their racism which even to their potential customers was barely disguised – "they're out of their cotton-picking minds", was one illogical expression he'd heard that very evening; and throughout the long shift in a cold, dark and obscure part of town, during which he'd had to trudge from door to door, he hadn't been able to obtain anything to drink but Coca-Cola, which he detested. Maybe that was why we went to California, I don't know, but perhaps the reality of having a job proved too much for him; better to keep on the move, to provide an easier illusion that something was happening.

Daddy must have been in funds because we began by staying at a decent enough hotel called the Shattuck, on Shattuck Avenue. Though I didn't know it at the time, he was trying to make himself more respectable because one of the first things he did after we had settled in was to arrange for me to go to the local free school. This was the George Washington Elementary and it, too, was on Shattuck Avenue. It was a delight to go there, be normal, get out of Daddy's claustrophobic company, the only trouble was that I was perpetually embarrassed by my clothes, as my grey flannel shorts had started to get holes in them between the legs and anyway I did not have much of what you would call a wardrobe, not having been bought anything to add to the few things we had hurriedly packed before leaving England. But none of this mattered very much because as I say it was such a delight to be among children my own age and our teacher, Mr Yoshida, was fantastic. He gave his life and soul to the job and was particularly sympathetic towards me, sensing, perhaps, a troubled background; or maybe it was because, like so many others in Berkeley with Japanese origins, he too knew the difficulties of living in an adopted country. I think it was the former. At that time my puppy fat was in danger of turning into obesity, and it was always a trial for me to be in the playground with the others during physical education classes. President Kennedy had ordered a rigorous program of exercises to be performed by all children in all schools across the land, perhaps to toughen them up for their anticipated roles as cold war warriors, which meant I always struggled to keep up, but Mr Yoshida generously pretended I had reached, say, the twenty press-up mark when I had done nothing of the sort, even going so far as light-heartedly to hold me out as a shining example to the others – not that they were in the least bit fooled, but they took it in good part.

Inside the classroom it was a different story; at that stage of education the British system was apparently two years ahead of the American, but even if that had not been the case I would still have excelled because I was a bright boy; (yes, Giles, you were such a fucking bright little boy). My essays were regularly read out and pretty soon Mr Yoshida was extolling all things British, perhaps to the bewilderment of the class but certainly to mine and to my then suspicion that perhaps I was not so very good after all, it was just that, Mr Yoshida being an anglophile, favoured me above the others. 'It's a sprawling city, sprawling...' he would say about London, emphasising its nature with eloquent movements of the arm. And, 'They're way ahead of you, way ahead,' referring to the British educational system.

Of all the teachers I ever had he was perhaps the most memorable, this man who was ethnically Japanese, who lived and worked in California but who clearly was a bit of an anglophile. Yet to look at he was nothing much, by which I mean only that with his spare build, his average height, his glasses and unremarkable haircut, his unexceptional white short-sleeved shirt and dark well-pressed trousers of some synthetic material, he could just as easily have been a bank clerk as a teacher, or anybody for that matter who would not stand out in a crowd.

Attending George Washington Elementary put a routine into my life and it was, therefore, a pleasure to go there every morning, made more so by the fact that things were strangely different from those to which I had been used in London. For instance, we always started by singing one or two patriotic songs. Mr Yoshida would get the battered old portable xylophone from the cupboard by the door, open it up and strum along to a chorus of childish voices "... and those caissons keep rolling along..." were some of the words. I bet Mr Yoshida only knew how to strum these few patriotic tunes and I never knew what a "caisson" was; still do not, really. Afterwards, came the ritual of water drinking: a ritual because a tap or faucet, as they called it, would be turned at the back of the class and the water allowed to run for twenty minutes before the first child put his mouth to the stream. The idea was that the water would not really be cold and pure unless you let it run for twenty minutes, which was oddly paranoid, like the obsession the Americans and, therefore, their children, had with their teeth, cavities and fluoride in the water. Next came bomb practice, which usually just consisted of us getting under our desks and staying there until Mr Yoshida blew a whistle. On sterner occasions an alarm would sound all over the school and we all would have to go into the big auditorium across the playground and stay there until someone told us it was over; then we returned to our classrooms. Somebody asked why we had to do this and Mr Yoshida explained that there were no windows in the auditorium and, therefore, if an explosion caused flying glass we would not be in danger of being injured by it, but in the event of a nuclear attack that surely would be the least of one's worries, or so it seemed to me because on the night when the Cuban Missile Crisis was at its most critical, Daddy had said to me, 'You do realise, don't you, that we might not be here in the morning?' There was an accusative gloat to his voice and a haunted look in his eyes, but somehow I felt detached at that particular moment.

By then we had moved our stuff and ourselves to a rooming house at the other end of town, walking the distance under the weight of our possessions; money again, you see. The Shattuck was proving too expensive and this rooming house was as cheap as they came, even the university students could afford better, which was why its residents were at the very bottom of the ladder: drunks and the semi-mad, drifters, hopeless types who had gone wrong or who had never had a break in their lives. It was approached by a staircase at the side of a shop, as was usual for accommodation in that town, the shop taking up the ground floor and the higher floors given over to living space. Our apartment was immediately to the right as you reached the first floor; it consisted of a bedroom and a combined living room and kitchen. The shared bathroom and toilet were down the passageway. Opposite, lived a young man who was clearly not quite right in the head but harmless. On the other side of the bannister was a communal telephone. When we first arrived I heard a decrepit man say into the receiver, 'I'd dearly love to see you again, you know.' He said this over and over again; it was like a sad but welcoming chorus for us.

Once inside our apartment, we unpacked. Daddy obviously got the creaking double bed that stretched into the middle of the room, which he immediately lay down upon, while I made do with an equally creaking single bed by the window. I remember I was sick out of that window more than once, not knowing where else to discharge it and I also started to pee at night without bothering to get up and use the communal toilet down the passage. It was not bedwetting as such, it was worse because I was aware of what I was doing and could feel the increasingly unpleasant warmth of my urine as it spread over the grimy undersheet. But it was less unpleasant, I imagined, than going all the way down the passage in the dark and possibly encountering some strange type who wanted to harm me. Afterwards, I would arrange myself so that I was as little as possible in contact with the urine and tried to go to sleep. The stain was always dry in the morning.

11.
Narrative, 1979

Of all the fanciable women who worked at the Huffington Club – whether as croupiers or otherwise – the one who attracted Giles Jones the most was an Oriental whose broken English, on the few occasions he heard it, was oddly Spanish-accented. He could not quite work it out. Yet because he was shy in relation to women he found desirable he had never yet managed to engage her in conversation, and simply had to make do with her appearances as she came to work in the evening and walked hurriedly past reception, where he made sure he was always present when she did. Sometimes she would nod at him, sometimes she would not; for his part he tried very hard – too hard, obviously – to give her a warm and encouraging smile of greeting. But as it was forced, the expression upon his face was more of a rictus than anything amiable, and it was perhaps for this reason that she was sparing with her own response.

What always happened, however, was that once she had passed reception and was approaching the grand staircase that led to the gaming room she would stop at the ornate mirror on the wall and stare at herself for a good few moments before continuing. The way she stared, it was as if it was in disbelief of herself and who she was; it was curious, but at least it gave Giles the opportunity of coolly surveying her trim but shapely figure, her lovely long black hair and her neat, symmetrical features.

This evening he was doing just that when he heard a voice from behind him.

'Dreaming again, Gentry?'

It was Pete, the out-of-work actor, and his remark was apposite because it had taken Giles a moment or two to realise he was being spoken to.

'Oh. Sorry.'

Pete was busy sorting out the hangers in the cloakroom where the members' hats and coats would be deposited. Giles went to give him a hand.

'Hello, chaps.'

It was Sandy; he came bristling into work, bustling like a mother hen, as well as being bright-eyed and bushy-tailed. At the start of the shift he was always like this; it was only towards the end of it that he would get morose and stare crossly at his fingers, which by then would have become dirty through too much reading of next day's newspapers that were always delivered free of charge some time after midnight.

A couple of croupiers came through the front entrance. They smiled briefly at the receptionists but no more than that. It would have amazed the latter if they had known that they were being looked down upon. As it was, Pete gave a suggestive noise which the croupiers ignored. Sandy was oblivious of this because he was fussing over his appearance in a mirror. He actually produced a tiny comb which he used on his moustache. He carefully smoothed his already neat hair with the palms of his hands. He turned and instinctively looked at his wristwatch. Marlene was never late exactly but always managed to be the last of the receptionists to arrive. She had to make her entrance. It was one of a number of affectations she had, of which there were so many that Giles often wondered who she really was.

Later, the telephone rang and Sandy answered it. He listened for a moment and frowned. He turned to Giles Jones and said, 'It's for you, Gentry. Better take it next door.'

Pete and Marlene were busy greeting a middle-aged couple who had just arrived but even so they were distracted and became curious at the intrusion. It was not really acceptable for staff to take private phone calls at work but Sandy saw the value of allowing some latitude to those immediately under him in this regard; and in any case, for historical reasons there was an extension in the little room behind reception which otherwise was not used. Giles Jones had also frowned when told it was for him but he did not think to ask who was calling. Instead, he simply walked into the little room and closed the door behind him. He picked up the receiver and waited till he heard a click on the line, which meant that Sandy had rung off.

'Hello?'

'Mr Jones?'

'Yes.'

'My name is Mort Sloane, I work at Bradshaw's.'

The voice on the other end of the line was thin and distant, precise but hesitant. The words themselves so far meant nothing to Giles Jones.

'I'm afraid I don't...'

'Bradshaw's is the firm of solicitors handling your father, Damien Jones', estate. I work as a managing clerk there, have done for a long time.'

Oh – Giles Jones remembered the name now. Over the years he had largely succeeded in ridding the heartbreak of his father's sudden death and its mortifying financial consequences from his mind; but strangely – which made this phone call a coincidence – those distant events and the oppressive and continuing silence in relation to any inheritance he might receive had recently become matters which, try as he might, he could not stop thinking about. That was why he had started to write his diary.

'What do you want?'

There was a pause; maybe this Mort Sloane was startled by the sharpness with which the question had been asked; or maybe it was the question itself, which indicated a quite unexpected reaction to this more than equally unexpected phone call. But he answered, 'I want to help you, Mr Jones. There are things you need to know.'

Giles Jones said nothing. He did not know what to say.

'I'm sorry, I...' the man continued, but left off.

Giles Jones did not know why, but he had the impression that Mort Sloane was somehow or other wiping his forehead in sorrow and regret – and indeed embarrassment and shame – for a failure to do things which should have been done many years before. He thought he heard the sound of liquid being poured into a glass on the other end of the line. Otherwise, except for the hum of the phone, there was silence.

He became suspicious. 'How did you get this number?' he asked.

'I spoke to Mrs Mary Jones, your mother. Her details are on our files. She would not give me your home number but she told me where you worked.'

'I see.'

That was some confirmation that the man was bona fide.

'Look, can we meet? I wouldn't keep you long. I feel it really necessary that I give you certain information, but it's not possible without a face to face.'

'All right', said Giles Jones noncommittally.

'I could come to you tomorrow morning, wherever you like.'

'But why are you putting yourself out so much?'

'I'll tell you, I'll tell you.'

There was a pleading note to Mort Sloane's voice. It crossed Giles Jones' mind that it might be himself who would be doing the other man a favour in agreeing to meet.

'Alright.'

'Tomorrow morning, say ten. Where?'

'I can't make the morning. That's when I sleep.'

'The afternoon, then. Say two. Where?'

Giles Jones thought for a moment.

'There's an Italian coffee bar on the corner of Queensway and the Bayswater Road,' he said. 'Not far from the Coburg Hotel. I'll be there at two.'

He put the phone down.

Immediately afterwards Giles Jones asked himself why he had ended the phone conversation so abruptly. He scarcely remembered the man's name, nor had he sought confirmation that the place and time he had suggested would be acceptable to him. Furthermore, he had no idea how they were supposed to recognise each other in a coffee bar which was always busy, when so far as he knew they'd never met.

Most of all, he assumed, albeit unconsciously, that he himself wouldn't necessarily turn up. On the other hand the tone of the man's voice made him sure that he would be there. Beyond that he could not analyse, not least because as he waited by the phone in the cramped, airless little room just in case the man rang back seeking further clarification, he felt a headache coming on, which reminded him of the ones he used to get in adolescence at Selwyn Mauberley College.

He shook it – his head that is, just as he had done all those years ago in an effort to rid himself of the discomfort; and waited. But Mort Sloane did not ring back, so he returned to reception looking a bit shaken. Sandy had been carefully waiting to gauge Giles Jones' demeanour when he should open the door; he looked, but said nothing. As for Giles Jones, the rest of his shift passed in a dream. When it finally finished, the dream did not; it stuck to him like a succubus all the way along the Bayswater Road, into Brunswick Gardens and his bedsitter, where unusually he went straight to bed, his head thumping as if he were about to get a bad dose of the flu.

He felt better when he woke about twelve. However, it took him a

58

while to remember the appointment made the night before; the memory of it startled him from his usual lazy lie-in; and he sat up, perplexed. Did he really want his past to be raked over for him by a stranger? For that is what the meeting would involve, he suspected. Having forgotten some of the impressions he had had when on the telephone, he asked himself, what were the man's motives? He had no idea. But whatever they were, did he really want to go down that road? He thought of ringing his mother, if only to ask whether she'd been contacted by him, but he recoiled from that road too. He got out of bed, the narrow, single bed with its oddly named "American Mood" sheets which he'd bought for a song at Whiteley's, and was as usual quite oblivious of his shabby, narrow surroundings, because he was exclusively preoccupied with his own thoughts. Mechanically, he put the coffee on and washed, shaved, cleaned his teeth while waiting for it to brew. The bubbles started, and he poured himself a cup. He lit his first cigarette of the day, and sat back on his chair in front of the desk by the window, with the grey light outside. He was still in his underwear. It was quite cold.

The trouble was, he thought, that he'd reached an emotional equilibrium which he didn't want disturbed. It had been hard going and he didn't really know how he'd achieved it but that is what he had done, at the cost, perhaps, of other more material rewards. It was not only that, but he felt frightened of his past being dredged up, of what such a process might do to him and what it might mean he would do to others. For there was hatred buried within him, of that he was sure, buried because he had not known where else it could go. He had not known what else to do with it, short of breaking the law, because if he hadn't buried it, if he hadn't buried it...

Suddenly, Giles Jones leapt to his feet, giving his knee a hard bang on the edge of the table and displacing the coffee cup. He had suddenly become aware of the direction in which his thoughts had been drifting and he didn't like it. His heart was racing and he was gasping for air. He told himself to calm down. He smoked furiously then stubbed the cigarette out.

Luigi's was a popular coffee bar cum restaurant with good food and cheap prices, obliging staff and a cheerfully careless atmosphere. Giles Jones liked it for those reasons, but also because he could breakfast there in the afternoon if he wanted, or sit for an hour over a single cup while he read the newspaper or a book. Today it was so busy that he had to share a table; the couple didn't mind – they were too engrossed in each other. That left the seat next to him free. He ordered a coffee and waited, he'd deliberately not brought anything to read because he wanted to keep his eyes peeled. All he saw, however, were a lot of people enjoying themselves, talking animatedly when they were not eating or drinking. Faces of the regulars were familiar to him; the waiters and waitresses were too. He felt at home. The coffee was good, as always, far better than what he could make in his bedsitter. He was savouring it carefully when he heard a man's voice say, 'Hello. Haven't seen you in a while.'

Giles looked up and felt a spasm in his head. Standing above him was a neatly dressed man in his sixties, with gingery hair and mauve spectacle frames that were too prominent. He was holding a document case to his chest but for a moment Giles thought he might produce a gun from a shoulder holster.

'You won't remember me, I expect, but I remember you as a little boy. Mort Sloane. We spoke yesterday evening. May I sit down?'

Giles Jones said nothing but Mort Sloane sat down anyway, with a minimum of fuss. The couple opposite did not notice. Giles Jones was somehow shocked. He had suddenly been reminded of the gingery man in the Automat in New York all those years ago, but this could not be the same person. The voice was different, clipped and reticent (and English-accented), just as it had been when they had spoken on the telephone. It was the hair, that's all. It was exactly the same colour, but apart from that there was no similarity. This man's complexion was florid, his eyes behind the glasses beady. Plus a weak chin, thought Giles; and thin lips that wobbled a bit. He'd noticed a spindly frame but also a paunch which a natty waistcoat did not conceal. Mort Sloane put his document case on the table and appeared to be thinking hard for a minute. He did not seem in the least interested in ordering anything for himself.

Because they were seated next to each other, the two men's faces were at an angle. Giles looked at him curiously out of the corner of his eye but Mort Sloane merely studied the table top.

'I suppose I'd better get right down to it,' he said, opening the document case and extracting a thick file. 'I want you to take this with you when you go home. If you look at it you'll see that it proves what I am about to tell you. Not to put too fine a point on it, everything has

60

been stolen from you.'

'How so?' asked Giles, almost with an air of scientific detachment.

Mort Sloane gave him a brief quizzical look and continued, 'My boss Derek Bradshaw with the connivance of the administrators Graham Greene and Aylmer Jones have been selling off valuable assets of your father Damien's estate and pocketing the money themselves. I know you haven't received anything because it's part of my job to raise cheques and I've never been called on to raise one for you.'

Giles Jones' quite inappropriate air of scientific detachment was now changing to one of bewilderment. It seemed that Mort Sloane was growing impatient.

'Look, it's quite simple,' he said turning to Giles Jones so that he could see him properly. 'Take Emrys farm, for instance, one of your father's holdings, prime Herefordshire land. It raised six hundred thousand pounds in 1969, a lot of money in those days. A lot of money now. The cheque for the proceeds of sale was paid into Bradshaw's client account where it should have stayed for eventual distribution among the beneficiaries, but instead he wrote further cheques drawn on that account for two hundred thousand pounds each to Aylmer Jones, Graham Greene and himself. These cheques were duly credited to the gentlemen's private accounts.'

Giles Jones was now mystified. He had never been good with money and had always found it difficult to follow any description of its movements.

'But surely,' he asked, 'there would be a record of this, so that...'

Mort Sloane was growing more impatient. His face assumed an owlish, professorial air, his voice became more clipped. 'That transaction and others equally lucrative were never entered into the estate's account book. It was as if they never happened. Others less lucrative were, just to make things look reasonable, but that money went on lawyers' fees, tax, your stepmother Coral's nursing home fees, incidental expenses and so on. You really have been ripped off good and proper, you know.' With that, Mort Sloane sat back a bit and waited for the effect of what he had said to sink in.

Eventually, Giles Jones asked, 'Why are you telling me this?'

'Guilt,' was the straightforward reply. There was a prim, defiant look on his face now.

'Why? Are you involved in all this?'

'No.'

'Well, if you knew, and how did you know, why didn't you do anything about it?'

Mort Sloane didn't falter one bit. He gave the appearance of a man who was determined once and for all to rid himself of every last drop of a concealment he'd harboured for a very long time. 'As to your first question', he began, 'I was a policeman once, but had to leave the force in disgrace, I won't go into details, but it concerned a certain addiction of mine.' He coughed. 'But I still retain links and was able by certain contacts to gain access to the personal bank accounts of Aylmer Jones, Graham Greene and Derek Bradshaw. It's all in there.' He patted the file in front of him. 'And as managing clerk of the firm that was handling the affairs of your late father I had access to the estate's account book and an original inventory of all his assets at the time of death, which document has been tampered with, by the way. That's in there too.' He patted the file again, and continued, 'As to your second question, I was compromised. I'd left the force in disgrace and was very lucky to get a job with Bradshaw's. I needed the money. If I'd blown the whistle that would have been it and I doubt whether anybody else would have wanted to employ me. Added to which...' here Mort Sloane did falter and started to look ashamed.

'Yes?' Giles Jones prompted.

'Oh, well, here goes. You asked me why I was telling you all this and I told you that it was guilt. That is because when your father died it was one of my jobs to make an inventory of the contents of his London home and also to make sure that the locks were changed, because even then they wanted to shut you out. I did as I was told and was going through the house as instructed and – and...'

Giles Jones waited. He knew what was coming.

'I took certain things, some silver, jewellery, an antique gun, photographs; things which were obviously valuable which I knew I could easily pass on for a few quid and nobody would be any the wiser. Your stepmother was more or less mad, see, and you weren't going to be allowed in any more. Plus, your own mother was out of it, she wasn't an administrator, she would never know, they'd been divorced for years anyway. I sold the stuff and, well, as I say that's where my addiction comes in.'

Giles Jones decided not to tell this man that having broken into his own home he had known that certain items were missing. In fact he decided not to say anything.

'Well, I've told you everything now and I'm glad I have. I don't care if I get into trouble for this. It's been on my mind for so long and now it's finally off my chest. Take a good look at that file there Mr Jones, and see what you want to do. But I tell you I'm not going to the police and if they come to me I'll say nothing. The ball's in your court now, Mr Jones. Goodbye and good luck.'

With that Mort Sloane rose abruptly from his chair and marched out of the coffee bar, taking his empty document case with him. Giles Jones watched him as he went but he didn't once look back.

He spent the rest of that afternoon and early evening before work going through the file Mort Sloane had given him. Its contents were neatly arranged, with explanatory tabs to divide the different sections. Cross-references had been inserted by hand, to highlight and make plain the real movements of very large sums of money and their end destinations. The estate's account book itself, the thing which, if necessary, would be shown to the world as a plausible financial picture of the administration, was, if read in conjunction with the other materials, nothing but a pale reflection of the truth. It was not even that; it was a travesty of it. Giles Jones was engrossed. Mort Sloane had arranged matters so well that reading the file was like reading an exceptionally good thriller; in doing so he lost all self-consciousness about the activity but, also like a thriller, he himself did not really feel that he was involved, this was not happening to him, the excitement lay in what was happening to others. True, there was some mention of him in the estate's account book – outstanding fees of his minor public school, for instance – but that was not the real story. That lay in the carefully collated bundles of bank account statements, a paper trail that even to a layman could only lead to one conclusion: that Aylmer Jones, Graham Greene and Derek Bradshaw had been crooks all along, no matter how much they might try to justify their activities to others, or even to themselves. It was with gradual astonishment, therefore, that Giles Jones began to realise that the victim of all this was himself. Because Mort Sloane had been such an apt spoonfeeder, his ease of reading meant that he could identify with the characters on the pages but that he could not grasp that he was one of them. It took a sudden, final spasm of concentration for him to appreciate that, not only was he involved in all this, but that, being his father's son, he was the principal victim. At which point his heart started to pound and he felt a choking sensation in his throat. A curious agony of mind assailed him, but at the same time he was paralysed and could not move. Something was happening to his being which would change him for ever.

He was aware of this but powerless to do anything about it. More immediately, try as hard as he might he still could not move; it was terrifying. Suddenly he had the idea of a refusal to fight the dark forces that had been unleashed within him. Instead, he would adopt them, since he could not do otherwise; and make them his own. The paralysis then passed.

12.
Giles Jones' Diary

Daddy would do nothing these days but lie on his creaking double bed and whenever I was around demand that I go down to the drugstore and buy him another "thirty-five center", as he called them – cheap, trashy paperback novels with lurid covers which he read avidly. I told him with very much a little boy's primness that I thought there was too much sex in them but he only laughed, shrugged and said, 'It's what makes the world go round.'

It was fun, though, to go to the drugstore, except that I kept on seeing dubious things which I didn't quite understand, like a magazine cover that showed a naked woman being held down by men while one of them carved a swastika on her back with a knife. Nobody seemed to mind. A man was sitting at the soda fountain quaffing his Coca-Cola and saying, 'Gee, that's so refreshing!' while I watched the man in the white bumfreezer behind the counter make me a banana milkshake.

This Cuban Missile Crisis was worrying and frightening. President Kennedy's television address to the nation was watched by people standing shoulder to shoulder in crowded coffee bars and soda fountains all over town; those who couldn't fit inside watched the black and white screens through the windows from the sidewalks, which in turn were crowded. The people strained to hear what he was saying, their children cried on the way to school on the bus; or they remained silent and glum, as it were turned to stone by eavesdropping on what their parents had been saying; yet Mr Yoshida remained upbeat, I think because he honourably thought it right to be like that in front of his charges; also maybe because he had a racial memory of this sort of thing, and appreciated just how disastrous the consequences for all could be.

When the crisis appeared to be receding he invited the class to a discussion about it. It was the only time he got cross with me, I think because when we were asked who would volunteer an account of what had been happening I took the lead; and it was too much even for him to have a British child give an opinion before that of an American one. So, I was interrupted and contradicted, with Mr Yoshida giving the definitive account of the events. All the other children had been strangely silent anyway; perhaps at the age of ten or thereabouts they were simply too young to conceptualise their fear.

I had, on another occasion, told the whole class that when I grew up I wanted to be a "Sir" and then had to explain what it meant to be knighted in England. I only mention this because patriotism was a large part of my mental make-up at that time, and it seems to me that this feature helped me not to be frightened of world events in the way, perhaps, that the other children were, since it was a necessary part of a little English boy's patriotism in the 1950s to feel that his country was the most powerful in the world and as mighty and resilient as any could be, more so, even, than the Soviet Union or the United States. But when I voiced something like this to a group of young male UCLA students in the launderette which was round the corner from our rooming house, they were amused but politely did not agree.

'Maybe fifty years ago,' one of them said good-naturedly.

I was disappointed by this and reported the conversation to my father, who to my even greater disappointment ruefully confirmed that that indeed was the case.

He then proceeded to do a ludicrously bad imitation of the American soldiers he had seen liberating Munich, toward the end of the Second World War. He himself had just escaped from his prisoner-of-war camp and had walked the twenty-five miles or so to that city under cover of darkness.

How they slouched! How they chewed gum! It clearly had been an eye-opener for him, coming as he had from a pukka British army background, in which such casual behaviour, even after heavy fighting, would have been deplored.

Daddy took an interest in a project I was doing at school. We all had to do one and could choose whichever subject we wanted so I chose the Industrial Revolution in England. I don't know why I chose this, maybe it was because a longing for my country and its history had been kindled by a visit to Berkeley by the Duke of Edinburgh. I can still remember him standing in an open-topped car and politely raising his hat to a curious crowd as it passed. The next day the front page headline of the local paper carried his quotation, "Odd place, this Burr-keley", and it only confirmed to me in an amusing way the obscure feeling I had always had that the town's name was not being correctly pronounced by its own inhabitants.

But when the project was finished – a bundled together portfolio of colouring drawings, pictures cut from magazines and my oversized babyish handwriting – Daddy looked at it and got very angry. I thought he was going to hit me.

'Of course the Industrial Revolution didn't have to happen!'

I didn't really believe in the conclusion I had drawn either, but hadn't known how else to finish the text of the project, and had thought it would be a good flourish to end with an assertion of the subject's historical inevitability. In any case, I don't know why Daddy got so cross; it was frightening and these moods of his were becoming all too usual, bizarre and unsettling for a little boy; and his behaviour not just towards me but also towards others was, well, off.

One evening we went to a really friendly meeting of the Parents and Teachers Association and as we sat with others in the audience the principal of the school on the stage in front welcomed "our British friends" while looking directly at us. I was faintly pleased and proud, and it was natural that we get to our feet to acknowledge the mild but warm applause. I looked up at Daddy but he was scowling while they clapped, one of those grin-and-bear-it scowls he had, with his lips pursed and his tongue forcing its way between them, as if everything was wrong with the world and he hated it but had to put up with it.

By this time Christmas was on the horizon, and it had got very cold. The young man in the apartment opposite had put a wreath on his front door, but it was not very cheery, and a long time had passed since I solitarily celebrated Thanksgiving Day in the Ground Cow, a hamburger restaurant on the other side of the crossroads, near our rooming house. For months a film called Peeping Tom had been showing at the cinema further down the road, but this was avowedly adult entertainment and me and the friends I had made went to other things like science fiction and horror. We also went out washing people's cars for fifty cents a time, and spent our money in the local department store or at the movies. We watched Reptilicus, which was about a giant lizard that terrorised the world but could not be destroyed because it would always simply replicate itself if any part of its loathsome body were cut away; and another one about alien invading bats which killed human beings simply by wrapping themselves around their heads and squeezing until the blood came. The poor victim was inevitably doomed but would nevertheless struggle frantically to get the thing off his head but would eventually succumb and drop to the floor in a pool of blood. It was horrible.

I am telling you these things because on one level I was a cheerful little boy who integrated well with his new environment, but on another there was the most hopeless anxiety and dread, a sort of billowing smoke which threatened to engulf me and which I could only keep at bay by pretending it wasn't there. The smoke of course emanated from my father and I tried to ignore him as much as possible. But it was not always possible, as when one evening he flew into a rage because I was reluctant to read the manuscript of a novel he had been writing and had asked me to read – reluctant only because at first glance I could not make head or tail of it – and in any case there seemed to be far more dots than words in the text, together with strange-looking hieroglyphics scribbled in the margins, things which disturbed and oppressed me. I had more or less immediately put the manuscript aside, saying I thought it "quite good" and further thinking that that would be an end to my involvement in the matter; but that was when the rage started. There was a small table just to the side of my bed on which I kept my comics and other materials, this he took with both hands and started violently to bang it on the floor. The comics – including Mad Magazine, my favourite – went everywhere. I was sitting on my bed at the time, with the manuscript, right next to it. I took fright and ran to the other end of the room, maybe scattering the manuscript, where I cowered against the wall. He didn't say anything, he just kept on banging the table on the floor and giving me such a fierce look that I thought he was going to kill me. 'Just keep banging the table on the floor,' I said to myself, because I thought that if he took his rage out on the table he would not take it out on me. He did not take his wild, fierce eyes off me for one moment, but he did just keep on banging the table on the floor; and it became surreal, particularly when he started to calm down, because his movements became ones of slow-motion, and eventually petered out altogether. He put the table back on the floor, almost gently, and turned to give the ceiling and its bare light bulb one of his customary haunted looks. Next he started to pick the pages of his manuscript off the floor. He arranged them neatly on a shelf. Then he picked the comics up too, and put them back on the table. As he was doing this he muttered something about my forcing him to live in a slum. I was still where I was, my knees trembling so badly that I had no idea how I managed to stay standing. I cannot remember what happened after that, maybe he took one of his thirty-five centers to read in the latrine down the hallway.

I didn't know it at the time, but Daddy's purpose in coming to Berkeley, and indeed his putting me in a school, was so that he could plausibly contact some influential relatives living in Oakland, the other satellite town of San Francisco. I think he thought that they would help him, or, to put it in a more flowery but somehow more accurate way, that they would give him succour against what he considered to be the dark forces ranged against him in England. In this he was quite wrong, as perhaps anyone with a reasonable degree of common sense could have told him if he had bothered to ask. Also, if that was his purpose I have no idea why he waited so long before contacting them, because we had been in Berkeley for several months before a meeting was arranged in a Chinese restaurant near where they lived. The evening meal itself I don't remember at all, except that there was a painfully studied atmosphere between the adults as they conversed in stilted phrases. I was not listening. I cannot remember what I was doing, but it seems to me now that I was probably trying to ignore them. I had no interest in this peremptory woman with very large lensed glasses, almost like television screens, or this small, softly spoken man with a drooping moustache. Nor even this twenty year-old woman, their daughter, my cousin, who, like me, said nothing at all and remained sullen and sulky, most of the time hiding her face by pulling her long brown hair across it.

When the meal was finished, Daddy and I left before they did; I don't know why. He'd got used to carrying around this cheap black briefcase, of the floppy sort you hold under the arm. Now he hurled it on the pavement and shouted 'Damn!' I was startled; because I had not listened to the adult conversation, I had no idea what was going through his mind. He picked it up and carried on walking, some way ahead of me, muttering to himself. I followed nervously. We had to take a long bus ride home, and during the journey it became clear that Bob and Decca – as were the names of the relatives – had refused to help and thought we ought to return to England. Daddy had gone cap in hand to them and been rebuffed. It never occurred to him that a couple of responsible adults, relatives or not, would obviously turn down a man on the run with a child.

When we got back to the rooming house Daddy simply sat on the side of his creaking double bed and put his head in his hands and wept. The overhead naked light bulb hung over him in a dreary way. He appeared to be inconsolable, but even if he could have been cheered up I would not have had the least ability to do it, for I was alarmed and bewildered by his behaviour, and these feelings produced in me a sort of paralysis. All I could do was wait in the hope that things would change. This had always been my strategy and, even then, I was not particularly proud of it, because I sensed its impotence in the face of forces against which I was powerless. Nevertheless, he did eventually collect himself, by starting to wipe the burning tears from his face with his hands. He did not carry a handkerchief; nor did it occur to me to get him one. His eyes were abject and engorged, and he would not look at me. He seemed the picture of misery as he shuffled about the room making feeble efforts to keep himself occupied by tidying up. He muttered to himself as he did so – strange, incomprehensible words which reminded me of the hieroglyphics I had seen in the margins of the manuscript of his novel. He cut a pathetic and shambolic figure, with his long white hair awry and his shirt tail hanging out of his trousers. I never admitted it to myself, but I was ashamed to be his son.

Later, we sat in the kitchen over mugs of the very strong tea he liked to make. He was not saying anything but brooding inwardly, and was as remote as ever, leaving me uncomfortable, particularly as, as was usual, a drunken couple who lived across the way were threatening each other with knives. A bottle smashed, the sound coming from their direction. After a while, even Daddy became aware of their noise and was alarmed. He shut the window and drew the plastic curtains. It had been cold anyway, the window kept open only because otherwise it would get so stuffy. Then he gave me a sly look and asked, 'Do you want to go back?'

'No,' I said, the monosyllable uttered almost involuntarily, coming out like a croak.

It had always been like this. I wanted to go home very much but always denied it when asked, which he did from time to time, because that is what I thought he wanted to hear. It was like a test, a test of my mettle; and I was not going to let him down. He usually asked the question in an abrupt, accusatorial tone, implying its own answer in the negative and brooking no dissent from that. But this time it was different.

'Perhaps we ought to go back,' he muttered, looking into his mug of tea.

'Don't you think that would be rather throwing in the towel?'

I cannot believe I said this, but that is what I said. He eyed me uncomfortably. He hadn't been expecting that.

'There is no hope, no hope,' he muttered.

Now it was my turn to become uncomfortable, if that were possible, in the sense that it was not exactly an unusual feeling for me these days anyway. After a bit of fluster, I got to my feet and banged the table.

'There is always hope!' I cried staunchly, looking him straight in the eye. Again, it was as if someone else were doing the talking, the behaving; not this cowering ten year-old boy. He didn't answer and looked away guiltily. Silence overcame us once more, a silence that was both troubling and profound, and which lasted a long time. The drunken couple must have passed out, or at the very least given up on each other, because no sound came from their direction either. Only the rumbling traffic in the distance, on the other side of the block, produced a continuous moan, as if it were a natural sound, like that of the wind or the sea. I think we went to bed after that, Daddy going out like a light as usual, thanks to his Nembutal.

13.
Narrative, 1979

Aylmer Jones was not the world's brightest man but that did not prevent him from regretting his own shortcomings. For instance, the fact that he had failed even to get into Eton rankled him all his life. Instead he had had to go to a minor public school situated quite close to the family estate. That rankled too, because it meant he mixed with boys whose parents were in some cases little better than servants of his family's, or worked behind the counters of shops whose freeholds belonged to the Jones'. When in turn he became a man, sometimes his ex-schoolmates, also grown up, became frightfully over-familiar whenever he had occasion to deal with them, which he made sure happened as little as possible. One of the consequences of all this was that, throughout his life, Aylmer had been a stickler for protocol; people had always to address him as "Mr Jones", for example, or, if a relative, just "Jones". The more familiar "Jonesy" he didn't mind so much, if the mood and company were sufficiently jovial. Even his own wife Venetia had had to sign a deed whereby she agreed to address him by his surname only. Originally, he had wanted to stipulate that she call him "sir" but that particular demand had been given the bum's rush by her own family, who had thought that this would be going too far.

It is a happy fact that in the early years of their married life, when their love-making had been intense if not particularly artistic, she would sometimes dare to swoon and murmur, 'Oh, Jonesy...'

But the period with which we are now dealing has left these background details far behind; Aylmer Jones is well into middle age and his wife has left him. She took her brats with her. He is now corpulent and alone. Not that he minds; he sees his fat as muscle and his obligations under the divorce settlement had been surprisingly modest. That was because – his, by then, solicitor Derek Bradshaw had told him – Venetia was a very wealthy woman in her own right, being descended from a successful line of brewers. So far as Aylmer was concerned, he and Venetia had been well fed up with each other. Now that he was free to do as he liked, his only concern was that people should not think badly of him. However, that old sense of form constrained him from going the whole hog, a summary of whose grosser parts his imagination was wont to provide; so he thought he would go to London and look around. Money for this was now happily plentiful as, true to his word, Derek Bradshaw had continued to provide him with the wherewithal for the nurture of his farm. Of course other things had to come first; his own contentment, for example. It was the least owing to him as Venetia had always refused to put up any cash of her own. Her inherited business sense clearly told her that it would be throwing good money after bad.

One morning well after nine o'clock, he was luxuriating in bed, intermittently drowsing and consciously basking in the sunlight that made the window impossibly bright and hazy. His superbly voluptuous sheets enveloped his fat body, which soon would be wholly submerged in a hot bath foaming with all sorts of goodies bought from the best shops. A smooth shave would be followed by breakfast. He always looked forward to a refreshing pint of orange juice and flask of coffee with which to wash down the eggs, liver, bacon, toast and marmalade Mrs Harrison, his housekeeper, who always arrived first thing in the morning, come rain or shine, was a dab hand at preparing.

Once dressed – in a dark suit, since he would be travelling to London for high jinks and considered, therefore, that he'd better look as much like a respectable businessman as possible – he descended the oak-panelled staircase of Badfield Court and entered the dining room. Some of the room's older pieces of furniture looked a little shabby in the sunlight, but he could not be bothered with that. Mrs Harrison was fussing with the hot plates on the side table and did not see him at first, but when he sat down at his usual place she saluted him with a customary, 'Good morning, Mr Jones.' She began to serve him. He had not replied to her morning's greeting, but he kept staring at the space between his neatly laid-out knives, spoons and forks until it was filled with a steaming plateful of offal. She poured a generous measure of orange juice into his habitual tankard (made of silver, complete with family crest). Coffee would come later. She murmured, 'Will sir be taking anything this morning...' Her voice had trailed off, but what she meant was, did he want a nip of something with which to start the day?

He was already eating but he considered as he munched. Better not, he thought, I don't want... but as she withdrew he grew suddenly irritable and looked sideways at her. With mouth full, he mumbled loudly, 'Brandy.'

'Very good, Mr Jones. Shall I bring the post in with it?'

There was a time when Aylmer Jones never opened his mail, because invariably it contained nothing but bills, but nowadays he didn't mind, knowing that the sums demanded would probably be met; so having returned to his food he muttered into it, 'If you please, Madge.' An old schoolmaster of Aylmer's had always used the phrase "if you please" and he had adopted it at an early stage as his own, thinking it the acme of old-world politeness. However, "Madge" was not what Margaret Harrison was called by anybody but himself. She would have corrected him had she thought her job was worth it. When she returned with a large glass of brandy she deposited it and a solitary letter on the table beside him, and withdrew again. He did not look at these until he had finished his food and poured himself another cup of coffee from the pot. He took a swig of the brandy and took up the letter, which he now looked at incuriously as he slid his thumb under its sticky flap. Actually, he was thinking that Mrs Harrison should have brought it on a silver salver, together with a letter opener, but she had relinquished that particular habit when told to, because it had not seemed to him that bills were worth such ceremony.

He was never a good reader, so he was glad at least that the contents were typed, although as he furrowed his brow in a paltry effort of concentration a strange and disturbing sense of familiarity overcame him. He knew this man, he knew who had written it, yet at first he could not quite think who it was. The letter read as follows:

"Aylmer Jones, you will remember me from many years ago when you took it upon yourself to become an administrator of my late father's estate. As you know, Damien Jones your cousin died intestate and I was told at the time by you and others that his financial affairs would take a very long time to sort out. That was twelve years ago, but since then I have heard nothing from you, nor have I heard anything from Derek Bradshaw, the solicitor, or from Graham Greene, my stepmother Coral's father. Now, I have very good reason to believe that you and the others have been systematically plundering the assets of this estate and dissipating them for your own purposes. These assets as you well know should have been mine, because I am Damien Jones' only son and heir, yet as I say, and as you also very well know, I have received nothing. I have been wondering what to do about this. I thought about going to the police but came to the conclusion that that would not be a good idea as they probably would not believe me and even if they did and you were prosecuted such punishment as you would be likely to receive would be quite pathetic and wholly inadequate to what you have done. I also thought of demanding the money back but I have no doubt that you would repudiate such a demand and even if you were prepared to accede to it on pain of exposure I very much doubt that you would be able to return the money. In any case, that is not really the point. The real point is that by your actions you have insulted me and the memory of my father so profoundly that by way of a reply I feel I can do nothing other than terminate your existence. As well as yourself, this also goes for Derek Bradshaw, Graham Greene, and his wretched, wretched daughter Coral, Damien's second wife, whom I absurdly assumed would look after him following their marriage. I look forward to seeing you on the occasion of your death.

Sincerely, Giles Jones."

Aylmer Jones finished reading the letter as slowly as he had started it, but even so he could not quite take in its contents. He had a sense of disbelief about them at first, then thought it must be some sort of joke. However, the deadly seriousness of the letter's tone persuaded him otherwise, and his final feeling was one of intense anger. He remembered Giles Jones all right, that young whippersnapper with the hideous hairstyle. He hadn't liked him from the start, had rather thought he would cause trouble sooner or later. Why, he was just like his father Damien, Aylmer's cousin, whom he had always hated because he was so – well – so bloody eccentric. He wouldn't conform. And so high fallutin' with it, just because he had been to Winchester and Cambridge and called himself an intellectual! How intellectual was it to go and die of a drugs overdose at the age of fifty without leaving a proper will? Having married some idiot of a woman only three months before? Quite frankly, old Damien Jones' son deserved all he got and more.

Aylmer Jones got to his feet, having crumpled the letter into a tight ball, and began to pace the room, muttering to himself, his breakfast quite forgotten. 'I bet he's on drugs, on drugs in some garret somewhere, a hopeless case, feckless, yes, quite feckless, just like his father, a whining little namby pamby who's now threatening me! I was quite entitled – I had every right – Derek told me I could get my expenses, I've done nothing wrong, I've helped, I mean I've helped clear up this business at considerable cost to myself, how dare he...'

It was quite in character for Aylmer Jones to react to a complex dilemma with an emotion that was more blunderbuss than appraisal; yet he did realise that Giles Jones' writing of this letter might well be a criminal matter – after all, he had been threatened – and he asked himself whether he should go to the police. In helping himself to a large part of Damien Jones' estate he didn't for one moment think he had done anything wrong, and, perhaps even more surprisingly, he did not now feel frightened for his personal safety but he did feel affronted at being threatened with death by someone whom he had always thought of as a complete nonentity; it was quite outrageous, and he wanted the law on his side. So, he went to the telephone in the hall and was about to dial the local police station when he thought better of it. He put the receiver back. 'Shouldn't I talk to Derek and Graham first?' he asked himself. 'See if they've... Oh to hell with it!'

He looked at his watch. It was time for Guthrie to take him in the runabout to the railway station. Next he looked at the crumpled ball of the letter which was still in his hand and absent-mindedly stuffed it into one of the pockets of his astrakhan coat before marching with it out into the sunshine.

Guthrie drew up at the entrance to the railway station, got out and opened the rear nearside door for his boss.

'Will Mr Jones require to be collected this evening?' he asked sententiously as Aylmer Jones emerged.

'No thank you, Guthrie,' was the reply.

'Very good, sir.'

After an uneventful journey Aylmer Jones took a black cab from Paddington station to a small, discreet, smart hotel off Ladbroke Grove, which was called the Flamingo. He checked in, as always under a false name. The receptionist was a supercilious young fellow, no doubt a student of some kind who thought a lot of himself.

'The bridal suite, I see,' he said, looking sniffily at the register. He looked up, took off his glasses. 'You'll be glad to hear, Mr Lugg, that the room is specially sound-proofed. We think that other guests get jealous when they hear the sounds these love birds make, if you know what I mean.'

Aylmer Jones ignored the fellow and took the tiny lift upstairs. Once inside the bridal suite – which was of some opulence – he drew the curtains and fetched a half bottle of champagne from the minibar. He popped the cork, poured himself a glass, put the bottle back in the fridge and removed his jacket and tie to make himself more comfortable. He sat on the screaming bed and waited.

Presently the telephone rang and he answered it with some alacrity. The receptionist informed him that a Miss Horniblow was below and desirous of ascending.

'What?'

'She wants to come up.'

'Oh, why didn't you say so? Yes, show her up.'

But there was no room service and, in any case, Miss Horniblow knew the way perfectly well. This was not the first time this arrangement had been made.

She eschewed the lift and took the staircase and after only a minute or so was knocking at the bridal suite door. Aylmer Jones opened it and there she was – pert as ever in her coat, slim and attractive, her blonde hair in a bob, her striking blue eyes sparkling even in the dim light of the passageway. She was carrying a vanity case. She seemed genuinely pleased to see him and when he let her in and closed the door behind her they embraced with sincere affection. Then she stepped back from him.

'What's the matter, Nigel? You seem worried about something.'

'It's nothing.'

He helped her off with her coat and she sat on the bed while he poured her a glass of champagne and replenished his own. He joined her. When they had finished drinking they stood up and each started to undress, much as if it had been a solitary act; but their love-making was very tender and quite long-lasting, she being the more proactive party. He kept on thinking what a lovely little body she had. Afterwards, they showered and put their clothes back on and went down to the basement bar restaurant for a bite to eat. They were hungry after their love-making.

It was not very crowded, it being only five in evening, but food and alcohol were served twenty-four hours a day, which was one of the reasons why they always met at this particular hotel. It had been Angela Horniblow's idea. Mercifully, the garish rock music being played was not too loud, but the bamboo and mirror décor always grated on Aylmer Jones' senses – not so much as it might have done, however, because he was feeling sexually replete and looking forward to his food.

He had a glass of wine in his hand. Angela Horniblow was looking around the room, as she always did just in case some minor celebrity or other were there to be spotted. It was that type of hotel and she, after all, was still in her twenties, at an age therefore when such things mattered. Neither felt the need to talk much, which did not mean that they did not exchange pleasantries whenever the occasion arose. But she did always ask him how business was, to which he always replied evasively 'Oh, all right,' before looking away.

Aylmer Jones had always to remind himself that on his first encounter with Angela Horniblow he had told her that he was an accountant, a rash and stupid piece of self-important lying because he knew nothing and was not capable of knowing anything about that particular occupation. This turned out never to matter because she was always satisfied with his brief answer to her perennial query and really, she was not in the least interested in what, if anything, he did for a living – she was just being polite. It was money that brought her to him, payment for services rendered, but there was nothing wrong with that, nor did it mean that they could not be friends, which they were after a fashion; in fact there was arguably something pure and genuine about their relationship which contrasted pleasantly, if obscurely, with that which he had had with Venetia. It was only when he was with Angela Horniblow that Aylmer Jones did not feel a complete fool. Further, he always felt himself to be a different person when he was in her company, he couldn't say why exactly. As for Angela Horniblow, she felt comfortable with him because in no way was he threatening or even violent like some other clients, and because her intellectual gifts such as they were, rendered his lack of them charming. She was also pleased that they always transacted towards the end of the month, just when the rent on her tiny working flat in Marble Arch became due.

When they had finished eating they returned to the bridal suite where she got an evening dress from her vanity case and changed into it. He merely freshened up a little bit. They ordered a cab at reception and took it to the Huffington Club in Mayfair, which they entered just as it was opening. Sandy came forward and started to make a great fuss of Aylmer Jones:

'Good evening, Mr Lugg,' he enthused. 'How nice to see you!' It was as if he were greeting a long-lost friend.

'Gentry! Gentry! Take Mr Lugg's coat! And Marlene! Marlene! Drat!

Where is that woman? Ah! There she is! Marlene, say hello to Mrs Lugg and take her coat!'

Marlene had finished buffing up her nails so she came forward all smiles, her black evening gown clinging apparently with discomfiture to her skinny frame.

The reception area was not big, and all three employees were now so falling over each other to greet their first guests of the evening that the effect of their bousculades was quite comic. Aylmer Jones and Angela Horniblow smiled good-naturedly but they never thought that their aliases really deceived anyone. Nevertheless, they went through the motions, signing themselves in under their assumed names and Aylmer Jones allowed his astrakhan to be taken by the man called Gentry, whom he recognised as being one of the receptionists at the Huffington Club; but that was as far as his recognition went. It was more than ten years since he had met his second cousin Giles Jones for the first and – as he had thought – last time; and it would have been beyond his powers of recall to match the two men in his mind. The same was almost true in reverse for Giles Jones, but for a different reason. He simply did not expect to encounter a more or less distant relative through the prism of his job. Had he been shown the man in a different context and told, 'This is your second cousin Aylmer Jones whom you have not seen for ten years,' he would almost certainly have recognised him as such. As it was, his eyes gave merely a flicker of something or other as they met those of Aylmer Jones. He murmured, 'Can I take your coat, sir?'

Aylmer Jones did not answer but allowed his coat to be taken and put in the cloakroom to the side of the reception counter; at the same time he was being asked by Sandy whether sir would care to dine now or later?

Aylmer Jones looked at his watch. 'Later,' he said. 'Eleven thirty.'

'Got that, Michael?' asked Sandy.

Michael di Napoli, the restaurant manager, was hovering at the entrance to the restaurant, which was directly opposite reception. He was a stocky, intimidating man who must have been in his fifties. One of his eyes was permanently closed and generally he had the look of a reformed pugilist. 'I will see,' he said in his broken English, and disappeared into the dark and cavernous bowels of his domain.

'Should be all right midweek, Mr Lugg,' said Sandy. 'Otherwise…'

But Michael di Napoli returned nodding his head and the reservation was made. Aylmer Jones and Angela Horniblow smiled at the others and made their way along the hallway towards the staircase which led up to the gaming room.

When they were safely out of earshot Marlene said, 'I wonder where he picked her up?'

'Maybe here,' quipped Gentry.

'I don't think so,' said Sandy primly, carefully scrutinising the photographic gallery of prostitutes caught soliciting on the premises, who were, therefore, to be refused entry in the future.

This gallery was discreetly housed where it could not be seen by customers, as was another photographic gallery of gamblers who were known to "pull strokes", as the jargon had it – in other words, who cheated, often making off with large sums.

'You know we don't allow…'

'Yes, Sandy,' said Gentry, with a touch of sarcasm.

Just then, the second punter of the evening entered. He was a weedy little man called Mr Al Noman over whom far less fuss was made by the receptionists than over the Luggs as he did not leave tips and did not even throw away too much money upstairs. In fact the management was seriously thinking of barring him too, as his membership was not worth the candle to them.

With an acid smile, Gentry took Mr Al Noman's coat – noting as always that it was of a rather unpleasant thin material and smelt faintly of chocolate and tobacco – and got a hanger for it from the cloakroom. As he was doing this one of his hands accidentally brushed against one of the pockets of Aylmer Jones' astrakhan and he noticed that there was something inside it, a hard but yielding ball of some sort. His curiosity was aroused. As he was putting Mr Al Noman's coat away he made a mental note to have a look to see what it was when no one else was around. Such inquisitiveness among receptionists is not uncommon, but in any case something else was at work in Giles Jones' mind. Perhaps after all he had found something familiar in the persona of the man who had just entered with the sexy young woman, and he wanted to explore further.

For the next few hours Sandy, Gentry, Pete and Marlene were occupied with taking the punters' coats, generally greeting them and hopefully taking tips. Some of the latter were superstitious enough to give a big tip beforehand, because they thought that it would bring them luck on the gaming tables. Other members treated the receptionists with off-hand contempt, as they did the expensive prostitutes who were accompanying them. Even so, the receptionists were invariably polite, and left their sarky remarks, if any, until well after the punters had disappeared up the staircase. Curiously enough, if some of the members of the Huffington Club were superstitious, so were some of its employees. Marlene, in particular, would sometimes refer to a new arrival after he'd been dealt with as "bok" or "bokky"; by which she meant that he was a bringer of bad luck. Gentry could never understand this, but when he asked her why she thought as she did she would not answer but merely pursed her lips and frowned, casting her head down so that her thin blonde hair covered her eyes.

It was after eleven when Gentry next saw Aylmer Jones and Angela Horniblow, because they came down to have a pre-prandial before their late dinner. She had that flushed, excited look which signified that she had won something on the tables, perhaps not very much. He, on the other hand, seemed rather anxious; his face was white and sweaty, and more jowly than Gentry remembered, no doubt he had been a loser, perhaps of a very large sum.

The appearance of these two reminded Giles Jones of his earlier curiosity, and when with a not unfriendly nod in his direction the couple disappeared into the restaurant, he realised he was alone. He decided to act, because he might not get another chance, and in any case he had to do so quickly. He fished through the coats at the back and came across the astrakhan, immediately behind Mr Al Noman's piece of schmutter, and quickly located what he was looking for, which appeared to be a scrunched-up piece of paper. It was strangely familiar. He put it into his trouser pocket just as Sandy returned with a tray of tea and biscuits – the receptionists' light refreshments at this hour. Mr Al Noman was just leaving, as it happened, and when he saw the tea and biscuits and realised that they were for the staff he exploded into laughter, showing all his gold-capped front teeth. Gentry had not meant to put the scrunched-up piece of paper in his pocket but read it there and then, and only did so because he had sensed that others were coming. Now he attended to Mr Al Noman by getting his coat, while Sandy, startled by this gambler's reaction of hilarity to the modesty of what he was about to partake, deposited the tray on the counter and smoothed back his thinning hair.

Gentry saw Mr Al Noman out onto the doorstep, where one of the red-jacketed car jockeys, a diminutive but swarthy fellow from Cyprus, looked at him and looked away. Once back in reception Gentry noted that Marlene had returned, and was helping herself and Sandy to a cup of tea. Pete was nowhere to be seen. He joined them and they chatted for a bit; until a man in a trench coat brought all the morning newspapers, including the green ones from the Middle East. Sandy and Marlene had their usual tussle over the Daily Mail, which gave Giles the opportunity to remove himself, ostensibly for a call of nature. It would get busy again soon, but Pete had finally tired of flirting with one of the soft drinks girls upstairs and come back to his duties.

Seated on one of the plush loos reserved for customers at the back of the hallway, Giles removed the scrunched-up piece of paper from his trouser pocket and opened it. He couldn't believe his eyes, but at the same time he immediately realised who the so-called "Nigel Lugg" was. What an extraordinary coincidence! With heart thumping he read his own words, some of which were difficult to decipher because the paper was so creased. This caused him annoyance because in a vain sort of way he always liked to read and re-read anything he had written, but this time the annoyance quickly changed to fury; here was this man, this loathsome individual, gambling money away which should have belonged to him – Giles Jones of Jones Place; while the latter was forced to work at a lowly job in the very casino in which it was happening! Not only that, but later he would have to return to his squalid bedsitter while the usurper Aylmer Jones would go on to enjoy a sexually satisfying stay in London somewhere with that attractive young woman; it was too much.

Giles Jones looked up suddenly, but all he could see were the blank walls of the cubicle. He was sweating profusely and his heart was still pounding but he felt as cold as ice. He was also shaking, and he felt like crying out in despair, but he was also intellectually in command of himself, as always. What he was thinking was that soon this man and his hired woman would be finishing their dinner and then going on somewhere – he needed to know where that somewhere was. Also, what should he do with the letter? Should he try to replace it in the pocket of the astrakhan coat? He thought he should: for all he knew his second cousin Aylmer Jones would notice its absence and start to wonder what had happened to it; and start to think curiously about that young receptionist whom maybe he had seen before somewhere. Giles

Jones got quickly to his feet but immediately stopped himself from leaving the cubicle; he needed to think. He must act quite normally when he returned to the reception area. Now that he had made up his mind to take this unlooked for opportunity of killing Aylmer Jones, he must act as if nothing had happened.

14.
Giles Jones' Diary

We did return to New York after Daddy's unsuccessful attempt to engage the assistance of his late brother's widow and her second husband, but I have no recollection of the journey, except that it must have been in the new year, as it had been in Berkeley that we'd had a big debate about whether to send Mummy a Christmas card; we decided not to. I have no idea if George Washington Elementary was informed of my imminent departure, but I remember chancing to see Terry Kinoshita and some of the other boys in the street just as we were leaving, and I took it upon myself to go and say goodbye to them. They were the ones with whom I went washing cars at fifty cents a time. It has to be said that they didn't seem particularly bothered when told that we were going away and would not be back, their farewells being casual to the point of indifference. I returned to Daddy, who was fiddling with the suitcases, and regretted having approached them at all.

We went to a hotel in New York that in lay-out was much like the one we had originally stayed in, but that is where the similarity ended as it catered for a different economic stratum entirely; though a skyscraper it had the feel and look of a commercial traveller's digs. There was an enormous bar and lounge on the ground floor where tired salesmen congregated and forced themselves to laugh over their drinks, as if having a good time. Whenever a woman entered, I noticed, she was mobbed. In a far corner there was an enormous black and white television which showed nothing but baseball. Our own quarters should have been on the thirteenth floor but they weren't because, in keeping with practically every other establishment in New York and elsewhere, the number thirteen was omitted as being unlucky, so we were on the fourteenth, immediately above the twelfth. There were no room numbers with "13" in them either. Again, there was a bedroom for Damien and a bedroom for me, connected by a passage which led to the apartment door. There were no cooking facilities but we did have our own bathroom.

We settled in, and I went to another school that was just down the road. It was called the Emily Dickinson, after the poet, but its other more bureaucratic name was Public School 75, or just PS 75. The first morning I was there I got pulled up in the auditorium for not singing along to the "Stars and Stripes" as everybody else was doing – even though we had been in America for something like fifteen months I had never had to learn the words. The orchestra came to a halt and it was explained to the very beaky woman who was conducting that I was British and, therefore, couldn't be expected to know them, but while she more or less had to accept this she was very grudging about it. She was quite a terror, maybe she was the headmistress, she certainly looked like one, with a severe mien, scraped back black hair in a bun and thick, heavy, black-framed glasses, through which you could see, and be frightened by, bright beady eyes, which were also of a dark colour. She was not at all like Miss Singer, my class mistress, who was in her spinsterish forties, and who was quiet, very kind and as self-effacing as it was possible to be in front of a room full of girls and boys who, although all aged eleven or twelve, differed greatly in terms of their sexual development. Those who sat at the back tended to ignore her because they were too busy bragging about their exploits of the evening before, while those who sat at the front were still children and listened attentively to what she had to say. The snippets I sometimes heard from the back of the class led me to ask another boy – who sat somewhere in the middle – what sex was. What did it mean when you were told that a man and a woman had had sex? He looked at me thoughtfully for a moment then told me that it was when a man put his penis into a woman's vagina. Those may not have been the exact words he used but whatever they were I got the picture all right, albeit in an obscure way; and was disgusted. It was strange that I had asked this particular boy, because he was not someone I had spoken to before nor, so far as I recall, did I ever speak to him again – he just had seemed to me like the sort of boy who might know these things, that's all, but who was also non-threatening, so that I would not be laughed at for my ignorance.

Apart from the headmistress, such figures in authority as I came across were a kindly lot; the cop, for example, who shepherded us across the road toward the school gates in the morning was always smiling; and when I asked him what the buttons on his tunic were made of he said, 'Brass! Just like you have in England!' This surprised me, not only because I did not know that he knew that I was British, but also because I had been reliably informed in a comic I had read in London that theirs were made of nickel. Equally, one of the sports coaches approached me and was obviously genuinely interested in what games we played at school in England, but I was embarrassed because, apart from occasional sallies to the gymnasium, we just ran around in the playground during breaks and didn't play any outdoor games, certainly not organised ones and certainly not the ice hockey he taught. I think as an ambassador for my country I was useless, more than useless as it turned out, when I stupidly let it be known that I could play chess, because immediately I was commanded to go to the home of another little boy who also played it and he beat me hollow. This produced a bad taste in my mouth; I was made to feel I had been used. The apartment, though ill-lit and to an extent gloomy, obviously belonged to a bookish family, and therefore I should have felt at home in it, but there was nothing on offer by way of candy, cookies or Coca-Cola; also – I cannot well describe it – there was somehow a mean atmosphere, which had nothing to do with the wealth or otherwise of the residents but everything to do with the undoubted fact that this family didn't care about others, only themselves, their own little unit. I was placed opposite a boy with a pasty complexion and a sullen face who never once spoke to me and always kept his eyes on the chessboard. Neither he, nor his parents, made any welcoming noises at all, and you felt not only that the boy was being selfishly groomed for high educational attainment but also that in the process his parents had forgotten about all the other things, if they had ever known about them in the first place. I felt – and was made to feel – uncomfortable and awkward, and knew that it was just a matter of time before I lost the game, which I duly did. It was a relief for the ordeal finally to come to an end, it had lasted quite a long while; and afterwards, there was no conversation, nothing. I was simply dismissed from the apartment without more.

The days went by and, apart from school, nothing seemed to be happening. Daddy was making himself scarce; he hardly ever came out of his bedroom and when he did he looked dishevelled and morose and he wouldn't say anything, just walked around the passageway and my bedroom with an abstracted air, hardly recognising his own son. On these occasions I would be embarrassed and would wait patiently for him to go, so that I could go back to the periodical in which I had been absorbed. I think he had, by now, engaged the services of a lawyer, because a conventional-looking man of about forty in a dark suit would come to the hotel and they would talk, either in his bedroom or at the bar downstairs. This lawyer once fixed the television set in my bedroom for me. I was surprised that such an ordinary person would have wished to associate with my father but they must have struck up a friendship because I often heard them laughing, even singing songs together, in the room next door – "Brother, Can you Spare a Dime?" being the most repeated.

As for myself, I had lost all interest in America as such. Sure, I made a few friends at PS 75, and went around with them after class, to donut bars and so on, and was even briefly and disastrously elected president of the class; but long gone were the solitary walks I had undertaken in Chicago and Berkeley, just in order to explore. To tell you the truth, I was repelled by this part of New York; and it was cold. I didn't have a coat to wear and whenever I walked the streets of the locality I couldn't help noticing the practically universal habit men had of spitting on the sidewalk as they hurried along. I wondered why they did it, but it seemed they thought the activity perfectly natural, like tossing a cigarette butt into the gutter.

Daddy was still trying, I think, to get support – financial, moral, whatever he could – for our continued stay in America. To this end we were invited to a very grand apartment belonging to a woman who must have been distantly connected to him in some way, perhaps a friend of a friend whose job took her to New York, I'm not sure; but it was an uncomfortable experience for me because she would not stop cross-questioning me and demanding to know why I did not have a coat. I said I didn't feel the cold very much and didn't mind. She also gave me some sort of present, a model of a Spanish conquistador complete with metal helmet and breastplate which had been hanging on the wall and which I had taken a shine to.

A few days later Daddy received a letter from her, parts of which he showed me. I really wasn't that interested, and found it difficult to read anyway, but it was obvious that she disapproved strongly of what we were doing; I put it like that but, obviously, it was of what he was doing, and what he was doing to me. She would not, I suppose, have assumed that I, an eleven year-old boy, was in any way complicit with his actions.

She was particularly incensed that I was "forced to go coatless in cold weather", as she put it, and I think it was this that made Daddy finally throw in the towel. At any rate not long after the reception of this letter we were back in London.

I do not remember our return journey at all; my recollection starts with our booking into the Grosvenor Hotel just by Victoria Station. Our own home was only just up the road, but it did not seem odd to me that we did not go back there. I understood that we were still on the run, and wanted to avoid any situations which might lead to detection. The hotel was also near where Michael Alexander lived in Eaton Place. He was the friend of my father's who had largely bankrolled our stay in America. I remember he and his wife, Sarah, coming to lunch with us in this hotel and when asked by the manager whether everything had been alright he enquired whether he could have another slice of beef, which request was granted.

As my father was never an early riser, I used to have breakfast on my own in the grandiose dining room, but stopped doing that when a waiter asked me to finish up all my bacon because he said he might get into trouble if I did not. He was quite urgent about it, leaning over my shoulder in a complicit way, but I was at a loss to know why he should be so concerned and rather resented his blandishments, which seemed to have more to do with him than me. Instead, I tried one of the new Wimpey bars across the road, but its hamburgers were so disgusting after America's that I gave that up too. I still remember the urge to vomit after the first mouthful.

It must have been shortly after that that I was boarded out with my old friend from the Orange School, David Calne. We shared bunk beds in his bedroom at his parents' mansion flat in Earl's Court. David's father was a businessman, a very substantial, florid character who chain-smoked small cigars. He had a horribly constant hacking cough and would leave catarrh-ridden handkerchiefs about the flat and in particular between the cushions of armchairs in the sitting room, where we ate dinner off plastic trays that could be attached to the armrests while watching black and white television.

'There was a bit about it, not much,' he had said, a propos newspaper reports of our escapade in America.

I think he and my own father got on quite well, but Daddy once complained to me that he had been expected to pay for his share of the lunch he had once had with him in one of the chain of coffee shops he owned. Mrs Calne, on the other hand, was a very petite woman with a not unpleasantly pink, pinched face and curt, tight lips. She used to chase David about the flat with a piece of flex in her hands if she thought he had been naughty, and whip him with it if she ever caught him, which was not often. 'Oranges from Gorringe's,' was what she said when I told her Daddy and I had been to that department store to see about a school uniform for me, for the school which Michael Alexander had recommended to Damien that I go to. He knew the headmaster slightly – Michael Alexander knew everyone – and said he was a "muscular Christian".

Daddy was very gruff with the assistant in the store, and most put out when he learnt that some parts of the uniform were not in stock and would have to be ordered specially, causing a delay, it being term time. This meant that I would be without certain important items of clothing when I arrived there. Apparently Michael Alexander had fixed it with the headmaster so that I should be given a place at very short notice. Daddy also sent off with a flea in his ear a booted and suited tout who had approached and asked whether he had ever considered Seaford College as a suitable future public school for his son. It all seemed highly odd to me, but I wish I could say that I felt even such a mild emotion as resentment at the fact that decisions about my life were being taken over my head. I just accepted whatever happened and might happen to me, that's all.

When the day came to leave for school, Daddy offered to travel with me on the train as far as Hayward's Heath. The school itself was on the Sussex coast, so after that I would have to continue the journey on my own; but at the time I thought even this partial offer was a magnanimous one; it was only years later that I realised it had been pure cowardice on my father's part, because he feared meeting with this "muscular Christian" and perhaps having to give an account of himself and his actions.

The journey was long and tedious, and Daddy was in a somnolent mood, saying nothing; this was caused, I suppose, by a mixture of depression and pills. I was detached from him and everything else, possibly in an alarming way. I had even given up on that sense of foreboding I had been feeling at the prospect of going to an all-boys English boarding school, something I had never experienced before. I knew from my reading of comics and other literature that fat boys were often teased mercilessly or even bullied at such places and I had made myself determined to avoid this; my strategy was to make myself as popular as possible, so that people would warm to me and not regard me as an object of derision to be tormented. But I was in for a shock; never before or since have I so much felt like an unspeakably singular animal in a cage at a zoo, but that is what happened when, after dinner in the school dining room later that day, I was surrounded by boys who simply would not stop gawping at me. They were standing, as I was; and not a word was uttered (the masters had all left); but I accepted their curiosity and tried to return it. I kidded myself that had I been wearing the correct uniform their curiosity would not have been so intense; but that was a lie. It was me who was the spectacle, not the inappropriate games jersey, me; this pasty-faced little fat blob of a boy who had descended upon them as if from outer space in the middle of the term.

It is extraordinary how parochial English boys' boarding schools are, or at least were when I went to Swindell's. The first sign of this, as I discovered, was that the dormitories were all named after famous public schools: Harrow, Rugby, Marlborough and so on; mine was Uppingham. It was cold in there, and the blankets were an incongruous red colour against the black metal bedframes. My own was in the corner, next to that of an Indian boy called Karimjee. He was alright, but it took me many hours to get warm enough before I was able to sleep. As I tossed and turned I heard an incessant noise which was worrying and inexplicable to me; I later realised it was the sound of boys grinding their teeth remorselessly as they slept. In the morning Matron and her helpmate (a shabbily dressed, thin woman of far lesser stature, who had her right hand bent permanently at a right angle to her wrist for some reason), would go about the dormitories vigorously ringing handbells in order to wake the boys up. It was our cue to get out of bed and go to the washbasins where we cleaned our teeth. This was always a horrible moment for me because I did not want to get out of bed and preferred my slumberous dreams to anything Swindell's had to offer; nevertheless I had no choice but to do it. I tried, but found it morbidly hard, not to look at the other boys in their dressing gowns as they stood at the row of basins while water and toothpaste oozed from their lips, their faces contorted with having to accommodate the toothbrushes they were using.

At breakfast everything was quiet except for the somehow unreal and certainly distant clatter of spoon upon plate, and the occasional scraping of a chair. This was because it was not until – usually about halfway through the meal, or when he felt like it – the headmaster, Mr Albert Charles Swindell, clapped his hands, that anyone was allowed to speak, the masters, one of whom sat at the head of every table, included. Extraordinarily, the room would then burst into chatter, the sound like a sing-song time bomb. So this was the "muscular Christian" Daddy's friend had referred to, I thought, as he made a point – as he always did – of striding into the dining room last, when everybody else was seated and silent; his face not just severe but menacing. He was a tall, good-looking and surprisingly young man but that face of his revealed considerable tension, for he had a habit of mastication even when not eating. His wife, Mrs Albert Charles Swindell, always accompanied him. She too was young and attractive, and in high summer would sunbathe naked on the balcony of their flat in the school building. At considerable danger to themselves the boys in the dormitories above would lean out of the windows as far as they dared to get a good look at her. So far as I know, this peeping activity was never discovered.

It is also extraordinary how malleable children are, because after a while I began to get used to, what was for me, this wholly novel environment, even to enjoy it to a limited extent. At first I was placed in a class two years beneath me, to reflect the fact that certainly at that stage American education lagged far behind the English model, but I quickly progressed, until by the end of my five terms at Swindell's I was regularly coming top of the appropriate class in every subject. I don't know whether fortnightly reading had anything to do with this, but let me tell you what it was anyhow, for the sake of completeness.

Every fortnight the whole school would enter the huge, purpose-built lecture hall cum theatre in the new block and sit cross-legged on the floor, class by class. The senior masters, with Mr Albert Charles Swindell in the middle, would be sitting on the raised stage, facing them. One by one the class marks that every boy had attained that fortnight would be solemnly read out. Those who had done particularly well would be hand-clapped; but those, on the other hand, who had done particularly badly or not as well as was expected would be told to stand up and would receive a dressing down from Mr Charles - as he was known - in front of the whole school. That happened to me at first.

It was humiliating. I still remember the way in which I gripped my hands together behind my back and bit my lip in order to deal with what I took to be his ferocious onslaught upon my character. But worse was to come: I had been in the habit of listening at night, quietly and under the bedclothes, to the cheap transistor radio I had bought in Chicago. I did not know this was against the rules but must have been wary of getting caught because every morning I would hide it under the mattress and leave it there until the following night. One day, I received a message that I should go to the headmaster's study at once. I did so; and knocked. The single word "Come!" came from beyond the door. I entered; a very vindictive-looking Mr Charles was seated behind his pompous desk. I do not remember his words but they were to the effect that Matron had reported to him that she had found a transistor radio under the mattress of my bed. He told me to stand at a certain place in the room with my face toward the window. I did. I heard him unlock a drawer of his desk, open it and remove something. Even then I wondered whether boys were told to stand facing away from the desk so that they could not see which drawer the strap came from, otherwise some of the braver among them might have known where to steal and then dispose of it. I heard him approach; next he fiddled with my shorts, shirt tails and pants so that my bottom was bare. I next felt six hard whacks to that part of my anatomy, in quick succession, but each one more painful than the last. Finally, I was told to get dressed and get out. I had not been called upon for any explanation I might have had as to the presence of the transistor radio underneath my mattress.

I tried to leave the room with as much self-composure as I could muster, but when I opened the door I saw another frightened-looking boy waiting to go in, no doubt to be met with the same treatment as had just been meted out to me. Incidentally, I never saw the transistor radio again. I went immediately to the library and sat on the large, yielding sofa there, because I thought it would the most soothing piece of furniture in the circumstances; and I burst into hysterical laughter. Other boys who had been reading or playing with their jigsaw sets looked at me curiously. I explained that I had just been beaten and that there was really nothing to it. 'It didn't hurt at all,' which was a lie; but my laughter was an expression of extreme relief at the fact that I was not whimpering or howling like a coward.

For a long time I had been concerned at how I would react if ever I received this punishment, which many boys did, many times. It was an everyday occurrence to see the tell-tale stripes on the buttocks of boys in the shower and changing rooms, and if you passed by the headmaster's study at any time of day there would often be one or two of them waiting there to be summoned inside. The fear was that you would not be able to take it, and would screech and howl and dissolve into tears as some did, for which they faced ridicule from the rest of the school. That above all was the priority; that you did not let yourself go into a funk. It was neither here nor there whether you deserved the punishment. That you did deserve it was taken for granted; which was the only reason why, I hope, it never even crossed my mind to remonstrate with Mr Charles, to say: look, this radio kept me going in Chicago, look: I didn't know it was against the rules; still less to say: don't you lay a finger on me, you filthy bully – for that is what he was. I do not believe that Mr Albert Charles Swindell was a sadist, still less a sexual sadist, but a cruel bully he most certainly was, a paid one at that, as Swindell's was an expensive private school with a good reputation to which the rich middle class of Sussex flocked to have their thick sons educated. His bullying nature was motivated, I believe, by his own fear; fear of losing control, of losing his precious school, its reputation and all the financial advantages for him that went with it.

One hot afternoon on the gravel drive at the front of the school but not on the manicured lawn which lay beyond it, I saw him mercilessly drilling a group of boys through a string of gymnastic exercises. He was shouting and barking at them and demanding that they go faster; he would not let up; the boys obeyed as best they could but as the afternoon wore on they started to flag, which only made him barrack them the more. I watched but of course did not intervene. Some of the boys were clearly exhausted, panting for breath, and with that frown on their faces with half-closed eyes that signifies extreme physical distress.

One of them, a lanky, pale-faced creature, collapsed gasping and badly grazed his knees on the gravel. At that point Mr Charles walked away, towards the front door of the school and his ground floor study whose windows overlooked the drive. He didn't even bother to dismiss them, just contemptuously walked away from the source of his earnings. Curious, I approached the lanky boy who was still lying on the gravel and asked him whether he was alright. He did not answer. He was still gasping and in pain. He was hugging his legs in a foetal position. So I tried again, and asked him what it had all been about. He mumbled that the group had been caught committing some misdemeanour or other, I forget what, I only remember feeling relief that I had not been among them. I only mention this episode because years later, after I had formed the murderous thoughts based on revenge which from then on were to guide my life, I wrote to Mr Albert Charles Swindell telling him what I thought of him, mentioning in particular the beating he had given me for possessing a transistor radio, which punishment had been a travesty of all that was fair and reasonable. I got a nice letter back, but not from him: it was from the present headmaster, assuring me that things had changed a lot since my time there, and regretting to inform me that some years ago Mr Charles had suffered a painful and premature death from cancer. It seemed a fitting end.

As I say, after a while I gave the appearance of fitting into Swindell's quite well, just as I had done at the George Washington Elementary in Berkeley, but as with the latter there was always the dark side, meaning my father. One day I was told to go to a certain room in the school where there was a telephone; he was on the other end of the line waiting to speak to me. I hurried to see what the problem was; it was unusual during term time for a boy to take a telephone call from anyone, and anyway it did not occur to me that it could be anything other than a problem. I was of course right. He was weeping, soft, low, mournful sobs which for several long moments proved an impossible barrier to his speech. I grew anxious, but waited patiently. Finally, he managed to collect himself enough to tell me that my mother was divorcing him. I suppose I expressed some sympathy but really, I had nothing to say about the matter. It was nothing to do with me, or so I thought, and anyway, what did he expect? I knew enough about such adult things to realise that once we had left for America, or even earlier, such a turn of events was inevitable. Furthermore, my patience began to run out when I asked myself, why is he bothering me about this? what on earth am I expected to do? I was only a child and, therefore, appreciated that it was not right for an adult to bother a child in this way. His self-pity as it came across on the telephone was outrageous and pathetic. Surely, he had someone else to tell all this to, someone better equipped to listen than me?

I grew weary of standing at the telephone and my knees had started to ache but he managed to tell me that he would be visiting Swindell's the following weekend to "take me out", as it was called. 'Oh good,' I thought sarcastically, or said with as much plausible sincerity as I could muster, I do not remember which.

When he turned up he could scarcely avoid meeting with Mr Albert Charles Swindell, and to my embarrassment he presented a cringing, fumbling front to this man, who I think regarded him with some polite condescension. My father had always been known for giving eccentric presents to unlikely people and this occasion was no different, as he had brought with him a copy of The Spanish Civil War by Hugh Thomas, which he hoped would be a suitable edition to the boys' library. Of course it was nothing of the kind, being far too grown-up but Damien pressed on with his gift, explaining that he himself had played a small part in that conflict, having been a volunteer in the International Brigade and was even mentioned in the book in a couple of places. All this, of course, meant next to nothing to Mr Albert Charles Swindell (who probably would have been on the Fascist side anyway, given a choice), but he nevertheless remained polite, with a faint twinkle of amusement in his eyes. I, too, was now cringing, but with embarrassment for my father and wished, above all, that we would simply leave this situation as it had unfolded outside the front door of the school and get into the car which he had hired from the station and go – it didn't matter where.

We went to a small seaside town nearby. As it was lunchtime we entered the dining room of a large hotel on the front to eat; I cannot remember what I had but Damien ordered roast beef and ate it mechanically and without any pretence of manners when it arrived. He was uncommunicative, indeed had not said a word and was thoroughly wrapped up in himself. This was my father of whom, truth to tell, I was a little bit frightened. Afterwards, we walked along the esplanade and came to a pier, at the end of which was a small fun fair. As was appropriate for a parent and child in these circumstances, he gave me money so that I could go on the rides while he stared at the sea. But I took no pleasure in performing this role, because whenever I returned to him from, say, the Ghost Train, his mood infected everything, the ride having provided little or no respite; the outing was joyless.

I learnt that we would be staying with friends of Damien's who lived on the other side of the county, so it was a long drive to a grand house set in remarkable grounds which were peopled with endless rows of utterly white statues in the classical Graeco-Roman style. Our hosts – whom I had not met before – were very nice, friendly and welcoming; but I could not understand how they were good enough to put up with my father, who after the greeting immediately flung himself down on one of the sofas in the main drawing room and went fast to sleep. He was still in this condition when several other guests arrived for drinks; I was praying that they would be received in another room so that they would not see my father like this, but no: whilst I sat at a table with a jigsaw puzzle or something like that they all stood around his recumbent form chatting away, their gins in their hands. I think someone tried to wake him up but was not successful; so they joked about it and thought they would leave him to his dreams. The conversation turned to politics, and in particular to Harold Macmillan, the prime minister of the day. Suddenly, Damien woke up and uttered with the utmost vehemence, 'That man is a sly opportunist!' He then went back to sleep. The others were disconcerted, said nothing for a moment or two, then carried on as before. I do not remember anything at all about the rest of the evening; except that when it came to my bedtime I was shown upstairs to a little room, where I undressed and went to bed. I read for a while then put the light out and settled down to sleep in profound darkness. Later, I heard my father enter. 'Giles?' he enquired, not knowing whether I was asleep or not. He sat on the edge of my bed and said, 'I've come to say goodnight.' I stirred; and burst into uncontrollable sobs, which alarmed him. 'What on earth is the matter, Giles?' he asked, with genuine surprise. I continued to be helpless, quite unable to control myself. Not only could I not stop sobbing, but I couldn't begin to express the reason for my sorrow, because I didn't know what it was. He hugged me and kept on asking what was wrong, his concern and alarm mounting; but I couldn't help him. He must have given up after that, for there came a time when he left the room and I continued to cry. It seems to me now that the state I was in then was a premonition of what was to come, for in a few short years my father would be dead.

That same term, I was in the changing room one day after games. No doubt I was loitering with the others as we now had nothing compulsory to do until evening prep. Someone came along and told me that I had to go to the headmaster's study at once as my mother was there, waiting for me. I was told to hurry up, and of course I did, pulling my day clothes on as fast as I could; but I did not want to see her and was full of apprehension at what the meeting would be like. When I got to the headmaster's study I knocked and went in – surprisingly not waiting for the booming permission to be given from beyond the door – and Mr Charles was sitting behind his desk, smiling, as was natural for him in front of parents. It wasn't that long since, grim-faced, and in more or less the same spot, he had beaten me for keeping a transistor radio under my mattress in the dormitory. At a greater distance was my mother, also seated. She too was smiling and she said, 'Hello, Giles,' but did not get up.

I do not remember advancing toward her and giving her a kiss on the cheek or saying, 'Hello, Mummy,' or anything like that. In fact, she was scarcely recognisable to me, except for the remembered charm, dark hair and pale face. Apart from anything else, I had been overcome by extreme shyness.

There followed some desultory conversation which would probably not be worth recording even if it could be remembered; and we went out into the sunshine – it was a fine Spring day, almost like summer – where her friend Reggie Kilmartin was waiting, having driven her down from London. I did remember Reggie a bit, a perfectly pleasant if ineffectual man. Years later he told me that he had worn his Old Etonian tie especially for the occasion, so that the two of them might make a good impression. I was told to show Reggie round a bit, as Mummy and Mr Charles had more to talk about (no doubt concerning me), and I remember pointing out to him the narrow covered walkway which led down to the playing fields from near the front of the school. I told him, just as a matter of conveying information, that only masters were allowed to use this walkway, the boys having to use the longer route at the back of the school, but he misunderstood the point and said, 'I daresay we'll be allowed to use it, as I am here.' It must have been St George's Day, because the flag of England was flying from the rooftop.

15.
Narrative, 1979

When Aylmer Jones and Angela Horniblow had finished dining they returned to the reception area and immediately Sandy set about getting their coats. By this time Gentry had managed to replace the scrunched up letter without being noticed.

'Call a cab, sir?' Sandy piped, in that falsetto voice of his.

'Yes, please.'

Marlene was attending to "M'damn" and enquiring whether she'd had a good evening. Angela Horniblow smiled. 'Yes, thank you,' she said.

Sandy was about to summon one of the doormen to hail a cab when Gentry butted in.

'I'll get it!' he said.

He ran out into the street before anyone could stop him and within a very few moments had commandeered an available black cab to the front door of the Huffington Club.

'Don't ever do that again!' hissed one of the doormen at him.

He was a big fellow with a moustache. That was because Gentry's actions had constituted an incursion into the proper sphere of activities of the doormen, who could expect tips for such things.

'Just this once,' Gentry had hissed back.

He stood his ground, keeping the door of the black cab open for the exiting couple. When they appeared he smiled at them, hoping against hope that the scrutiny he was directing toward the so-called Nigel Lugg would not be noticed.

As it happened, Aylmer Jones did not so much as give him a second glance, although Angela Horniblow smiled at him. He heard Aylmer Jones say, 'The Flamingo Hotel,' to the driver as he was about to close the door.

'Where's that, guv?' the cabbie asked.

Giles Jones momentarily kept the door open and heard Aylmer Jones say, 'Ladbroke Grove. Top of Ainslie Gardens.'

Giles Jones shut the cab door with a cheery 'Good night sir! Good night madam!' and went back inside.

At the end of his shift Giles Jones put on his coat, said goodnight to Sandy (who always insisted on being the last to leave), and walked out into the cold night air. It was just after four in the morning and whenever there was a lull in the traffic in Park Lane he could hear an early bird or two chirruping in the trees overhead and in Hyde Park. He pulled up the collar of his coat as he walked. He thought he'd hail a cab. When after a few minutes he managed to find one it took him straight to Brunswick Gardens, where he paid the cabbie off. Once inside his bedsitter he did not even remove his coat but searched in the drawer for the sharp kitchen knife he used for slicing beef. He found it and put it in the pocket of his coat. Ladbroke Grove was not far from where he lived; he knew the way of old as he often shopped in the markets of North Kensington on his days off. Yet even so it felt strange going on this night errand; he felt a stir in his body which told him that he was used to going to bed at this time. He also felt a quite terrifying sense of the enormity of what he was about to do, if he thought about it at all, which he tried not to. Instead, he concentrated on looking down the deserted alleys and round the dark corners as he passed, just in case anything was there. But he was alone; apart from a rat which he saw scuttling away from a rubbish bin when he approached. He couldn't help wondering, though, what it was going to be like. A quick murder would be best, he didn't want to hang around any longer than he had to. Of course she would have to go too, he didn't want anyone left behind to tell on him. He'd already thought of the ruse by which he would gain access to their room; but then what? This was unknown territory; he'd never done anything like this before; that was the frightening bit. Yet he'd thought about it many, many times.

The Flamingo Hotel was discreetly situated, being just another of the substantial terraced houses which lined the small street off Ladbroke Grove. It had no sign to exhibit itself, only its large glass door with the name of the establishment printed upon it revealed it for what it was but, as expected, it was locked and, looking through, Giles could see no sign of anyone about. So he rang the bell and waited. Nothing. He rang again. Eventually a sleepy young man in jeans and a white open-neck shirt appeared within the golden gloom of the interior. This man unlocked the door, opened it and ushered Giles in. The latter smiled faintly, thinking that his black tie must put him in the category of guest who'd had a posh night out, and mumbled something about having forgotten his room number. The receptionist's shift had not started until the last guests had returned, so he was in no position to verify Giles' identity when the latter gave his false name. In any case the man was too sleepy to make any proper enquiries. He merely squinted at the bookings chart, haphazardly asking, 'What did you say your name was?'

'Nigel Lugg.'

The receptionist gave a puzzled look but eventually found the name. 'Room 34, third floor.'

'Thanks.'

The receptionist looked into the corresponding pigeon hole but Giles quickly said, 'It's all right. I've got my key.'

Giles turned swiftly to the staircase and was halfway up it before any further questions might be asked, but they weren't, and as the staircase turned in on itself it was natural for him to look down, and when he did he saw that the receptionist had already returned to his makeshift bed on the sofa in the lounge that adjoined the lobby. Giles smiled, and went on. When he reached the third floor he looked about him and saw that number 34 was well along the narrow passage, far away from the top of the staircase. He had to go through two doors each marked "Fire Door" to get to it. Well and good, but now was the tricky part. Taking a deep breath, he knocked loudly on the door of number 34. At first there was no response, but then he heard a sleepy rustling coming from within, and a deep male voice which he recognised asking, 'Who is it?'

'Room service!' he said in a raised voice.

'At this time of night? What do you want?'

'It's an urgent matter, sir.'

Giles heard what sounded like grumbling coming from within, and a movement, as of someone – quite a large person – shifting himself. Giles was breathing deeply. Inside the room, Angela was stirring, coming awake. She saw that Nigel was getting out of bed and asked him what the matter was.

'Room service,' he muttered. 'They say it's urgent.'

Aylmer Jones had turned a small bedside light on, the better to see what he was doing. Angela Horniblow sat up in bed, frowning. She was also squinting at the light. She said, 'There isn't any room service in this hotel.'

But it was too late. Aylmer Jones was already at the door and opening it. The moment he did, Giles Jones barged in and punched him in the solar plexus, very hard. Aylmer Jones gasped and tumbled back, clutching his stomach. At that moment Angela Horniblow let out a loud, piercing scream, so Giles leapt over to the bed and punched her hard in the face. She had been about to avoid the blow but was not quick enough. Nevertheless, that did not stop her screaming, so he punched her again, shattering some teeth and causing blood to seep from her mouth. Her screams turned to a whimper as she clutched her face. Aylmer Jones was on his knees, still clutching his stomach, quite at a loss to know what was happening. Giles returned to him, kicked him in the head and closed the door. Now Aylmer Jones was struggling on the floor, his hands having moved to cover his head. He too was whimpering. Giles could not be sure that others had not been woken and heard what was happening, but in any case it was too late to go back on what he was doing. If he were to leave now – run out of the hotel, for example – that in itself would surely raise the alarm even if nothing else had. He would just have to trust that the rest of the hotel was too deeply asleep to have noticed this kerfuffle. Aylmer Jones and Angela Horniblow were in shock and struggling to make sense of what was happening. They were also trying to deal with the pain that had been inflicted upon them. Giles said in a loud, clear voice, to neither in particular, 'If either of you make any noise, I will kill you both.'

This appeared to sink in, because neither protested. Giles was going to kill them anyway, but he knew that they didn't know that. Surely they would now be compliant, realising as they did that their lives depended on their being so? However, Aylmer Jones managed to ask, still holding his head, 'Come to rob us, have you?'

'Not exactly.'

Aylmer Jones said nothing more, so Giles told him to look up. Aylmer Jones did not move.

'Look at me.'

Aylmer Jones did now do as he was told but his face wore a blank expression. In exasperation Giles turned on the overhead light, so that the room was flooded with brightness. Angela Horniblow's continued whimpering could be heard in the background.

'Look at me!' he hissed.

Aylmer Jones blinked at him, looking hard.

After a few moments he said, 'I remember you from the Huffington

Club.'

'What is going on here?' Angela Horniblow now managed to ask. She had wiped some of the blood from her face and was sitting up, her chest exposed.

Giles turned on her and hissed, 'I told you to not to make a noise. I won't tell you again.'

Angela Horniblow didn't say another word, for already her professional experience was telling her that the situation was potentially deadly and she had begun to think desperately of how she might escape. She wasn't sparing any thought at all to the man she knew as Nigel Lugg, much as she liked him.

Giles turned again to Aylmer Jones.

'You remember me from the Huffington Club, do you? Anywhere else?'

'No.'

'I'll tell you, then.'

Giles Jones started to kick the sprawling form of Aylmer Jones hard and was pained to note that its squashy mass yielded in a quite sickening way to his booted foot. He recoiled in distaste as Aylmer Jones clutched his sides in pain.

'I'll show you!' screamed Giles Jones. 'My name is Giles Jones, remember me? Your fucking little cousin whom you've been ripping off all these years! Your fucking relative!'

There was a quality of naked hatred to Giles' rage that Angela Horniblow had never seen or heard before, and that left her gaping. She did, however, realise that their quarrel was nothing to do with her and that gave her some hope for her own personal safety.

'I don't know what you're talking about,' muttered Aylmer Jones, in answer to his second cousin's assertions, 'I'm no relation of yours. My name is Nigel Lugg...'

But Aylmer Jones' face betrayed him. As he looked at Giles he had indeed seen a likeness to someone he had met years before, someone important... and it clicked, and the flicker of recognition that had crossed his face had not gone unnoticed by Giles Jones.

'You liar. You're Aylmer Jones.'

The man on the floor said nothing. Giles Jones kicked him again, causing him to wince.

'Admit it, you bastard.'

Aylmer Jones was thinking as hard as it was possible for him to do, given the circumstances in which he found himself and his own intellectual limitations. Better own up, he thought. Then he might go away.

'All right,' he said in a low voice. 'If that's what you want. I am Aylmer Jones. Now what more do you want?'

'I always knew his name wasn't Lugg,' said Angela Horniblow in a shrill voice, thinking that if she took their assailant's side, things might go better for her.

But, faced with this admission, Giles Jones could simply do nothing but look at his quarry. It did not even cross his mind to repeat to the girl his threat as to her noise.

'There's money in my wallet, over there,' Aylmer Jones continued, gesturing with his head toward the bedside table. 'Take it and go.'

His voice was surprisingly cool; the upper class county burr had a throaty sound to it.

Giles Jones ignored Aylmer Jones' last remark and asked, 'You got my letter?'

He of course knew perfectly well that he had, but asked the question as a matter of course, almost politely.

Indeed Giles Jones' fury had practically vanished, thanks in part to Aylmer Jones' even tones – a fact about his mood that he himself was beginning to notice with dismay. It was now impossible not to carry through the task he had set himself; he simply had to keep going. If he left now with his tail between his legs, in time Aylmer Jones would undoubtedly call the police and that would be it. He and the others would escape scot free.

Aylmer Jones was about to say yes in answer to the question but thought better of it, just in time.

'No,' he blurted out but it was obvious that he knew what was being talked about. 'What letter?' he added weakly.

Giles Jones looked around the room, searching for any sign of the astrakhan. He saw a wardrobe and went to it. As he was doing this, Angela Horniblow thought she saw her chance and leapt from the bed quite naked and made for the door. Unhappily for her, the path took her within a few feet of Giles Jones, but she had reasoned that while he had his back to her as he poked about in the wardrobe she could get by without his noticing in time. She was wrong. He turned quickly just as she was by him and grabbed her. She spat at him and tried to claw his

103

face. She would have screamed so that someone might hear if she'd thought about it. Giles Jones had in his hand a wooden hanger and in the brief struggle that ensued he managed to slot this over her head, whereupon he wrenched it fiercely to one side, breaking her neck. There was a sickening muffled crack. Angela Horniblow looked at Giles Jones in total astonishment and died within moments, falling against him as if in supplication. He stepped back so that she could continue her passage to the floor, where she lay lifeless, her eyes and mouth wide open in eternal shock.

Giles Jones was puzzled. He couldn't quite appreciate what he had managed to do, he certainly hadn't intended her to go this way but before he could collect himself an angry shriek came from behind, and movement, and next he felt himself being hurled forwards so that his head hit the bridal suite's door with great force. It hurt; he blacked out for a moment. Aylmer Jones was seething with anger. Moreover he was stronger than Giles Jones had ever allowed for. Aylmer Jones was now pinning his younger relative by the shoulders against the door and muttering darkly into his face.

'You've killed her, haven't you? Have you no shame? She had nothing to do with you and me. She was quite innocent. She was the only thing that ever meant anything to me.'

Aylmer Jones, though speaking quietly, could not hide his rage. He was heaving with it, shaking with it, as if he might explode. Again, Giles Jones had not been prepared for this. He felt frightened. He hadn't given a thought to how Aylmer Jones might react to Angela Horniblow's death and, if he had, he wouldn't have supposed that it would be any big deal.

'…the only thing that ever meant anything to me...' Aylmer Jones was repeating. 'She made me feel so different.' He now had his hands round Giles Jones' throat and was throttling him. 'Don't you see that whatever I've done is as nothing compared with your behaviour? Why, at school...'

But he got no further. With an almighty effort born of terror as much as anything else Giles Jones had managed to release Aylmer Jones' hands from his neck by punching his forearms with his own. He followed this through with an uppercut which stunned his adversary and had the effect of disorientating him. Even so he repeated the assault by punching him hard in the stomach for good measure, which caused

Aylmer Jones once again to fall to the floor – incongruously beside Angela Horniblow's corpse. Very quickly, Giles Jones removed the kitchen knife from his raincoat pocket and returned with it to the incapacitated Aylmer Jones. He proceeded to stab him with it over and over again, indiscriminately.

'Die! Die! Damn you!' he screamed, even as Aylmer Jones, it seemed almost half-heartedly, raised his arms in self-defence.

'Go on, then, you bastard,' muttered Aylmer Jones. 'Kill me. Let's see how far you get.'

'I'm gonna get this far…'

So saying, Giles Jones rolled his second cousin over and stabbed him where he thought the heart was. He did this because it had come to him rather late in the day that he would not get very far simply by lunging any old how with the knife. Nevertheless, blood had oozed from many different places in the now grotesque body that was gradually ceasing to be that of a living person. It shook and rolled, its pyjamas awry, its hair dishevelled. Giles Jones watched in horrible fascination. Eventually what remained of Aylmer Jones was still.

Under an hour passed, before Giles Jones was back in his bedsitter. On the way home he had disposed of the knife by dropping it down a drain. It might well be found but how could it be connected to him? He had carefully wiped it. True, they would almost certainly think that the visitor in the middle of the night was to blame, but how were they to find out who he was? Giles Jones didn't suppose that the sleepy receptionist would be able to give a very good description. And of course he had looked for the letter, found it and taken it with him, just so that no immediate connection could be made between himself and the couple in the bridal suite of the Flamingo Hotel. Leaving had been a cinch. He had not known it, but at the end of the narrow passage, through yet more doors each of which was marked "Fire Door", was a fire exit. This had led onto a metal staircase which he had descended pretty rapidly because a loud alarm had sounded when he pushed it open.

At the bottom of the staircase he had found himself in a private garden, but it had been an easy thing to jump over its wall into the street. The only thing was, it was now light, and there were a few passers-by. Giles Jones had had to act normally. One man in office dress in particular had passed and given him a funny look. But, reasoned

Giles Jones, this man could not possibly have known what he had just done. If only he could!

Giles Jones exulted in the thought; it was his little secret. Indeed as he walked home he had never felt such a lightness of being, such a freedom from fear. It was as if a great weight had been removed from his shoulders, simply because he had accomplished what he had set out to do. Over and over again he relived the murderous situation in his mind, acting it out, embellishing the details – to the point where the construction of it in his head achieved a greater reality for him than anything that had actually happened. He thought he should go to bed and get some sleep so that he would be fit for work in the evening. He downed a couple of glasses of vodka but did not fix himself anything to eat, tore his clothes off and left them where they fell on the floor, and got into bed where he fell fast asleep.

16.
Giles Jones' Diary

I now turn to the autumn of 1964, and the most forlorn occasion of all, when my mother drove me to Selwyn Mauberley College, which was to be my public school, for the first time. As usual, whenever faced with a prospect I did not like I burst into tears and whimpered that I did not want to go. We were seated in the Austin 1100 she had hired for the journey and parked against the large, drab and dusty so-called junior house that was to be my home for the next three terms. The place was a tip; I could see that. More to the point, I could feel it. I knew it was going to be terrible, just as the last long leg of the journey along the Bath Road had been.

'It's all right, Giles,' she had said. 'If after a few days you really don't like it you won't have to stay. We can think of something else.' This cheered me up a bit, but only a bit because I knew she was lying; in good faith perhaps, in order to soothe me, but still lying. Once beyond the portal to this house I knew that that would be it; I would remain there a prisoner. In any case, Selwyn Mauberley College was not the public school I had been entered for; to everyone's surprise, including my own, I had not done well enough in the Common Entrance examinations and had been turned down from elsewhere. So here we were, at this relatively modern dump.

The reason why, apparently, Selwyn Mauberley College was so called was because its founder had once dipped into the poetry of Ezra Pound, had come across the poem of that name and thought it sounded rather grand. And so he had adopted it for his school.

It was a source of considerable irony to me that, a few days later, one of the new boys did just get up and leave. He was a young African prince, I believe, and clearly he found that the privations this junior house had to offer were just too unbearable. Also pretty clear was the fact that he must have had very amenable parents, because there is no doubt that had I called in my own mother's insincere offer I would have been given the bum's rush. I wish I could say that by then anyway I had settled into the barbarous mix of savagery and boredom that Masher's House – such it was called – embodied, but I can't and never was able to. To this day I cannot understand why parents, or more probably in the case of Selwyn Mauberley College, trustees of funds set up specifically for the purpose, pay good money for this sort of thing. A prime example: it became known that as new boys we would have to undergo an initiation rite called "swinging", which entailed exactly that: swinging at night, naked, from bars which were fixed above the beds in the dormitories. The purpose of these bars, apparently, was so that curtains could be hung from them, thus affording the boys some measure of privacy from each other while they slept. But they had never been installed. All the boys who had been at Masher's for more than a term watched with their torches trained. These latter had had to do it themselves at the beginning of their first term, when they had been the new boys. Curiously enough – or perhaps predictably – the boy who gloated most about our forthcoming ordeal was himself a perennial object of bullying; because he was odd and had the most incandescent temper. His name was Harry Cumberbatch but we all called him "Cucumber Patch".

'For the sake of the show, men, give it a go!' he would cackle at us, in anticipation of the spectacle, which however kept on getting delayed because there was an unusually large intake that term and we were seriously thinking of rebelling. Eventually, there was a showdown, by which I mean a fight in the dormitories which went utterly unnoticed by the doddery old housemaster and his wife, who slept in another part of the building. Of course, being more numerous and a little bit older than us, the boys who had been at Masher's for more than a term won; and we were made to swing from the bars while everybody else watched. Like gymnasts we each clung to the bars and pulled ourselves to the other side with our hands while boorish remarks were made about our physical accoutrements. I had been particularly apprehensive about having to do this because I was fat and under-developed. 'What a castrate!' somebody yelled when it came to my turn.

Another source of irony to me was that the new boy who had been the most instrumental in fomenting the ultimately unsuccessful rebellion against "swinging" that term became the ringleader of it the next; the prime mover in getting the then new boys to play their part in the initiation ceremony. So much for human nature, I thought. The boy in question, a Richard Beggs, was a bully anyway, and repulsive at that; also he was a hypocrite, because when he led the rebellion he had kept on saying by way of a defence, 'It's the principle of thing,' meaning, I suppose, that it was just not right to be bullied in this way; yet he went on to do the very same thing to others.

The boys at Masher's behaved for the most part like little savages – in fact they were little savages; but I cannot pretend that I was any different. This was particularly so in relation to Harry Cumberbatch, whom I have mentioned. He was mercilessly bullied – by me and others; and although the doddery old housemaster knew as much, he did nothing about it. I know this because one day at lunch in the main hall of the college, where each house had tables to itself, he intercepted a note that had been passed around among the boys. I think he only did this because he wanted to know what was causing so much hilarity.

The note had been written by a grimy little character called Field, and it invited everyone to a grand 'bate' – that was the word we used – of Cucumber Patch that afternoon. As it was a Saturday there were no classes and it was free time. Mr Smithers – the housemaster – read the note and said nothing. He put it in his pocket and went back to where he was seated at the head of the table. I can still remember the look on his face; he had a silly face anyway but now it had a sort of vacillating impassivity about it. It was the look of sheer impotence. He didn't want it to be known that he could not control the boys in his care in case he lost his position. Instead, he would simply turn a blind eye.

It was known that Harry Cumberbatch couldn't bear to have any of his possessions interfered with, so after lunch when everybody had returned to Masher's, a structure was built out of the tubular-framed chairs in the school room and his satchel thrown on top of it. The idea was that he would be anxious to retrieve this important possession but would only be able to do so by climbing the precarious structure, which hopefully would collapse, causing him to fall and hurt himself. An added bonus, it was discovered, was that he had received a letter from his parents that morning but, like the note at lunch, it had been intercepted and was to be waved in his face but not handed to him. This would goad him to distraction, it was understood, and would make up for the disappointing possibility that he might retrieve his satchel unharmed.

When the solitary Harry Cumberbatch came into the schoolroom, everybody else was standing at their desk, waiting for him to react. At first he did not understand what was happening, but when he recognised his satchel at the top of the structure he gave a bellow of rage and ran towards it. Next he realised he could not reach his satchel without climbing. So, he started to climb, and had almost reached the top, all the time being watched with scarcely suppressed excitement by the others; when someone kicked away one of the chairs. The structure had been wobbling perilously anyway, but now it toppled, causing Harry Cumberbatch to fall with it. By a stroke of luck one of the chairs was dislodged in such a way that it fell directly onto his head. He let out a howl of pain and tried to shield himself from any further blows.

By now everyone else was cheering and jeering at him. The noise was intense; a chorus of voices, some broken, some not. Harry Cumberbatch got to his feet, holding his head. 'That hurt,' he muttered; but he was now trying to grin, as if to show that he was taking the undoubted rag against him in good part.

He dusted himself down, picked up his satchel (which also had fallen to the floor), and was about to go grinning to his desk when he realised he would have to drag one of the chairs with him in order to sit at it. So he turned to fetch one; only to be shouted at by the boy Field, 'You've got a letter, Cuke!'

Field waved the missive at him. 'Let's have it then,' said Harry, nonplussed, forgetting about the chair and walking towards him. 'It's quite thick, a lovely long letter from your people,' remarked Field casually, turning it over in his hands before making as if to give it to him; but when Harry tried to take it from the other boy's grasp the latter ran off, shouting and screaming with mirth.

The audience joined in. Harry was enraged, and must have been wondering why another boy had possession of a letter which was meant for him anyway.

He ran after him, but it was no good; whenever he got near enough to snatch his letter it was simply passed to another boy who ran in a different direction. How they were enjoying this, but any trace of the false camaraderie which Harry Cumberbatch always tried to display in situations like this in order to protect himself was gone: he was reduced to a trembling, desperate wreck and had started to mutter strange incomprehensible things to himself. Yet he persisted in his efforts to get back what was his, and would not let up. Frequently, he or others stumbled on the chairs which were still strewn about, occasioning even more hilarity. Once or twice he very nearly succeeded, but just as it looked as if he might, the letter would be thrown like a paper dart to another boy, slicing through the air. It would be caught, its recipient cradling it in his hands, then thrown again, the maddened Harry having turned this way and that to see where it might land. Then a boy who had caught it ran out of the schoolroom and into the grounds of the house; everybody else followed, like the pack of savages that they were. If Harry Cumberbatch had had an ounce of wisdom in his small frame he would have left them to it, no doubt realising that sooner or later they would tire of their cruel game and his letter would be discarded somewhere where he could retrieve it; but he didn't have any such maturity, so he followed them out and saw that the pack had run round the muddy curtilage of the building and into the changing rooms via the back door.

This door had glass panes so that you could see through the upper half of it. The boys gathered round the doorway inside, shut the door and locked it; from where they taunted the impotent Harry Cumberbatch, who was on the outside. They waved the letter in his face, which was only a foot or so away from them, albeit separated by glass. Curiously, this face of Harry Cumberbatch's had become pale and still; the whole of him was very still indeed. Also there was a blank look to his eyes. He now had such an extraordinary appearance that for an appreciable moment all the whooping and catcalling died down, and the other boys became still too. An ocean seemed to separate the boy and his adversaries; but suddenly and in a strangely deep voice Harry Cumberbatch shouted, 'I know I shall be redeemed by the Holy Ghost!' whereupon he pushed his fist through one of the glass panels of the door, shattering it entirely. The boys were amazed by this. After a moment the letter was dropped to the floor and they all scarpered in different directions. None of them wanted to get into any serious trouble, which they would if blame were attached to anyone for the breaking of the glass. Harry Cumberbatch's frighteningly unexpected act of desperation proved to be the end of the afternoon's sport, and he got his letter back.

Hell such as this lasted for three terms; then I moved to Prasher's, my senior house, which was worse. There is a reason why Masher's and Prasher's had the names they did, but it is too boring to tell here; suffice to say that the latter was a mere continuation of the former, except that it was larger and even more collectively thuggish. Furthermore, homosexuality took centre stage, abusive homosexuality at that, for it concerned the unwelcome attentions that the older boys lavished on those younger whom they found sexually attractive. I tried to ignore all this; certainly I was not involved and there were other factors at play which monopolised my concerns; I was so desperately unhappy but I had no idea why, though perhaps the reasons for it were obvious.

Prasher's was the furthest away of all the houses from the college, which meant a walk of thirty minutes or so just to get back there after morning classes and lunch in the great hall. You had to go along the main road, through a field, along a track and over a bridge crossing a river, which led to a path that ran through a graveyard next to a church, then up an incline towards the house, which was really a collection of separate buildings. You next passed the housemaster's quarters through one of whose front windows he could invariably be seen seated, hunched forward, intently watching sport on television, clutching a golf club, racquet or cricket bat between his legs, depending upon what was being played, as if by that means he could believe himself to be participating in the action he was watching.

Finally, you got to your little desk, one of a large number of squalid wooden things in a large, long and ugly block on the other side of the track from the squash courts; and if you were lucky there would be a letter from home waiting for you, since the morning post came too late for it to be collected before leaving for college; but I was never lucky, or hardly ever. Once I think my mother sent me a tub of cold cream after I had complained of chapped legs incurred on frosty sports grounds; and very occasionally one of my father's sad and self-pitying epistolary efforts in his usual bizarre handwriting lay there on the desk before me; but that was all.

Even these disappointing offerings were better than nothing, however, for they meant contact – contact from people I knew if did not love, contact which I craved but never got from Selwyn Mauberley College. It went further, because the academic success I had achieved at Swindell's, which had given me so much pleasure and which had itself been a kind of contact, proved a mere flash in the pan which I could not repeat, I don't know why. On the contrary, at Selwyn Mauberley College I became the dunce of whichever class I happened to be in and would simply loll at the back, quite unable or refusing to follow whatever the teachers were saying. I hated them all and I think they must have hated me, because they habitually left me alone and would only ever order me out of the room if my behaviour became particularly sullen or disruptive. What I meant to say was that on those lonely walks back to Prasher's from college I longed for a letter to be waiting for me: news of home, such as it was; but I was invariably disappointed.

The situation was not helped by the fact that I had made no friends and could not get myself to try to make any. And, like the teachers, the other boys left me alone, as I did them. For me, everything was solitary and then adolescence crept up, complicating things. I did not know how to cope with it; I started to get strange headaches, some of which were imaginary. My solitary walks grew longer and longer, and a sort of desperation overtook me, which I did not know what to do with. It turned into anger, but against whom could my anger be directed?

The one activity at Selwyn Mauberley College which I enjoyed and became moderately proficient at was shooting. There was a rifle range on the other side of the river from the science labs, in front of which was a large parade ground for the cadets' square bashing, a small naval gun and an armoury. It seems strange now, but you were allowed to practise on the range without supervision. The teacher in charge, a retired army officer called Major Milner, would simply give you the key to the armoury in exchange for your signature on a piece of paper, if you were someone he knew as an enthusiast. I don't suppose it was ever thought that anyone might abuse this trust, but looking back it seems a rather naïve state of affairs. Anyhow, most Wednesday and Saturday afternoons – which was when we had free time – I'd be up on the range with a rifle if the weather was fine. Sometimes other boys were there too, sometimes not; on some occasions there was an adult instructor present, but not usually. The range itself was remarkably laid out; instead of regularly spaced circular targets all at the same distance, there were thick rectangular plywood mock-ups of attacking soldiers coming at you from all directions, at least they appeared to be; in reality they were static, of course, but they were so life-like they were frightening. Their background was of a mustard yellow colour, the image of the soldier itself was black and white, its face a picture of deadly intent. They were at different distances and some were partially obscured by trees or bushes, as if perpetrating an ambush. The weapons they carried looked fearsome, awesome; certainly far more formidable than the antiquated bolt actions we had. But ours were real and if you

113

scored a direct hit, the plywood image would topple backwards and disappear.

When other boys were with me we'd obviously compete to see who could score the most kills, but if I was on my own, having obtained the key to the armoury from Major Milner, I wouldn't even bother with these plywood cut-outs. I'd hunt around for small animals; or hide and wait for them to come to me. The former required stealth, the latter patience and the ability to remain quite still for a long time. I think I preferred the latter because despite my best efforts my movements were often clumsy; at the sound of a breaking twig, or something like that, a startled rabbit would run away at such speed that it was impossible to aim and fire with any chance of success; or a disturbed bird would go screeching into the distance, flying low, its wings beating furiously. On the other hand I found I had the ability to keep perfectly still for long periods of time, either by lying on my stomach or crouching halfway up a tree. If the latter, I'd make myself comfortable and wait, my rifle resting on a branch, its sights very near to my eye. I very much fancied myself as a sniper; I fantasised about being a silent, invisible but deadly assassin. Whenever I killed anything I simply left the small corpse where it was, or hid it in some bushes.

One afternoon I was like this when I saw a slight but unmistakable movement in the field about two hundred yards away, near a clump of trees. There was no wind, otherwise it could just have been a blade of grass. I felt that familiar tautening of my body which I always hoped would not give my presence away and lifted the stock to my shoulder. I took aim at the spot where I had seen the movement and sure enough the outline of a rabbit appeared. It was only just visible. I waited, tense; knowing that if I fired now I would miss and not get a second chance because the rabbit, startled by noise, would run for cover too quickly for me.

Nothing happened for a while. I remained absolutely still but straining. Still nothing happened, except that I could no longer see the rabbit and thought that its appearance might have been an illusion. Nevertheless I continued to wait and after fifteen minutes or so I saw it again, this time much closer. It was actually making its way towards me in the long grass, utterly unaware of the mortal danger it was in. My body tautened still more. This was the bit I enjoyed: having unseen power over life and death. I continued to wait, and the rabbit continued to approach, looking for that extra juicy leaf of grass which to me would have tasted no different from any of the others. You could now see its face; rather a gentle, inquiring face it had, like all rabbits. As usual I decided to shoot when the animal was within ten yards or so of my sights; that way I could be fairly confident of a kill. At the moment it felt as if I were luring it towards me, because it kept on coming closer, bobbing up and down, so that sometimes its floppy ears appeared to bounce on the tips of the long grass. Now was the time to pull the trigger but just as I was about to do so I heard a boy yell in the distance; which startled the rabbit and caused it to dive for cover and disappear. By then my reflexes had kicked in so I fired the gun anyway, but it was too late: a spray of earth appeared just where the rabbit had been.

This lost opportunity made me furious – furious with the boy who had caused it. I looked and in the distance I could see someone in shorts mucking about in the clump of trees where I had first seen the rabbit. It was his bare legs which made him visible. I wish I had been able to contain my fury but I couldn't; without for one moment supposing that I would be able to hit the boy at this distance I swung my gun round, took aim at him, and fired. Nothing happened for a moment; and then there was another yell, and I now saw him clutch his leg and go to the ground. It turned out to be Harry Cumberbatch. Trust him to be mucking about on his own. It turned out he had been pursuing his usual solitary pastime of collecting edible fungi and probably yelped the first time because he had found an unusually rare one.

In the normal way such a matter wouldn't have been reported, but this was just too serious. Harry Cumberbatch had to be taken to the sanatorium and have the bullet extracted from his leg, the wound cleaned and dressed. He was in a state of shock and had to be laid up for several days. Naturally the school doctor wanted to know how the accident had happened – for it was inconceivable that such an injury could have been inflicted deliberately. At first Harry Cumberbatch had not wanted to tell him anything about it, or at least so he later told me, but the doctor had persisted and eventually he told him the circumstances. Maybe his reluctance to do so had to do with the fact that it involved admitting that he had no companions and was therefore hunting for mushrooms on his own. However that may be, the truth came out; and I was identified as the only boy who had had access to the rifle range that afternoon. So I too was questioned. I must admit that at the time when I had realised what I had done I panicked and ran with the rifle back to the armoury where I deposited it. But I still had the key, and hadn't dared return it to Major Milner, which was pure irrational funk as it would be known anyway who had it. Sure enough, it was found in my desk where I had put it when the housemaster searched the same.

17.
Narrative, 1979

That evening at work Giles felt tired. He'd missed about half his quota of sleep that day and he'd also missed his usual afternoon diary session, an exercise which had become strangely therapeutic. That he had become a killer did not, however, appear to concern him very much; at least not from moment to moment when he was preoccupied with other things. This evening was particularly quiet, though; in fact for some time the manager had been worried by the relative paucity of the takings and as there were others at reception Giles thought he might wander to the top of the building where the staff quarters were. It was possible to grab forty winks on one of the sofas in the men's or women's changing rooms, but this was frowned upon as they were there simply for relaxing on during short breaks. To his pleasant surprise he saw that the girl with the funny accent whom he fancied was on her own in the women's changing room as he passed by its open door. She was sitting on the edge of a chair doing her make-up, holding a small mirror at arm's length, a picture of concentration. Again, it was frowned upon for staff to enter the changing room of the opposite sex but people did it; it was okay if you maintained your respect and made sure you were not bothering anyone. So he went in. She looked at him and smiled. She put her compact away.

'I'm not disturbing you?'

'No, I just finish.'

He sat down near her. There was a silence.

'It's quiet.'

'Yes. I would like to be home.'

'Where do you live?'

'South.' The way she said it, with a downward motion of the arm, he took her to mean somewhere very far south in the city.

'You?'

He told her. Again, there was a silence.

'I never like to be at home,' he continued.

She frowned. 'Why not?'

'I live alone.'

'So do I, but I like.'

He was startled. He hadn't got her down as a loner.

'Don't you have family?'

'In Ecuador.'

'Boyfriend?'

She smiled. 'Not right now.'

He smiled back.

'I go down now.'

She got to her feet. Disappointed, he got up too.

'What time do you finish?'

'Four.'

'Do you want to go on somewhere afterwards?'

She smiled again.

'Maybe.'

'I'll wait for you at the door.'

'No. You wait at corner. People talk.'

'The corner of Park Lane?'

'Yes.'

'See you there, then.'

'Maybe.'

She continued to smile at him as he let her leave the women's changing room first. He waited for a few moments, before wandering into the empty staff kitchen to make himself a cup of coffee. That was easily done, he thought as he boiled the kettle on the tacky old stove; so unlike his usual awkwardness. Why? He thought he'd take her to the Grecian Grill off Tottenham Court Road. You could get whatever you wanted there at any time of the day or night. It was one of the few places in London that, by tradition, catered almost exclusively for casino workers.

At four, Giles Jones put on his coat and walked the hundred yards or so to the corner of Huffington Street and Park Lane; and waited. It was a cold, clear night. After as much as half an hour, when most of the staff had left the casino, he saw her coming towards him, a smaller figure than he had expected. She wore a modish faux-fur coat and her complexion was strangely pale in the darkness. He told her what he had in mind and she nodded, so he set about looking for a black cab with its orange "For Hire" sign illuminated. One came along soon and it took them to Tottenham Court Road, turning into an obscure cul-de-sac. The bright lights at the end were those of the restaurant. When they got out of the taxi both were conscious that they had scarcely said a word to each other and both were worried that it would continue like this inside.

But the atmosphere in the Grecian Grill changed all that. Once installed in a booth with their drinks they started to relax. The ethnic music was soft and the lights were dim. There were a few other parties around but business seemed slow, the waiters were attentive but a little jaded perhaps. He realised he didn't even know her name, so he asked.

'Jessica Wu,' she answered. 'Yours?'

'Giles Jones.'

They were smiling at each other.

'Why they call you "Gentry"?'

He laughed.

'My accent, I suppose.'

'What that mean?'

'The way I talk.'

She looked puzzled.

They talked less as they ate but she told him that she had been in London for less than a year and was still unhappy with her English. She also told him that she had found it hard to get a job and that her wages were so meagre she had to rely on tips. Luckily, the punters were generous to her too. Then she frowned.

'We pay this half half?'

'If you like.'

'How I get home?'

He looked at his watch.

'The tubes will be starting up soon.'

'Where do you say you live?'

He told her again, and added that it was not too far from where they were. She did not ask anything else until he said, 'Do you want to come back with me?' She didn't answer, so he continued, 'Just for a coffee or something. Then I can walk you to the tube.'

Jessica Wu was not at all impressed by Giles Jones' bedsitter. She sat on the edge of his bed and refused at first even to remove her coat. Instead she looked gloomily around her, but nothing she saw made any difference to her feelings about it. She could not see Giles because he had the door to his kitchen cupboard open and was on the other side of it, making her coffee. He had surreptitiously taken a few swigs of the vodka he kept there but had thought it better not to offer her any. They were not speaking, but he had put on a little background music to improve the atmosphere, as he supposed; but it did nothing of the sort, being at once repetitive and difficult to hear. He realised this and apologised to her about it as he gave her the coffee. He asked whether he should turn it off.

'No, s'alright.'

He sat down on the bed beside her but she moved slightly away from him, even though she had the mug of coffee precariously balanced on her lap. It nearly spilt.

'Here, let me…' With a brusque movement he took the mug from her lap, causing her to move again, and placed it on his desk by the window, meaning she would have to get up to get it, so he said, 'You might be better off on this.' He indicated a chair, which he dusted down. It was an old black thing with a wrought-iron frame and a round leather cushioned seat which needed patching. He had bought it for next to nothing in a junk shop on the Portobello Road but it was quite comfortable. She made an awkward movement as she walked self-consciously towards it, and he thought he would take this opportunity of asking her for her coat.

'It cold here,' she said.

'Oh, all right, then.'

He sat on his bed and watched her as she perched on the chair and took a sip of her coffee. She looked uncomfortable, very much out of her environment; and he wondered what he could do about it.

'I'll put the heater on.'

She did not say anything but at least had started to look as if she were enjoying her coffee, while he pulled the little radiator from the cupboard and turned the switch, which as usual caused a faint but continuous buzzing noise.

'Do let me take your coat. You'll be more comfortable without it.'

She smiled; but without acknowledging his suggestion she then frowned.

'Why you live here?'

'I have to live somewhere. I…'

But it was Giles' turn to frown.

He didn't really know why he lived in this grotty bedsit, except that with the death of his father he had lost everything and for some reason needed continually to remind himself of that fact.

'It's difficult to get a place round here,' (which begged the question as to why he wanted to live in North Kensington anyway), 'somewhere cheap enough, that is.'

'It not nice. It sad.'

He winced.

'It's all I have.'

'Coffee is nice.'

She smiled again.

'Well, that's something.'

He laughed self-consciously.

'What you writing?'

She had turned to his desk and was fingering the hand-written sheets that lay scattered on the surface.

A feeling of alarm overtook Giles Jones and at first he had an instinct to grab them from her, and put them away somewhere from prying eyes.

'Oh, nothing. It's just a hobby of mine.'

But her curiosity was not satisfied. She continued to look at the sheets, while Giles Jones became worried.

'I like books,' she said finally.

'Do you?'

'You write a book? I would like to see.'

He smiled. 'You couldn't read my handwriting.'

'I kun read English anyway. You tell me what it's about.'

He hesitated. In fact as he looked at her his mouth opened and closed like that of a fish.

'Tell me,' she insisted.

Why not? he thought.

She obviously had found something of interest in him, and she had done him the kindness of coming to his flat, at considerable discomfort to herself, it would seem.

'It's about my past.'

'How funny!'

She laughed. He was taken aback, even offended.

'It was hardly that,' he said drily.

'No I mean, why you wan' write about your past?'

'I… er… to get it off my chest, I suppose.'

'What that mean?'

'To get rid of it, to stop it bothering me.'

'Why it bother you?'

Giles Jones became restless, got to his feet and walked about the little bedsitter nervously.

'Because it does, that's all.'

'I sorry.'

'Look, do you mind if I have something to drink?'

'No.'

He poured himself a large glass of neat vodka.

'Would you like one?'

'No.'

He sat down on the bed again with his drink. She waited.

'Look, I'm sorry…' he began; but what was he sorry about?

'You robbed?'

Now how did she know that?

'Yes,' he said.

'It happen to me. I get over it. I try to run stall. Fashion goods. I collect stuff, lot of time, lot of waiting, money. Then it all gone. Somebody take. I know who.'

'Who?'

'It a girl in casino. I thought she was my friend. She come home with me, see my stuff, hear my plan. She offer help. She have boyfriend. I have pitch in market, she offer get boyfriend drive me there. He come in van, collect stuff, drive off. I no see him again. All stuff gone.'

'Did you have it out with her?'

'What that mean?'

'Did you tell her what happened?'

'She say know nothing. She not see him either. But I do not believe.'

'Which one is she?'

'She tall, dark, croupier.'

'Did you go to the police?'

'They no help. They tole me could do nothing. Then…' Jessica Wu flinched.

'Yes?'

'I threaten by girlfriend. She tole me stop making trouble. She tole me…'

122

'Yes?'

'Could get me sack. I need job.'

A look of bewilderment and sorrow came over Jessica Wu's face. She also looked troubled and as if she might start to cry. She had been duped by someone she had thought a friend and had lost an investment of a great deal of time and money. She had wanted to set up in business on her own account and it had come to nothing.

'I'm sorry. Are you going to try again?'

'My savings gone. I kun…'

She looked at her empty cup of coffee.

'Maybe I write,' she said, brightening up a little.

'About it?'

'Yes.' But then, sorrowfully, 'I kun write.'

'In your own language?'

'Maybe. If I go home.'

'Will you go home?'

'I no want. Nothing there. Nothing to do. So I don't know.'

Giles Jones touched her on the shoulder as gently as he could. 'I'm sorry', he said; but it had been an equivocal gesture. He stayed where he was, leaving his hand on her shoulder.

'I no want sympathy. I like you but I no want sympathy.'

'All right.'

He let his hand drop to his side and stood back a bit.

'What do you want?' he asked.

'Friend.'

'Okay.'

'I need friend.'

'Okay.'

She looked at her watch.

'But I go now. It late. I sleepy.'

'Stay.'

'It too late. I go home.'

'Do you want me to come with you?'

She looked at him.

'Not now', she said. 'Maybe then.'

'I'll walk you to the tube.'

'Okay.'

It was in fact eight o'clock in the morning, the rush hour. They were dazed by the light and activity in the streets, but also because they now

123

almost seemed strangers to one another, they had never seen each other in daylight before. As they walked along they kept on casting surreptitious sidelong glances at each other, as if unsure it was they who had been conversing so intimately but a few moments ago. At the entrance to the tube they held hands and kissed several times on the lips, brief pecks which were more affectionate than anything else. Then she pulled herself away from him and with a worried expression was swallowed up by the human maelstrom descending the escalator.

18.
Giles Jones' diary

A word about Mr Tompkins, the housemaster of Prasher's. I have told you that he could often be seen through the window of his living room clutching an appropriate sporting instrument as he watched the box; but he himself was a fanatically successful player – of cricket, golf, squash, real tennis and squash rackets particularly; and it has to be said that the reason why he went to work as a teacher in a country public school at all was because such a place would be guaranteed to afford him the facilities for those pursuits, unlike, say, a desk job in London, which in any case he would have wrongly thought beneath him. As to anything else, the man was useless and wholly deserving of contempt. I never had the misfortune to be taught by him, but once I passed by his classroom and couldn't help but look through the window to see what he was doing, which was chalking up some mathematical equation or other on the blackboard; and simply by his movements I could tell that he went about this tedious duty much as he went about the housemastering part of it: in a dull, plodding unimaginative way, and only because it was a necessary part of the deal which allowed him to do what he loved. He also had the most boring face and physique I have ever seen: sort of like an upright tortoise, only blander, but enough of this. My animosity toward him cannot obscure the fact that, as was to become painfully apparent during the next few days, he was in the driver's seat and I wasn't.

On the day of the incident, I had been summoned in the evening to Mr Tompkins' study on the first floor of Prasher's. This room was long, low and narrow, and it could only be reached by an awkward, winding staircase. He was always seated behind his desk, which was at the very far end of it, at a relatively great distance. I was made to stand by the door, facing him, as if he were too important a personage to suffer any proximity from others. He took his time consulting some document, his glasses absurdly halfway down his nose. I think he thought that in that position they gave him an intellectual look. After several minutes of this charade he looked up and surveyed me with distaste.

'Take your hands out of your pockets.'

I wasn't even aware that I had them there, but I took them out and left them dangling uselessly at either side.

Mr Tompkins cleared his throat. I could see his favourite number nine iron leaning against the wall behind him. 'Never in all my years as housemaster of Prasher's have I come across such an episode as this.'

He spoke with that characteristic, gnomic primness, characteristic but acquired; a mediocrity's affectation of authority.

But now he barked: 'What? What?'

'Yes.'

'I can't hear you, Jones!'

I had forgotten: 'Yes, sir,' I said.

'Harrumph.'

No, really. He did mutter that.

He looked again at the document in front of him and grimaced. Next he started to read, and in order to do so had silently to mouth the words to follow them in his mind. It was excruciating to watch but again characteristic. I waited.

'It says 'ere...' the accent had dropped, becoming really rather common, 'that you shot young Cumberbatch with a rifle. In all my...,' he continued to squint at the document, 'you do realise this is a very serious matter, which could mean expulsion?'

'I didn't shoot him, sir. He got in the way.'

'What do you mean?'

'He got in the way, sir. I was up on the shooting range.'

'I know where you were. Major Milner told me. And I found this...,' with a flourish he plopped the key to the armoury on the surface of his desk. '...in your desk. Why didn't you give it back to him?'

I didn't say anything, because there was really nothing much to say.

'You were going to try to deny it, weren't you?'

Again, I said nothing.

'And get some other poor sod into trouble.'

His wording could have been more felicitous, but still I said nothing.

In exasperation, Mr Tompkins beat the document with his hand and said, 'What I want to know is why you did it!'

'Like I said, I didn't mean to, sir, honest.'

'Don't say "like I said".'

126

'Yes, sir.'

It was true that I had thought of denying the whole thing, denying even having been at the rifle range earlier that day, but something told me I would be found out, and that would only make matters worse. On the other hand I didn't give a fig, really; or at least I thought I didn't.

'You surely must have meant to… people don't just go round…'

'All right. I meant to.'

I said this quietly, even though I felt my temper rising. I wanted to blot out this absurd little man.

Stopping in mid-flow, he gave me an astounded look. I too had stopped, and returned to my normal sullen, recalcitrant self. But inside I was shaking with rage.

After a pause, Mr Tompkins said quietly, 'And why did you mean to, Jones?'

I looked away, embarrassed. I could hardly say, "Because he got in my way", but that is what I did say. Another pause.

Finally he asked, again in that quiet tone of voice, 'How?'

I explained the circumstances, muttering my way through their description without looking at him, as if it were all some ghastly dream in which I had been the principal victim. He listened, then said, 'At least you have admitted what you have done, and why. There may be some room for manoeuvre. You will go now, Jones, and in the meantime I will consider how best to deal with this matter.'

'Yes, sir.'

I skulked out, closing the door behind me.

I went back to my study and smoked an illicit cigarette, making sure to exhale the smoke through the open window to avoid detection.

A few days later I was again summoned to Mr Tompkins' study. Harry Cumberbatch was sitting next to him at his desk: It was an odd and unexpected sight. The boy at first looked older and more authoritative just because of his setting; and the housemaster had one of his very bland looks about him, as if he were about to pull off a famous coup.

'Sit down, Jones', he said.

This, I suppose, was good news. I sat gingerly on a rickety chair by the wall next to the door. I noticed that Harry Cumberbatch was embarrassed and would not look me in the eye.

Mr Tompkins cleared his throat and began, 'Jones, you will recall the other day I impressed upon you the seriousness of your behaviour in relation to… ah… young Cumberbatch here' – he prodded the fellow in the ribs, causing him to squirm; in any case he was, in fact, slightly older than me – 'and I raised with you the possibility of your removal from this institution, a draconian step perhaps, but one which would have been fully justified in the circumstances.' He paused and cleared his throat again. He was fixing me with a "beady eye" as they say, and happily for him his glasses were fully up his nose.

'Er, however, I have discussed the matter with young Cumberbatch here' – again, he prodded the boy in the ribs, causing him once more to squirm – 'haven't I, Cumberbatch?'

A fraction belatedly, Harry Cumberbatch realised that this was his cue to agree, so he turned to Mr Tompkins and said, 'Oh – yes, sir.'

'And – and – you may be pleased to hear, Jones, that surprisingly he bears you no ill will whatsoever for what you have done, which is very sporting of him, God knows why, I certainly would. Isn't that right, Cumberbatch?'

'Yes, sir.'

I looked briefly at Harry Cumberbatch, who seemed to be in a state of some excruciation, and still would not look at me. Moreover, he was now squirming continuously, as if he had been thoroughly got at, or even bullied to the point where even he might have been embarrassed for his tormentor's sake.

'So, so…,' again, Mr Tompkins cleared his throat,' I have decided that the best way forward is this. No, wait a minute. Let me get this right. Stand up, Jones.'

I did so, curious as to what would be said next. 'Jones, er, clearly some punishment needs to be imposed. So you are banned from the rifle range for the rest of your time at Selwyn Mauberley College. Got that?'

'Yes, sir.'

I tried to act suitably chastened but in fact the effort came easily enough, because not to be able to go to the rifle range ever again – the only activity I enjoyed at the school – would indeed be a blow. I remained standing. 'And…,' he continued, 'I have talked this over with Harry Cumberbatch and have suggested to him that the incident could be closed suitably – bearing in mind his quite extraordinary lack of ill will towards you – isn't that right, Cumberbatch?'

'Yes, sir,' croaked the boy, staring at the floor.

He always had a croaky voice anyway, it was one of the many things that made him such an object of fun to the other boys.

'Good. By – ah, come forward, Jones.'

I approached the desk, on the other side of which they sat like a most improbable double act. I had no idea what was coming next, and felt a little trepidation. 'By apologising. You will apologise to Cumberbatch for what you have done, Jones.'

'Yes, sir.'

Now it was my turn to clear my throat. I looked at Cumberbatch, whose face was only a few feet from mine, but who was still looking at the floor, and said, 'I'm very sorry, Cumberbatch.'

He did not reply.

Mr Tompkins said, 'Go on, Cumberbatch.'

'That's all right, Jones,' muttered Cumberbatch, his heart not really in it.

'Good,' said Mr Tompkins, looking pleased with himself. 'Now shake hands. Get up, boy.'

The housemaster was of the view that it was impossible to shake hands with any sincerity if both parties were not on their feet. So, Harry Cumberbatch was made to stand up and for the first time he faced me. We shook hands – with reluctance on his part, I thought. His hand was scrawny and moist; it was not a pleasant experience to have to touch it.

'Good, good,' said Mr Tompkins. 'Sit down, Cumberbatch. Go back to your seat, Jones.'

We did so; Mr Tompkins now looked at some papers in front of him, causing his glasses to begin their perennial descent down the bridge of his proboscis. He appeared to have read something which caused him to snigger.

'You know, Jones,' he said, a propos of nothing, 'Doctor Hunter and I did wonder whether in view of your behaviour we ought to refer you to a psychiatrist, but we decided against it, because it had always seemed to us that you were mad anyway!' He threw the papers aside and heaved his upper torso across the desk and looked at me with glinting eyes, and bellowed with laughter. It was the sort of behaviour of someone who thinks he has said something funny but hasn't. I looked away, embarrassed for him.

Mr Tompkins pulled himself together and said, 'You may both go now.'

Unreal, I thought; as Harry Cumberbatch slowly got to his feet while I waited for him to reach the door. We were both about to leave (backwards, as was the requirement) when, as if as an afterthought, Mr

Tompkins said, without looking in our direction and while restoring his papers to a neat pile on the desk, 'It goes without saying, I suppose, that neither of you need tell your people about any of this, since it has been resolved to my satisfaction. Do I make myself clear?'

'Yes, sir.'

'Yes, sir.'

We left the room and closed the door behind us; having done so, however, we had nothing to say to each other, so the moment we reached the bottom of the winding staircase we went our separate ways.

As I say, the banning from the rifle range was a great loss to me. It was from that moment on that I started to have real trouble getting to sleep, which had always been a difficulty, but now the whole night would be spent just lying in my narrow dormitory bed and staring at the dark but moonlit ceiling. In the daytime, I would be even more morose and tired than usual; would nod off in class, not that anybody cared or maybe even noticed; and in the afternoons would fall asleep when I had been dragooned into, say, scoring at a cricket match. Nobody wanted me in their team, you see, so it had to be me who did the scoring; but they did notice this particular sleepfulness, of course; so I was dropped even from that. I became such a nuisance to myself that even I felt I had to do something about it; so I rang up my Aunt Felicity, the doctor.

'Tell you what, Gee,' she said, with her usual bubbly enthusiasm, 'there's a new drug on the market, absolutely safe, non-addictive, you take one at night and you'll be off like a top.' She said she'd send me a prescription. Again, looking back on things, it seems extraordinary that a fifteen- year-old boarder at a public school could simply walk into the town and obtain a bottle of strong sleeping pills from the local chemist without any questions being asked; but that is what happened. They were called Mandrax, and I took to them immediately. I discovered that if I took more than the correct dose but did not go to bed I would begin to feel very relaxed and curiously light-headed; and inhabit a strange and new but highly pleasant world I had not known before; which I relished. Moreover, it was my little secret: this was something nobody else knew about. I took care to hide the bottle in a place I judged Mr Tompkins would never find, no matter how much snooping he liked to do; and at first I told absolutely no one about this new habit of mine. At night when everybody else had gone to sleep I would slip out of the dormitory and make my way to the squash courts across the drive. There was an old, low wall there, plenty of whose bricks were loose; it was behind one of these that I kept the pills, having carefully removed the label with my name on it from the bottle in case it should ever be discovered. I would swallow a couple whole and go into one of the squash courts, the one with the open roof so that I could see the night sky, the stars and the moon. After a few minutes the pills would begin to work, and I would simply walk around in diminishing circles, growing ever less steady on my feet until my dizziness forced me to sit cross-legged on the stone floor and simply enjoy the feeling of weightlessness that accompanied a glorious absence of self-control and sense of dissolving which the pills engendered. Yes, it was flowery; so the words are apt. I started to see strange shapes – looming things which achieved colour in the moonlit darkness; they were my friends.

For maybe an hour I would experience this delight; but of course there always came a time when I would have to get back to the dormitory, and so I stumbled along the driveway, into the building and up the stairs. Once I fell over and bit my tongue very badly; it was painful for the rest of the term. On another occasion I felt I might get found out because I had just got back to the dormitory and fallen asleep (the pills did do what they were supposed to do, if you let them), when the fire alarm sounded. It was an unannounced drill and we all had to put on our dressing gowns and shuffle down to the courtyard where we stood in rows to be counted. I had to stumble past a watchful Mr Tompkins and another master; the former gave me a curious look but that was all. When my name was called I think I slurred the words "Yes, sir" but again I suppose that if this was noticed at all it was put down to mere sleepiness.

I continued to take these pills for the rest of my time at Selwyn Mauberley College and beyond. I had been worried that Aunt Felicity might stop sending me prescriptions for them but she never did; I think because having nailed her colours to the mast it would have been too dreadful for her professional pride to admit that she had been wrong to prescribe them in the first place; this despite the fact that Mandrax began to get a bad reputation as a malignant barbiturate substitute and were often used – illicitly acquired – by teenagers at rock festivals and so on.

When I had been at Prasher's for a year I became entitled to a study of my own, which was good news as it meant a great deal more privacy for me. I set about decorating the smelly little room – one of a number along a corridor in the main building. To my dismay, cockroaches scuttled into hiding when I removed some sacking that a previous boy had left. I also noticed, when I stripped the wallpaper, that the bare walls underneath were covered in graffiti and garbled messages, of the sort you get in public lavatories. But I was undeterred. My ever obliging aunt and grandmother had provided me with silk cushions, sofa, a desk which I had chosen from a department store in York; and some William Morris wall hangings, among other things. The room looked quite cosy when I had finished; except that I took a dislike to the desk and wished I hadn't chosen it. Mass produced, it had a prim, genteel look, as if intended to give tone to whatever its surroundings may have been; but the intention appeared to have failed in this case, for it was thoroughly out of place and whenever I looked at it I thought of the provincial department store where it had been bought, and of the fact – as it seemed to me – that that establishment was really its true and only home. Anyway, one afternoon as I was leaving my study, the boy next door happened to be leaving his. We of course knew each other by sight and had even exchanged friendly words from time to time and often passed each other in the corridors and on the playing fields; so I was startled when he turned and introduced himself, as if we were strangers to each other, and offered his hand to be shaken.

He had a broad ploughboy grin on his face and his whole manner was of someone who might have said, "Welcome aboard!"

Still startled, I took his hand and shook it; but did not feel it necessary to give him my name.

'You're Jones, aren't you?' he continued, still shaking. 'We should look out for each other now that we're neighbours!'

'Ye-es,' I said tentatively.

His name was Snape, and he had the reputation of being a bit of an oddball; not that that mattered to me as, after all, I had no friends and didn't particularly want any.

He always looked a bit sickly, particularly from a distance, as he was quite thin and pale, and had floppy, straw-coloured hair which Mr Tompkins was always telling him to get cut. His movements were awkward and angular. However, close up, one sensed a certain hilarity about him, as if he thought everything a bit of a joke, including anybody he happened to be speaking to. He was no good at games and did not shine academically.

'Come in, come in,' he said, beckoning me into his study. 'I want to show you something.'

Against my better judgement I followed him; I had earlier been aware of a lot of banging and crashing going on next door when I was decorating my own study, and had become a little curious.

Inside, all along one wall, were shelved row upon row of Kilner jars containing coffee grounds. He started to take each one from its place in turn and explained to me which part of the world its contents came from, including the precise geo-botanical conditions in which the beans grew, their strength and flavour, etcetera, etcetera. As he did, he would unscrew the top and invite me to savour the aroma. I did once or twice – politely I hoped – but I then had no interest in coffee and was anyway bemused by his obsessiveness. After quite a while of this I cut him short.

'Look, I must be going,' I said. 'It's been jolly interesting.'

Snape seemed pleased, and invited me to return when I had more time so that he could finish his demonstration. With some insincerity I said I would. This encounter hadn't been for me the most auspicious of starts to a friendship of sorts, but such it became.

19.
Narrative, 1979

Derek Bradshaw was seated at the breakfast table reading a copy of the Daily Telegraph. His wife sat opposite him, reading the Daily Mail. Both were engrossed. They had finished eating, and their cups of coffee were nearly empty.

It was a pleasant enough morning for the time of year; pale yellow sunlight streamed through the window of the dining room of Cornwallis Lodge, their large, detached house in Carshalton, Surrey, albeit that it was extremely cold outside. The central heating was on. Derek Bradshaw looked at his watch. He would have to be making tracks soon. First, the drive in his Rover 3 litre to the railway station, where it would be parked in the permanent space he had there, then the train to Victoria, followed by a tube journey to his offices in Lincoln's Inn Fields. Shirley Bradshaw, on the other hand, could afford to let the morning idle until her meeting at the Women's Institute at eleven. She had not yet dressed. She was a large woman in a pale lemon dressing gown. Her brown hair was still tousled.

Derek Bradshaw turned the page of his Daily Telegraph and gave a start. There in front of him was a poor colour photograph whose unmistakable subject, however, was his client and co-conspirator, Aylmer Jones, underneath which was another photograph of an attractive young woman whom he did not recognise.

"Grisly double murder in fashionable hotel", went the headline.

He read the details with mounting fright. When he had finished reading and composed himself as best he could he looked at his wife.

'Good God,' he muttered.

She looked up.

'Pardon?'

'Seems a client of mine has been murdered. You know, that man who's been administering old Damien Jones' estate. Aylmer, his name is.'

'Really? I've just been reading about that.'

She came over to have a look.

'Yes,' she said. 'The article is more or less the same as mine. I thought I'd heard the name.'

Derek Bradshaw was prone to gossip with his wife about his clients, usually in a bitchy sort of way. He had not, of course, told her about his and the others' defalcations.

'Are you all right, Derek? You're trembling.'

'It's just the shock of it, that's all.'

'What are you going to do?'

'What can I do? I don't think I could give the police any…' he looked again at the article.

'They haven't a clue who the murderer is, nor why he did it.' But Derek Bradshaw was beginning to form a ghastly idea. 'Says the woman was a high-class prostitute.'

'Well, I never. He doesn't look the type.'

'Yes,' answered Derek Bradshaw thoughtfully. 'He was divorced some time ago, of course.'

'This Jones' estate of yours,' said Shirley Bradshaw, who had heard about the bare bones of it for many years now, 'I daresay this will mean more delays?'

'Yes, I suppose so.'

'Good,' she said. 'We need a new summer house in the garden. The present one is falling to bits, as you know.'

An hour and a half later Derek Bradshaw was entering the building in Lincoln's Inn Fields where his firm's offices were housed. It had been a difficult commute, not because the train was late or overcrowded or anything like that, but because of the inner disquiet he felt at the possibility that his client's murder as reported was connected with their joint theft of the proceeds of Damien Jones' estate. He had considered ringing Graham Greene when he got to work but dismissed the idea as alarmist.

Fiona Keene, his secretary, was seated at her desk in the ante-chamber to his own suite of rooms when he entered; she looked up at him expectantly as he passed by her with a murmured, 'good morning.' She was an attractive, middle-aged woman who had retained her good figure.

'May I have my breakfast now?' she asked.

'I suppose so,' he said absent-mindedly, closing the door behind him. She followed, and closed the door behind her too. Then she locked it.

135

He was already by his desk but instead of sitting at it he turned to face her, while she approached and knelt before him. She removed the braces from his trousers and undid them, pulling them down to his ankles. His shirt tails idled at the sides. She pushed back these and kept her hands clamped on his hips. Next she pulled his underpants down with her teeth. Despite this morning's worrying news, he as usual became erect very quickly and allowed her to plant her mouth over his hard penis. She proceeded to move her mouth forwards and backwards over the full length of it, tonguing, sucking and gently biting as she went; he began to feel dizzy and weak, and had to lean back against the desk for support. She continued what she was doing without pause; he felt that if only she would stop for a moment everything would be all right, he would not have to come in her mouth as she wanted. But she did not stop. Rhythmically she continued, building up a slow pressure in his loins which eventually burst. He shuddered and gripped the edge of his desk with both hands. She gulped a bit; then swallowed; and withdrew from him.

'Thank you for my breakfast, Mr Bradshaw,' she said, getting to her feet.

He did not reply, but simply watched, fascinated, as she walked to the door, unlocked it and left, closing it behind her. He, as always after this episode, had to re-dress himself but whilst he was doing this she came in again and said, 'Oh, here's the morning post.'

'Thank you, Miss Keene.'

She deposited the letters on his desk and walked out again.

One of the letters was not of the usual type; its envelope was handwritten for a start, and bore a stamp rather than being franked, which was more common in business correspondence these days. Curious, he put the others aside and opened it with his silver-handled letter opener, a birthday present from Shirley. He pulled out a folded piece of A4 paper and spread it out on the desk in front of him. Again, it was handwritten, in black ink, and in neatly spaced paragraphs, but it was not so easy to read. So, he looked first at the bottom to see the signature. It was that of Giles Jones. Derek Bradshaw started to frown. How did he get my professional address? was a question that flitted through his mind, but that was easily answered in lots of ways: Giles' mother had it, it was on the files. Even so, what the devil was he writing to him for? His eyes went back to the top. There was a date – yesterday's

– but no sender's address. He started to read.

"Mr Bradshaw, you will remember me as your client Damien Jones' son, whom you met all those years ago on the occasion of the interment of his ashes at Jones village church. You have not taken the trouble to communicate with me since and, indeed, I had forgotten all about you until recently. I have been given to understand that you and others for a very long time have been systematically defrauding my father's estate for your own benefit and to my detriment. In fact, I know this to be the case. To be honest, I had given up on any idea of an inheritance for me and had not pursued the matter because it would have meant delving into a past which has always been painful. But certain things have changed all that. I am writing to tell you that I never felt such a rage as I do now and that you and the others – you know only too well who they are – are the object of it. I have considered more conventional modes of revenge such as taking you to court, but I have not the time, the patience or the money for that, and in any case any positive result would not be good enough. I also thought of going to the police but what would they do? As a solicitor you would no doubt be plausible with them and even if you were arrested, charged and brought to trial the outcome would be uncertain. And even if convicted I couldn't bear it if your sentence turned out to be a derisory one, which it might very well be.

So, I have decided to kill you. You will probably have read of the death of Aylmer Jones and his girlfriend by the time this letter reaches you and you must brace yourself for a similar ending. I am very sorry about this but this rage inside me will not be abated. You simply should not have taken me for a fool.

Sincerely, Giles Jones"

Derek Bradshaw put the letter down with a limp wrist. Like Aylmer Jones before him, he at first thought that its contents must be some sort of a joke. This was because, if taken seriously, their meaning was too horrible to contemplate. Yet he realised he was shaking, and there was cold sweat upon his brow. His heart had started to thump and his hands were clammy. Gradually though, he started to accept the sincerity of what had been written him. He looked at his watch – it was far too early for a drink but that is what he needed to have. He rang through to Miss Keene and told her that he was not to be disturbed until further notice. Next he went to the ornate cupboard in the corner and poured himself a very large glass of brandy and gulped at it. The liquid was immediately warming, calming and perhaps paradoxically started to clear his head. He tried to be analytical of the situation he found himself in. yet he could do nothing but pace up and down the room, before he forced himself to sit again at his desk. Glass in hand, he considered the matter. His first thought was that it was not going to happen to him, not him, Derek Bradshaw, who had survived and prospered for so long that his imminent demise was inconceivable. He looked at the wide, broad window that faced Lincoln's Inn Fields and considered that extra security should be installed at Cornwallis Lodge. Shirley was always worrying about burglars anyway, so she would welcome the prospect and ask no awkward questions about it. Of course, Giles Jones' letter was a police matter but as a lawyer Derek Bradshaw knew he daren't take that course, unless he was prepared to run the considerable risk of his own wrongdoing being exposed. He tried to weigh in the balance the respective merits of the saving of his life as against the few years in prison he would undoubtedly serve, but for him this was an artificial exercise to the point of unreality: because his ill-gotten material gains were his life.

A sudden anger rose in his breast at this thorough little wanker Giles Jones. Why couldn't he be behaving more reasonably? Take the lot of them to court for example, or even contact the police himself? People didn't just go round killing others because they had a grievance. But he knew that they did. He'd seen it in his own practice. Then he had an idea. He would write to him, try to reason with him, suggest a compromise. Since Derek Bradshaw's primary, if not sole, motivation in life was money he made the elementary mistake of assuming that it was everyone else's too. Surely if a substantial sum were offered? Without any admission of liability, of course.

He rang through to Miss Keene and asked her to dig up Giles Jones' most recent address.

'His mother will have it,' he said when she queried where she was going to get it from. 'It'll be on the file.'

'Right.'

'And Miss Keene?'

'Yes?'

'On no account must you give my home address to anyone who asks for it, you understand?'

His home address had always been a talking point, on account of the fact that the famous but failed British general was reputed to have once lived on the same spot.

'Yes, Mr Bradshaw.'

When Miss Keene put the phone down she started to bite her lip. Derek Bradshaw of course could not see this. But it was because only the other day she had given her boss's home address to a very nice-sounding young man. She had thought nothing of it at the time.

Next Derek Bradshaw took a piece of headed notepaper from the top right-hand drawer of his desk, unscrewed his fountain pen and started to write. He paused and frowned, looking again at the window which faced Lincoln's Inn Fields. He scrunched the paper up and deposited it in the waste paper basket. He started again with a plain piece of typing paper which bore no heading.

As for Giles Jones, he thought he would kill Derek Bradshaw with a gun. It would make a change, and in any case he had found the Aylmer Jones debacle rather messy. Things had happened in the hotel which he hadn't expected and he had been in very great danger of losing control of the situation. With hindsight, it had perhaps been rash of him to act on the spur of the moment like that, without having thought things through. But with a gun, he reasoned, all he had to do was aim properly, pull the trigger and flee. He had discovered where the man lived, so with a bit of planning the kill should be quite quick, easy and simple. He also knew where the man worked, but a moment's reflection satisfied him that it would be unwise to try to do it there; these days high-end solicitors' firms crawled with security, and it would have to be in daylight, just as Derek Bradshaw was arriving for work or leaving it. Lincoln's Inn Fields would be full of people like him at those times of day and he would assuredly get caught. As against which a leafy suburb at night would afford excellent cover. True, the Bradshaws' drive opened onto a main road, but with a car left idling there he could be away in no time.

Giles Jones did not possess a car, so he would have to get one. The alternative, as he had reconnoitred, would be to walk the twenty minutes or so it took from the nearest railway station to the Bradshaws' house, do the deed and return to the railway station on foot, discarding the gun as he went; but that would be risky too: even if he managed to kill Mr and Mrs Bradshaw the sound of gunshot would obviously cause an alarm to be raised and the police would have ample time in which to track him down. The gun would be found nearby. So, having worked and lived in London for years without the need of a car he would now have to obtain one; and a gun, of course, although he had not yet thought about this at all.

He could not just go and buy one legitimately, he reasoned, because he would have to get a license for it and that would mean being identified as someone who owned such a thing, quite apart from the fact that the gunsmith would keep records and no doubt would require his name and address before he sold it to him. Besides, he had heard that guns sold on the open market – particularly of the type he had in mind – were very expensive; and he did not see why his efforts at revenge should cost him too much money – money which he didn't have. On the other hand, something told him that the area where he lived would not be right for a clandestine purchase. Queensway, or more generally North Kensington was many things: it was raffish, it was seamy, it could be sordid but, strangely, it was not violent. In any case it would be safer to go further afield. He had heard of a pub in North London which by repute swarmed with members of the IRA; to visit such a pub would of course not be without its own dangers. As a stranger he would be stared at with suspicion and hostility, and when he asked for a gun – well! Maybe though, his presence there would be explained and indeed regularised by that request. So, on one of his evenings off he got a cab all the way to Willesden, got off at the High Street and went in search of the Shamrock Tavern.

Meanwhile, Derek Bradshaw was seriously thinking about what he should do to protect himself. Not himself and Muriel, and Graham Greene, but just himself. He had waited many days for a reply to his letter, sent to Giles Jones' last known address, but had received none; and something now told him that he never would, even if it had ever reached him. He again toyed with the idea of contacting the police, he didn't quite know why – it was just to, well, see if there was anything he could find out which might help him avoid the risk to his life which patently now existed – anything which might unwittingly be revealed by a police officer who had no reason to suspect that the man he was talking to was guilty of anything at all. He would of course present himself merely as the murder victim's solicitor, a professional man who was concerned about the matter and wanted to know certain things should they have legal implications for the deceased's estate.

At this point Derek Bradshaw frowned at the circularity of his own thoughts. It was at times like these that he wished he had someone to talk to. He wished his marriage to Shirley was more – well – intimate; but he knew she would leave him immediately if she thought he had been behaving dishonestly and would almost certainly go to the police herself if she realised her own life was in danger. Giles Jones hadn't spared the prostitute, so why should he spare Shirley Bradshaw? Perhaps they should go away – on a long cruise somewhere, so long that in all probability the murderer would have been caught by the time they got back. But he might not have been caught and anyway Shirley – and indeed others – would be instantly suspicious at the suggestion of a cruise and she would know very well that if he neglected his clients for any length of time it would mean that his practice would be jeopardised and she wouldn't stand for that, because their lifestyle, to which she was just as enslaved as he was, would be adversely affected, possibly even killed off altogether. For similar reasons, it was not realistic to move house, just supposing Giles Jones had discovered their home address; so all he could do was make Cornwallis Lodge as secure as possible. He made a mental note to see about that the next day. In the meantime, he continued to experience that extreme mental torment which accompanies a sense of imminent and mortal danger, fuelled by his shuddering and self-repeating recollection that, as reported, Aylmer Jones had died of multiple stab wounds, which must have been the work of a frenzied individual whose heart was filled with hatred. It was too awful to contemplate.

He really thought that he ought to go to the police after all, and come clean about everything. Surely a few years in gaol would be better than… but no; he just couldn't do it. The moment his hand reached for the telephone it stopped in mid-air at a halfway point, where it wavered before changing direction toward the tumbler of brandy on his desk. He gulped again, but it was no use. The numbness the alcohol induced was no match for his preoccupations. He felt he had to speak to somebody or die anyway. Without for one moment thinking he would be at home on a weekday afternoon he dialled Graham Greene's number, knocking the brandy over in the process. The phone answered after just two rings; had Derek Bradshaw known that he would be there he would probably not have called at all.

'Graham Greene speaking.'

'Graham, it's Derek.'

'I wondered if you'd call.'

'So you've read about it?'

'Of course.'

'What do you think we should do?'

'We? It's every man for himself. Anyway we don't know young Giles did it. It's nothing to do with me.'

'What about the letter, then?'

'What letter?'

'You haven't received one?'

'No.'

'I mean from Giles Jones. He's threatening to kill me.'

'I haven't received one. Anyway he's not going to get past me.'

'Don't you think we ought to go to the police?'

'You're the lawyer.'

'I'm in two minds.'

'Well, don't.'

There was a pause.

Graham Greene resumed, 'Look, Derek, you know and I know that Aylmer or Mr Jones as he insisted on being called was a complete fool. He had no business letting Giles anywhere near him, supposing it was Giles. I can look after myself. If you go to the police I shall deny everything. It's not my fault you gave me too much money. How was I to know it belonged to Giles? You're the lawyer, not me. Now, if there's anything else…?'

'I suppose not.'

Derek Bradshaw had by now realised that it was no help having called Graham Greene and he wished he hadn't. Furthermore, there was a tone of gruff hostility to the man's voice which made it clear that he would not be in the business of offering help or of collaborating in any way.

'One more thing…' said Graham Greene.

'Yes?'

'Have you got a gun?'

'Of course not.'

The very thought of owning a gun shocked Derek Bradshaw.

'Well, get one. For protection. Do as I do.'

'I don't think…'

'Goodbye, now.'

The phone went dead.

Derek Bradshaw sighed as he mopped up the brandy with his handkerchief and poured himself another. Well, that was it; he was on his own now and he didn't like it. He poured the brandy back into the bottle. Better not get home reeking of alcohol, Shirley'll think something is up. There was a knock on his door.

'Yes?'

The door opened. Miss Keene stood there with nothing on but her bra and panties. There was a little-girl-lost expression on her face, and a tone of enquiry to her voice.

'Is it time for my afternoon tea, Mr Bradshaw?'

'Yes, Miss Keene, it is. Come in, and close the door behind you.'

She did so, and approached.

Anything, anything, thought Derek Bradshaw, to rid these infernal thoughts from my mind.

20.
Giles Jones' Diary

I think the next time I saw Snape I was lying on my sofa in my study late one afternoon listening to music, which was playing very loudly. This didn't matter: practically every boy who had a study of his own turned his radio or record player up to its maximum, just to drown out the sound of everybody else's; but his knock reverberated irresistibly against the thin panelling of my door and I shouted, 'Come in!' I also turned the music down. The door opened, and Snape popped his head round the frame, bashfully. He seemed genuinely surprised to have been admitted to someone else's world, but truth to tell I resented the interruption the moment I saw who it was. His jaw kept on dropping, and he blinked at me behind his glasses.

'What do you want?' I asked pleasantly enough.

He didn't say anything for a moment, then asked, 'What are you listening to?'

'Bob Dylan,' I said.

There was nothing unusual in that – practically all boys my age at Selwyn Mauberley College listened to this crack-voiced crooner of genius, at least until they discovered Leonard Cohen. Snape didn't say anything more.

'Ballad in Plain D,' I supplied helpfully, although I doubted whether the name of this particular song would carry his understanding very much further. Snape just stood there, half in, half out, the door concealing most of him.

'Look, are you coming in or what?'

Snape gulped, then took the plunge. He stepped forward and closed the door behind him but remained standing like a sentinel.

'What's so odd about it anyway?' I asked. 'Everybody listens to Bob Dylan.'

'I don't. I've never heard of him.'

'You must have done.'

'I haven't.'

'What do you listen to, then?'

'Not much.'

'Well, sit down and listen.'

I turned the volume up again. Snape sat gingerly on the desk chair, the only other place to sit. I rummaged around and found a half-drunk can of flat shandy, and offered it to him. He declined, so I drank it myself. He continued to sit primly on the desk chair, his back quite straight, as if he were at a formal concert and had to behave himself, even though he would rather be elsewhere. But nobody had forced him to come in and listen, so his behaviour was a bit of a mystery. Eventually even I grew weary of the music, so I turned it down again and said, 'Now you've heard Bob Dylan.'

'It was jolly smashing.'

I winced. His language was so uncool.

After that he kept on looking at me but clearly was having difficulty thinking of anything further to say, so I asked, 'How's the coffee?' I wished I hadn't, because no sooner had I done so than he started to babble robotically on about – so far as I recall – a new variety of Blue Mountain he'd had delivered from a fancy delicatessen somewhere; I cannot repeat what he said about it not least because I simply was not listening. I suddenly got to my feet and interrupted, 'Look. Do you want to go for a walk or something? It's stuffy in here.' He stopped talking as quickly as he had started, and that open-mouthed look returned to his face.

He blinked, appeared to be thinking furiously for a moment, then said, 'Okay.'

We walked all the way into town in silence. It was a hot day. Just as we were passing the church he asked, 'Where are we going?'

'You like coffee, don't you? There's a tea shop I know on the other side of town. You should be able to get some there.'

Snape was intrigued. It was remarkable to me how few of the boys ever bothered to explore the ins and outs of the small market town which bordered the college grounds, contenting themselves with the High Street only, where the tuck and sports shops were, and the hotels their parents stayed in.

We walked the length of the High Street, past the Town Hall where the road forked around it and began to incline steeply upwards until the two prongs met before turning into the main highway leading out of town. In this area there were many narrow side streets which seemed to have been forgotten by anyone not living within their purlieus, except that you saw nobody anyway, and no cars. The place was dead, and not even charming or olde worlde like the centre of town, because it was so drab. Snape was getting restive.

'It's here somewhere.'

Even I had forgotten exactly where it was; we had to retrace our steps several times, noticing gloomily that the sun was disappearing and now everything was in shadows, curious cigar-shaped things that bulged then tapered towards the street corners. Snape seemed to be getting scared: he had started to sniff audibly and repeatedly. It was annoying. But I was determined to find this tea shop.

"Mrs Parfitt's" was its name, as I recalled.

Finally, I found it; a drab, dusty shop with a few cakes on cake stands in its unlit window.

'Here it is,' I said.

'This?' asked Snape, peering dubiously at the cakes, which in any case were imitations. 'It looks shut anyway.' There had been a hopeful tone to his voice when he said that.

'It's not shut,' I said, pushing open the dusty glass door, which took some doing. 'It's just that nobody ever comes here.'

A bell tinkled as we entered. There was a strange smell inside, an old marble counter and an atmosphere of stillness, as if none of its contents had been used for years.

'Come on,' I said.

He followed me up a creaking staircase; things were better when we got to the first floor. There were tables, and more light was coming through the window, by which we sat, on chairs which wobbled. Doilies had been placed upon the tables, which were of old, stained but overly varnished dark wood, of the sort you get in poverty-stricken rural cottages. No attempt had been made at cheeriness. Snape, sitting opposite me, was looking embarrassed; more, as if he had been committed to a mental hospital in error, and would shortly have to partake of bad food in the company of people with whom he could not possibly communicate. I lit a cigarette.

'You can't do that,' he said, shocked.

'Why not?'

'It's not allowed.'

'So?'

'Someone might come in.'

I laughed.

'Who's going to come in?' I challenged.

'The owner. She might tell on you.'

'Mrs Parfitt? She wouldn't know how to. Anyway, I'm her best customer.'

I smirked and exhaled; and tapped the cigarette ash into the cheap metal ashtray provided.

'Do you want one?'

'No, thanks.'

He looked away; and just then Mrs Parfitt herself came through a swing door and approached. She was an elderly, shapeless woman with glasses and a perm.

She smiled and said, 'Good afternoon, Master Giles.'

'Hello there,' I said.

'I see you've got company.'

Her eyes twinkled a bit.

'Yes, this is… but I don't know your first name, Snape?'

'William.'

Snape muttered this while frowning at the table surface beneath the doilies.

'Good afternoon, Master William, I'm sure.'

'Good afternoon.'

Snape said this grudgingly, still looking at the table surface; but it was a start.

'I'll have a pot of tea, please, Mrs Parfitt, and William will have a cup of coffee.'

At this, Snape did look up; and asked, 'What have you got?'

'Just the Nescafe, sir. Blend 67, I think they call it.'

'Oh, all right.'

'Very good, sir.'

She went off.

'You hungry?' I asked Snape.

'Not particularly,' he said. And then, 'Look, I wish you hadn't given her my name.'

'Why?'

Snape's jaw dropped characteristically.

'Because,' he said, it being obvious to him, 'she might tell on me, that's why.'

'She wouldn't do that, I told you, and anyway you're not doing anything wrong.'

He winced.

'I'll try a cigarette, if you like,' he said. 'Only you mustn't tell anyone either.'

'Of course I won't.'

When the tea and coffee came we drank it without complaint, Snape demurring at the darkened swill that loured in his mug; and he took the proffered cigarette – I was on my third – which I lit for him. Gingerly, he held the smoke in his mouth for a moment but then puffed it out without inhaling. He coughed slightly.

'You've got to inhale,' I said. 'It's no good if you don't inhale. That's the whole point.'

'Why?'

'For the buzz.'

So, again very gingerly, he held the smoke in his mouth, but this time he drew his breath in. The result was spectacular. He gasped and put his hand to his mouth, nearly overturning the coffee; and had a coughing fit. I thought he was going to be sick. He turned his face to the window and continued to retch, his hand to his mouth. I quickly put his cigarette out, which he had dropped, and saved it for later. He collapsed into another coughing fit.

I was worried that Mrs Parfitt might come and see what was wrong, but she didn't.

Eventually, Snape managed to collect himself, while I watched.

'Jesus Christ, Snape.'

'Sorry.' And then, 'I don't suppose I'll be trying that again.'

'You will, you will. It's always like that the first time.'

He looked at me curiously.

'Come on, let's get out of here,' I said. 'I'm bored with this.'

I put some coins on the table and we left, shouting goodbye to Mrs Parfitt, but she did not respond. Maybe she'd had enough of customers for the day. We walked all the way back to Prasher's without saying very much, and got back just in time for evening prep.

After that we spent a lot of time in each other's company – it was quite easy: we didn't feel we had to say anything to each other if we didn't want to; and neither of us were bothered about all the competitive things that boys did, like games and lessons. Illicit smoking was more our line; as it turned out I had been justified in supposing that Snape would take to it. After lunch when we got back to Prasher's we'd pretend to be playing tag down by some disused sheds at the bottom of the back garden, but when we thought no one was looking we'd go behind them and light up. The back of the sheds faced some tall undergrowth before the drive started, so we were reasonably safe from discovery. Snape, particularly, would inhale as if his life depended upon it. It was quite startling to watch: his entire power of concentration was directed toward getting the stuff into his lungs as quickly and deeply as possible, then getting it out so that he could take another greedy gulp. His whole pale face puckered with the effort of it, his cheeks drawn in, giving it a sunken look. I suppose he wanted to ensure that he finished the cigarette as quickly as possible before being alarmed by anyone's footsteps. Watching him, I was in a sense shocked to have introduced him to something which he now appeared to value even more than I did. Not only that but just as with his coffee, he took delight in experimenting with different brands. On one occasion he offered me a strange-looking one; it was black, with a gold filter.

'Blimey,' I said. 'What's that?'

'Balkan Sobranie.'

He gave the name with shy pride, as if he'd been storing up the moment of its revelation.

I lit and took a puff, but it was not to my taste, so I gave it back to him.

One afternoon we were lolling about in my study – our venue of choice these days as it was more comfortable than his and, anyway, I told him I couldn't stand the smell of all that coffee. We were listening to music, to which he'd become accustomed, and I think I was also reading a magazine when he suddenly asked, 'What do you do at night?'

'What do you mean?'

'I've seen you leave the dormitory at night. Where do you go?'

I looked at him. I thought I had always made sure that everyone else was asleep before I crept out, but apparently not. In any case, why should I not tell him?

'I go to the squash courts. I've got a stash of drugs there.'

'Get away!' He grinned. Of course, he didn't believe me.

'I have.'

Then he frowned. It must have been the way I said it, because now he was not so sure.

He didn't say anything more, just had that open-mouthed look again. 'It's not really a stash,' I continued. 'Just a bottle of pills legally prescribed. But Tonkers would go ape shit if he knew about them.'

'What are they?' he asked curiously.

'Sleepers. I get them from my aunt. She's a doctor.'

'But why don't you take them in the dormitory when you go to bed?'

'Because if I take them in the squash courts I find I can loon around for hours.'

'What's loon?'

'Get high. You know.'

He didn't know.

'Well anyway,' I said. 'You asked and I told you.'

I went back to my magazine; Snape didn't say any more. But that night as I was leaving the dormitory in darkness I heard a whisper coming from the direction of Snape's bed. I thought it best not to respond and carried on my way, but on the creaking staircase I became aware of being followed; and outside he caught up with me, a little breathless. He seemed thinner and paler in the moonlight; a very slight, bewildered figure in pyjamas, slippers and dressing gown. His tow-coloured hair was tousled, his glasses awry.

'What do you want?' I asked.

'I want to try some. Please.'

'You can't. They're not for you.'

'Please.'

'We can't talk here. You'd better come with me.'

We must have cut two guilty figures in the moonlight and I kept on looking at the high windows in case a light were turned on; in which case we would be in trouble. Nothing happened. The night was a little cooler than the last time. As we approached the wall I made Snape stop and turn and look away because I did not want him to see where I hid the pills. He was quite willing to do this; I had the impression he would have done anything so long as he was allowed in on the act.

Once retrieved, I took the pills into the squash court with Snape following, it seemed, at a respectful distance. There was nowhere to sit, and it was cold.

'It's cold in here,' whispered Snape unnecessarily.

'Yes, but you can see the moon. Look.'

I pointed to the roof, which did not cover the entire building, and sure enough a bright silver sickle lit up the night sky in the gap, its surroundings electric blue. Snape squinted but did not seem particularly interested. He had started to shiver. We could see each other easily in the moonlight.

'Here, take one,' I said, handing him one of the pills, not then realising that I had flatly contradicted myself in my attitude to him with regard to them.

He did so and gulped. I did the same.

'Can't we go to your study?' he asked. 'There's nowhere to sit.'

'We can sit on the floor.'

'I don't want to.'

I sat down with my legs crossed but he remained standing.

But then he said: 'I feel funny.'

'You'd better sit down, then.'

Awkwardly, he fell to his knees and managed to arrange himself so that he now had his legs crossed in an upward position.

'Feel anything?'

'Yes. I feel dizzy.'

'Relax. Enjoy it.'

He did not look as if he were doing either. On the contrary, an expression of anxiety was clearly discernible in his face, a look almost of distress. Despite the warmth and haze I was beginning to feel, at the back of my mind there was the undercurrent that it had not been a good idea to give Snape one of the pills. What if he were to react in the same way that he had to his first cigarette?

But then to my astonishment he said, 'Man, this is good!' He said it in a low, dreamy voice.

It was so unexpected, I burst out laughing, but the moment I realised what I was doing I suppressed it, because I was making too much noise. Or at least I tried to, but then had a fit of the giggles, largely because of the new look on Snape's face, which signified that he felt as if he were in the seventh heaven. I covered my mouth with my hands but could not control myself. He turned to me and said, 'So good!' having apparently forgotten the cold and the hardness of the floor. It was ludicrous. I could not make up my mind whether he was acting or not but if so, I had never seen him like this before. 'Ha! Ha! Ha!' he mimicked, as I continued to heave with mirth. He had pushed his face near to mine, so that I could feel his hot breath on my cheeks and see his glittering eyes, his pale skin even paler in the moonlight. I could do

151

nothing to shut him up. 'I feel like flying!' he shouted and got in a wobbly way to his feet, whereupon he ran unsteadily about the court, his arms outstretched, as if he thought he could take to the air that way. His dressing gown had become undone, so that it billowed in the comparative darkness of the corners of the court.

'Ha! Ha! Ha!' he continued to shout. I became greatly alarmed; such euphoria as the pill I had taken had caused in me was now nothing compared to the fear of being discovered – which is what would happen if he continued to behave like this.

'For God's sake keep quiet and sit down!' I hissed. But Snape would not listen, so I too got unsteadily to my feet and went and grabbed him and pulled him back to the centre of the court where we both collapsed in giggles on the floor. Its concrete surface hurt but that did not matter.

'We've got to keep quiet,' I managed to say.

But this only made us laugh the louder, I don't know why. We couldn't help ourselves.

We were like this when the heavy wooden door of the squash court opened and a torch beamed its light across the concrete floor, flooding us with it. We froze; and waited, knowing that we had been caught in the most guilty of circumstances.

'I think you two had better come with me.'

Mr Tompkins' prim voice was unmistakable, though neither had dared to look in the direction in which the torch was being wielded.

'And bring that bottle with you,' he commanded. 'Whatever it is.'

21.
Narrative, 1979

Giles Jones found the Shamrock Inn, an unprepossessing building down an alleyway off the main road. As he surveyed its dingy exterior, before entering, he felt like crossing himself, even though he was not religious. He had no idea what to expect, but it was the sort of place that would make anyone feel superstitious. The interior was nothing but distinctly low-key, dark and drab. It was practically empty, too. A few middle-aged men propped the bar up, they all had nicotine-stained grey hair and wore leather jackets that had seen better days. A sad old barman had a look that was both lugubrious and cadaverous. Nobody was saying anything and no music was playing. In fact, as Giles Jones blinked in the darkness, he had the impression that nobody was even moving, that he had entered a rundown house of waxworks. Nevertheless, he approached the bar and in his best conversational fashion asked for a pint of Guinness.

The barman gave him an odd, harassed, thunderstruck look. It was as if for him nothing but disbelief could have heralded the arrival of this new face. Without saying a word, he slow-motioned his way toward a glass and put it under the tap. He pulled the pint with the sort of ambulation one associates with graveyards at night. But at least he was complying with the new arrival's orders, and for that Giles Jones was grateful.

A pint of Guinness takes a relatively long time to pull anyway, but this one went on and on, to the point of embarrassment, particularly as the others at the bar were not saying a word but seemed at least to have come to some sort of life of their own. Through the corners of his eyes Giles Jones could see that they were being as studious as they could be, without in the least betraying their interest in the new customer with anything so obvious as bodily movements. Hunched over the bar, they studied the mirror, bottles and optics straight ahead, and were motionless. Yet if you looked closely you could see that their ears were twitching.

While the pint was being pulled, Giles Jones had been asking himself whether he should retire with it to one of the gloomy tables at the back or stay at the bar and try and hold his own with the others. The latter was clearly preferable if he really was going to ask about a gun, but he was frightened of these men, of their impassivity, of their almost complete absence of body language. He would have to keep his nerve. Once the pint was pulled and paid for – the barman did not etch a shamrock on the head – Giles Jones remained rigidly where he was, as if nothing could be more ordinary than coming into this strange pub and standing four-square with the presumed locals.

After fifteen minutes of silence, Giles Jones turned to the man on his left and muttered conversationally, 'Nice place here.' The man ignored him. This was disconcerting – it had taken a supreme effort on Giles Jones' part even to open and close his mouth so that something approaching coherence would come out of it and he had drawn a blank. He would have to try again. He turned to the man on his right. This man was somewhat different from the others. He was older, scruffier – if that was possible – and wore a tatty overcoat that was too long, its hem draping the beer-stained floor. He had a cringing manner and, Giles had noticed, would occasionally look furtively at the barman as if he were about to ask for credit. But the barman had, in any case, returned to his waxwork mode. Despite the fact that Giles Jones had come to the conclusion that this particular man would have no guns to sell, he was about to open his mouth to him but panicked when he realised he had not thought of anything to say.

Worse was to follow, because he misjudged the distance of his pint of Guinness from his hand and, therefore, succeeded in knocking it off the bar and into the space behind. The glass broke with a very loud report but one piece of luck was that it did so in one of the sinks. In dismay, Giles craned forward and could see that the dark, frothy liquid was gurgling down the plughole. The noise had been a thunderbolt but absolutely nothing happened in consequence, except that with practised nonchalance the barman came to life and reacted as if to the inevitable by clearing the mess up.

'Sorry,' muttered Giles.

The barman did not answer, so he continued, 'I'll pay for another one, of course.'

The barman looked at him as if he were mad.

But Giles Jones had had an idea. If he could get the scruffy man talking he might have a chance with the others. So, he turned to him and said, 'And while I'm about it, I'll get you one too. What will you have? I see your glass is empty.' Which was an understatement, if that were possible. The man's tumbler was as dry as dust; it clearly had not been touched for a long while. The scruffy man's eyes twinkled.

'That's very good of you, mate,' he said appreciatively – he had a heavy Irish brogue – 'I'll have my usual. Six shots of Black Bush.'

Possibly once a month this man was offered a free drink, so obviously he had to capitalise while he could. The barman had already been pulling another Guinness, but he left it to pull itself while he went to the back of the bar for the whiskey.

'I don't mind the same glass,' said the scruffy man, in a consummately generous gesture.

'You'll get what you get,' hissed the barman.

'Steady on.'

It was Giles Jones who said that, but he hadn't meant to. It was just that he felt that the barman was being rather rude to this poor fellow on his right. The reaction was instantaneous.

'What's that you said?'

The barman came towards Giles Jones in a menacing fashion. The latter felt that he was going to grab him by the lapels of his jacket and pull him across the bar. So he backtracked. He still couldn't believe he had said that when he was trying to be nice to these people. 'Nothing. Sorry about the spillage.' The barman glowered at him but let it go. The others were watching. The drinks served, Giles Jones computed that he was being charged about twice what he should have been, but he didn't demur. He felt as if the barman were testing him and a moment later he was proved right.

'What brings you here?'

'I, er…'

The barman, whose name was Ricky, had shed his corpse-like mien and was now behaving with aggression – of the spitting, scratch-you-in-the-eye-if-you-come-any-closer sort. His eyes were dancing in their sockets, yet all the time remained trained on their object, a sure sign.

Giles Jones started to feel distinctly uncomfortable.

'You're not Irish.' It was if he had said, you're a scumbag.

'Well, no…'

'You're not from round here.'

By now, Giles Jones had decided to cut his losses. He did not like the vibes. He had need of a gun, but at this moment he was more concerned for his own personal safety, so he took a sip of his new pint, placed it firmly back on the counter and said, 'No, I'm not and I'm sorry if I've intruded, but I thought this was a public house. I'll be going.'

He turned to the scruffy man beside him who was nursing his whiskey as if it were a newborn baby and was about to say something by way of goodbye to him when he felt a meaty hand on his left shoulder. It was unmistakably a restraining act.

'No, you won't.'

The voice was deceptively gentle. It came from the man to his left, a very large, powerful man – a bit gone to seed, maybe – in one of the leather jackets. Giles Jones turned to look at the man but also sensed that others had crowded around him. He felt sure that someone was right behind him.

'It's a fair question Ricky has asked. What are you doing here?'

Unlike Ricky's, this man's eyes did not flicker. They were grey, set deep in their pale sockets and completely unreadable. Giles Jones, who had effected such murderous destruction upon Aylmer Jones and Angela Horniblow, now felt his knees tremble and a wave of nausea cross his stomach.

'I've come to buy a gun,' he blurted.

He would have liked to think that this utterance resulted from a conscious decision to come clean as to his motives, but in reality it was simple fear that made him say it.

This time the man did blink. Just fractionally. He also relaxed his grip on Giles Jones' shoulder, but not by much. His voice became even more deceptively gentle.

'You want to buy a gun, do you?' he whispered.

'Yes.'

'Well, fancy that.'

Silence.

The man let go of Giles Jones' shoulder and pushed him back a bit. As he had thought there would be, he felt another body behind him.

'You hear that, Paddy? He wants to buy a gun.'

From somewhere within the knot of men now tightening itself round Giles Jones there was a wheeze of laughter.

'A gun, eh?'

'Yes.'

'What type of gun are you looking for, squire?'

'I rather thought a sawn-off shotgun.'

The man's eyes glinted. He had a hint of a smile on his thin lips, beneath which nested a dimple. This dimple resembled a small black hole within the pronounced cleft of his ill-shaven chin. He parroted, 'A sawn-off shotgun, eh?' as if he were slow-witted but it was because such repetition gave him time to think.

'Yes,' answered Giles Jones; and added, 'one that would be difficult to trace.'

The single, solitary wheeze of laughter now proved to have been but a prelude to a general babble of mirth, accompanied by guttural coughs.

'How much money have you got?' the main man asked, very deliberately.

His face had returned to its studious, immobile self, its grey eyes set in stone. Giles Jones did not quite know how to answer this. He had no idea how much such an item would cost on the black market. He had imagined that he would not be able to negotiate but that he would be allowed to make sure that the gun was fully working and accompanied by ammunition. He certainly had not counted on having to bring the money with him at first meeting.

'How much money have you got?' repeated the big man, a little louder and with menace.

'I – er – rather thought…'

But he did not get any further.

The man pushed him savagely in the chest so that he fell back against the man behind, and as quick as you like the meaty hand which had been so recently on his shoulder now searched for his wallet. Of course, its owner had seen exactly where on his person Giles Jones had put it after paying for the drinks, so it was not hard to find.

'You – er – rather thought, did you?'

The man retrieved the wallet, opened it and contemptuously counted the notes; whilst the other man behind Giles Jones held him firmly by the arms so that he could not resist. The others, abuzz with curiosity, had crowded around even more tightly.

'You won't get far with this, squire,' said the man, 'but we'll keep it anyway. We'll call it a deposit.'

His eyes lit up.

He stuffed the notes in a pocket of his leather jacket and

contemptuously forced the wallet back where he found it. It hurt.

'Now fellows, let's get rid of this boyo, shall we?'

At this suggestion, to a man the others lifted Giles Jones above their shoulders, carried him to the door, opened it and threw him through. That hurt even more. Giles landed on the pavement in a daze. He was just about aware that the main man was approaching him with the others looking on and he thought he was going to get a good kicking.

'Here, boyo, you better have your bus fare home.'

The man contemptuously threw a few coins at Giles, most of which came to a rest in the gutter beside him, having first made a pinging noise as they landed on the pavement.

'Never let it be said that we Irish kick a man when he's down!', he heard someone say, to a general guffaw of amusement.

Another man shouted, 'Begorrah!'

The pub door closed. In near total darkness, Giles tried to collect himself, which took several minutes. Though he was hurting, so far as he could tell nothing was broken, and this conclusion helped him get painfully to his feet, having gathered the coins. He walked awkwardly back to the High Street and set about finding the nearest tube.

On his next day off he thought he would try his luck in South London somewhere. That was where all the blaggers were, surely, or so he had heard. He set off for Brixton, by tube this time, and having scouted around a bit, walked into a likely-looking place. It was called the Duke of Clarence but its interior was not like that of any pub he had seen. It was that of a vast discotheque, with stroboscopic lights, a dance floor, comfortable groups of foamy seats coloured purple set apart from each other, and cheerful but high-tempo reggae music which, surprisingly, was not too loud. A bar went right along one of the walls to the end. It was not crowded, being about ten o'clock on a weekday evening, and most of the crowd were quite young; they stood around in small groups and chatted away. No one was dancing yet. A few sat on the seats and drank from bottles of lager or cocktail glasses which they placed on the glass tables in front of them. The light was good enough to see the expressions on their faces, which were amiable and relaxed – indeed, even a little subdued. It was all surprisingly civilised and Giles was pretty sure he had come to the wrong place but by this time he had bought a drink at the bar and was standing by it, soaking in the scene.

He thought he would hang around a bit anyway, because the atmosphere was so good. Nobody had paid any attention to him; he liked this place. He bought another drink – off one of the affable and efficient barmen – and stayed where he was, feeling relaxed.

After about an hour of this he became aware of four young men standing together by the far wall, who were all looking at him in a not unfriendly way. They were smiling, and quite possibly had been talking about him. Giles Jones smiled back, and continued to look in their direction until it seemed inappropriate – or unwise – to do so any longer. They seemed different, he couldn't quite work out why, but they formed more of a pack than the other groups, and as such were more self-contained. Also unlike the others, they appeared to be looking for something, had come here with a purpose beyond mere socialising, though Giles Jones had no idea what that might be. It surely could not involve him, though, he thought; yet after another lapse of time one of their number approached and leaned casually against the bar beside him.

'Hey, man, you lookin' for something?' he asked.

Giles was startled; he did not say anything.

'You want to score?'

'What?'

Giles had looked at him. The young man continued to smile.

'E? Spliff?'

'Oh – no thanks.'

'Trade? You lookin' for trade?'

'What's that?'

'Sex, man, sex.'

'Oh…'

'Boy? Girl?'

'No.'

'What then?'

Giles thought for a moment. He might as well say it.

'A gun.'

'A gun?'

Now it was the boy's turn to be startled. He was still friendly, but was looking around to make sure nobody was listening, which they weren't.

'What kinda gun?'

'Sawn-off shotgun.'

The young man whistled softly and thought for a moment.

'Don't go away, man.'

'I won't.'

The young man walked back to his group. The hopeful Giles purposefully did not follow him with his eyes, nor did he look at them. Instead, he affected a nonchalance and ordered himself another drink. A while later the young man returned and said casually, in a low voice, looking straight ahead, not as if he were really speaking to Giles at all, 'We can get you a sawn-off pump action, man, but it'll be two hundred.'

Giles nodded.

'You want a contract too? It's an extra fifty.'

'What do you mean?'

'You want someone to pull the trigger for you, or you think you can do it yourself?'

The boy was articulate, casual and it would seem endlessly patient with his interlocutor, who however, must have appeared to him to be from another planet.

Once the meaning had sunk in, Giles did not need too long to consider it. He wanted to do the dirty work himself, so he said, 'No.'

'Cash on exchange. We can get it for you by tomorrow.'

'You sure it'll work properly?'

'It'll work prop'ly.'

'Ammunition?'

'Twelve cartridges. We throw them in.'

'Where do I go?'

'You got a number? We'll call you.'

Giles Jones gave him the telephone number of his bedsit, which the boy surreptitiously wrote down, shielding what he was doing from view with a cupped hand.

Afterwards, Giles muttered, 'I have to be at work by eight in the evening.'

The boy laughed. It was a curiously high-pitched sound.

'We'll call you in the morning.'

'Thanks.'

The boy casually walked back to his group, none of whom appeared to have had the slightest interest in the transaction. Giles slowly drank up and left, nodding at the barman as he went.

The next day Giles Jones' phone rang at just after twelve. He woke and answered, and a very deep male voice asked, 'You the guy who wants the piece?'

'Yes.'

'You got the dough?'

'Yes.'

'You know the flats at the back of Wilberforce Close?'

'No.'

'Find them.'

'What's the nearest tube?'

'Brixton, man, Brixton. There's a line of garages in the basement, down a ramp. We'll be there at two, we'll wait ten minutes.' The phone went dead.

Giles hastened to collect himself. He went to the bank on his way to the tube, taking his A to Z with him. At Brixton he followed the directions he had memorised from the book and arrived at Wilberforce Close far too early. He found the basement garages and went to the end. It was not very well-lit; a couple of youths were loitering in a corner and eyed him suspiciously when they saw him. There was a smell of hashish. A lot of the garages had their doors broken off, and you could see bits of old junk inside.

Having made sure he knew how to get back, Giles left Wilberforce Close, very conscious that he was almost certainly being watched by the two youths. He did not want to get mugged, particularly as he was carrying over two hundred pounds in cash. It was a fine day – funnily enough, for the first time Giles realised that he had a spring in his step, despite the circumstances. Having time to kill, he thought it would be provident to go to the High Street and look around for a holdall to buy. When it was approaching two he returned to the garages, where to his dismay the boys were still loitering in the corner. But almost immediately the sound of a high-powered car came from behind him, and he saw a white three-litre Capri screech to a halt at the far end. Two well set-up men in long leather coats emerged, and one of them shouted at the two boys to fuck off. They obeyed, but in a sulky, mulish way, walking the length of the bank of garages with their heads down and their hands in their pockets. The other man carried a bulky object wrapped in black bin liners. It was as if Giles were watching a film in slow motion; it seemed to take forever for the boys to disappear. He could hear nothing but the car's sound system emitting soul music above the growling engine. When the boys had disappeared the two men approached. They both were heavily whiskered and tall, with the

161

usual impassive faces.

'You got the dough?'

This was asked by the one who had told the boys to fuck off. With a jump Giles produced the cash and while it was being counted he noticed that the man with the bin liners had been smoking and now flicked the butt across the way.

'That's cool, man. Where's your car?'

'I haven't got a car. I came by tube.'

The two men looked at him thoughtfully. One pocketed the cash while the other handed over the object in bin liners. Giles had not allowed for its weight so his arm sagged as he took it.

'You need a car, man. You need a car.'

'Yes.'

'We can get you one, clean. A hundred.'

Arrangements were made.

'You take care, now.'

With that they walked back to the Capri and were off, with a roar of the engine and a screech of tyres. The whole transaction had not lasted more than five minutes.

Giles put the gun in its bin liners into the holdall and made his way back to Brixton tube.

When he got back to Brunswick Gardens he wondered what to do with his new possession. He didn't dare test the thing because it would make too much noise and besides, where could he? The idea of taking pot shots in the gardens below crossed his mind, but that would be absurd. So he would have to make sure to get it right the first time, which would mean learning how to handle it. He removed the gun from the holdall and its wrapping of bin liners. It was surprisingly small, and could easily be hidden inside a man's coat. It was clearly old, too; the wood of the stock was worn and smooth, and a once elaborately engraved pattern on the fascia had all but faded away, as had the maker's name and mark. There was a stubby attachment underneath the barrel, which with some fiddling he realised was the pump action mechanism because it could be pulled forward, revealing an empty chamber. There were grooves to it, suggestive of where the hand should grip. He also realised that this was where the cartridges went, and surmised that by pulling the attachment backward and forward the pump action would be engaged. He quickly looked among the bin

162

liners and found them – twelve shiny new things coloured pink, cylindrical, with a ring of brass at the bottom. He would not put them in now, of course. He examined the shotgun further and found the trigger, which he had not yet noticed because it was tucked away on the underneath, inside a metal ring. He made sure the cartridge chamber was empty and pulled it. It did not move. Why? Had he been sold a pup? Had this gun been disenabled in some way? With mounting annoyance he examined the weapon further, turning it over and over and closely inspecting every part. Finally, he came across a small switch behind the guard of the trigger. Could this be a safety catch? He remembered that even the old rifles at Selwyn Mauberley's had such things. He pulled the switch and tried the trigger again. It moved, and there was a satisfying click. He also discovered that with the safety catch in the "off" position the pump action mechanism and the trigger were synchronised. You pulled the latter, heard it click, with the other hand pushed the underneath attachment forward then backward, thereby presumably loading another cartridge into the barrel, and pulled the trigger again. This could be done at some speed. Also, the stock fitted nicely into his hip, as he discovered when practising standing in front of the mirror. The gun was held with his left hand on the underneath attachment, his right was on the trigger, whilst his hip steadied the whole weapon as he shunted the attachment backward and forward.

22.
Giles Jones' Diary

The upshot of all this was that I was expelled, but Snape was allowed to continue at the school under certain conditions. It was thought that I had been a bad influence on him, which might have been true. Certainly his parents were of that view, apparently. In any case, the black mark of the shooting incident was already on my sheet. On the other hand, Snape had never done anything wrong before, to anyone's knowledge. I think Mr Tompkins made such a fuss about it because he wanted it to be known that he would not tolerate such drug-taking behaviour. Added to which, we had been caught in the act, so his hand had been forced. Of course, the situation mortified me but at the same time I felt curiously detached, I don't know why. It was arranged that I go to the local grammar school in York; and live with my grandmother and aunt in their large gloomy house on the outskirts of that city. This was ironic, as it had been the latter person who had supplied me with the wherewithal with which to disgrace myself. First, however, I had to go and see my father, Damien.

I was not quite sure why I had been summoned by him, probably to be told off about Selwyn Mauberley College; but whatever the reason I was not looking forward to visiting 15 Pimlico Road again. This was because he and I had grown distant from each other since the start of my adolescence; and I hardly ever visited the house in which I had spent my early years. It is fair to say that he and it gave me the creeps.

After my parents were divorced the court had decided – to everyone's surprise – that I should spend half the school holidays with my mother and half with my father; "surprise", because the lawyers had told us that it was an "unwritten rule" that the mother always got complete custody of the children. So one year not that long before he died it fell to my father to take me in for Christmas. It never occurred to me that I should ever have any say in the matter; and anyway at that stage I was not so concerned about him, or rather not so concerned about any adverse effect he might have on me.

The moment I had presented myself at 15 Pimlico Road it was obvious to me that Damien had made a tremendous effort to make me feel welcome and also to give everything – including himself – the air of being normal. I was a little bewildered to see the house looking so tidy and Damien himself had had a haircut and a shave, and was even dressed reasonably smartly in one of those sleeveless jerseys of his and trousers from one of the many bespoke suits he owned. God knows where from, but he'd also got in a cook for the festive period and an au pair student, which was in addition to our char, Mrs Hyam, who still came in daily from Battersea, and an odd-job man called Mr Sutherland, who was always hanging about for no apparent reason (both of whom would be away on Christmas and Boxing Day). The cook, however, was not what you might call a normal sort of cook; for he was a middle-aged, white-haired, rather paunchy man who came from Scotland, who so far as I recall did very little cooking but preferred to spend his time ironing in the kitchen in the evening. I've no recollection whether the clothes he was ironing were ours or his but anyway that did not seem to be the point; it was merely the repetitive motion of the iron on the ironing board which appeared to induce in him a feeling of almost spiritual calm. I would watch him, fascinated. He also smoked while he ironed, Embassy cigarettes, the thing hanging from his mouth and occasionally being drawn on, ash and smoke spilling on to the board beneath him. He was aware of my presence but hardly ever said anything to me, and when he did it was only to mutter, through clenched teeth, 'I like a good, strong cigarette.'

One evening, no doubt in order to continue the illusion that this period was nothing but a happy and normal holiday arranged by a father for his son, we went to the West End to see a Frankie Howerd show, which was exceedingly funny; we both laughed a lot, as did the rest of the audience (the house was packed); and then we got a cab home. Turning on a light in the hallway, my father noticed a piece of paper propped up on a vase on the hall stand. On closer inspection it turned out to be a scarcely literate note left by the cook, who had left, claiming that there were just too many stairs in the house for him to cope with. My father became thoroughly deflated when the meaning of the note was finally absorbed (I remember the light in the hallway was not at all good and we had had to stand there close together for some time, hunched over while we struggled to decipher the note's contents); although it was nothing much to me. I don't think I had a clue as to who was going to cook the Christmas lunch, and had certainly never seen the Scotsman as a candidate for such a task. In any case, come Christmastime, my father seemed to live off nothing but the boxes of marrons glaces he always ordered from Fortnum & Mason's. It was more of a concern to me that he had come up with such a pathetic excuse for leaving, but I think my father took it personally in the sense that he felt insulted by the man's departure, and was perhaps asking himself why it had been made in such a hole-in-the-corner way. Whatever, the next day or the day after, I cannot remember which, I had reason to make an unexpected visit to the drawing room, where of course I assumed I would see Damien spread out on his studio couch by the window as usual, with his pills on the table in front of him; he was there all right, but so was Gaby, the au pair student, who'd managed to perch herself on the bit of the sofa that was left after Damien's body had been catered for. Her blouse was undone, but only so that you could see the line of her bra and some cleavage. I remembered taking a peek in the bedroom she'd been allocated – the small one at the top, back, facing the well of small gardens down below – and seeing underwear she'd carefully washed in the sink and laid out to dry in front of the gas fire, which had been left full on. I'd not had much to do with her, she seemed nice enough, not much older than me, attractive but certainly not stunning - German or Austrian, I cannot remember which. Now she just was expressionless, so far as I could tell, but Damien was clearly embarrassed and discomfited – I even thought I saw a reddening of his cheeks, which was most unusual because normally his colouring was to me that of ash and charcoal.

Whatever had been going on between them was no business of mine, so I affected a nonchalance and went to my desk in the corner and collected something; and left the room as quickly as possible without saying a word. Nor did either of them say anything; but that afternoon I went to South Kensington to have a look around – that part of London always remained a favourite haunt since my days at the Orange School – when by chance I bumped into her, Gaby I mean; she was standing on the tube platform as I was. We recognised each other and approached; she told me that she had left 15 Pimlico Road for good and that if she had wanted "any of that" – as she put it, rather sneeringly – she would have gone for someone younger. I did not know what to say, although I guessed that she would have been quite happy to have had "any of that" provided the not so young man's son had not become aware of it; and not having known what to say I simply put my hand into my pocket, withdrew two pound notes and gave them to her, I don't know why. Somewhat to my surprise, she took them, and walked away, never to be seen again.

All of which left me in a quandary, or at least it did when I gradually realised that I would now be on my own with my father over Christmas; the thought was not an attractive one. When I had been much younger I was sitting late one evening at my desk which was at right angles to the end of Damien's studio couch in the drawing room, albeit set back in an alcove; he was in his usual position. We had been quiet for some while – and it was way past my bedtime – when he suddenly leapt up – or at least sat up, which was much the same for him – and started to berate me with I cannot remember what set of circumstances in which I was supposed to have played a shameful part. I burst into tears, I think because I thought that such a display would be a sign of great weakness and therefore would cause him to leave me alone; but not a bit of it: his voice grew louder and deeper and he started to shout, as if this extraordinary behaviour were the only way in which he could assure himself of his own animation; and I cried all the more intensely, as a sort of chorus to his ranting. As I say, I cannot remember at all what it was about, but he did say, 'I'm just going to have to bully you for the time being' – which is exactly what he did do; for hours.

I shuddered at the recollection; and at the same time I recalled that my mother would be spending Christmas in the house in Bayswater which had been bought for her as part of the divorce settlement, together with other relatives. No sooner had that thought come into my mind than I guiltily supposed that I could sneak off there and then and leave my father to stew in his own juices. It would be a rotten thing to do but preferable, perhaps, to staying with an ogre who happened to be my father. I knew Mummy would be pleased to see me and would ask no awkward questions. Equally, Damien would not dare to, or perhaps demean himself – as he saw it, by ringing to find out where I was. The moment I began to consider the possibility of such flight, a personal mental process was set in train whose inevitable result would be the flight itself, although I'm not sure I appreciated that at the time. Anyhow, that is what happened although I cannot remember anything about the mechanics of leaving 15 Pimlico Road stealthily, nor indeed of the festivities in the house in Bayswater; save that, a few days after

Christmas, with great trepidation and guilt I telephoned the Pimlico Road number in the hope of speaking to Damien and finding out how he was. Actually, the real reason for my making the telephone call was in order – hopefully, but in vain – to return the situation to what it had been prior to a hiatus which had been of my own making, in other words to try to regularise and patch up relations which had always been difficult with my Dad. It proved an excruciatingly inept diplomatic initiative which was always going to be doomed to failure. He answered; remained silent when he'd established who the caller was; and listened to my no doubt fumbling enquiries as to how he had been and excuses as to why I had left. Then he cut me short. 'Listen, Giles,' he said, 'I have one thing to say to you and one thing only. If you carry on behaving like this, you will end up a weakling. Goodbye now.'

He put the phone down. I was mortified.

Now I would be seeing him again; and all those memories as it were walked before me when I entered the house. I did not know what to expect; would he be in a good mood? Whatever, the man shouted at me to come upstairs when he heard the front door close; he was in his study, the door open, at his desk, his ancient Remington in front of him, with a blank piece of paper inserted. He'd maintained the recent spruceness of appearance I remembered, but he did not look at me: he was in profile because his desk formed a line with the doorway; nor did he invite me to sit down or anything else, so that I was left hovering just inside the room, awkward as hell. Silence, while he continued to stare at the typewriter; and even when he finally spoke he remained in that attitude, his speech preceded by a noise that was half growl, half chuckle.

'I hear you've had a little local difficulty.'

Consciously or otherwise, he was quoting the now famous phrase of a British prime minister whose character he had slated all those years ago on a visit to Swindell's. I guessed he was referring to my expulsion from Selwyn Mauberley College but I did not say anything, just continued to stand awkwardly. Suddenly, he got up from his desk and started to pace about the room, uncharacteristically for him. Years before, I had seen him lie on the double bed which he kept in the study and practise stabbing himself with an imaginary knife, as if it were a joke. That seemed more in keeping. But on both occasions – then and now – a common feature was that it did not really seem as if he knew or cared whether anyone else was present. I watched him go to the window and stare out of it. He was gasping hard, as if an unspeakable anxiety were about to overwhelm him, causing an utter loss of self-control; of self, even. I became frightened, and began to wish that I could do exactly what I had done that Christmas and simply walk out. I suppose I felt that he would start to berate me for my bad behaviour at school. Having to an extent collected himself, he turned and faced me for the first time. His eyes were wild.

'I expect you've heard that I shall be re-marrying.'

I hadn't.

'No.'

This was something of a surprise, not just because I hadn't in the least expected the news, but also because Damien appeared to have completely forgotten about the "little local difficulty" of mine he had mentioned. On the other hand, I had never spared a thought for his private life, and if ever asked about it, I expect I would have said that I didn't think he had any. What a mistake.

'Well, I shall be.'

His tone had softened.

I did not say anything; there seemed nothing appropriate to be said, or nothing I could think of at any rate. He approached me, trying to be nice, the same softness in his tone, and asked, 'What do you feel about that?'

'It doesn't make any difference to me,' I hissed.

It was the first time I had said anything, and it was like someone else said it. I had no idea that would be my reaction. But Damien backed away slightly, and seemed pleased. He even managed a faint smile. Later, I considered that I had given him the answer he wanted, that I had given him a green light of some kind. He returned to his desk and typewriter, and was in profile once again. I had not changed position at all since being in the room. I didn't know if he meant to signify that this interview was at an end but I certainly took it as such. So, with a croaked, 'goodbye, then' – to which he did not answer – I left.

But on my way downstairs I heard him shout, 'Now go back to those witches of yours!'

I met Coral a few times. She was twenty years younger than him, very bubbly and good fun, but hopelessly scatty. She had a good figure, but her hair was mousey and her facial expression in repose was one of extreme vapidity. Also, she would make the most bizarre suggestions – meaningless, clueless, although I cannot give you any examples. I wondered what the attraction was and supposed it must be sexual. For him, at any rate. And for her? I had no idea. I also wondered how they had met and heard that it was through a psychiatrist, of whom they were both patients; which did not seem particularly auspicious, but better than nothing. I remember thinking, Oh good, he'll have someone to look after him now – which was a comforting thought for me to have because I felt perennially guilty at avoiding him, my own father; but that thought could not have been more wrong. There was also a question mark about why they wished to get married at all; I can only think that at least so far as my father was concerned it was because he would then feel, in an old-fashioned way, that he could treat her as he liked; that they could do as they liked; that she was his property. As for her? Again, I have no idea; maybe at thirty she and her parents were thinking that she'd better take her chances otherwise she would end up on the shelf; also maybe it was thought – daftly – that marriage – any marriage – would be good for her mental health, which, as it turned out, was far more precarious than anyone had realised. Looking back on it, their legal union should never have been allowed; but who was to stop them? Damien had no one to tell him what to do; as for Coral, well, I never met her father until afterwards, so I don't know what his reaction was; in light of subsequent events, he probably thought about the financial advantage. Also, no one was invited to their marriage, which was a hole-in-the-corner affair in a registry office, with people invited off the street to be witnesses.

The truth was, as I had told him, that I was not that bothered; the next thing for me was to acclimatise myself to this grammar school in York, which turned out to be easier than expected. The "witches" were very welcoming and I remember Aunt Felicity complimenting me on my alleged courage the first time I walked up to its gates in a new blue school blazer. I did not know what she meant; to me, school was just school, fee-paying or not; with luck you might find one or at most two teachers who would inspire you, and maybe elsewhere there might be better facilities (which you would probably not use anyway); but that was all. Curiously, I did not miss the rifle range, I suppose because the ban had weaned me off it. I think what Aunt Felicity had meant was the drop in social standing that going to Bishop Grosseteste's Grammar School, York, entailed; certainly Henrietta, her mother, would not stop making noises about this, to my annoyance. I had a great deal of freedom, could roam around the large gloomy house as I liked and the streets of central York were an enchantment after those of Selwyn Mauberley's small, dusty town. There was of course a large inter-school teenage community, of both sexes – a novelty for me; after school we'd get together in little groups in the new coffee bar at the local theatre and gossip over cigarettes and drinks. Sex was the primary topic of conversation; who was going out with whom, who had had who; and so on; but there was no malice in it. Next came work, which university was to be tried for, what grades at 'A' level were needed for it, whether the teachers were up to their task and if not, what could be done about it. Anyhow, I made friends, was accepted and was never asked – what I had most dreaded – any awkward questions about my past, an absence which to me now seems a curious but gratifyingly universal feature of youthful human nature. People knew I had been to a public school but I think they thought that my parents had just run out of money; which illusion, however, should have been quickly shattered by the enormous number of pop records I was known to buy at W H Smith's in Coney Street, courtesy of my grandmother's account there. She had accounts at other shops – clothes and so on – which I could also freely use. Being doctors, their strategy had been, apparently, that I should be given everything I wanted and more, otherwise I might have a nervous breakdown. The Mandrax kept coming. I took everything as my due. The one thing I seemed unable to do was get a girl into bed but I was working on it.

Then as I have told you, something disastrous happened. I was lounging about in bed late one Saturday morning when Aunt Felicity came in and told me she had some bad news.

'Your father's dead.'

She left the room, closing the door behind her.

It was the unexpectedness of the news that was the most explosive part of it. I felt as if someone had kicked me in the stomach, very hard. Then I burst into tears, and could make no sense of it. Surely they had only been married a few months and were now in California on honeymoon. Only the other day I had written him a letter in which I had tried to communicate with him in a different, more mature way. I had wondered whether I would get an answer, but never did. Besides,

I had never thought he would actually kill himself because he had taken so many overdoses before and recovered – it was his little game. I felt sure, though, that it was drugs – although Aunt Felicity had not told me that – and had considered, as I have told you, that marriage would be a refuge for him, a haven from his dark thoughts.

I spent the rest of that day sipping from a bottle of sherry, just about the only alcohol they had in the house; I carried it around with me and cried all the while. But the genuine sorrow gradually became mixed with tedious self-pity and, oddly, not a little self-importance. I was the head of the family now. I sought out a piece of black ribbon and ostentatiously tied it round my arm, as a sign of recent bereavement. The truth was, that I couldn't really understand what had happened. Henrietta and Felicity were most sympathetic and allowed me to behave just as I wanted; Felicity muttered something about "life has to go on", to which I disagreed. Then it occurred to me to ask how they had heard the news. She told me some friends in a village nearby had read about it in a local paper. Immediately, I wondered whether there was any doubt about the matter, so I got hold of the number and rang the police station in Berkeley, California. A dry American voice, having first told me it was five-thirty in the morning where he was, confirmed the facts: that the dead body of a man identified as Damien Jones, a Briton, had been taken from the Shattuck Hotel (he even stated the room number), following an unannounced visit by a woman purporting to be his wife, name of Coral Jones, to a physician they had already consulted, having been in need of sedatives. This physician heard what she had to say: that they had both taken large quantities of pills and been "out for the count" for many days but that she had "pulled round" and now feared that he was dead. The physician immediately rang the police, who in the course of their duties visited the hotel and on approaching the room down a corridor noticed a "strong faecal smell". On entering they discovered the naked body of a "heavy-set" man under a blanket on the bed. A number of empty pill bottles were found both on the bedside table and on the floor.

The dry American voice was careful to relay the information that all these bottles bore the labels of English pharmacies. No doubt there were other questions I could have asked but I merely thanked him and hung up. This was because I had already formed the idea of flying out there to see my father for one last time, although it would just be his corpse; and the American police officer had mentioned that Coral had been taken in by relatives of her husband's living in Oakland. For some reason, which I did not understand, I thought that I would have to act very quickly, so again I got hold of Bob and Decca's number and rang it. To my surprise, because it was still so early in the morning, Decca answered, sounding a little groggy.

'But Giles,' she explained, a little tentatively, when I had told her of my plan, 'Damien was cremated days ago.'

I wish I had said to her, 'But why? Why have you not bothered to get in touch with anyone in England to tell us what happened? Why have you had him cremated when you might have realised that his son would like to see him one last time?' But I did not. Such conversation as we had was all so terribly genteel, compounded in part by the weird-sounding upper class Edwardian accent she had obviously carefully preserved throughout her decades in America.

It was as if she had said, 'Giles, your dad's dead, we had him cremated straightaway and decided not to tell you, because it might have caused complications. You'll never get to see him again, so sorry about that.' And I had said, 'Right-o,' accepting it all so matter-of-factly; as one does. It makes my blood boil to think of it. But again, what was the motivation in my desire to fly out and see the body of my father, see him for one last time? Was it so that it would have been something noble to do, something grand, a gesture of caring, drawing excited but sympathetic attention to myself? I don't know.

I had had little desire to see Damien anyway these last few years, so what was the big deal now that he was dead? But anyway, the trip was off. At least travel arrangements would not have to be made, and money spent – not that I ever thought of money those days, it was always going to be somebody else who picked up the tab, my grandmother and aunt probably.

23.
Narrative, 1979

A few days later, Giles Jones got a call to say that the car was ready, but that he must collect it at the precise time given, otherwise the guys would not be responsible if it disappeared. He duly returned as instructed to Wilberforce Close and to the seamy garages in its basement. An old black Vauxhall was parked at the end, its keys in the ignition. Upon closer inspection he saw that the car was validly road taxed but that the bodywork was badly dented and the unkempt interior far from congenial, exuding as it did a strange smell, with all sorts of unidentifiable droppings in the console and over the floor. The passenger window was cracked in several places and there was, what looked like, a bullet hole in the windscreen with the tell-tale spider's web effect; also the driver's door had to be slammed and re-slammed before it shut properly; but at least the engine gave off a low whine when the ignition was turned, and when he gingerly pressed the pedal the car moved forward. The gears looked simple enough; he remembered to lift the stick before being able to put the car into reverse, which he did, and the driving wheel turned the tyres smoothly. All the lights worked. Pretty soon he was on his way, driving carefully, and pleased that his driving skills did not seem to have deserted him, but he was fearful that he might get stopped for some reason. He'd already taken the precaution of hiring a small lock-up garage off Talbot Road, which he had seen advertised in a local newspaper. This was not as near to where he was as he would have liked, but on the other hand he knew that if he left it parked in the street near his home he would need a resident's permit and he didn't want to be officially associated with this car in any way.

When he got to Talbot Road he turned into a small, unremarkable side alley and found the lock-up, easing the car gently into its interior. He stopped the engine, got out and locked the sliding metallic door behind him with the key given him by the landlord. He looked around; no one appeared to have been watching and the drive across London had passed without incident.

Late that night he returned to the lock-up carrying his holdall with the shotgun inside it. He was dressed in his casino clothes because, if all went well, he would abandon the car somewhere on the outskirts of London and make the rest of his journey home by tube; he wanted it to look as if he had just come from work should that be necessary. Painstakingly, he had charted and re-charted the route he would take from Talbot Road to Carshalton, where Derek Bradshaw lived, carefully noting the one-way streets in the A to Z so that he would not get caught out by them. He was pretty sure he now knew the way by heart and would not have to stop and consult the map further by torchlight. He wanted there to be as little risk as possible of a nosy policeman, or anyone else, seeing him and the dilapidated state of his car and making further enquiries. For the same reason he had dismissed the idea of going on a dry run, which had appealed to him because it meant there would be less chance of any hitches on the actual night but, again, he wanted there to be as little scope as possible for detection and that meant keeping his association with the car to a minimum. He was about to put the holdall on the back seat but decided it would be better if he put it in the boot, out of view. So, he did that, and set off.

In Cornwallis Lodge, Derek and Shirley Bradshaw were already asleep in their double bed in the master bedroom whose wide windows overlooked the front drive. Shirley was a very light sleeper, being sensitive to the slightest noises, so it was she who was woken first by the banging on the front door below. She sat up, turned on the bedside light, looked at the wristwatch which she wore even in bed, saw that it was a quarter past three, and shook her husband. He stirred.

'Derek! Derek! There's somebody at the door!'

After a short silence, the banging started again; then stopped.

'What?'

'There's somebody at the door!'

'Well, go and see who it is.'

'At this time of night?'

'Anyway, it's impossible. The alarm would have sounded.'

Derek Bradshaw was fully awake now.

The banging started again, six emphatic strikes of the antique knocker, a present from Shirley's mother. Then, for the first time, the doorbell rang.

'What is going on?' asked Derek Bradshaw.

Shirley Bradshaw flinched.

'I turned the security system off,' she said.

'You did what?'

Derek Bradshaw started to feel that pumping sense of fear in his gut, an experience he had got to know so well recently.

'It always makes such a dreadful buzzing noise, I can't bear it.'

He couldn't believe his ears.

The doorbell rang again; then more banging.

'You'd better go and see who it is.'

'How could you have turned it off without telling me? How could you?'

'I'm sorry.'

'You see who it is. Who could it possibly be at this time of night?'

A crestfallen Shirley Bradshaw got out of bed in her nightgown and went to the window and opened it. She leant out, but could see nothing.

'Who it is?' she shouted.

'Police, madam,' an authoritative male voice came from below. 'We have reason to believe a burglar has attempted to gain entry to the rear of your property.'

Shirley Bradshaw was alarmed by this and turned to consult her husband. She was surprised to see him cowering behind her.

'What's that?' he asked.

'It's the police. They say we've been burgled!'

Derek Bradshaw was shaking.

'What can you see?' he asked.

She turned again to the window and looked out.

'Nothing,' she said.

Giles Jones was standing well within the framework of the front door and Shirley Bradshaw could only make out a slightly built man in a dark coat, nothing more, certainly no police helmet. She could not see that he was wearing gloves.

Immediately, he said, 'Can you let us in, madam? We need to make sure the house is secure.'

It was the authority in the man's voice that tipped Shirley Bradshaw's mind in favour of compliance. Besides, it just did not occur to her – or to her cowering husband for that matter – that a criminal would be so bold as to impersonate a policeman in order to gain an entry.

'I'd better go,' she whispered to her husband.

'All right. But be careful.'

'Coming!' she shouted out of the window.

She put on her dressing gown and left the bedroom, leaving the door open. On the landing she turned the dimmer switch and flooded the downstairs hall with light. She descended the staircase and crossed it, approaching the front door swiftly, her slippered feet making no noise on the polished wooden floor. While she was doing this her husband had cautiously approached the window and peered out, but could see nothing.

It took her fully two minutes to unlock the door, not being familiar with its new system of security, although her husband had laboriously shown her how to use it. Next she pulled the door back, which she had to do with both hands as it was so massive and heavy; her intention had been just to open it a little bit, so that she could peer through the gap and satisfy herself that it was indeed a policeman who was standing outside; but she wasn't given that chance because the moment she managed to pull the door back she felt it being kicked wide open and a shotgun blast at close range tore a hole the size of a tennis ball in her chest. She was dead before her body touched the floor. Instantly, Giles Jones jumped over this obstruction and ran like the clappers across the hall and up the elaborate staircase. It was a marvel to see how fast he moved, his coat billowing behind him, the gun shaking at his side. On the landing he went straight for the open bedroom door and entered; it appeared to be empty; but he was not deceived: a moment's intuition told him the man was hiding. There were some fancy inlaid wardrobes running along the wall to his left; he opened one and pulled the clothes back: sure enough, Derek Bradshaw was cowering foetally on the floor, his eyes closed, his hands over his ears, like one of the proverbial wise monkeys. It was as if by that posture he could persuade himself that present reality did not exist. Even so, he muttered, 'Money. I have money...' Giles Jones had raised the shotgun so as to take aim; but for a moment – just for a moment – he paused; not at the prospect of getting money from this man – his money, money that was rightfully his – but because he wanted him to suffer before he died, he wanted to play with him for a little while; but he realised that he did not have the time in which to do this, if he were to accomplish his task and get out before an alarm would undoubtedly be raised. Already this might be happening; but to Giles Jones' disbelief the lawyer had taken this split second of indecision on his part to effect an escape. He did not know how this had happened: one moment Derek Bradshaw was cowering in the closet, the next, slippery as an eel, he was racing toward the doorway and through it on to the landing which ran right along one side of the house.

Giles chased after him, caught up and whacked him hard with the barrel of his gun; the lawyer fell against the bannister clutching his head, whereupon he put the muzzle straight and close to the pyjamaed figure and repeatedly discharged the shot into his body by drawing the undercarriage backward and forward while pulling the trigger. There were several phenomenally loud reports and the stock kept on recoiling hard into the crook of Giles' arm, causing him pain. Nevertheless, Derek Bradshaw had been despatched; as was obvious from his immobility and the fact that several large holes in his body had appeared, each oozing blood. Giles Jones stepped back to examine his work but noticed he was trembling so much that it was scarcely possible for him to stand or even hold on to the shotgun. So he dropped it, because he remembered that he had determined not to use it again anyway. He leant back against the bannister, exhausted. He was breathing very quickly but deeply, panting. It took him several moments to recover. As he was doing so he kept watching the prostrate form in front of him, which to his fear and amazement had started to convulse violently, as if it were coming back to life. It was a ghastly sight. Not realising that Derek Bradshaw was simply in his death throes, he picked up the gun and fired. Once again the noise was deafening and he realised he had to get out of this place as soon as possible.

He again dropped the shotgun and ran out of the house, leaving the bodies where they lay in the bright electric light and the front door wide open; down the gravel drive, from where he saw that lights in other houses were already on; through the gate and on to the road; he stopped. He thought he heard the distant whine of a police siren and wanted to ascertain which direction it was coming from. He could not tell, but it was a long way off anyway so he continued towards the Vauxhall, which he'd left parked in a state of high visibility by the side of the road. By the time he got to the driver's seat he was again panting, this time from his exertions; he was exhausted, and could not help but slump forward against the driving wheel, in which position he waited for a minute or two, trying hard to get his breath back.

The police siren was getting louder and louder, and he thought he saw some flashing lights in the distance ahead. With a supreme effort he composed himself and tried to start the car. He had to turn the ignition several times before succeeding, and in those few seconds he felt panic rise like vomit, but even so he managed a sedate three point turn in the middle of the empty road and then, with as much nonchalance as possible, drove in the direction of central London.

The road became reasonably well lit but bordered on each side by grassy banks and tall trees whose foliage dwarfed the street lamps, throwing everything into occasional shadow. It was at one of these points that the police car passed Giles, going in the opposite direction. He knew that his face would be lit up by the police car's headlights, but he did not know whether anyone had managed to give a description of him. If they had, it was unlikely that they had seen much of his face anyway, and seated in his car, of course, his general physique could not be determined so easily. Even so, he could not help looking into the eyes of the two police officers in that moment when the two cars passed each other; and he had seen that they were returning his gaze, with inquiring looks on their faces. But it all happened so quickly because whilst he was being careful not to go too far above the speed limit, the police car was travelling at a considerable pace. His heart thumped as he considered that he might next hear a screeching of brakes and the squeal of tyres as the police car turned round to chase him, but this did not happen. Maybe, however, the policemen would relay what they had seen to their control room and another car would intercept him further down the road, but this did not happen either.

After forty minutes or so of careful but frenzied driving Giles finally reached the well-lit Brixton High Street, chosen by him, not because it had the nearest tube to Cornwallis Lodge – it didn't – but because he knew that he could merge easily into the area's busy nightlife and become inconspicuous. It had been a calculated risk to have driven further than he needed, but so far it was proving a risk worth taking. Also Giles had half a mind that wherever he abandoned the car within the environs of Brixton it would probably be more traceable to the thugs who had sold it than to him. Nevertheless, he drove round and round the blocks cautiously before making a move. He parked the car in a side street, took off the pale mackintosh he had been wearing and exchanged it for his usual dark overcoat, which he'd put in the boot. Giles left the mackintosh in the unlocked car and walked to the High Street, with that nervous, dancing tread of his.

Suddenly, he felt relief and an overall lightness of being. It was extraordinary to him that something like an hour ago he had been engaged in the brutal murder by shotgun of two middle-aged people in their own home; and now he was walking down a crowded thoroughfare almost with a cheery step. And he was in his work clothes, as if nothing had happened! He almost felt like going into a bar and having a few quiet, celebratory drinks, but he judged that that would be too dangerous; better not push his luck. So he entered Brixton tube, bought a ticket and skipped down the escalator. His luck remained: he just managed to catch the very last train.

24.

Giles Jones' Diary

Maybe Aunt Felicity was right: life did go on as before; but after the interment of Damien's ashes at Jones Place and when I got back to York nothing would ever be the same again. Something had happened; I mean apart from my father's sudden death obviously, something structural in my mind had collapsed, not even taking into account the usual distortions of adolescence.

The damage took the form of an implosion, so that I don't think others really noticed; in any case the seeing of ghosts is surely a subjective experience: it would be wrong to assume that it could be universal. I say this because my father popped up everywhere, even though dead; his favourite place was at the end of the hallway, just before you got to the kitchen and scullery and beyond, at the point where the green baize door remained permanently open, next to the antique linen chest with the telephone upon it; yet his appearance there was always unexpected, and would catch me by surprise. He always looked as he had done when he came back that evening in Chicago, having managed to sell a set of encyclopedias to that couple in the suburb: sort of pleased with himself, almost triumphant, his grey overcoat wrapped tightly around him, his untidily long hair meeting the collar and blending with it in terms of colour, or the lack of it.

I'm not sure I knew then quite how much my father wanted to be dead, but his ghost should have conveyed that to me: for it was – initially at least – a benign presence, but I also saw other things, whose meanings were, and have always remained, mysterious. For example, a pale ring of obscure yellow flames in danger of being blown out by a light breeze, their tips wobbling precariously, in a setting that was otherwise black and void. Maybe they were candles in a church, and in fact I think I saw a dirty, black metal stand supporting them, and an impression of a grey stone pillar; but if they were extinguished there would be nothing but darkness. This was troubling: I could make no sense of it, but the image seemed to me a very sad and desolate one.

Outwardly, I carried on as best as I could, but there was no doubt that a melancholy self-absorption, to which I had sometimes been prone, now engulfed me completely; so much so that it could be described as the real ghost. A perceptive English teacher at Bishop Grosseteste's noticed this and suggested I take up acting. He was looking around anyway for someone to take the lead in a school production of Hamlet he was contemplating and thought I could do it, which was flattering. To be fair to myself, I had slimmed down enormously – and very quickly – over the last few months, and my grandmother, fearing that my frizzy Jimi Hendrix hairstyle betrayed a touch of the tar brush somewhere or other – hopefully not on her side of the family – had insisted that I get my hair straightened at the most upmarket salon in York, at considerable expense to herself. The result was a lanky, long-haired young man with a good profile, very much of a type in the '60s, complete with tight bell-bottomed trousers and a kipper tie if required.

I had turned into a good-looking young man. But could I act? That is not so stupid a question as it might seem as very often young people who have had no formal training in the art can take to it like a duck to water. Mick Newton – the English teacher – was very encouraging; as with others in that position before him I felt he was on my side but, although I had no difficulty in learning by heart the considerable number of lines that the part entailed, I found the constant rehearsals in the draughty school auditorium to be the hardest work I ever did. They were always in the evenings, of course, after a full school day and as they progressed the burden, even of getting there on time, became wearisome. Moreover, there seemed no interaction between myself and the other players: the difficulty simply of saying the lines to the required standard was all that could be done: as for mastering the art of facial expression or even physical movement beyond the merely mechanical, forget it. Nevertheless, Mick Newton urged us all on. I still remember him following the proceedings underneath the front of the apron stage. Only his bowed head with its shaggy black hair was visible to us, together with the pool of light that illuminated the text he was reading from. The rest was darkness. He would shout instructions while still looking at the text, although he was always clearly aware of what was happening above him. This he would do over and over again, his voice becoming harsher and harsher. 'No! No! No!' he would shout; and then explain what was required more clearly. We would gamely repeat the particular action in question until in his mind it had been got quite right. He was a perfectionist. It was a shame that the human material he had to work on was more or less adolescently slapdash, yet such was his zeal that he did succeed in making a silk purse out of a sow's ear, as the final production largely bore witness to. I think the whole project was a cause celebre for him because for the first time in its history he had managed to persuade the local girls' grammar to take part, so that real females as opposed to boys dressed as such were involved. However, some of the females were drawn from the staff of that school, I'm not quite sure why – maybe it was thought too ridiculous to have, say Hamlet's mother played by a piping adolescent girl. Or maybe so many of the girls were just too shy and more willing teachers thronged in. It didn't matter, because they were almost as young as the girls themselves, and usually they had the minor roles – ladies in attendance and so on.

One in particular caught my fancy, but I was just too wimpish to do anything about it. She insisted on having screens to change behind, when all the others would crowd into a room separate from the boys and change there. The screens could only be placed in the boys' changing room, don't ask me why; nor ask me why, either, the boys didn't take surreptitious peeks at her while she undressed, except perhaps because they were more polite and grown-up than their public school counterparts. I took my cue from them, although I was sorely tempted; particularly when a tell-tale rustle and stamp of the foot would suggest that at that moment she was quite nude.

The weeks went by, and finally came the dress rehearsals, followed by the production itself, which only lasted three days. It seemed funny that all that effort was spent simply to provide entertainment on a Friday, Saturday and Sunday evening; but there it was. I think it went reasonably well; the audience, of course, was packed, mostly with pupils and their parents, but also others, all conscious perhaps that they were there to enjoy a serious, artistic experience.

Except that on the first night a roar of laughter rose up during the sword fight with Laertes and at first we couldn't understand why. The scene had had to be the most meticulously rehearsed of all, and was not without its dangers anyway, but we thought it was going well and strictly to order when the laughter arose, even among some of the others on stage.

Laertes and I faltered; and looking down I discovered that a packet of

Number 6 tipped cigarettes had fallen from my doublet, where it had been secreted by me in case the opportunity for a few quiet smokes ever arose off-stage. I remember failing to understand quite why the audience found it so amusing but after a moment's indecision I kicked the packet aside and that produced even more laughter. I did this so that it would not get in the way, obviously; and so that we could get on with the fight; but the renewed merriment – fuelled perhaps by the spite of those who had not been selected for the cast – caused Laertes and myself to stop altogether. We simply stared at each other, slack-jawed, paralysed. Mick Newton thought it right to turn all the lights off, so that the entire auditorium was plunged in darkness.

As the laughter subsided slowly into an interested murmur he hissed sharply at us that we would have to start all over again. He was not at all pleased, but we did as we were told and the rest of the evening passed without incident. There was prolonged, if muted, applause from the audience at the end and several curtain calls. Saturday and Sunday went without a hitch and were equally well-received, I am glad to say, but the episode of the cigarettes entered school lore and my gossip stakes went sky high. The thing was written up in the end of term magazine, by which time many girls, who would not otherwise have bothered, approached me looking to be my girlfriend; for which once again I was flattered, although I could not seem to capitalise on this unexpected bonus. Sometimes, however, all they wanted were giggles: they would stand in groups as I passed and fall about with mirth. Occasionally there were catcalls, and I couldn't help noticing that their words were always framed in fake posh accents, picked up no doubt through lengthy exposure to my voice on stage. I tried not to mind, but as in previous academic institutions a sense of social uneasiness made me too anxious to court popularity – which was how I came to give a disastrous party at my grandmother and aunt's house. The idea of a party did not strike me as being a good one at all, but everyone knew I lived in a very large house (although it had never crossed my mind to consider that hardly anybody else did), which was why it universally seemed such a good choice of venue. I was eventually persuaded by the callow ringleader of a group of youths during break, in the field in front of the school. I still remember his skinny frame and thin, almost expressionless face, pale and immobile as he waited for my response. His dark grey trousers were shabby and unpressed, his blue jacket torn in places. I could not back down: I had been noncommittally talking about it for weeks; and now came the crunch. I agreed to host the party; and having so agreed, I could not backtrack.

Nor did I even have the grace to consult with my grandmother and aunt about it; the first they knew was on the evening itself – I suppose they were compliant, but there was an edginess to their generosity which I had not seen before. They decided to sit the matter out in Henrietta's locked bedroom on the first floor. As for the rest of the house, it became mayhem, but more of that later. I and some others had dismantled the Sheraton table and created a very large dancing space in the dining room. My powerful hi-fi was installed there, together with some stroboscopic lights. Apart from that, there had been no preparation except the purchase of large quantities of alcohol, most of which was put in the scullery.

During the course of the evening I went in there, to discover that a couple I did not recognise were busy removing the bottles and placing them in a suitcase which they obviously were planning to take away with them. 'Can I get you a drink?' I asked sarcastically; but they did not reply, albeit that they were embarrassed. They started putting the bottles back. I left the room, closing the door, not caring whether they took them or not, because other things of greater concern were happening. I'd already gone into my bedroom and discovered another couple I did not know, naked, having sex in my bed. I was shocked, but said and did nothing. On my way up there a valuable wall clock was dislodged by a drunken passer-by but I managed to catch it before it fell to the floor.

For a reason which I didn't understand, a hefty male teenager had installed himself as a bouncer at the front door; by which time the drive was covered in parked scooters. The only place of refuge was the dining room, which was in darkness except for the stroboscopic lights. The blaring music – 'Jumpin' Jack Flash', that sort of thing – practically drowned out speech. A group of about ten girls were dancing in a ring in the centre of the floor, their handbags all carefully placed in the middle where they could see them. Others – males, mainly - were standing by the walls. I think by then I had given up on the house; it was just going to be too difficult to police it all the time. So I joined in. Some of the girls I knew; others I did not. One I did was Kate Binns, a pretty blonde with an impressive bust and very shapely legs revealed by a mini skirt. Altogether, however, she was quite petite. I think she'd been one of the ones who'd taken a liking to me because one afternoon in the theatre bar she'd offered to buy me a coffee and had stood over me provocatively, so that I had had to look up at her breasts. She knew what she was doing.

Anyway, we paired off and danced. Out of the blue, she asked me at the top of her voice whether I was a misogynist. I did not know what to say, but made a clawing gesture at her as if to confirm that I was. She was amused. I don't remember anything about her after that, that evening I mean, but I took the question as a challenge. Come the early hours of the morning I thought I'd look in to my grandmother's bedroom to see how they were doing. There was a steady thump of music from below and boys were sitting on floors in groups getting drunk from brown bottles. Couples, also on floors, and on sofas and chairs, were necking with abandon, quite oblivious to anything else that might be happening in their immediate surroundings. It was pretty revolting. Objects were smashed or broken all around. It had become, as I say, mayhem. I was later to discover that a number of valuable items had been stolen.

On entering my grandmother's bedroom, having unlocked the door, I saw that both she and Felicity were sitting together, looking very scared and worried. At the same time they had that set demeanour which betokens stoicism, a willingness and an ability to wait things out, no matter how bad they might be. I felt terrible: these were good people who had taken me in when they had had no real obligation to do so, and I had stretched their generosity too far. Apart from anything else, they had to be up in the morning to attend to their surgeries, for they always worked Saturdays as well as weekdays. I backed out of the room and determined to bring the party to an end. Luckily, the fornicating couple in my bedroom were now gone. Quietly but firmly, I asked everyone else to leave, one by one, and in the dining room I switched the lights on and turned off the music. People got the message, and sulkily shuffled off into the night. I subsequently discovered that on the evening of the party one of the local shopkeepers had allegedly been made ill by the sheer number of teenagers entering his premises and demanding directions to my grandmother's house. I had no idea half of York's youth would appear on her doorstep.

The next day a pale green Morris Minor drew up outside, braking sharply to a stop, crunching the gravel. I looked through the drawing room window and saw Kate Binns get out. She was in jeans and had a business-like air about her. I was startled but pleased. She approached the glass front door and was about to ring when she saw me approach from the other side. She smiled through the glass. She was looking very pretty as always but had put a lot of make-up on, which was unusual for her. Her blonde hair was quite pale and she had accentuated this by pale, almost white, foundation. Her lipstick was of a pale pink colour. I let her in and kissed her briefly on the cheek while she touched my arm. She was wearing scent. Immediately she apologised for turning up unannounced but claimed that she had left her handbag behind the night before and wanted to retrieve it. We had a look around, in fact we had a thorough look around, but it was nowhere to be seen.

After about half an hour of this, she said, 'Oh well, I must have left it somewhere else.' It was unconvincing. I had already started to disbelieve the reason she had given for her arrival.

'Come into the drawing room anyway, and have a cup of coffee.'

'Yes, I could do with that.'

What she meant was, it had been a long night and she needed a restorative, which I prepared.

We chatted about our lives, such as they were – she on the sofa and me in the armchair nearest the grand piano with all of my mother's family photographs placed upon it. She blushed when she told me her grandfather had been a butcher. She clearly had a suppressed sense of outrage about that, also she asked me rhetorically where on earth she could get in the world with a name like Kate Binns. But I was nonplussed. I was more concerned about the rest of the clearing up that needed doing. My aunt and grandmother would be back in the evening and I felt it a point of honour to have the place ship-shape by then. She said she would help me. I moaned about the fact that a valuable silver-topped walking stick belonging to my late grandfather was missing. She said she would ask around about it in the town. I thanked her.

Actually, during all this small talk I was transfixed by her sexiness. She kept on moving her body about as she sat, as if she were uncomfortable with the sofa, but she was merely advertising herself, although that is not to say that she was in any way being vulgar. There was a lightness about her being and personality that was enchanting; quite apart from her physical allure. As I listened, and watched her – she was something of a chatterbox, employing her body in the service of her speech, as it were – I gradually realised I was becoming deeply aroused and did not know what to do about it. The embarrassment of course would have been that she might notice; but she seemed too engrossed in what she was talking about. So I let it happen; and after a while my concealed erection reached bursting point. Again I let it happen; and almost immediately had to close my eyes as that familiar sense of overpowering post orgasm weariness took over.

She stopped what she was saying and asked, 'Are you tired?'

I came to my senses. 'Sorry', I said. 'It's just... '

'Me too.'

Silence. Strange, that, when she had been so talkative.

'I suppose we'd better get on with some clearing up,' I mumbled, 'if you would still like to help me.'

'Yes,' she answered; but she looked doubtful.

Another silence. She got to her feet and I followed suit. There was another almighty pause, following which we did not go about the house but simply approached each other. There was wariness on both sides but we tentatively touched hands and, that being all right, embraced and kissed passionately. Our tongues explored each other's mouths. We then reluctantly withdrew and she asked, 'Is there somewhere we can go?'

Now it was my turn to look doubtful. I knew my aunt would kill me if she ever found out. But my desire for Kate Binns was so strong that I was prepared to take any risk, so I said, 'Yes.'

I turned and she followed me into the hall and up the staircase. There was a door on the left which opened on to a little-used part of the house, at the end of a passage of which there was a small bedroom, before it led to another staircase. We entered. Very bright sunlight streamed through the window, making the edges of the single bed and its dull cover, and the rest of the furniture, seem jagged. We had been facing each other but I went to draw the curtains and as I did so she exclaimed, 'What's that?'

Startled by the tone of her voice I turned and saw that she was pointing at my jeans, in the area of my groin. I looked down and immediately realised what she meant. There was a large stain there. I said nothing – what could I say? I just looked up at her hopelessly.

She was thrilled.

'You've creamed your jeans!' she hissed enthusiastically, adding to my embarrassment; but it was clear that she had been thoroughly aroused by the sight. She was in an ecstasy of anticipation. We lunged and tore at each other's clothes after that. Somewhere along the way I managed to draw the curtains before pulling her on to the bed. There was a narrow public pathway on that side of the house. Despite my lack of experience – I could not speak for her – the sex between us I would have thought was good, perhaps because of my earlier premature slaking, and because it appeared that she came easily, giving little gasps whenever she did. But as the intercourse wore on I began to realise that she was no longer really communicating with me: she had become less responsive and simply stared at the ceiling, as if wanting to be in some other place. I stopped and said, 'You have to go now. My grandmother and aunt will be back soon.'

She agreed; and we put our clothes on in silence. There seemed to be a guilty atmosphere about.

'Post coitus tristum est,' she said.

'What's that?'

'Post coitus tristum est. One is sad after sex.'

'Where did you get that from?'

'My Latin teacher.'

'He told you that, did he?'

'Yes.'

I frowned. I was faintly troubled by this, but didn't enquire any further. I showed her out of one of the back doors that opened onto a yard with garages. I told her how to get back on to the main road. It would not appear as if she had come from the house. I was terrified that she might bump into my grandmother or aunt on their return home, or be seen by a nosy neighbour who would no doubt make the right inference. Just before I opened the door we kissed and I said, 'We'll be seeing each other again, I hope. Like this.'

It was quite obvious what I meant.

'Yes,' she said simply, looking straight up at me, but her blue eyes were distant.

I closed the door on her with an intense feeling of relief. I felt I had got away with it. Walking back into the main part of the house, I saw what else needed to be done in terms of clearing up. There was not so much as I had thought. Still, I set about the remaining tasks and after a while heard the front door slam but noticed that it was without the usual accompanying cheery "hello!" that my aunt was in the habit of shouting. But it was her. She greeted me with a vague smile and with no

189

further acknowledgement immediately started to make such domestic corrections as were obviously needed, like turning a table the right way up, for example. I watched her with dismay.

'I'm so sorry, Fee,' I mumbled. 'I had no idea...'

'That's quite all right,' she said perfunctorily, not pausing from what she was doing. 'Let's just not do it again, shall we?'

Then she did stop, faced me and said, 'All day I've been worrying what it would be like when I got back. I didn't have time to take a good look this morning. Your poor grandmother was so alarmed. You should have told us and we could have hired a hall or something. Really, we're not used...' Just then the front door slammed for the second time and to our intense surprise the sound of laughter came from the hall. Henrietta came into the Aga room – where we were – shouting 'More ale! More ale!' whenever she could control herself.

She sat down and as usual Aunt Felicity started to make her evening China tea, together with a tot of sherry. Henrietta fell into a dry chuckle and kept on muttering, 'More ale! More ale!' Aunt Felicity looked grim but managed to explain the perfectly obvious to me, namely that her mother was imitating what she thought she had heard last night when locked in her bedroom. Suddenly, Henrietta got to her feet and grabbed one of the many empty brown beer bottles that were still lying on the floor and surfaces and raised its neck to her lips in a mock show of emptying it to the lees. Meanwhile, she started to dance a jig, to the astonishment of myself and Aunt Felicity.

'Mother!' chimed her daughter reprovingly; but this did nothing to stop her. She continued to dance in a tight circle in the middle of the room while wielding the bottle to her lips. One would not have thought that a woman of seventy would have so much energy, particularly after a hard day's work. Also, it looked so incongruous because she was dressed in her habitual charcoal grey suit, thick stockings, black shoes and odd blue-grey hat which she always had pinned to her silvery hair, and which she never took off except when going to bed.

'More ale! More ale!'

I was laughing affectionately at the spectacle but Aunt Felicity had become frozen and slack-jawed, and continued to stare at her mother, with a look on her face which suggested that she felt she simply must do something to stop this unconscionable display of bad taste, but didn't know what. For a moment I thought she was going to get her in a straitjacket-hold but instead she finally managed to collect herself and turned to look at me; as if to say, 'See what you have done! It's all your fault!'

'Oh, dearie me! Oh, dearie me!' Henrietta was now saying to herself; and having discarded the bottle she had placed the palms of her hands on her knees and was knocking them together while changing her hands from one knee to the other, giving the illusion that they were passing through her legs. I too was now getting worried. I had never seen my grandmother like this before; she seemed to be having a fit of some kind.

'I'll get her something,' said Aunt Felicity, leaving the room in search of her doctor's bag, which she usually left in the hall. The moment she was gone, however, Henrietta slowed down, eventually stopped what she was doing and walked unsteadily back to her chair, with that discomfited look that suggested she had no idea what had come over her. But when she was seated – and as we could hear Aunt Felicity's equally sensible shoes tapping on the wooden floor of the hall – she became very serious, almost deadly, and while looking at me put an index finger to her lips, as if about to impart a matter of the utmost secrecy. Then she whispered in conspiratorial fashion, 'Between you and me, Giles, all the men in our family – all the men, including you – it's either the neck of the womb or the neck of the bottle that gets them in the end.'

I was bewildered. Aunt Felicity returned, but saw at once that her mother had calmed down, so put the small brown bottle she was holding to one side and resumed her tea-making, as if nothing very much out of the ordinary had happened. She even started to whistle when, having filled the heavy old kettle with water, she put it on one of the Aga's hot plates.

25.
Narrative, 1979

Giles Jones was no great follower of the media, so he came across few of the reports of the shocking murders that he had committed in Carshalton. Further, to an extent, his working hours insulated him from the daily excitement of lurid news; and in any case he was not interested: what gripped him now was an obsession with getting the rest of the job done. He took serious delight in making up his mind who should be next. His stepmother, surely: that way her father Graham Greene would have the grief of having lost a daughter before he himself was killed (Giles did not know that the stockbroker didn't care tuppence about his daughter). In any case, Graham Greene must also know by now what was happening: the systematic extermination of those who had connived in defrauding Giles Jones. He must be quaking in his boots. Yet he must also be wondering what, if anything, he could do about it. Surely, fear for his own safety, as well as that of his daughter, might lead him to go to the police and name the obvious culprit, even if such a course would almost certainly mean the exposure of his own wrongdoing? Giles Jones didn't mind being caught and sentenced, in fact he rather enjoyed the thought of a prolonged and formal self-vindication in court. What he did mind and indeed was most frightened of was being caught and sentenced before he had finished the job to his satisfaction. He was terrified of this eventuality, which was why he was transfixed with a sense of urgency so pressing that he simply didn't have the time to think of the consequences of what he was doing.

Gaining access to Coral Jones proved to be easier than he had thought. He knew the name and general location of the private institution in which she was lodged and, late one morning, simply rang Directory Enquiries and asked for its number. This was given. He dialled. After a few rings, a woman answered and said, 'Kane House, June Simpson speaking. How may I help you?'

In horror, Giles Jones put the receiver down as quickly as possible. It had belatedly occurred to him that, despite it being a natural thing for a stepson to want to communicate with his stepmother no matter how mad, in the circumstances it would be folly to announce himself before making a visit, which is what he had planned to do. The last thing he wanted was to give anyone any warning of his existence, particularly as Kane House might have been alerted to the fact that one of its charges might well be in danger for her life.

Having thought about the matter, he re-dialled the number, and again there was the cool female voice. 'Kane House, June Simpson speaking. How may I help you?'

'So sorry about that. We must have been cut off. It's simply that I need to know the address of Kane House.'

June Simpson gave it, allowing time for Giles to write it down, and added, 'Would you like a brochure?'

'Yes, please. I would.'

'If you will kindly give me your address I will put it in the post.'

Giles Jones gave a false address, details of which were the first plausible ones he could think of.

He could hear her writing them down, then she said, 'I'm sorry, I need your name, of course.'

He gave a false name.

'Thank you, Mr Johnson. Visitors' days are Tuesdays, Thursdays and Sundays, in the afternoon. We have ample parking but should you come by train, the nearest station is Dartford.'

'Thank you. That's most helpful.'

'I think you'll find our rates are very reasonable.'

'Thanks.'

June Simpson had even given him unasked-for directions from the railway station before ringing off.

That was on a Monday. On his next free day Giles Jones got up early, washed, shaved, combed his hair and polished his black lace-ups. He put on a sober suit he hadn't worn in years, together with a matching shirt and tie. This ensemble, he thought as he looked in the narrow, cracked mirror on the inside of his wardrobe door, gave him just the right air for a dutiful stepson who had come to pay his respects to a woman who, most unfortunately, had gone quite bonkers. He put on his overcoat.

He felt light-headed as he walked to the tube. The weather was cold and grey and the other pedestrians took no notice of him. Giles Jones' light-headedness turned to breathlessness as he descended the escalator. He realised he was running, but could not help himself. He tried to calm down but could not. Once on the platform he worried that he would jump onto the tracks just as the train appeared from the tunnel. He very nearly did, but with a gasp managed to pull himself back. Other passengers were looking at him curiously. He realised this and wondered paranoically whether an alert had been put out for him. Perhaps his image had been plastered all over the newspapers. Just before the train passed, he saw on the wall opposite a poster of a male model smoking a pipe. He thought it was him. He thought – but what was he thinking?

His next fear was that in the carriage there would be a selection of people from the Huffington Club, who would all ask him where he was going. He would have to lie. Actually the carriage was practically empty, the rush hour having passed, and in typical London fashion those who had looked at him curiously and entered the train were now indifferent to anything but their own preoccupations. Just as he himself was.

About an hour later, he was standing outside Dartford Railway Station and feeling, so he thought, quite normal again and in full control of himself. He was consulting the directions June Simpson had given him, which he had written down on a piece of paper. He looked up, spotted a street sign and crossed the road towards it. He had no idea how far away Kane House was, June Simpson not having told him, nor he having asked, but he had determined to walk, because he thought a cab driver might with hindsight be able to give valuable and incriminating evidence against him; which was illogical: if he'd thought about it at all, which he hadn't – and which was why he wasn't quite as normal as he hoped – he would surely have realised that if, by any chance or guile, he succeeded in seeing Coral and killing her, they would know who the culprit was.

Who's they? The police, of course. Giles Jones shuddered. After a longish walk along a straight, dull road he finally reached an entrance whose sign directed him to Kane House. He had to go up an incline bordered by trees before he saw the mansion, which was large and sprawling and surrounded by woods and grassland running down to a lake at the front, which was peopled with a multitude of Canadian geese and a few swans. There did not seem to be any real people about.

194

As he approached, always having to go up a bit, for the building was at the top of a slight hill, he began to see how dilapidated it was, with crumbling turrets, lopsided chimneys and even the odd broken window. A whole wing seemed to be on the verge of dereliction. Nevertheless, when he got to the main front door he noted that, like a sticking plaster over a bad wound, licks of paint had judiciously been applied here and there, and the shiny new cars parked at the entrance gave the establishment an air of prosperity.

He rang the doorbell and immediately an electronic buzzer sounded so that he could walk in, after which he felt as if a great distance separated him from a large, formidable desk behind which sat a blonde woman. The floor was covered with cheap, poorly laid linoleum of a green colour, which made a disconcerting sound as he approached. It was almost as if he were not walking on anything substantial at all, but something which could give way at any moment, the noise it made under his feet triggering the sense of unreality he had felt before.

But it was vital to keep his composure; he tried to smile. She was smiling at him expectantly, and he wondered whether she was the June Simpson he had spoken to the other day.

'Good morning, Oh, so sorry,' she laughed, looking at her watch. 'I mean, good afternoon.'

Instinctively, he looked at his watch too. It was twenty-five past twelve.

Obscurely, he was aware that there was no one else about, even though this was supposed to one of Kane House's visiting days.

'Good afternoon,' he said, smiling. 'I've come to see my stepmother. Ah...'

'What is her name?'

'Coral. Coral Jones. Well, she was Coral Greene before her marriage.'

The young lady frowned. It was only because her facial expression changed so dramatically that Giles began properly to notice her at all.

'Have you made an appointment?'

'No. I was just passing and...'

'We have strict...' having interrupted Giles Jones, the young lady proceeded to stop herself. 'Would you take a seat, please? I'll just go and...'

Already, she'd got to her feet. She'd also waved in the direction of some uninviting-looking moulded polypropylene chairs in dark grey, ranged along the far wall. Giles Jones couldn't help noticing that the paint on this wall was peeling and there were patches of damp.

'You are?'

'Giles Jones. I'm the son of Damien Jones, who married Coral.'

Her tone had been brusque when she asked the question; now she muttered something to herself and disappeared down a corridor to the side of her desk, her shoes clacking on the linoleum.

There was a cheap coffee table in front of the polypropylene chairs, upon which rested some out-of-date magazines and a copy of yesterday's Daily Mail. Otherwise the vast room was quite empty. Had Giles Jones not had it verified that he was in the right place, he wouldn't have thought for one moment that this was indeed the institution in which his stepmother was housed at such great expense.

After a few minutes the receptionist returned with a real battle-axe of a woman dressed in a light blue nurse's uniform. She was squat and ugly but with very bright eyes behind glasses which turned their beady gaze on the man seated on the polypropylene chair, as if at the very least he had the clear look of a child molester.

He got up. The receptionist went back to her desk.

'Mr Jones?'

'Yes.'

'You've come to see your stepmother?'

'Yes.'

'It's your first time here?'

'Yes.'

She did not ask, 'So why have you come now?' although the question was evident in the way it silently hovered above her forehead.

'Do you have any identification?'

'Yes.'

He had thought he might be asked for this, and now fished in the inner breast pocket of his jacket for his passport, which he produced. She took it and thumbed it through, her bright eyes scanning the pages, for all the world as if she did a bit of moonlighting as an immigration officer.

'You were born at Kington, I see.'

'Yes, I...'

'Tell me, Mr Jones, do you always carry your passport with you?'

'Why no, I...'

'Miss Simpson told me you were just passing.'

The implication was clear. He would not have had his passport unless he thought he might need it.

'I'm sorry, but whom do I have the pleasure of addressing?'

The nurse was taken aback. In fact she did step back a bit, somehow revealing that she had bow legs. For once, the bright eyes behind the glasses blinked.

'I'm the matron here.'

Out of the corner of his eye, Giles Jones saw that the seated Miss Simpson was biting her lip. She clearly had been listening to the interrogation and maybe she was dismayed that she had not effected an introduction. In a curious way, this possibility gave Giles new heart, because until that moment he rather thought he would be shown the door.

'Well, Matron, what I said to your colleague was not quite true. I – ah – was not just passing, I came here deliberately. You see, I have not seen my stepmother since – well, you may know something of the background, and I feel rather guilty about that, so I...'

Matron visibly relaxed a little bit. Even something like an understanding smile crossed her prominent, colourless lips. Giles Jones noted this and pursued his advantage.

'To tell you the truth,' he continued, 'I was so appalled by what happened that I... well, I mean...'

'There's no need to go into all that,' she put in perfunctorily. 'I'm sure it was a great shock. Come this way.'

She turned, and he followed her down the corridor from which she had come; and up a staircase of the sort you get in cheap hotels: the linoleum bounded by metal at the edge of the steps. Her bow legs carried her up swiftly.

'Afraid the lift's not working,' she barked in front of her.

'Good exercise,' he muttered.

They went right to the top of the building and along another drab corridor with gloomy brown doors on either side. She appeared to pick one at random.

'In here, please.'

It was a small office, stuffy, unkempt, and littered with dog-eared folders out of which bulged papers of varying degrees of desiccation. A few magazines were strewn about. She kicked these aside as she made for her desk, a movement that was somehow grotesque because it looked as if she were about to pick it up and throw it out of the window, which, he noticed, looked as if it had not been opened for years, ever since an indifferent decorator painted over the frame, careless of any future need for ventilation.

'Sit down, forgive the mess,' she commanded. 'It's just that we get so few visitors.'

Was that a reason for working in such a slatternly environment? Giles Jones asked himself this but was too polite to voice it. And, of course, he had other things on his mind. He had to move some of the magazines – 'put them over there!' – before he could sit on the hard-backed chair opposite her.

'Doesn't anyone come to see Coral?'

'No, not a dicky bird. Mind you, I'm not surprised. Between you and me, she's a mess. But you'll see that for yourself. Now let me see…' she rummaged around – 'ah, here we are.'

She produced a file which had the appearance of being quite empty.

'No one at all?'

'No.'

She was not really paying any attention to him because she was looking at the file suspiciously, as if its contents had been filched.

'And…, but doesn't anybody ring up for her, or send her cards and things?'

'Nothing of that kind. A trust of some sort pays the monthly bill, is all.'

Giles Jones felt relieved. It meant that neither her father nor anybody else had bothered to notify Kane House that she might be in danger.

'Wait a minute!' Matron was squinting at a solitary post-it note that was gummed to the inside of the folder. 'There was a call quite recently. Hm.'

She read aloud: 'The caller hung up, a Mr Graham Greene, representing himself as her father. Unusual number – Knighton is it? no, Kington 2371. I wonder where that is. Thing is, he asked to reverse the charges and we couldn't accept that, could we?'

'No, no.'

Giles Jones quite understood. Yet he felt a frisson: Kington 2371 was the number of Jones Place, Kington being the nearest town of any size.

'Now let me just take down a few of your details and I'll take you along to her.'

She took his details, which she wrote in a sloping hand with a cheap biro, her fingers curling toward her wrist; then eyed him warily.

'Now, I don't want you to bother her too much. She's in a very fragile emotional state and she hears voices. Well, she says she does. Since we can't hear them, we can't be sure, can we? But these skits are all the same. They need cossetting. The moment she gets alarmed, you just push the button you'll see by the door. It rings a bell and we'll come running. Got that?'

'Yes.'

Giles Jones decided, without being faintly interested, that there was something childish about this woman, despite being the bright-eyed battle-axe she also undoubtedly was.

She led him down the corridor and through a couple of swing doors whose concertinaed middle section was reminiscent of the link between railway carriages. The next shock was that, once they had entered the further corridor, there was a gaping hole to their left: the outer wall had quite fallen away, and it seemed as if a precipice were coming to meet them. A sense of giddiness made Giles step back from the view he now had of the grassland beneath the institution and the shimmering lake beyond. Broken bricks formed a ragged frame to the picture. If he lowered his gaze he could see the shiny tops of the parked cars by the main entrance. He was appalled that Kane House could be in such a state of disrepair, yet Matron skipped ahead almost blithely, as if she were in her element now that they had entered the most dilapidated part of the building.

'Sorry about all this,' she breathed cheerfully. 'The hole and all that. We're in dispute with the builders. You'd better mind how you go.'

He did not say anything but continued to follow her, his mind having strangely left any thought for his own immediate safety and gone on to what he could expect to find when he saw his stepmother, which surely must be only in a few moments' time. It was – what – twelve years or so since he had last seen her, at his father's wake, and she had then seemed repulsive to him, a sort of angry bird whose wings took the form of human elbows as she carved and carved at her food, while she laughed madly at whatever piece of nonsense came into her head, or whatever she thought anybody had said, or not said, to her from any direction. He thought of the quite inappropriate joke she had made about the erection of buttresses and flying angels around his father's tomb and he reminded himself of how much he hated her and, in so doing, realised perhaps for the first time how good it would be to kill her, to wring her neck like the bad, ugly, repulsive chicken that she was.

'Here we are…'

They had reached a door at the far end of the furthest corridor in the topmost quarter of the building; as she spoke she produced a key and unlocked it and went inside, repeating to herself, 'Here we are, here we are…'

26.
Giles Jones' Diary

I suppose the time has come to tell you a bit more about my grandmother and aunt. To a child, their behaviour seemed perfectly natural but, in fact, they were regarded as eccentrics in the town. Aware of this, they struggled hard to appear normal to their patients and others, but this only heightened the sense of oddity one had about them. Certainly, Henrietta was always supremely conscious that she was an Irish immigrant and went to great lengths to proclaim her allegiance to England, even going so far as to hang a portrait of Queen Elizabeth in pride of place above the mantelpiece in the main drawing room. This was not so false a thing to do as it appeared because the reason why she and her husband left their own country was because they couldn't stand their compatriots, with whom they had grown steadily exasperated due to their ignorance and irrationality, as they saw it. Yet that did not mean that they did not bring with them what was perhaps, the most defining characteristic of their home country, Catholicism. To the end of their days they remained profoundly devout in a way that was different and perhaps inimical to the easier Anglican ways, and it was this that marked them apart and gave them curiosity value to whoever they dealt with.

Henrietta's husband spent eleven of the twelve years it required training to be a Jesuit, only to discover at the eleventh hour that he did not have a vocation; so he became a doctor instead. They met at medical school in Dublin, where Henrietta had been one of the first female students. Later in life, her mind was not as good as it had been. She became suspicious of others to the point of paranoia and hysterically suppressed any part of her own self which she thought might be perceived as outrageous. There was no such part, so it was the suppression that was evident, not, as is usually the case, the thing being suppressed. Like my father, she had to take Nembutal at night to get to sleep, and she was always terrified that the one person that she needed, whom she could not do without, would leave her.

Like her sister, Felicity could have been expected to have wanted a life of her own in the conventional sense – a husband, children, a home of her own and so on; but this did not happen: I am quite sure that my Aunt Felicity is, and remained to her dying day, a virgin. She told me once that as a young woman shortly after her father died – an event which affected her very much, leading her to the brink of suicide – she had been misdiagnosed as a schizophrenic, which was why she never married. Whether this was true, or an excuse, or both, it meant that she had never had, and never would have, any sexual relations, since it was inconceivable that so devout a Catholic woman would have such things outside marriage.

Once when I was a very small child I wandered into Henrietta's bedroom quite late in the evening – even then I think I had trouble getting to sleep and wished for any distraction – and to my surprise saw her on her knees on the floor, propped against the bed, her back facing me. I was further surprised when, self-centred creature that I was, she took no notice of me, even though I was standing but a few feet away from her.

She was utterly lost in prayer. She seemed apart from the world. There was a quality of stillness about her which was maddening, because she would not acknowledge me. Yet, at the same time, I was troubled because I did not understand what she was doing – and maybe still do not.

I stood my ground and waited and after what seemed a very long time she must have become aware of my presence because slowly she started to turn her head in my direction, but she only got halfway, so that she was in profile. Her lips were moving. She was saying things but no words were coming out. Her eyes were, I think, closed. As she continued to move her lips she made sweeping motions with her left hand. To my mortification I belatedly realised that she was shooing me away – so unlike my granny who, together with my aunt, I thought always had all the time in the world for me. I backed out of the room, closing the door as I went.

I think this experience contributed to the sense of strangeness I had about my grandmother's bedroom, but it was also tinged with fear because I began to recognise that there were things in the world which were not only beyond my understanding but even my knowledge. I was not able at that time fully to distinguish the person – my grandmother – from what was obviously her own private environment – her bedroom. The latter was far more indicative of her than any of the other rooms in the house, in the sense that it contained her private things, and was the place where she could behave, as elsewhere she could not, as she wanted.

On my next visit, my curiosity having been aroused, she was in bed early one evening, her rosary on the table beside her, the crucifix on the wall and the commode at the far end of the room. The rest was heavy Victorian furniture, equally heavy brocaded curtains and a thick, stultifying carpet. There was a gloomy atmosphere but because she was not praying she was quite happy for me to be present and I took advantage of this by burrowing around under the bed to see if there were anything there other than the chamber pot I had seen before. I was not disappointed; I came across a hard, prickly object which my hands could not recognise. I dragged it out so that I could examine it further. I could not lift it without a great effort.

My first impression was a fearful one; it was made of wood – brown, black and shiny – but hard as stone. It looked like the branch of a tree, but unlike such an object, with which I was of course familiar, it had clumps upon it as hard and round as cricket balls, each of which contained sharp spikes that bristled from the surface. The largest of these was at the end, and at the other end the wood had been fashioned into a handle, so that the whole thing could be held, although it was too heavy for me to do so, and it toppled forward when I tried.

I asked my grandmother what it was and she told me it was a shillelagh. I had not heard the word, which was as strange to me as the object itself. So, I asked her what it was for and she told me it was a weapon they used in Ireland, where it came from. Still puzzled, I asked her why she had it and she said she kept it for self-protection. What's self-protection? The questions went on and on. She said there were bad people in the world and you never knew when they might be coming to get you – all of which was very troubling to me. I think for the first time in my life I was made aware of the potential danger to be had in being alive. Looking back on it, it seems obvious to me that this shillelagh if used with sufficient force would either kill, or at least completely incapacitate, depending upon which part of the body it struck.

I thought Kate Binns had let it be known that she wanted to be chased a little bit and I was more than happy to oblige. At first it seemed as if we had not been intimate at all, because we met only as other teenagers did, and did not speak about it. Sometimes a look from her or myself betrayed a secret between us, but we did not want others to know what that secret was; we feared gossip and, most of all, exposure. I had no idea what her parents might think if they knew; I knew my aunt and grandmother would be ashamed. Yet she was a physically mature and intellectually capable young woman, and I – well – there's the point, as it turned out. The truth is, I became obsessed with her, but had to mask that obsession with an air of indifference, which I think she found misleading. There followed the cat and mouse game which I have described, but between her and myself there was one big difference; that she was capable of understanding that there were many other boys whom she might fancy who were after her, and I was not so capable in regard to girls, don't ask me why. Anyway, it was frustrating that the apparently very natural way in which we had come together could not be repeated. More, that arrangements for its repetition could not even be made. I could not ring her for fear of her parents answering, she could not ring me for a similar reason, we could not speak openly because we were always in the company of others. I thought we dared not be seen together because there might be talk.

Then one day I saw her sitting on her own on a bench in the little-used footpath that stretched along the River Ouse from the centre of town to an outskirt, the outskirt where I lived, in fact. She was reading a book and appeared to be waiting for someone. I was in the habit of taking that route home and stopped when I saw her; and the pleasurable impression that she was contriving a chance meeting with me entered my mind, because she knew where I lived and maybe also guessed that this was the route I sometimes took. Nevertheless, I remained at a distance of a hundred yards or so just to make sure it was her, which it was; but to my surprise another young man approached her and she got up to greet him, casting her book aside. I could see them smiling at each other before they kissed, her arms around his neck while his were round her waist. He then led her off the footpath and onto the grass bank which went up to a large copse.

This copse had a certain notoriety among the local teenagers; it was surprisingly untended, so that parts of it were densely overgrown while others were not. It flanked one of the old city walls and it was impossible, without taking a really good look, to see what, if anything, was going on inside. So it had the reputation of a knocking copse, although I always doubted whether anything more serious than heavy petting went on in there. Sure enough, with a quick look to right and left, the scope of which did not include me, they made their way carefully through the tangled bushes and thorns and disappeared.

I was shocked and angry; what was more, I recognised the boy – a freckly, red-haired, stocky fellow who always wore white jeans that were too tight for him. He wasn't at Bishop Grosseteste's – was a bit too old anyway – but was always hanging around the theatre coffee bar bragging about the girls he'd had or the stuff he'd nicked from shops. I remembered him for the way in which his meaty chops would always settle into an inane grin whenever he felt himself to be the centre of attention, and he was one of these cheaply good-looking but utterly empty men who, I had learnt, always seem to be a success with girls, don't ask me why. But then my anger returned to her; how could she? What a two-timing little hussy; for all I knew, a three, four, five or six-timing one, and, therefore, a slut to boot. In an instant her sexual appeal for me was buried within a feeling of disgust, but this change was caused by nothing more than a sleight of mind, designed, I dimly realised, as a self-protective mechanism to minimise my very great and gut-wrenching hurt.

Equally, the realisation that I had been wrong about Kate Binns was no consolation, because it had not been for me to demand fidelity from her and anyway, I had not demanded it. It was just that one had certain expectations, that's all; and these expectations had been confounded. It is an extraordinary thing for one's intelligence to have to do battle with one's feelings, but that was what was happening to me as stiffly I carried on my way along the footpath, having decided that I would behave as if I had seen nothing and go home. For a moment I had had the urge to follow them in to the copse and – what? make some sarcastic remark? have it out with them? But again a self-protective mechanism kicked in; it would have been too painful, whatever the outcome might have been.

It was troubling to me how I would react when I next met with Kate, because pride dictated that there should be no appearance on my part of loss, dismay or hurt; just an easy manner which betrayed nothing – after all, she did not know that I had seen her with that boy, to which extent it would be interesting to see how duplicitous or otherwise she could be. Of course, given the nature of the town, our paths were bound to cross again sooner or later, despite what I thought had been a mutual reluctance to arrange a rendezvous by telephone; and it happened very quickly. A few days later I went to the theatre coffee bar after school with some friends and saw her sitting with a group of older boys and girls, none of whom I knew but some of whose faces were familiar. Next to her was the red-haired fellow and their arms were crossed against each other because he had a hand on her leg and she had one on his; they were openly canoodling. They were not the only ones and noises of brash hilarity were coming from the group, partly because they were enjoying themselves so much over their coffee and soft drinks but partly also because they wished to draw attention to themselves, which they were doing. The rest of the young crowd, and even the waitresses, seemed cowed and over-awed by them, also nervous, although everyone tried to carry on as if nothing were happening. But you felt that there was danger in the air; that at any moment a glass might fly or even a chair be thrown; I certainly felt it, but for the moment I was at a standstill and simply stared at Kate Binns and her friend. The people I was with moved on, to one of the few empty tables in the far corner. Perhaps surprisingly her amazingly clear, blue eyes caught mine and held them for a few moments; and nothing happened. It was as if the rest of the world and the noise had disappeared; but then they started to twinkle at me, as if she knew something that I didn't, or as if she were playing a game; and she got up and walked towards me with an irritatingly practised stride. I was fit to burst but could not move.

'Hello Giles, long time no see.'

There was an ironic tone to her, not just her voice but the set of her eyes and a mischievousness of disposition generally which I was beginning to find insufferable. I did not answer. She frowned a little bit, as if this were not in the script. Only now did I notice that the red-haired fellow had joined her, and was giving me a cool, even look. He was taller than me and certainly stockier. I also noticed that the others in their group had fallen silent, and were watching.

Having become aware that he was beside her, Kate Binns said, 'Giles, meet Keith.'

Still I said nothing, but the other man, true to form, began to leer at me, in that inane, triumphant way he had. Kate, however, continued to frown, because she could not get a reaction, so she said, 'Keith, this is Giles. He's that misogynist I was telling you about.'

Even then I wondered whether he knew the word. This man Keith's grin grew wider even as I felt my right arm tighten into a hard piston. I had clenched my fist so that it became just like one of those spikey cricket balls on Henrietta's shillelagh; my forearm was at right angles to my upper arm. Suddenly, and with all my strength, I punched him in the stomach, keeping my fist and forearm as rigid as I could. Keith gasped and went down, clutching his stomach. Kate Binns screamed. A commotion started, but Keith remained on the floor, apparently in an agony. He was gasping and struggling to breathe. Others went to help him. I felt myself being pulled back. For all I could sense, the commotion had turned to pandemonium. It sounded as if a table and glasses had been overturned. A very upset Kate Binns was being comforted by a few girlfriends. They had made her sit down and were standing over her and encouraging her to drink some water. A male shouted, 'What did you do that for?'

I tried to struggle free but too many people were holding me back. I wanted to get at him but at the same time worried that he would collect himself and come at me. It was only later that I discovered that the wall of his stomach had been ruptured and that he was suffering from severe internal bleeding. There was no chance of his getting off the floor. But I did not know that at the time. Nor did I realise that 999 had been called and an ambulance and police car were on their way. All I can remember before they came is that everyone – including the people I had come with – were looking at me as if I were the most shocking thing that ever came out of a womb.

So, that was that. Shame had been brought on the House of Henrietta in exactly the sort of way she most feared – a scandal in the town. She and Felicity grew more distant with me every day that passed; except that, whenever Henrietta did speak to me it was with a kind of shrill menace, implying a threat that if I did not do the decent thing and leave she would not be responsible for her own sanity. As always, her daughter Felicity backed her up in this, albeit tacitly. In the past, whenever someone had come to live or work in the house to whom Henrietta took one of her obsessive dislikes, it would be Felicity who did the dirty work and told her she must go. I use the feminine because it usually was a cleaning lady on the receiving end, but I foolishly never thought that the same treatment would be meted out by them to one of their own.

This situation, (which was intolerable to me), grew more and more tense the nearer the day of the court case came, for Keith had pressed charges and the matter was viewed as one of some seriousness by the authorities. I was quaking in my boots. I did not want to go to gaol, although the solicitor had told me that that was most unlikely as I was still a minor. I, too, felt the shame of it but I couldn't really accept responsibility because I did not feel at fault. On the contrary, in my wilder moments I almost felt I had done the community a service in decking the loudmouth Keith Thompson – as I discovered his full name was; and I had no regrets.

There was something else, though; a few days after sexual intercourse with Kate Binns I had noticed a soreness in the tip of my penis which would not go away, in fact it got progressively worse and eventually a nasty, viscous, green discharge appeared, which stained my underpants. The head of the penis was also engorged and of an angry dark red colour and hurt like hell. I was shocked when I belatedly acknowledged to myself what would have been obvious even to a disinterested layman very much earlier; that I had the clap, and really ought to do something about it. But what? It was this contemporaneous predicament that occupied my mind far more than the Keith debacle, because I knew that the medical establishment in York was a mafia and that news of any consultation and treatment I might receive would immediately get back to my aunt and grandmother. They would, of course, be appalled – far more so by this further scandal than anything to do with Keith Thompson. Nevertheless, I was terrified into seeking treatment by reading up the relevant sections of medical textbooks in the local library; having identified the symptoms, it was quite obviously not an option to hope that they would just go away, because they wouldn't; and the books left one in no doubt as to the seriousness of the consequences for health if they went unchecked. So, one afternoon with great trepidation I entered the portal of a small, modern, redbrick building at the further end of Musgrave Street; "York District Hospital Department of Genito-Urinary Medicine" was discreetly printed on a plaque on the door. Inside, it was institutional; a long, drab corridor, painted green, with notice boards, on the immediate right hand side of which was the reception area. A pleasant enough woman asked me whether I had ever attended the clinic before. I said I hadn't. She asked my name and I gave a false one, irrationally thinking that all the while she knew my real name anyway and would mirthfully point this out. But she didn't; she simply opened a file, gave me a printed number on a slip of paper and directed me to the waiting room opposite. Here came the next dose of anxiety; would there be anybody in there I recognised, or who recognised me? Mercifully, none of the five men waiting showed any sign of such a thing and nor did I them. They seemed quiet, embarrassed and eager to keep themselves to themselves.

From time to time a man in a white coat would enter and call out a number, at which point one of the seated men would check his slip of paper and follow him out. Eventually, it came to my turn. Nervous as hell, I was politely asked to be seated. The room looked much like an ordinary doctor's consulting room; with one of those tall, rigid couches behind a curtain at the side. Like the receptionist the man in the white coat seemed pleasant enough, if a bit garrulous. After introductions and a few questions, he told me that it really didn't bother him what was the matter with me, but that – contradictorily – the last man he'd seen would be needing "a very thorough investigation indeed". He gave me the impression that he was jaded, possibly been in his job too long or been overlooked for something better; but then he looked at me more closely – he had a broad face with a buttery complexion, was stocky and could not have been more than forty-five – and said, 'You're Doctor Henrietta's grandson, aren't you?'

I was startled. This was exactly what I had wanted to avoid, but I answered yes.

'Marvellous woman, Doctor Henrietta. And her daughter. Great doctors. Done such a lot of good in this town. Salt of the earth, they are...'

I just wanted to get on with the consultation, get the treatment and get out. I was mortified that he should recognise me, that he should want to talk like this.

'...but I'm so sorry,' he continued. 'We all heard about why you had come up here, about your father's untimely death, so deeply sorry. Not that we knew him, of course, but we were sorry. Must be a change for you, that grammar school. How's it going? Are they looking after you all right? I thought you were superb as Hamlet, I really did. Very well done.' Then his tone changed a bit. 'I heard you clobbered that chap Thompson, good for you. He's known as a trouble maker round here. Mind you...,' his tone changed again, 'he had very extensive injuries. Was a day in A&E and then moved to a ward where he spent – let me

209

see – a week was it? – in care. Had to be patched up quite extensively inside. You don't know your own strength, boy. You shouldn't...'

But then he stopped and frowned. This was because he had finally noticed that I had put my head in my hands and was convulsed with tears. To me, it had always been a depressing feature of my by then sixteen years of existence as a male that anyone, be they intimate or stranger, had only, deliberately or otherwise, to pull the right verbal levers in my presence for the floodgates to open. 'Oh dear. I'm most terribly sorry – what's a matter?'

I couldn't say anything.

I think he thought that it was the condition which had brought me to his clinic that was getting me down; because he shut up like a clam and produced a glass of water in a most conciliatory way.

'Here, drink this.' He waited patiently while I collected myself, which I did eventually; then took a sip of water.

'Now what – I'm sorry if I got carried away, I don't need to tell you that everything that goes on in here is in the utmost confidence – what seems to be the trouble?'

Still faltering, I told him; but before he did his examination he wanted to take a detailed history of the events which had caused me to come and see him in the first place; which annoyed me because it seemed to me that all he needed to know was that I had had sex with someone, not the whys and wherefores of it, nor whether I had a "regular partner" as he put it; among other things. He was writing it all down in the newly created file.

Eventually, I was led into another, smaller room where a swab was taken by another man in a white coat, a technician of some kind. I then had to have another wait in the waiting room, where there were now different faces all of whom, again, were mercifully unfamiliar. I started to worry about what might be found in the swab.

At long last my number was recalled and I re-entered the consulting room, where the first man in a white coat was sitting studying a slide under a microscope. I sat down.

'It's as I thought,' he said, without looking up. 'You have gonorrhoea.' He carried on studying the slide.

I did not say anything; what was there for me to say? Anyway, everything was so very worrying that I would probably have choked on my words if I had tried to speak.

'You'll need a shot of penicillin. It won't take a minute. Please go over to the couch, take your trousers and pants down and lie down on your stomach.'

To my surprise, he then started to whistle through his teeth, as if about to carry out a duty which required only a fraction of his attention. But I did as I was told, and heard him washing his hands. A minute or two later I felt a sharp stinging in my left buttock, followed by a curious lingering sensation, as of cold water entering my system. While this was happening, he asked casually, 'Who was she, by the way?' I paused, then said, 'Someone called Kate.'

'Oh, yes?'

Another pause, and he started to whistle again. The needle removed, I heard it thrown into a bucket. He washed his hands again while I pulled my jeans up with alacrity and turned to see him remove a large brown bottle from a cupboard, which he gave me.

'It's an alkaline mixture. You swallow a dessert spoon of it three times a day for a week, all right?'

I nodded, feeling ashamed.

'And then I'll need to see you again, to make sure the gonorrhoea's cleared up, which it should do.'

He was now seated at his desk, and writing something out. I remained standing, clutching the bottle to my chest, vaguely realising that it would be conspicuous in the world outside.

He looked up, as if distracted by my continued presence.

'Run along now, Giles, and make an appointment with reception, there's a good fellow. And Giles…'

Though somewhat resenting this dismissal, I had already started to leave, but turned again and faced him.

'Yes?'

'Don't go with this Kate again, will you? Otherwise you'll get it again.'

'No, no.'

27.
Narrative, 1979

'Here we are...' Giles took a moment to recoil from his thoughts, then followed Matron in.

The room was enormously hot and small. A single bed lay against the far wall; in front of it there was a hard wooden chair. Above the bed on the wall, which was otherwise bare like the others, was a crucifix. The bowed head of Jesus was tilted toward the ruffled pillows below, as if looking over, guarding and protecting whoever might sleep there. Giles was unspeakably shocked by the sight of this, so much so that he had the utmost difficulty in following what the matron was saying.

'Here we are – here we are – you have a visitor, Coral. Quite a surprise for you, eh? I expect you're pleased. It's your stepson Giles. He's come to see you after all these years. I hope you're not – I mean I hope you haven't...' Matron had initially gone into twittering mode, but she wrinkled her nose and looked about the room as if she had noticed a bad smell and wanted to find its source, '...done your business where you shouldn't, have you?'

While she was looking Giles was staring at his stepmother. She had become a very fat woman, with a pale face and vacant eyes, and a shock of hair quite drained of colour. She was wearing some sort of yellowy smock, from which her bulging legs hung like large grainy balloons. She sat in a groaning, stuffy, institutional armchair, furrily upholstered. There was a table at her side which was covered with pills and well-thumbed magazines.

She made no signal that she was remotely interested in what the matron was saying to her, or even that she had heard anything that she had said at all. However, when she noticed that Giles was staring at her she blinked almost imperceptibly. He sat down on the hard chair by the bed and faced her.

Matron, having given up on her search for what she had described as Coral's "business", turned to Giles and said, 'I'll leave you both to it. Just ring the bell when you've finished and I'll be along.' She thought for a moment. 'I'll come along in half an hour anyway, but ring the bell before that if she gets violent.'

With that, and quick as a flash, she removed herself from the room and locked the door behind her, something which startled Giles as she had not told him that she would do this.

He returned his gaze to his stepmother. She was now blinking rapidly at him, her grotesque cheeks wobbling. He continued to stare but did not say anything, not least because her ugliness was exerting a repelled fascination upon him, a sensation which was growing by degrees into that well remembered hatred.

She was such a fright, even more loathsome in appearance than when he last saw her. There was a bloated aspect to her pale face, and the whites of her eyes seemed made of broken china submerged in dirty dishwater. The eyes themselves stood out from her face as if on stalks. Her tongue, which was nearly as colourless as her complexion, protruded from her lips with the effort she was clearly making of trying to say something. Saliva – of the sticky, mucousy sort – hung from each corner. As for her body, it was just a vast shapeless cesspit encased in the slovenly smock which was streaked with dried food, having been slobbered over. She had no discernible breasts or hips.

Giles turned away: he couldn't bear to look any more. Instead, he consulted his watch, conscious that he should finish his work quickly; yet he was filled with horror at the thought that in order to kill her he would have to come into contact with this repulsive human being. Best get it over and done with as quickly as possible, he thought; but before he could make a move she managed to utter, 'Yes? What did you want to say to me?'

The voice was very high and sing-song. Both the sound of it and the words themselves caused him to be startled once more. He realised his limbs were shaking and he wondered whether he could carry out his task. Next, but for a reason which he would not have been able to fathom, he burst into a high-pitched maniacal laughter.

Matron, who had been listening on the other side of the locked door, thought, Oh good. They're getting on well. And she bustled off down the corridor.

Giles carried on laughing, his head flung back, apparently unable to control himself. Coral continued to blink at him expectantly. Suddenly, he turned his laughter off like a tap and lunged at her. He had to force himself to do so. His chair and hers scraped the floor as they came into contact. His intention had been to grab her neck with both hands and squeeze and squeeze until all the breath had come out for ever; but he could not find her neck. She didn't appear to have one, just a rubbery shapeless mass that was both head and torso. The sensation he had was one of dipping his fingers into warm, yielding putty. The revulsion he felt very nearly caused him to desist. But, as before, he could not go back down now. Coral was looking alarmed. Their faces were within inches of each other.

'What did I want to say to you? What did I want to say to you?' he hissed.

'It wasn't my fault,' she murmured in her sing-song voice.

'What wasn't your fault?'

'Your father. He's still alive, you know.'

Now Giles did pull back a bit, with something like disbelief.

'What rubbish. You know perfectly well…'

'He's alive, he's living under a different name, that's all,' she continued breathlessly. 'Somewhere outside Oxford. And he changed his sex. He had a sex change on the National Health. He's now living as a very fat woman on the outskirts of Oxford. He has dark stringy hair. He writes poetry. He calls himself Fleur Adcock. They'll tell you that if you ask.'

'You were at his funeral. You saw his ashes…'

'Yes, but they weren't his. They'll tell you that if you ask. They'll tell you that if you ask,' she repeated herself, the ripples of her body rising and falling with every quick breath she took. It was obvious that she knew she was in danger and was trying to lie her way out of her predicament.

'Your aunt was writing a book about the funeral industry and her cupboard was filled with all sorts of dead people's ashes. It was for her research. She just picked up one of the urns and sent it back to England, but it was the wrong one. It was an old urn, it had a funny colour, I seem to remember.' Coral's voice continued high and sing-song. She gave no hint of that violence about which he had been warned.

Giles' disbelief hardened into contempt.

She carried on, blinking rapidly, and without appearing to realise the extent to which she was contradicting herself, 'I hope he left you some money. I hope he did. I never wanted any of it.'

'You took it all. You and Graham Greene.'

'Who's he?'

'Your father.'

'My father died before I was born. It was most tragic.'

'Was it you who sent a wreath to the funeral with yours and Damien's names spelt backwards on it?'

'Yes.'

'Why did you do that?'

'That's what we said, that if ever one of us died without the other, we'd send a wreath with the names backwards.'

Giles again consulted his watch. He calculated that he had about twenty minutes left before Matron returned. He'd had enough of this woman's ramblings anyway and wanted to finish her off. He took the crucifix from the wall and examined it carefully, rolling it about in his hands. It was heavy enough to be used as a club and its edges were really quite sharp. Its maker – nor anybody else who might have had a use for it, for that matter – would scarcely have contemplated that it could be used as a weapon. Yet that is just what he was contemplating now. He looked thoughtfully at his stepmother. Coral clearly had divined the direction of his thoughts because she had got to her feet – if such they could be called – and was facing him, her body wobbling like a blancmange. They stared at each other for a few moments, her popping eyes caught as a rabbit's in a car's headlights. Giles' own eyes had an evil glint in them.

'No, no... ' she muttered, now looking toward the door.

'Yes... ' he hissed.

He started to thwack the crucifix on the palm of his left hand in preparation. Coral's gargantuan frame wobbled all the more as she tried to effect an exit from the room. She had started to make a strange whinnying noise. To Giles' surprise she did not make for the alarm bell but for the door itself, which she could not have noticed had been locked. Out of disgust he let her pass. He had decided that when it came to it he wanted to have as little physical contact with her as possible. Even so, he detected a nauseating smell emanating from her body, a sort of stale sweetness that made him want to chunder. Killing her would be the hardest thing he ever did. Nevertheless, he clubbed her from behind just as she was frantically scrabbling at the door. In her last few moments she finally realised it was locked and had started to scratch at its wood pitiably, as if she thought that by that means she could open it.

The first blow caught her on the back of her head, but it appeared to have no effect. It did not stop her scrabbling, although a low, whinnying moan came from somewhere within the heap of her body, which sounded like the wind that blows beyond the window panes when a storm is brewing. Giles struck again and again, in a frenzy, wherever he could; most of the hits were insubstantial because they landed on her ample shoulders. But his frenzy continued: at that moment he was not responsible for his actions. He grabbed her hair with his left hand – how disgusting it was; thick, greasy, matted stuff which in the ensuing struggle came close to entering his own mouth. By means of this he pulled her head back so that her ghastly blob of a face was facing his, albeit upside down. The crucifix in his right hand, he rammed and rammed its base into her face. Gradually, she fell silent. He would not stop; and eventually her face became a bloody mash, an unrecognisable thing. He could tell that she was losing consciousness and indeed life. She grew limp and, falling against him, he had to support her. It was only then that he realised how heavy she was. He let her slump to the floor, her body slithering against the door. He rammed the crucifix into her mouth and pressed as hard as he could, so that it went in further and further. He kept it like that, twisting the thing every once in a while. She started to gurgle. There was an imploring look in her eyes as they met his; yet there was nothing about her now that was human. He removed the crucifix and repeatedly stamped on her face, again as hard as he could. To his amazement, she found her voice and started to beg for mercy. Would this woman never die? He stamped again and again. Finally, she went still and said no more. But though unconscious, he could see that she was still breathing. Giles' frenzy was turning to panic. He simply had to kill her, but she wouldn't die. He knew his time was running out. He dropped the crucifix and plunged his hands into the bloodied mass of her face, searching for her neck. It must be somewhere. He was guided by what remained of her features, in particular the slobbering mouth and lolling tongue, which were just discernible. She wasn't resisting at all. But those eyes on stalks had become very bright and were staring at him. He couldn't bear to look at them and that made his task more difficult. Finally though, amid the rubble of her face and smock he came upon that sensation of warm yielding putty that told him he had reached flesh, and he put his hands around its mass as far as they would go in order to gain the best purchase. Then he squeezed with all his might and maintained the pressure for second after agonising second, each of which appeared to last a lifetime. Minutes passed before he was nearly there. He looked at her to see what effect he was having; and to his satisfaction her eyes now had a lifelessness about them, as if turning to glass. Her tongue and mouth were no longer moving at all; and Giles thought that if he could only maintain his grip for a minute or two longer, the deed would be done. He managed it. But when he was sure she was dead he heard a key in the lock and he knew that within a moment or two Matron would be opening the door.

He let go of Coral and, grabbing the crucifix from the floor, leapt back. He faced the door and crouched with his weapon, ready to attack. The door was unlocked and opened but its movement was partially blocked by Coral's corpse.

After a moment, Matron trilled, 'Is everything all right in there?' Giles did not answer.

Matron pushed and pushed, but the door would not budge any further and now she shouted, 'What is happening in there?' Giles knew that his only exit was by the door, so there would have to be a confrontation. Matron would have to get hurt. So he shouted, 'Hang on a second, will you?'

Matron was seriously concerned but at the moment she felt powerless. Giles dropped the crucifix once more and grabbed the dead Coral by her flabby ankles and dragged her away from the door. No sooner had he done this than Matron burst in; but Giles was ready for her: he now whacked her across the face with the crucifix. His action dumbfounded her; so, quick as he could he shoved her aside and ran through the doorway into the corridor. He sprinted back the way they had originally come, but when he got to the ragged frame of bricks where the hole in the wall was he simply jumped through it, hoping for the best.

Meanwhile, Matron regained her senses and saw at once that a serious assault had been perpetrated upon someone in her care, as she had originally suspected. Nevertheless, she thought she'd stay put for a few minutes while she nursed the wound to the side of her face where the crucifix had connected. As she did so, it was with mounting horror that she realised she was staring at the bloodied, bloated corpse of Coral Greene.

Giles' fall from the building was partially broken by a clump of tangled trees and bushes at the bottom. Nevertheless, he did hurt himself: his right leg was quite numb and he was surprised to discover that he could still run, which he did with a limping motion. He made

217

straight for the lake and jumped into it, displacing a gaggle of squawking Canadian geese.

The water was shallow and icily cold, but it got deeper as he waded toward the middle. When he reached it he was able wholly to submerge himself by kneeling on the bottom and tucking his head into his chest. He wanted to do this not only in order to hide but also to remove from his skin, clothes and hair as much of Coral's blood and other bodily fluids as possible. This would give him a fractionally better chance of avoiding unwanted attention when – as inevitably he must – he tried to return home; but also he had reached such a pitch of loathing at the very thought of any of Coral's remains being on his person that he must at all costs get rid of them. So, he rubbed himself frenetically – his clothes, his hair, all over; and he writhed and splashed around in that icy water, not for one moment caring whether he would be seen or not.

After a few minutes he waded out of the lake on the far side and reached a stretch of grass that ended in tall hedgerows which separated the grounds of the mental hospital from the main road. No one was about, but he dared not look back. He was shivering from the wet but he knew he must make a decision now whether to stay and hide somewhere or simply run back to the railway station. Both alternatives presented dangers but on balance he thought he'd wait till night because the state of his appearance would attract too much attention in daytime. He determined to walk all the way back to Brunswick Gardens when night came, which was going to be an arduous thing to do, not least because he had no idea of the way, but at least it meant that he could keep in the shadows and avoid any unwanted stares from other passengers on the tube or train.

It had further occurred to him that the authorities would probably expect the murderer to have fled the scene altogether, so if he hung around and hid somewhere he would be safer – at least so he reasoned; that might indeed be the case provided he hadn't already been spotted and his movements followed by someone in the building, but the nursing home was quite far away and, anyway, he had to take the chance. Already he could hear sirens and so he must act now; accordingly he ran as fast as he could to the hedgerow and simply forced his way into it, suffering numerous scratches in the process. Inside, the hedgerow was far deeper than he had thought and what was more, it was like a little forest to itself: in some places he could move, in others he couldn't. It was also tall, so tall that he knew he could remain unseen within it from the outside, even when standing. At the same time the ground beneath his feet was quite uneven; its surface of earth, pebbles, twigs and whatnot dipped and rose quite arbitrarily, in rough mounds and deep furrows. If he squatted in one of the furrows he could almost be hidden from view entirely. He would be as all right here as anywhere else.

As he dug with his hands to make one of the furrows even deeper he heard the sirens pass by him, but at some distance. Curiously, that did not frighten him, and he did not stop digging for one moment. A strange but powerful instinct of self-concealment had taken over. When his hands grew tired he found an old branch and dug with that. He made a mental note not even to try and peep and see what if anything was happening beyond the hedgerow, fearing superstitiously that to do so might itself somehow cause his discovery – the very thing he wished to avoid.

When he'd dug the furrow to a depth he judged to be sufficient he sat in it and waited, his arms crossed around his knees. It was still daytime, the late afternoon. His wet clothes clung uncomfortably to his body, so he took them off and waved them around as best he could among the branches in order to dry them; but it did not do much good. He put them on again and started to wonder whether he would be discovered. It was almost as a matter of intellectual curiosity that he thought about it. It would be sad though if he were, because it would mean a premature end to what he had set out to do. He thought it unlikely that he would be able to escape from prison and finish what he had begun.

He heard and saw nothing, however, no footsteps coming towards him, no voices, no torchlights as it grew dark; not even any flashing blue lights of police cars or ambulances. But later, when it had got quite dark, he did hear the chop-chop-chop of a helicopter flying directly overhead, and he saw its powerful searchlight sweeping the grounds. He made himself as small as possible in his furrow and put his arms over his head. His clothes were dark. He remained absolutely still until the chopper lost interest and veered away towards another assignment. Now was the moment. He stood up and pushed his way through the hedgerow towards the road and came across a high railing which he climbed, letting himself fall as gently as possible on to the pavement below in order to minimise any noise. The road was ill-lit but he'd made sure there were no pedestrians or cars around before he jumped.

When he hit the concrete he felt a stabbing pain in the leg which had already been compromised by his leap from the building, but on testing it seemed to work well enough. Having gathered himself up he could not resist a look in the direction in which he assumed the entrance to Kane House to be, and sure enough he saw a police car stationed there, its interior lit up and its lights flashing. A couple of policemen, also clearly visible, were loitering by it, at a distance of about three hundred yards. They did not see or hear Giles. Quickly, he started to walk in the opposite direction, keeping as close to the railing as possible.

28.
Giles Jones' Diary

I returned to Henrietta's as quickly as possible, concealing the bottle of alkaline mixture in my jacket, and making sure to hide it in my bedroom when I arrived; but as the days passed it became increasingly obvious that she and Felicity had been informed of my condition, and I was met with a stony stare in the hall or wherever I happened to pass by one or other of them. I avoided the drawing room, dining room, Aga room or indeed any part of the house where they might be, and kidded myself that I was doing them a favour by keeping out of their way so much, since I reckoned it would cause them great embarrassment to have to confront me face to face. But even in so large a house it was impossible not to have some contact and not to be aware of a perpetually thunderous atmosphere which hung like a heavy curtain between them and me: a possibly naïve trust had been betrayed and communication had been quite cut off.

It was therefore a relief, to be given the all clear the following week by the doctor at the clinic and to have made my mind up in the meantime to get out of York and go to London. My academic ability had not been improved by changing schools and it was obvious to me that I would not make university, so why hang around? The set-up at my grandmother's – and, indeed, everything else – was just not working and, most of all, I feared the imminent court case, this time because of the embarrassment it would cause me, not anyone else. I figured that if I didn't turn up at the magistrates' court the matter would be forgotten and eventually dropped, or even if it were not, the police would not be able to find me.

So, very early one morning before anyone else was awake I left my grandmother's and went on foot to the railway station on the other side of town – a long, ghostly walk in the deserted blue dawn in which I had the strange sensation that my dead father was accompanying me. I could almost hear his footsteps and see his profile at my side but little realised that this was the beginning of a haunting which would last all my life, until I entered my own grave, wherever and whenever that might be.

I had few possessions, very little money and, worst of all, no contacts. Another lack; I had no ideas, save that I would have to get a job and a roof over my head straight away. But, curiously, I was not apprehensive about all this, just light-headed; and in luck, because after a few days' sleeping rough I had both – a b&b in King's Cross and, having signed on to something called Industrial Overload, guaranteed daily work albeit menial and on low pay. A lot of it consisted in going up to Oxford Street and helping to move racks of garments from the interiors of vans to the interiors of shops. It was frustrating because nobody ever seemed to be in charge, with the result that effort was duplicated and quite often the rags – for such they were – were left higgledy-piggledy lying around and not accounted for. But that was not my problem and I was simply happy to collect the cheque that was made out to me at the end of the week.

Then another piece of luck: a foreign man in one of the shops asked me whether I would care to be a sales assistant there. As the money was double I jumped at it, but the work itself proved even more boring and frustrating than before: if you look inside a fashion shop you may think that everything is happening, but it isn't. There were many long hours when nobody came in and I started to wonder how on earth the place could make a profit; but, again, that was not my problem. With what I'd saved I was able to put a deposit on a bedsitter, the first of many I was to live in over the next ten years – I would simply move to another if I felt restless enough, and I never acquired so many possessions as would make it a difficult task. I had no desire to settle down, or even make friends; I suppose I had become what they call "a loner".

However, things did take off when I got a job as a wine waiter in a popular, fashionable restaurant in Mayfair. It was so buzzy and alive all the time. We had to wear green tops and dark trousers, or black dresses for the girls, and we were worked like crazy although it was terrific fun whizzing up and down the staircase, to the bar and to the tables, where we deposited the drinks. Loud, repetitive disco music played constantly. Quite often one or other of us would faint from the sheer adrenalin rush and excitement of it – particularly as, as often happened, the young person concerned had a daytime job as well – and he or she would be given a brandy and sent home.

There was another bonus; the hours suited me far more than the bleariness of a nine to five, I realised and, perhaps I should have realised this sooner, given the nights I had spent looning around at Selwyn Mauberley College; but there it was: I was happy; except that a little thing nagged: I had no girlfriend; or rather, to be honest, I had nobody to have sex with. Just a word about this; although I did not appreciate the fact, I had become what is called a hypochondriac, at the back of my mind there had been for a long time the conviction that the Mandrax I had abused on a daily basis had caused me irreparable brain damage (how else could I rationalise to myself the fact that I could not achieve the academic grades I wanted)? I had stopped taking them, of course (and now would certainly never get another prescription from Aunt Felicity, who together with Henrietta I had effectively abandoned, having no wish ever again to communicate with them); but the damage had been done, I was quite certain of that. Added to which, the episode of gonorrhoea had produced in me a morbid and overpowering reluctance to have any sexual contact with anyone at all. It went further: in my worst moments I was able to convince myself that I had been infected with a very special type of the germ, which had not only produced the original symptoms but was able, once there had been an apparent cure, to reproduce itself; in other words, that I was permanently infected and that at any moment hideous abscesses would start to form in my loins.

Naturally, I shrunk from the possibility of passing this on to anyone else; but it was mainly the sheer embarrassment of being discovered to have this condition which prevented me from undergoing any sexual relations. I knew all this was highly irrational, but I could not help it. So I didn't dare take up with any girl, which was a pity because certainly at the restaurant there were plenty of pretty ones who in one way or another let it be known that they would be interested. I think the furthest I got was to suggest dinner to one of them – an exceptionally striking, beautiful and curvy brunette; to which she had said that, 'that would be nice'; but when I did not follow this up she must have thought that I was odd, or just "queer", as it was then called. None of the men got a look in either, since those of them who might have been that way inclined were given no reason by me to suggest that I was too; because I wasn't. What a conundrum – it meant that for very neurotic reasons I was forced to endure ongoing sexual abstinence at a time of one's life when, as I could see all around me, others of my own age were at it like rabbits. It also meant that what had started as a dangerous dualism in my personality now verged on schizophrenia, because I was totally different on my own to when I was with others at work. I've no idea how they saw me – fey, perhaps – but they certainly did not see the darkness, self-obsession and sheer loneliness of that morbid individual in his bedsitter.

One evening I was at the restaurant, which was packed as usual, when I noticed a girl I had seen before but couldn't think where. She was only young like me but she was sitting with three middle-aged men in suits at a table by the heavily curtained window at the far end. She was very glamorous but all four seemed bored with each other's company and their lips were not moving, which would have been the only evidence of speech available in this din and at this distance. Nor were they making any effort at eye contact. They were neglecting their food and wine and one wondered why they were there at all; they stood out not just because of her appearance but also because, incongruously, they were not taking part in the bustle and enjoyment of the place.

Their untouched glasses did not need filling but I approached anyway with the excuse of seeing whether they did, my real reason being that I wanted to get nearer to her and, to my satisfaction, when I was standing over them she looked up and gave me a beaming smile which I shall never forget; but the men just continued to look away and apparently couldn't have cared less when she started to talk to me. She said that she remembered me from my working in a fashion store she had visited with a boyfriend. We talked or rather shouted a bit more, and the upshot was – to my surprise, for it had never happened before and could not have been expected to happen, that a member of staff get off with a customer – that we arranged to meet outside at the end of my shift. I was concerned that the men she was with might have something to say about this but they did not. In fact, they didn't even look as if they had been listening. Later on I saw them leave but when it came to my turn I saw her waiting for me in a taxi by the side of the kerb. The men had gone. I did not know what to do with my bicycle which I used to get to and from work; until to my further surprise I found that it fitted into the back of the cab.

We travelled to Cornwall Gardens off the Gloucester Road, where she shared a top floor flat with others. It was a cavernous, empty tip with a strong but stale, sweetish smell in the air. There was nobody else around and we just talked, she on a dilapidated, sunken sofa and me on an equally dilapidated armchair which creaked whenever I moved. I was struck by how different she was from her shabby surroundings, although she did not seem to care or even notice the contrast, and I do not remember much of what was said except that she chain-smoked and her body seemed slimmer in its shimmering white gown than before. She had a habit of continually holding the cigarette up to her lips and taking short gasps, so that her hand partially covered her face, which in any case was also partially covered by her long, straight hair whenever she turned to use the ashtray at her side, which had already been horribly full of stubs before she started. It did not seem to occur to her to empty it, not that there appeared to be anywhere where she could have done so. I was nervous, and did most of the listening. I didn't ask her who were the men she had been with, nor why they had not been communicating or why they had parted company at the end of the evening. She didn't say anything about them either, so that, without an explanation, an initially unreal if arresting situation in the restaurant had given way to another, but different, kind of unreality, that of me and her talking as strangers in the near darkness of this cavernous room. It was becoming more and more dream-like.

I was nervous because of that, and because our present situation seemed to cry out for me as a man to make the first move; yet as I have told you I was crippled in that regard and could not leave the hang-ups I had acquired in my bedsitter behind. It was becoming embarrassing, though she was displaying remarkable patience – maybe she had another agenda? She just kept on talking away – she had a slight lisp, which accentuated her sing-song cockney accent – and smoking. Suddenly there was a bang in the hallway where the flat door was and she looked up and behind her, to my disappointment with that beaming smile she had given me earlier; and in walked a tall, shabbily dressed young man with a ponytail and a very frightening-looking Alsatian dog, which at first eyed me suspiciously but then went to a corner and lay down, his head over his paws. The man gave me a steely look but otherwise there were no introductions; he turned to the girl and she asked him, 'Have you got any stuff?'

'Yeah.'

He fiddled with something in his pocket.

'Let's have it.'

He sat down next to her and started to roll a joint. While she watched she simpered at him and primped her hair, as if trying to make herself as attractive as possible, her cigarette quite forgotten. He remained intent on what he was doing.

The joint made, he lit it, inhaled briefly then immediately passed it to her, with true chivalry. She grabbed the thing with both hands and cupped it to her lips and dragged as much of the smoke into her lungs as she possibly could, keeping it there before she exhaled as a matter of relief. She repeated this activity several times before returning the joint to the man, who did likewise. The dingy room was now filled with their exhalations and a far fresher, more intense form of that sweetish smell I had noticed on arriving. The dog had gone to sleep.

When he had had enough to his immediate satisfaction, the man looked at me and asked, 'Want some?'

I had never smoked marijuana before, which was the reason why I answered, 'Yes.'

He passed it to me and I inhaled deeply several times, just as they had. Meanwhile, he was already rolling another joint, from a tin he had on his lap.

The girl's eyes were closed and she was smiling to herself in a self-absorbed way. We carried on taking it in turns to smoke the newly made joints in silence. The girl was in a world of her own and the man was not the chatty type, and anyway conversation would have seemed superfluous. As for me, I had begun to feel rather strange. But this feeling quickly turned to terror as I realised my heart was racing and my unknown companions had turned into wolves. They looked far worse than the dog quietly sleeping in the corner, though not unlike him. A stroboscopic effect was taking place in my mind. Snatches of vision were interspersed with black unconsciousness. The wolves were pointing guns at me and I was hiding from them by kneeling behind the armchair I had been sitting in. But at the same time I was clinging on to its back because I thought some frightful power would snatch me out of the world altogether. As it was, my mind had left my body and I was watching the scene below from the ceiling. I could see myself clinging on to the back of the armchair for dear life. I was screaming.

I woke up in a small room that I had never seen before, on a single bed which stank of urine. I was fully clothed. I had no idea where I was and felt profoundly sick. Daylight was coming through a grimy window and I could see a few tacky brown bits of furniture on a soiled carpet. Various stains with ugly shapes covered a closed door. When I tried to move I felt as if dead weights on my arms and legs were preventing me. I had to struggle to get off the bed, but immediately collapsed on to the floor, where I remained for several minutes, making a great effort to collect myself. From somewhere deep down an urge was telling me that if I did not succeed, I would be dead. From the state of my jeans I could tell that the stench of urine from the bed had been caused by me. In any case I needed a shit.

Eventually, I managed to get to my feet but had to lean on to the bedstead for support. I felt so weak that the slightest movement seemed an impossibility; and my head was buzzing. Another urge told me to cry out for help, but somehow I did not think this would be a good idea. I could only crawl to the door and open it, having to raise my hand to the knob, and when I did it was apparent to me that I was still in the flat where I had smoked marijuana with the man and the girl. It was quite obviously a squat, and looked even worse in daylight than it had at night. A long corridor led to the room where we had been sitting. There were other doors; mercifully, I recognised one as being the front door. The place seemed deserted. My only desire was to get out as soon as possible and return to my own bedsitter, which I did, but I have no recollection how.

It was a day or two later that I realised I had left my bicycle behind, but that was the least of my worries. For I had been out for the count for the best part of two days and of course I lost my job. Even after that, for many months I felt dizzy and unsteady on my feet, and could never get to sleep without at first seeing a gun pointed at my head. The episode could not, as a matter of wishful thinking, be dismissed as if it had never happened, although it remained unreal and I never saw the girl or the man again. On the contrary, it came to form another link in the chain of my mental undoing.

29.
Narrative, 1979

The walk back to Brunswick Gardens took Giles Jones many hours, made longer by the fact that he lost his way several times and became increasingly exhausted. His damp clothes clung to him with unnerving, irritating persistence, particularly as he was conscious that, even in the darkness, he should not draw attention to himself. But his ordeal went without any incident of that kind; and when finally he locked himself into his bedsitter he pulled off his clothes, leaving them on the floor where they fell. He threw himself onto his bed. He slept for twelve hours. It was only when he awoke that two things occurred to him. First, that he would have to hurry if he were to be in time for work – showered, shaved and suited, as it was now past six in the evening. And second, that it would be dangerous for him to continue to live where he did, for surely in time the police would catch up with him, now that they must know the identity of Coral Greene's killer.

True, he had given a false address, and so far as he knew nobody who mattered knew that he worked in a casino in Huffington Street, but he had no doubt that the police had their methods. He did not think of what he had done to Coral at all; he had got used to killing and would have said that it must have been another person who did it, since by now as a matter of survival he had dissociated himself from his actions; which is not to say that he would not have taken pride in them if reminded. Quite simply he had other things to think about, but was glad at least that his leg, which had hurt so much the night before, now seemed to be very much better. For the time being, he would have to get himself ready for work. But no, he thought again: perhaps he shouldn't turn up for work at all. Do a bunk now while he had the time. Get out of this place; disappear, go somewhere, but where? He had nowhere to go and very little money with which to start a new life.

He thought of Jessica Wu, the girl with whom he had become friends at the casino. He thought of her more and more. And in his indecision another thought came to him: that his priority was to finish the job he had started and that meant killing the last offender, Graham Greene. Which was best to do that, stay with his present life or get the hell out of it? The question required careful thought, but on balance he came to the conclusion that an escape to another life, even if it could be achieved, would be too much of a distraction, and that in order to try to achieve his aim he would simply have to run the risk of premature capture by remaining as he was.

At work he made a mental note of seeking Jessica Wu out and later that night their paths crossed on the grand staircase that led from reception to the gaming room. She was coming down and he was going up; as they passed each other he stopped and quipped, 'It's bad luck passing each other on the staircase!'

She stopped too, and smiled, but did not appear to understand what he was talking about.

'Look, Jessica, I have a favour to ask of you.'

She turned wary, but waited for what he had to say. She liked him but she was conscious that employees were not supposed to conduct private business while at work. She looked around in case any of the managers were within earshot.

'Can I stay with you for a while?'

'Why you wan do that?'

He told her the first thing that came into his head, that the ceiling of his bedsitter had fallen in and the place was uninhabitable until the landlord fixed it.

'You got nowhere else?'

'Well, no, not really, you see…'

'I think about,' she said, but she was stalling. She did not want him to think that she was always that accommodating.

'I go now.'

She walked on.

'I'll catch up with you later!' he shouted after her.

At the end of his shift Giles Jones waited for her at the corner of the street, which was where they usually met if they had arranged to do so after work, but he felt conspicuous and for the first time since getting out of bed the day before, his mind dwelt upon the possibility of being apprehended. So he withdrew as much as possible into the shadows, and called out to her in a hoarse stage whisper as she passed. She was startled.

'Why you hide like that?'

He looked at her.

'Is something wrong?'

'No.'

But the tone of his voice was unconvincing.

'Tell me.'

Why not, he thought.

'Let me stay with you and I will.'

'You in trouble?'

Characteristically, she looked around – almost as if she were being sucked in to whatever it was.

'No.'

But it was unconvincing.

It was not that Giles Jones felt the slightest remorse for what he had done, or guilt about what he still planned to do, but some guard had dropped in his mind, because it was difficult not to tell the truth to someone in whom he had placed an instinctive trust. The more important point, however, was that he had come to realise that he would need help if he were to evade capture.

Something was going on in Jessica Wu's mind too.

'You come to my home now,' she said. 'You pick up your things later.'

It was a long journey on the night bus and on foot to the little rented flat in Catford that was Jessica Wu's home. As he had expected, it was as neat as a pin but rather too cramped and crowded. A row of miniature cactuses adorned the window sill above the kitchen sink. The enamel of the bath was cracked in several places, and the bedroom had just one window which looked onto a brick wall that was only a few feet away. But she'd cheered it up with bright colours and picturesque ornaments, some of which had a decidedly Spanish flavour. There was no alcohol.

He sat on a pouffe in the dark little sitting room while she made coffee in the kitchen next door. He felt uneasy because he knew that there wasn't much else for them to do except talk; and what was he going to say? Being offered accommodation warranted a certain amount of self-explaining, but somehow he felt out of his depth with her and that, he thought, was dangerous. Nevertheless, in the course of the next few hours he told her everything. At first she was incredulous and told him to be serious, but when he persisted she began to look worried and silently asked herself if she had not invited a madman into her home.

Also, she gave thought to her position in this country, and whether by associating with this man she had not irrevocably destroyed her chances of staying here. But finally, and perhaps despite herself, she felt that she was being drawn into this elaborately murderous tale of privation and revenge. She quite understood how he felt. This was particularly so as Giles continued to speak with a troubled intensity that occasionally frightened her. She had started to yawn but it was an open question whether this physiological response was down to fatigue or anxiety.

Even the monomaniacal Giles Jones noticed this and asked, 'You all right?'

'I okay. I tired. I go to bed, I think.'

'Yes, of course.'

In a humourless sort of way Giles Jones quite understood that his friend would need time in which to digest what he had told her.

'You have sofa.'

'All right.'

This was good of Giles Jones, to have fallen in so quickly with Jessica Wu's directions.

She got to her feet in a rather embarrassed manner and went to the door, but thought better of it and returned in his direction; whereupon she stooped and, taking his head in her hands, kissed him passionately on the lips. He let her do this but was not responsive – that old feeling came upon him: that he was now made of clay, that he was brittle and could not behave as he should with girls. This did not deter her. She withdrew and said quietly, 'I see you later. I maybe sleep long time.'

'Yes.'

He watched her go. He did not hear her prepare for bed. Instead he tried to make himself comfortable on the sofa and clear his mind of all that had happened recently. Unlike before, he saw himself as the cause of what he had done, because simply to have talked about it at such length – as he had to Jessica Wu – made such clarity inescapable. However, another part of his mind wished to dismiss any growing self-acknowledgement of his responsibility. Quite simply, he wished to go to sleep. But it was no good.

He was as tense as an athlete on a starting block, and parts of his body were aching painfully. He thought of Jessica next door and wondered whether she would be annoyed if he joined her. He didn't think so, but it would probably mean waking her. Also, did he want to make that commitment? For that is what it would mean if he made that move. He couldn't decide – which further mental hiatus only compounded his general discomfiture. But suddenly he was aware of the door opening and next could clearly see the form of Jessica Wu on the threshold. This surprised and alarmed him but he waited. An age seemed to pass. Finally, she said, 'I have thought. You come.'

Now it was she who was waiting.

He said nothing, but slowly and with a great sense of weariness he left the sofa and followed her into the bedroom, where he undressed and got under the duvet beside her. They did nothing but hug each other close for a long while.

It was well into the afternoon when they awoke; when they did they were a bit shy of each other. Without speaking, she got out of bed and went into the kitchen. After a moment or two he followed. She was making yet more coffee. He got the impression that that was all she lived on. He joined her in a cup, but they remained silent.

Eventually, she asked, 'What you do now?'

This startled him: he really hadn't been thinking about it at all.

'I – er – don't know,' he said. 'I suppose I'll have to go back to my flat and get some things.'

'You going work?'

'I suppose so. I hadn't thought about it.'

'You ring in sick?'

Giles grinned. To do that would be as good as losing his job.

'No, Jessica, I no ring in sick.'

She did not take offence.

She said, 'I go to work later. I give you key. You come and go.'

'Thanks.'

Why was this girl being so nice to him?

And sexy too: her thin nightdress accentuated her figure, which was strangely voluptuous. Her black hair was lustrous, her features nimble. When she leant across the table to get more coffee her nipples and the globes of her breasts were clearly visible.

'I get dressed now.'

'Yes.'

Giles had left his clothes strewn around the sofa. He put them on with some distaste as he was fastidious and would have preferred clean ones. His suit was fetid and crumpled. He did, however, think that he

232

could go to work as he was; Sandy might notice, but no one else would. But what was he to do in the meantime? He had several hours to kill. He did not know what to do. Then he thought of his diary.

Next door Jessica Wu was pondering the situation she had brought upon herself while she dressed and made up. She liked him, he was quite dishy, but he was cold, as she had discovered. Also, now that it was the day after she had to re-examine what he had told her and ask herself whether it could be true. If it was not, then he was a weird sort of boastful liar, and which was worse – that or being a murderer? She was frowning but she was not fearful for her own safety. She felt she could control him – not in a bad way but so that he would be better. She had been lonely since she found this flat and moved in. Except for Giles she hadn't been able to make any friends at work; and there was no one round here.

She was about to leave her bedroom when she remembered that she had offered him a spare key. She flinched – had that been a wise thing to do? She could always pretend to have forgotten that she had made the offer but if he reminded her – well, that could be awkward. Anyway, she'd put her trust in him, so that was that. She rummaged around in the top of the cupboard where she kept the spare set. Then she thought he must have been lying when he told her that the ceiling of his bedsitter had fallen in, which had not occurred to her despite what he had told her the night before. He had not told her that he still had one more to go, so to speak, so she assumed his killing spree was finished and now he simply needed somewhere to hide. Would he have done the same for her? It was an intriguing question and she thought the answer was yes; but then, she was no murderer.

To her surprise Giles was nowhere to be seen when she entered the living room. She called out but soon it became obvious that he had left the flat. She frowned again. She had not heard him go, he must have done so quite stealthily. Put simply, she was offended that he had not said goodbye first. She herself left the flat in order to do some shopping in the High Street, but her preoccupation was with this strange man, and she wondered whether she would see him at work that evening.

When she reached the High Street all thoughts of Giles Jones were immediately replaced by the emotional armour she always had to wear there. Her ethnicity made her an object of distaste to the locals, a fact which when she had first moved to Catford she had found difficult to believe. But it was true, she had gradually realised, as she was habitually shunned or queue-barged in the shops or simply frowned at by passers-by. The flip side was that some men – labourers and the like – leered and wolf whistled at her but in a way they never would with a white girl. It was distressing and she couldn't say that she had ever got used to it; she was just determined to ignore it as much as possible, that's all. Ideally, she would have moved to a more cosmopolitan neighbourhood but she just didn't have the money. Today it was particularly bad, she didn't know why.

Giles was already on his way back to West London. When he reached the corner of Brunswick Gardens he slowed down and pressed himself against the railings of the houses as he moved, like a fox. He turned the corner and peered with extreme caution in the direction of number 59. He could see no police cars or policemen but his view was partially obscured by other parked cars and pedestrians, so he continued with care, trying successfully, as he mistakenly thought, to act as nonchalantly as possible. In actual fact his heart was pounding with fear and he felt sick. There was a sort of unreality to his emotions when he approached his flat front door and he came to the conclusion that for the moment at least the authorities had not caught up with him.

Once inside, he pulled his clothes off and went and showered and shaved in the bathroom down the corridor. Next he pulled on a jersey and jeans and combed his hair. His diary caught his eye. Its papers were lying in a heap upon his desk and it was not finished yet. He thought that there was no use hiding it for they would find it anyway if they came here, wherever it was. Besides, what did it show but the background of a troubled man?

Sunlight was streaming through the window on to the scattered pages. He'd written on them with the black ink he always used, by means of the fancy fountain pen he'd once filched from a large department store, just to see whether he could get away with a bit of shoplifting. It too lay on the table but he found that he was mostly staring at the pages which were covered with black squiggles; they didn't seem to be handwriting at all, and certainly did not appear to have anything to do with him. He was shocked: it was like looking into a mirror but seeing no recognisable reflection. But gradually he saw the face of his long dead father there, as it were swimming on the surface; and he thought of that manuscript his father had shown him all those years ago, of which he had been able to make neither head nor tail. The

234

weird hieroglyphics that had adorned its margins rose up in his mind too: they had been the work of a madman, but who was the madder – himself or his father? Damien had been no murderer, so far as he knew; but surely – surely – without him Giles would not have taken the path that he had? It was to avenge him. That's right, he had to remind himself – that was why he was killing all these people. Yet he realised now that that was not so. The real reason for his actions was because his past had filled him with hatred; and he was nothing without his hatred – quite simply nothing.

With an oddly furtive movement and a small squawk of bewilderment he swept the pages of his diary off the table top so that they scattered on the floor.

30.
Giles Jones' Diary

There is no use giving a blow-by-blow account of the following years I spent in London, for each blow was like the one before and the one after, so that there came to be a formlessness, almost a void, in my history which led me to question the point of everything, for nothing ever changed. By my late twenties I had nothing to show for my existence except a background string of bedsitters, dead-end jobs and an ever-deepening hollow where a soul should have been. That I might have had a soul I did not question; but this hollow was both inside and outside my being, the self being something I clung on to because it was the only thing I had. As for the rest – the outside world, even my own body – it was meaningless.

Needless to say, I remained very much a loner and even the possibility of emotional contact with others, the desire for which had always been fraught with fear, became out of the question; until, that is, the casino and Jessica Wu came along. As to the former, I got the job through the classified ads of the Evening Standard, their "situations vacant" columns having always stood me in good stead. (Sooner or later it would be boredom or the sack or both which led me to consult the newspaper again). I remember the interview very well – it's not that long ago; it took place in a tiny room at the top of a building that contained many small black and white TV screens which showed the comings and goings in many of the other rooms, something I had not seen before. I was told by the fat Frenchman who was the manager of the Huffington that a previous candidate had turned the job down because "the money was not right enough for her". I was nonplussed by this; but at that stage certainly did not realise that with the addition of tips the annual payment would effectively be twelve thousand pounds, a good deal of money. The manager, perhaps, didn't realise the extent of the tips either, otherwise he might have set the basic salary of four thousand pounds at something smaller. Later, I was told by Marlene that Sandy had wanted to "break me in for a while", as he put it; in other words to have withheld from me a share of the tips so that there would be all the more for him and the others, but that she and Pete would not have any of this idea, which was very big of them.

I was given a chit to take with me to Cecil Gee in Oxford Street, where for free I was kitted out with the dinner suit I have told you about, the most comfortable piece of clothing I have ever worn. And I took to the job like a duck to water, because of my night owl nature and because of the glamour, though I suppose others might have found the latter tawdry. Plus, it was a world I had never experienced before.

As for Jessica Wu, well, I flattered myself that she was a friend. She came to my bedsitter a few times, and we would occasionally eat out after work. I fancied her, of course, but somehow I couldn't get near her in that way. I think she was puzzled by this, but accepted me as an oddball who needed help. She didn't seem to mind that our relationship, such as it was, was not normal; and she herself had the characteristics and the circumstances of an outsider. Perhaps she also was flattered that a man could take an interest in her that was not purely sexual, a man who, besides, was a native of the country in which she was living. I suppose after a while one stops asking questions about a relationship which seems to work; but when I got the phone call from Mort Sloane, and certainly afterwards, I needed her more. In truth it took me a while to realise that I had needed her at all, and it never occurred to me to ask myself whether she had the slightest need of me. To this day I do not understand why I told her what I had done; it was such a self-evidently silly thing to do, but at the time I was more concerned about how she would react. All I can remember is that her eyebrows raised just a little bit. I think she thought I was lying, but she did not say so. In fact, she never said anything very much, confining herself to brief questions which I thought were a manifestation of genuine curiosity. She did at first tell me about the theft of fashion items which she had carefully collected at great financial privation to herself, and with which she had intended to set up her own business, but I thought this was in order to establish her credentials as a fellow victim, an outsider. I was wrong: I had not told her very much about my own situation by then, and, as she had told me, she did not want sympathy. If that was the only occasion when she spoke at any length, it was because she had had something to say, something which might be of interest; an underlying modesty meant that she usually confined herself to questions because she assumed that there was nothing about her own self that was particularly worthy of attention.

When I crept into that bed of hers in that little flat in Catford all I needed was a little human warmth and comfort. I felt so alone. My confessions had seemed a waste of breath because she had scarcely reacted to them, or if she had, it was in an oblique, oriental way. And I felt no better for having told her that I had committed a number of murders, indeed to have given a description of their circumstances had if anything robbed them of what little reality they had possessed for me. They were now just words.

But there was something more. She lay there in the dark, right next to me, motionless, but I could tell that she was thinking – what, I don't know. I would have loved to have held her close but I was paralysed, I don't know why. So I hoped and prayed that she would make the first move. But she didn't. I tried to, very hard, but couldn't. We were stuck there, within inches of each other but we might have been miles apart. And all the time I could tell that she was thinking – what, I don't know.

I left the flat the following day without saying goodbye to her, I don't know why; and went briefly to Brunswick Gardens where I collected my rucksack and the knife I had bought for the occasion. It was getting late in the afternoon and I did not know how long I would be, so I packed a change of clothes and some other things, including a sleeping bag. I made my way to Paddington station where I got a train to the West Country, descending at Kington. The journey had been awkward: I kept on getting strange looks I think because I was fidgeting so much. It was dark by now, and the once familiar streets were pretty deserted. I debated whether to check into a hotel for the night – perhaps the very same coaching inn where my father's wake had been held so many years ago – but decided against it as I wanted to get the job done as soon as possible and rather thought that the time of day would be in my favour. There was a cab stand on the corner but no cars. However, there was a phone box with a number in it which I rang, and within a few minutes an elderly Humber rolled up. The driver eyed me suspiciously without opening any doors or even winding down his window; so I got into the back and told him where I wanted to go.

'That's a good few miles.' He had a Welsh accent.

Actually, I had lied: I had said Mulberry farm, which was a mile or so down the road from Jones Place, because I did not particularly want him to know where I was going.

238

'You got the money for it?'

'Yes.'

I was about to show him when he said, 'That's alright.'

As we left the town, he asked, 'You staying there?'

'Yes.'

Another lie, but what else was I supposed to say? Obviously it would not look too good if I had said I intended to be left in the depths of the country without a bed for the night.

'You a friend of theirs, then?'

'I've known the Williams' for a long time.'

This was partly true, as I had met with the Williams family several times as a child. They were tenant farmers. Mulberry farm – or the home farm as we called it – was one of the properties belonging to the Jones Place Estate.

'Have you now?'

'Yes.'

All these questions! I had forgotten the curiosity of locals, innocent or otherwise. London was not like that.

By now we were on a narrow country road. Everything was dark except the lit up black asphalt ahead and the uncut grass at the side. The faint shock of a humpback bridge took me back years, as did the distinctively curved fencing of the fields, which glowed white whenever we turned a corner.

'Only, see, old Mr Williams died some years back, and his family gone to live in Kington.'

I did not say anything.

'You sure it's not the Jenkins' you were meaning? They've took over the farm now.'

'Yes, yes, the Jenkins'. Sorry. I get the names mixed up.'

'You're not from round here, are you?'

I would have liked to have told him that I was, having been born at Jones Place, but didn't.

'No.'

'Here we are. I'll just take you in.'

We had stopped by a gate, and he was about to get out and open it.

'No, no, it's all right. I'll enjoy the walk.'

'Suit yourself. Mind you take your rucksack.'

'Yes.'

He took the fare and drove off, at some speed I thought. When his

239

lights had gone I was left in an eerie darkness, with a cool wind on my cheek. The sound of his motor gradually faded, to be replaced by that utter silence you often get in the countryside, which is perhaps disturbing to a city dweller.

From memory I knew that the farmhouse was so hidden from me that for present purposes it might just as well not have existed. I turned and started to walk up the road, which again from memory I knew to follow a slight incline all the way to the entrance to Jones Place, before it turned and snaked up the hill to the village where my father's ashes had been interred. My leather-soled shoes made a curious flat sound with every step, like an echo. A horse whinnied nearby, and I could feel, rather than see, the presence of a large, curious animal. I have always been frightened of animals, so I gripped the rucksack hard and pressed on, pretending that it was not there. I stopped at the gate which opened on to the drive that led to the ruined manor house, and even from here I could see a dim glow in the sky, which meant that the lights were on in the cottage and someone was at home. Also, I could hear faint music, a song I recognised but could not quite place.

Suddenly the music stopped and was replaced by the barking of dogs. I froze.

I had not really thought through how I was going to set about killing Graham Greene, nor even about how I would get near enough to him to make the attempt. Equally, I had not tried to envisage the possible circumstances that might surround such an act; it would just happen, that's all. The din of the barking dogs unnerved me. Even so, I carried on. I reached the gaunt, grey facade of the manor house, and – a further surprise – saw that it was covered with scaffolding, very much as if it were being renovated. I could see it because a very powerful searchlight had come on in front of the cottage on the other side of the drive, on its own plateau, above me. It was so powerful that I could also see behind it the silhouette of a man, which I knew to be that of Graham Greene. Another flash of light, this time orange and yellow in colour, and almost instantaneously the crackling, startling sound of gunshot which pitched and pierced higher than the barking of the dogs. As I fell to my knees I also heard a spattering noise reminiscent of fireworks as they explode in the sky, their lights cascading away into the night. A moment later and there was another shot, producing exactly the same results; then a pause: I could see the silhouette crouching a little and realised he was reloading a rifle. He had missed first time and I would not get another chance. Even this opportunity was fraught with danger, however, because he might already have put the bullets in before I could get to him and, more, the nearer I got the better a target I would become. But I had to do it.

I hared the rest of the drive, crossed it and tumbled up the steps that led to the plateau where the cottage was, opposite the old kitchen garden. I had the knife in my hand, but was not conscious of having removed it from the rucksack. As I ran I could see him still fumbling with the rifle. He was desperately trying to get the bullets in in time. I launched myself at him just as he was looking up from what he had been doing. There was a look of shock and surprise on his face, as if he could not believe that his carefully laid plans had let him down. The blade went straight through his heart, I believe, and he fell down onto the stone slabs of the cottage forecourt, dying. At this proximity the noise of the dogs was deafening, added to which was the pounding of a cage. There were two of them – great black things – and they were hurling themselves at the walls of their compound in ferocious and frantic efforts to get at me. I will always remember their pure hatred of me, expressed in their eyes and the brilliant white colour of their bared teeth. As for Graham Greene, there was no sound or movement from his crumpled body: he was dead. I was standing, trembling, looking at the dogs, wondering why he hadn't let them at me, when I heard the screech of tyres on the drive behind and men hurriedly get out.

They were police officers. I was overpowered by them – not that I was putting up any resistance – and found myself on the stone floor on my stomach and my wrists handcuffed behind my back.

'What did you do that for, sonny?' I heard one of them ask, but I did not answer. I had dimly recognised the cab driver during the melee, but he was standing apart, watching.

'We'll have to wait for a van,' one of them said; then added, 'look at this mess.'

The dogs by now had quietened down, and were simply whimpering.

'We'd better take a look around. You got any more equipment, sonny?'

It was difficult for me to speak because my face was pressed against the floor and I was in pain. The cuffs were hurting and I think I banged my head on the way down.

'My rucksack's over there.'

'What's your name, sonny?'

'Giles Jones,' I managed.

I next heard the formal language of an arrest but was not properly able to take it in.

'Christ, sarge, look at this man. Properly skewered he's been.'

'Don't touch it. Keep away from the blood. Has he got a phone, do you know?'

'I'll go and see.'

One of the policemen went into the cottage, at which the dogs put up a feeble protest.

'We'll obviously need an ambulance, but tell 'em it's a death.'

'Right-o.'

There was a scuffling noise on the floor.

'Cartridges. He was using the gun in self-defence, I'd say.'

'Did he have a license for it?'

'I'll check.'

'What's his name anyway?'

'A Mr Greene. Been here a few years only.'

'Has he reported any burglaries?'

'No.'

The cab driver, whose voice I had recognised, said, 'I picked him up off the London train. It's a long way to go burgling. He said he was staying with the Jenkins' at Mulberry farm, just down the road.'

'What they call this place anyway? Jones Place, isn't it?'

'Used to be.'

'It's mine,' I heard myself saying.

'Is it now, sonny?'

'Yes. I…'

But the cab driver chipped in again.

'I'll be going now, I reckon.'

'To the nick, will you? Make a statement.'

'Yes.'

His car drove off. The policemen were now standing around, chatting desultorily. One of them, however, always kept a knee in the small of my back, which forced my arms further up than they would naturally bend.

'This place fair gives me the creeps, I don't know why,' I heard one of them say.

'I've heard it's haunted. A small, stout, grey man is seen to walk the fields. I got it from…'

But he stopped, preferring the noisome inhalation of tobacco to his speech. As I knew, it was indeed a lonely spot, the only sound now being that of the wind in the beeches high overhead. The dogs had gone to sleep. There was darkness everywhere, except for the bright lights in the immediate vicinity of the cottage.

Presently more vehicles drew up. Doors opened and slammed. There was a whirring noise.

'Let's be having you, sonny.'

I was unceremoniously dragged to my feet and frogmarched down the steps to the drive. Coming past me were, what appeared to be medical people, and more men in uniform and suits. They looked grim.

I was bundled into the back of a police van, the door slammed behind me and locked. There was a grille in front, beyond which I could just see the shadowy forms of a police driver and passenger. As we drove off down the bumpy drive I was thinking, I bet they think I'm miffed to have been caught on my burglary spree. And on a murder charge at that. But they're wrong.

So far as I was concerned, my mission had been accomplished.

31.
Narrative, 1980

Giles Jones had been in custody for some time, but still his trial seemed as far away as ever; anxiously he awaited the visit of his lawyers, but they never came. Until, that is, he complained; and an appointment was made for the following week.

He had written to Jessica Wu but got no reply. Nor had she ever visited him. It was as if he were in a cocoon; there were no newspapers and the television was always commandeered by others, who, in any case, ignored him just as he ignored them. They had nothing in common. Occasionally, loud London voices would erupt at mealtimes, impinging on his solipsism, and for a moment he would realise he was among other people, that he was one of them; but it made no difference.

A concerned guard had tried to befriend him, indeed had tried to winkle out the reason for his actions, but had eventually given up when Giles Jones' sullenness proved impenetrable. The guard had dismissed him as mad – whatever that means – but that was not the view of the experts who had come to assess him, and to whom he had been a little more forthcoming. "Seriously unhinged"" was the nearest one of them had got; "seriously unhinged but not mad", Giles Jones had read at the bottom of the report, and it had seemed to him to be a curiously unprofessional conclusion to have reached. But what did he know? He had only pleaded "not guilty" at one of the interminable earlier hearings because he wanted to have his own say in court. But then things became more complicated when the lawyers finally arrived.

That morning, awaiting their visit, he had been more than usually tense, anxious and preoccupied. He wondered what they would say; importantly he wondered what, if anything, he would say to them. Would they be sympathetic? Would they be good listeners? Or would they try to get him to change his plea? Later, he was escorted by two guards to the conference wing of the prison. There were three men in suits waiting for him inside a glass booth. They did not get up when he entered, but continued to study the legal papers spread out before them. Giles Jones sat down on the only other available chair and waited. The guards stood outside, within sight but out of earshot.

Giles Jones recognised the oldest man as being the solicitor who had represented him in the magistrates' court. But he had never seen the other two before and it was a long time before they were introduced. Even then there was an awkward atmosphere, in which silence reigned, as the gentlemen studied their briefs. In turn, Giles Jones studied them and decided that the middle one, who had finally got up to shake hands with him, was far too big to be a lawyer. He looked more like a rugby player and was just about young enough to be one. The third man – if such he could be called – was even younger, almost looked as if he were still at school.

'You know, the curious thing is, there isn't that much evidence,' the rugby player had said slowly, after another long pause, still not looking up from the papers.

'You were right, of course, to make no comment at the police interviews,' chipped in the solicitor, 'I'm glad you took my advice.'

Giles Jones realised he was being spoken to, and nodded. Inwardly, he congratulated himself on having been careful enough not to have made any admissions to the psychiatrists. 'The thing is,' continued the rugby player, still not looking up, and as if he were talking to himself, 'there is next to nothing to connect you with the murders of Aylmer Jones or Angela Horniblow, or Derek and Mrs Bradshaw. The shotgun was void of prints. As for Coral Greene, remarkably, the matron there and Miss – whatever her name is – the receptionist, failed to pick you out at the identification parades. There is of course the passport, but I think we can deal with that.'

The rugby player at last looked up, and gave Giles Jones a brief, narrow glance. The youngest of the three men was scribbling away in a large blue notebook.

'We'll say, obviously,' said the solicitor, in what appeared to be a creative outburst, 'that you killed Graham Greene in self-defence, that you had gone there to burgle and that he had shot at you with his rifle. You had a knife for cutting through bushes or something like that, but that on the spur of the moment you had to use it in order to avoid being killed.' The rugby player was looking intently at the solicitor, while Giles Jones said nothing.

'We can discuss this nearer the trial, but it would seem to me that it would not be in your interests to give evidence,' said the rugby player.

'What, not go into the witness box?' Giles Jones heard himself blurt this out and immediately became ashamed. He felt he had let himself down, because he had not wanted to reveal himself in that way.

The rugby player was now giving him a broad, candid look. He had a buttery complexion and untidy fair hair. 'We can talk about it nearer the time,' he said judiciously.

'So, it's a "not guilty", then,' said the solicitor, rubbing his hands. 'Should last a couple of weeks at the Bailey at least.'

He got to his feet and tidied the papers in front of him, prior to placing them in a large black bag. The youngest man put his blue notebook away and got to his feet too.

'Goodbye, Mr Jones. Till the next time,' said the rugby player, again extending a hand across the table. Giles Jones took it but had returned to his customary silence. Only a nervous tic around his eyes betrayed the confusing, conflicting emotions he was experiencing.

A few weeks later he was sitting in his cell one morning doing nothing but staring at the little barred window above him, when he heard the key in the door and saw the guard enter. Another guard stood impersonally in the passageway outside.

'You have a visitor, Gentry,' the guard said.

Giles Jones groaned. Why did everyone always call him that?

'Who?'

The guard looked at a form he was carrying and said, 'A Miss Jessica Wu.'

This was startling; the guard must have noticed the look of indecision on Giles Jones' face because he said quickly, 'You don't have to see her if you don't want to, Gentry.'

'No...'

Awkwardly, Giles Jones got to his feet and followed the guard out into the passage. His cell door was locked behind him. He was escorted without conversation to a part of the prison he had not been to before: the visitors' wing. It looked strange, a vast room with a snooker table at one end and, in the middle, tables fixed to the floor at which people sat, mostly couples, confabulating loudly, animatedly but indistinctly. He could see that most of the men were prisoners, wearing their intentionally distinctive orange jackets, as if they were workmen on a railway where a high degree of visibility is needed. The women were obviously their wives or girlfriends; some were accompanied by children, nearly all of whom, it has to be said, were making a great deal of noise by running around on the linoleum floor or simply wailing in their mothers' arms. Around the walls stood guards in their dark blue uniforms, impassive but intensely watchful.

In the middle of all this sat a lone figure: Jessica Wu. He recognised her immediately even though she had her back to him. Once he'd signed a form at a desk, Giles Jones was bidden to approach her, which he did, again from behind; so that it was only when he sat opposite her that she saw him. She smiled faintly.

She looked older, though it was really not so long ago that he had last seen her; and she had been trying to compose her nerves in a noisy environment that was presumably alien to her. They did not kiss or shake hands, or even talk for a while, but simply eyed each other warily. But when they did speak, they had, like the others, to lean close over the table to make themselves heard.

'I decide I come see you.'

'You could have let me know.'

'I sorry about that. It was sudden decision.'

'Did you get my letter?'

'Yes, but someone already open it.'

Giles Jones was puzzled by this.

'How are you, anyway?' he asked.

'Oh – lot of problems.'

'Like me, then.'

She looked surprised, then realised what he meant.

'I hear about you, I worry.'

'Well, don't.'

'You go to jail for long time.'

Giles Jones shrugged.

'I'm not sure there's much difference between here and the outside,' he said with bravado.

Jessica Wu didn't react to this; instead, she looked as if she were making a great effort to say something. Giles Jones hadn't asked himself – or her – why she'd come to see him.

'Anyway my lawyers tell me I've got a good chance.'

'That good.'

Jessica Wu looked down at her nails, uncomfortable.

'So, what are these problems of yours, then?'

'They come see me, they take statement.'

'What do you mean?'

'They say, cannot live here anymore if do not make statement.'

'What statement?'

'What you tole me.'

For Giles, the penny was dropping.

'They say I involved, cos I put you in my house. They say must make statement or else.'

'You told them I told you I killed all those people?'

'Yes.'

'But you didn't believe me, did you?'

'I dohne know. Dozen matter if true or not, they say. Just if you said.'

Giles Jones let out a snort of frustration.

'I make statement or else – or else will not stay in this country. I not wan go back my own country. I not wan make statement but I do.'

Jessica Wu started to cry. Giles Jones looked at her with gathering impatience. It was not exactly true that it made no difference to him whether he was inside prison or not.

'But don't you see you'll get me put away for a very long time?'

'I dohne know. They say…'

'To hell with what they say!'

Giles Jones had risen to his feet, in anger. He was gripping the edge of the table. 'I thought we were friends,' he hissed, conscious that he was drawing attention to himself.

'We not friends. You use me.'

Jessica Wu got the words out, more to herself than anybody else, and despite her tears.

Giles Jones was shocked.

'What?'

'You use me.'

Jessica Wu had dissolved completely by now. Giles Jones thought she was just attempting to justify her actions.

'I never used you!'

She did not reply, too engrossed in her tears.

Giles Jones banged his fist on the table and walked away. It was the last time he saw her before she gave evidence at his trial.

At which she had returned to her usual composure, when she entered the witness box. She never once looked at Giles Jones, whose abiding memory of the case was of how nice everybody was to her. The judge asked if she would like to sit down; demurely, she had said that she was all right standing. At least, her interpreter had said it for her. This interpreter, also oriental, also female, spoke clear English when not chatting to Jessica Wu in Cantonese; in an effort, apparently, to elucidate what she originally meant. In a kindly way, the judge ticked the interpreter off for this, pointing out that her job was simply to interpret what had been said to the witness and what, in turn, the witness had said by way of reply. But it was obvious that this was not the first time the two women had met, because they had a rapport which got in the way of the evidence. No matter: the court's indulgence was such that the acceptability of Jessica Wu's account of her conversation with the accused Giles Jones was a foregone conclusion.

Before she had gone into the witness box, the defence had been passed a couple of documents the study of which required, they said, a short adjournment. This was granted, the jury pompously retiring; and it was then amazing to see the way in which these wigged and robed types gathered round and pored over those bits of paper, as if they were sniffing each other's bicycle seats.

That was how it seemed to Giles Jones, who was seated at the back in the dock with an officer at either side – he was what the trial was all about and yet he was being excluded from this parley.

Again, no matter: he knew what the documents contained. His lawyers had brought copies when they came to see him in prison for the last time, after Jessica Wu's visit. They were headed "Home Office" and boldly stated that, in view of her cooperation with the police, Jessica Wu would be granted immunity from prosecution and allowed unconditional leave to remain in Great Britain.

Accompanying them was the statement she had told him about when visiting him. In that glass box of a room Giles Jones had read all sixteen pages while the three fellows looked on. So far as he could recall it was the truth, but so sexed up in a flowery way that the truth became irritating, maddening. The policeman who took the statement must have been a romantic novelist manqué, yet Jessica Wu had signed every page, even going so far as to correct certain passages and add others, which she had then initialled in her babyish handwriting. Giles Jones saw, too, that the interpreter had also made a statement verifying her translation and now recognised the name as being the same as that of the person who stood beside her in the witness box; so it was the interpreter, not the policeman, who was the romantic novelist manqué. She looked the part.

Having read the statement Giles Jones threw it contemptuously down on the table and said, 'It's a pack of lies.'

The three lawyers had looked relieved.

'Well then,' said the rugby player. 'We have a broad line of attack: that she will say anything the authorities want to hear in order to save her own skin and stay in this country.'

He had looked triumphant, inspired. The solicitor was rubbing his hands again. The youth was scribbling away. Now Giles Jones was wondering why they needed to look at the documents all over again, but later he was told that they were the originals and would become court exhibits, so it was important that they exactly matched the copies previously seen. In any case, in a very short period of time, he had come to realise that lawyers love adjournments, because they give the impression, if not the reality, that the trial will stretch into eternity and beyond.

Lunchtime had come – or the "luncheon adjournment" as it was quaintly called – and as usual Giles Jones had been conveyed to the basement and locked in a cell, which looked, felt and stank like a latrine. Luckily, however, he now had one to himself, because several times in the past he had had to share with nutters for some of whom, quite obviously, random ferocious violence was a way of life. He had narrowly escaped injury. On another occasion a grossly unkempt man of about six feet tall, who must have weighed at least thirty stone, had made homosexual advances to him. He only escaped the predicament by verbal guile and by the timely arrival of a gaoler. The verbal guile had been that he was a murderer and so his potential molester had better watch out. His complaints about these situations had not so much fallen on deaf ears, as been completely ignored, even by his own lawyers, particularly the youth, who more likely than not was always the one to have to visit him in the cells.

This time he knew nobody was coming to see him, so he would have had time to eat the miserable hamburger and chips in a Styrofoam container thrust at him through the wicket gate of the cell door. He looked at the food despondently. It was a disgusting sight, in a disgusting environment, and he decided not to eat it.

How he wished he were back at the Huffington Club, and remembered the delicious curries one of the chefs used to make for any of the staff who cared to partake. Even his bedsitter – no doubt let to somebody else by now – seemed to him to have been a haven, a heavenly retreat from the outside world, although it had never really been that. Of course, he acknowledged that he had brought his present predicament upon himself. He thought of his mother; for the first time in months he thought of his aunt and grandmother, from whom he was now thoroughly estranged. He thought of everything, including the case against him.

They had told him that the prosecution knew, and were prepared to accept in open court, that the people they called "the victims" – Graham Greene, Aylmer Jones, Derek Bradshaw et al – had all been thieves or their associates, but they also knew that Giles Jones had been born at Jones Place, which was, therefore, a funny place to burgle; and they knew that Graham Greene had installed himself there, giving Damien Jones' son a motive to kill. Clearly, the prosecution case was that none of these things excused his murdering spree; and no doubt the jury would feel the same should they accept that he was guilty.

At the thought of the jury, Giles Jones became frightened. It had been agreed that since the disclosure of Jessica Wu's statement, he would have to go into the witness box if only to refute its contents. But jurors never said anything, so by and large you did not know what they were thinking. Besides, he had never had to give an account of himself to so many strangers before, in such a formal setting. He had come to think that one of their number looked like Mr Tompkins, housemaster of Prasher's, but this was really just an illusion, serving merely to confirm his fear that, inevitably, he would be judged adversely. In a way, he rather wished that capital punishment still existed. He'd never had the courage to kill himself, so why not let others do it for you? Curious, that – he'd dispatched a number of people but drew the line at suicide. All the more curious, since the void that undoubtedly awaited held no fear for him; unlike so much in his life that did. Everything was trepidation; death, on the other hand, would mark the end of his sorrows, his turmoil. It would, quite simply, be darkness and nothing, an eternity under general anaesthetic.

For even if he were acquitted, his troubles would remain. He would no longer have a reason for murder, yet, as he now discovered, his spree had solved nothing. He did not feel any better just because Aylmer

251

Jones, Derek Bradshaw, Graham Greene and the others had been killed by his own hand. He had been told that the money could not be recovered and Jones Place was already on the market for a price he could not possibly afford. What would it be? Back to bedsitter-land and another dead-end job; on and on for the rest of his life. There would have been gossip, and that gossip would continue. The Huffington would never employ him again and he burst into weird laughter when he considered that he and Jessica Wu might resume their friendship. What an extraordinary thought! He choked on his laughter. But then he burst into tears.

'I've always been good at the old floodgates,' he muttered to himself.

He spent the afternoon in court thinking about his father, quite immune to the proceedings. More specifically, he was wondering what exactly happened during Damien's final hours, in that hotel room in Berkeley with his new wife. He wished he had been a fly on the wall. Since Coral had turned mad and was, in any case, now dead, he would never have a chance of knowing. She had been the only other person there. The matter preyed on his mind.

His self-absorption became apparent to his legal team, and it worried them, not least because their profession prized close attention to detail practically above all else. The rugby player would turn a full 180 degrees at his place in the well of the court and survey his client with apprehension. He would note the abstracted look on his face and the disturbing fact that Giles Jones would not stop chewing his lip and wringing his hands, as if trying to rid them of a fearful stain. He raised this during their next conference. 'You'll have to concentrate on the evidence, you know. There'll come a time when you have to deal with it.' Giles Jones said nothing. 'We can only do so much for you. The jury will want to hear you deny Miss Wu's allegations loud and clear.'

Again, silence. The solicitor chipped in.

'We did well with her, though, didn't we, Everet?'

Everet. It was the first time Giles Jones had properly taken in the rugby player's name.

'True. She came unstuck a bit. She got confused. But I think the jury will find that she is a witness of truth. Which is why...'

The rugby player became impatient. 'What is the matter with you, Mr Jones?'

Giles Jones scarcely realised he was being spoken to. His mind had grown cloudier with the mention of her name.

'Are you all right? You're not sick, are you?'

'No.'

The small, hollow word had been forced out of him.

'Good. Now, as I was saying…'

A gaoler rapped on the door. It was time to go up to court again. The rugby player went on hurriedly.

'…you have to cast doubt on the evidence of Jessica Wu. We were not there, in that sense we cannot speak for you. We can show up inconsistencies, as we have, but it will be your testimony that counts.'

The gaoler had opened the door, and everyone was scrabbling to their feet. The barrister's utterances had all been Double Dutch to Giles Jones anyway. What did it matter how he lied? The lying itself was the thing. They could take it or leave it. But for all he knew or cared, he would tell the truth.

When the time came for him to go into the witness box, whatever happened to him there, and afterwards, would be as nothing compared with his nightly torments, in his cell at the remand prison nearby.

Something was seeping into his head, something which left him terrified, something which made him unable to recognise himself. It was as if he were becoming another person, and he could not stand that. If he'd had the means, he would surely at least have tried to kill himself, despite his feeling that that was a line he could not cross. During the first few days of the trial there had been many statements read out loud, which detailed the deaths of the victims, their injuries, the stab wounds, the ballistics, how their bodies were found, the post mortem findings and so on, and as Giles Jones had listened he had a clear sense of disbelief that he, in any way, could have been involved. The junior prosecution barrister – a rotund man with a mellifluous voice – must be attributing all this to someone else. Another person should have been in the dock, not Giles Jones. But as the weeks wore on he had begun to feel that he must, after all, in some way be to blame; not that he knew how or why. He had forgotten all about his quest for revenge; or rather, he had simply blanked it out of his mind. And then had come the nightly torments in his cell at the remand prison. Having emptied his mind of the reason for his actions, it became filled with images of the faces of those he had killed. Worse, of their faces in the moments leading up to their violent deaths. He even caught a glimpse of Derek Bradshaw's wife in shock when she had opened her front door to him and realised he was not a policeman. At that time he had been in too much of a hurry to get to her husband to take much notice of her. When he did, up popped the lawyer's face, terrified, rat-like. As for Coral Greene, that ghastly, pleading blob with eyes on stalks that would not die continued to stare at him and continued to live with him forever. 'Come to take your revenge, have you?' Aylmer Jones was muttering, as he lay bleeding on the floor, his naked partner with her head askew by the wardrobe door. His sweating, distressed face in profile as he said the words. Even Graham Greene, a mere silhouette at the time, now haunted him with the flash of his gun, shot falling at the side, fireworks exploding in his head, just like the bad dreams he had. But who was he? Who was this man with the bad dreams, the torments and a seat in the dock of a court? It was him, Giles Jones. Giles Jones had done all this. It wasn't remorse he began to feel, exactly; more a terrible but pointless sense of responsibility.

Inevitably, the day came when he was due to go into the witness box. The day before, court had risen early – another adjournment – so that he could have a fresh start in the morning. Once again he had not slept at all, and was shaking. It seemed to him that he would not allow himself to sleep because the dreams had become so bad. Yet, perhaps, the insomnia was worse, because it detached him from reality. The trial had become a dream anyway, the black and grey backs of the lawyers bobbing up and down like seals. The judge had a ferocious look on his face, his eyes seemed as big as saucers. Giles Jones was convinced he carried a gun, and was toying with the idea of shooting him at any minute. The jury were all dead. Only their corpses lolled back uselessly, their heads rolling to the side, their mouths open. Their entrance that morning had been a mere trick of the light. Now that the usher had shown them to their places, she was sitting quietly at her customary seat, knitting. She was a petite, efficient woman, but now it seemed that she had pride of place at the guillotine.

'Stand up, Mr Jones.'

The judge was addressing him. The lawyers had turned so that they could observe the defendant, who got to his feet. This is the moment when he shoots me, thought Giles Jones. He has clear space between himself and his target. He bit his lip and clenched his hands.

'I have been told that you wish to give evidence in your defence,' said the judge. Giles Jones tried to nod his head but couldn't.

'I have been told that you wish to give evidence in your defence,' repeated the judge, more loudly. 'Is that right?'

Giles Jones' head was spinning. He knew he should reply but couldn't. The rugby player bobbed up.

'My Lord,' he said, 'my client is understandably nervous…'

'Sit down,' said the judge, sharply. The rugby player did as he was told.

Giles Jones' knees were trembling. He felt as if he would collapse at any moment. He put a hand on one of the gaoler's arms to steady himself. Unaccountably, the jury had all come back to life and were now staring at him intently.

'Mr Jones,' continued the judge, with a measured but testy patience, borne, no doubt, of many occasions such as this, 'I have been told that you wish to give evidence in your defence. Is that right? Answer yes or no.'

'Yes!'

The shriek came as if from the depths of a primeval forest, heartfelt but doubtfully human.

'Very well, then. You must bear in mind that you are not permitted to speak with your legal counsel from now on. Do you follow?'

'Yes.'

This almost a whisper.

'Very well. Step forward.'

The short walk across the courtroom to the witness box, accompanied by a gaoler, seemed a journey of a thousand miles. During this journey Giles Jones happened to look up at the public gallery and flinched when he saw Jessica Wu peering down at him, her distinctive face among a sea of others. Now that she had given evidence, she was allowed to watch the proceedings.

He remembered the efficient usher giving him a book to hold while he repeated the words she read to him from a board. Then he turned to his barrister who was standing, greeting him with a practised smile from across the way. The questions were sympathetic, the tone of voice reassuring. Gradually, Giles Jones began to tell his story.

ABOUT THE AUTHOR

Edmund Romilly was born at Huntington Park, Herefordshire in 1951. When he was ten years old, his mother walked out of the family home and his father moved to America taking Edmund with him. Upon their return to England, Edmund was placed in a boarding school. His father committed suicide shortly after having remarried, when Edmund had just turned 16. His father died intestate and his second wife subsequently became insane. Having read Philosophy at University College London, Edmund worked at a number of jobs before being called to the Bar in 1983. Thereafter, he practised in the criminal courts for 24 years before retiring to the Dorset coast with his wife, Deborah, where he now writes full-time.